REVEALING HANNAH

The Myth
of
Arachne

Laura Fedolfi

Illuminated Myth Publishing

This is a work of fiction. Names, characters, businesses, places, events and incidents are either the products of the author's imagination or used in a fictitious manner. Any resemblance to actual persons, living or dead, or actual events is purely coincidental.

Illuminated Myth Publishing
Chelmsford, Massachusetts
www.illuminatedmyth.com

© *2016 Laura Fedolfi*

Printed in the United States of America
First Printing May 2016
ISBN: 978-0990979333

www.revealinghannah.com

Cover art, *Arachne's Web*, © Amy Flannery, 2016
Book cover design by Richard Puorro, 2016

For Lily

"An envious heart makes a treacherous ear."

Zora Neale Hurston, *Their Eyes Were Watching God*

PROLOGUE

The Myth of Arachne

* * * * * * * * * *

Athena

Sweating it out in the Carpathian sun

Arachne, a young woman in Lydia, had been overheard boasting that her weaving skills surpassed even that of the gods, so Athena, Goddess of Wisdom, War and Crafts, disguised herself as an old woman and challenged the impudent mortal to a weaving contest. She would curb the girl's pride in the most direct way she knew how, with shame.

Leaning back from the loom, Athena admired her own work, the shuttle resting lightly in her gnarled hand. She was certain that the tapestry in front of her far surpassed the one being woven by the girl on her left. As the Goddess of Crafts, this was her contest to win, and she practiced in her mind the gracious look she would wear as the villagers around her exclaimed at her obvious superiority. Her luminous grey eyes would be serene, while a gentle smile would spread across her face as her disguise would fall away. She could already hear the gasps of the onlookers and the weeping of the girl. She would let the girl plead for mercy and proclaim Athena's superiority before being magnanimous and only punishing the girl *slightly*.

It took no effort on her part to be magnanimous because she was always superior to those around her. There was no work, complex or simple, which was beyond her. Her name, Athena, meant "of the mind," and it had both a literal and metaphoric context. The literal came from her birth out of Zeus's head. When Zeus had impregnated her mother, Metis, one of the last of the Titans, he had been worried about a prophecy that any child of Metis' would surpass the greatness of their sire. So after laying with her, Zeus had swallowed Metis whole. But Athena was already growing in Metis and was born inside Zeus. One day Zeus, suffering from an unbearable pain in his head, begged his son Hephaestus to split his skull with an axe. Once his skull was split, Athena, sprang forth fully grown and armed. She'd been ready to emerge and had been poking the inside of his skull with her spear. Maybe not the most traditional birth route, but it got the job done.

The more symbolic meaning of her name, "of the mind" was at the heart of this weaving contest. It wasn't only that she was beautiful and powerful, she was also a genius. No realm of thought was beyond her: philosophy, politics, science; it was all as easy for her as the weaving of this tapestry in front of her. She could lift threads of ideas up and slide her mind through them with the ease of her shuttle sliding through the warp and weft of her cloth. She was accustomed to being the most brilliant person in the room, and she preferred to handle her goddess gifts with grace and composure. Not like her idiot half-brother Apollo, always preening and posturing and *glowing*. No, she liked to make people, and other gods, for that matter, as comfortable with her extraordinariness as she could by remaining, if not modest, at least gracious in her acceptance of their awe.

So it was a moment beyond her experience when she glanced at Arachne's tapestry. Her breath caught in her throat as she stared at the cloth. It was finely woven, even and supple, not a thread out of place. And the colors— they had both used the same threads, but somehow the girl had combined her colors to illuminate and enrich the images flowing from her shuttle-cock. It was as if the images had sprung to life; the scent of the flowers wafted to Athena as the robes of the girl's figures flowed across their breathing bodies and the birds seemed to flutter across the fabric. The girl had chosen to depict Zeus's dalliances with humans, and she felt herself blushing at the verdant sensuality of the scenes. Athena's own tapestry was perfection, clinical in its precision, but this, this was beyond perfection. This ensnared the senses, mesmerized the viewer. This was *creation*.

How could this be? How could this human, this girl, weave beyond not only Athena's skill, but her imagination? Not one person was even looking at Athena's tapestry. All eyes were on the girl's work and the crowd was silent, raptly watching the girl's fingers fly. A new feeling filled Athena; it was foreign and uncomfortable and it made her jaw clench and her fingers tighten so sharply that the shuttle in her hand splintered. The sound of the shattering wood drew all eyes to Athena, even the girl's, and as the crowd looked from one tapestry to another there was an audible gasp as if the crowd became aware of the outcome of the contest as one. Athena frowned at the sound and the girl did the one thing which could make the situation worse. She smiled.

All of Athena's confusion coalesced into one emotion and she rose to her full height, shedding the old woman disguise and spoke, while pointing at the girl:

"You, Arachne, are truly a weaver of great skill, and yet look at what you choose to depict— the gods in their follies. You waste your gift and you don't even have the wisdom to acknowledge that you would be but dirt if it weren't for the gods and their gifts to you. What do you have when you have a weaver who weaves without wisdom? Naught but an insect, a creature to spin with no thought of their actions but only their own fulfillment. So, it is just that you, who weave thinking only of yourself, you shall spend your days like an insect, as will all of your descendants!"

And with a slash of Athena's hand, the girl shriveled and disappeared under her clothes, until from the pile emerged a small black spider. Raising her arm again, she slashed the girl's tapestry, the threads instantly dissolving their connections to each other and becoming wisps on the wind. Athena stared at the stunned villagers, "Let this be a lesson to you all." And with that, she left.

· · · · · · · · · ·

Closter

Sorrow, thy name is child

Closter flung himself to the ground, burying his face in his mother's clothes, the scent of her body filling him with the aching loss of her arms around him. He dug his fingers into the ground and felt the hot tears sting his cheeks, his shoulders racked with the suppressed sobs he kept locked inside. He felt the gentle hands of his grandmother lifting him up and as he turned into her shoulder, his small body suddenly went slack and weightless. She carried him away from the place of his orphanage, away from the loom covered in threads twisting in the wind of Athena's exit.

His pain and shock twisted inside him like the loose threads sifting through the air, catching on the trees, and he felt the delicate limbs of a small black spider move across his face, drying his tears. He lifted his hand and the spider ventured out onto his finger, seeming to look him in the eye, the small black body somehow the mirror of the sorrow he felt in his heart. He saw the spider and knew. No longer orphaned, his sorrow shifted in that moment, and his feelings clarified into one simple thought: Revenge.

CHAPTER ONE

The Best Laid Plans

* * * * * * * * * *

Hannah

The last Monday of August at the university library

Finally giving in to the urge to scratch and tipping precariously on the tall library stool, Hannah bent over to reach the mosquito bite on her ankle and absently noted that she needed to shave her legs. Reaching even further down for her bag, and wobbling slightly with the effort, she extracted her phone and scrolled through the screens until she found the cute little yellow notepad icon and tapped it. It opened to a file she had labeled "Greece or Bust" and added her personal grooming task to the list. Scanning the neatly checked items, she felt the anticipation bubble up inside of her. In exactly seven hours and nine minutes her plane would be taxiing down the runway. Greece, Greece, Greece! It would be her first trip outside of the United States. Six days and seven nights cruising the islands with her best friend, her *new* best friend and fellow Classics grad, Gretchen Holder.

She'd known Gretchen for four years, but as undergrads at Whitfield they'd only been acquaintances. This was due in large part to her own dysfunctional disinclination for engaging in potential conflict causing her to keep most people at arm's length. Rolling her eyes at herself, she tried to think that thought again. *Dysfunctional disinclination.* God, what a load of crap. Hannah acknowledged to herself that the truth was she had been somewhere on the spectrum between painfully shy and a cold bitch. Nice but aloof. She had chosen not to get to know people because her experience had taught her that people were stressful. So she cultivated space for herself by being *nice,* but aloof. Both parts had been necessary to avoid people. People tend to get curious about an aloof woman. They wondered if she hid some deep dark secret. But no one was curious about nice people. If she just smiled and nodded most people didn't bother to wonder what she wasn't talking about. It was how she had behaved for her entire undergraduate career. Well, almost her entire career.

She'd lived through a rather unusual graduation week. Sliding her fingers over the Gorgon necklace which always hung from her neck now, she pushed the memories of the week when she'd been gifted by the Greek gods to be the Speaker of Truth back into the safe, compartmentalized box she had made in her mind so that she could proceed with everyday life. That box held things like the memory of having the power to control people with her words, being cursed by vengeful gods, healed by Nereids posing as ferry workers, flying across the Cambridge skies in the arms of a demon, who happened to think you were his beloved, and lying through her teeth to the King and Queen of Olympus to keep her friends and family from ending up as shrubbery. Yep. All of that was kept in a tightly lidded box somewhere in her subconscious so that she could function in everyday life. Everyday life included normal things, like her job as the curator of the University's Rare Book and Classics Collection, and her plans to take a week of vacation with her new friend, Gretchen.

She'd run into Gretchen at a graduation party and unlike every other time she'd been around her, she'd actually talked to her. It turned out they had a lot in common beyond majoring in the same department. They were both only children. They both had at least one crazy parent. There was a lot of bonding that can occur when you unpack the insanity of a parent. But it was more than their upbringing that connected them. They both loved to read and had a weakness for cheesy science fiction TV, ice cream and hoppy beers. And they both wanted a career in academia, applying to the same classics programs for graduate school in the fall.

They had started talking and just had never stopped. It was like one long run-on sentence. Sometimes Hannah would answer the phone and Gretchen would be in mid-sentence, still debating some plot point from the recent episode of *Doctor Who*, complaining about studying for the GREs or digging for details about Hannah's recent date with Declan.

Declan; rebound boyfriend and Greek nymph. Hannah had started seeing Declan after she'd been forced by her mother, Elise, to join her parents in attending Hera's Fourth of July party. Yes, that Hera. Ancient Olympic Goddess of Hearth and Home, and current day editor-in-chief of *Ladies Home and Hearth*. Hera had a fantastically beautiful home on Martha's Vineyard and every year she hosted a Fourth of July party that, according to Declan, who had been going for years, always ended up in a drunken, brawling mess. Hera had invited Hannah's parents so that her mother, Elise, would bring the brownies that Zeus liked so much. Hannah had been shocked to learn that her mother, the embodiment of all that is proper, had a marijuana crop in her attic. Suffice to say that the brownies were not Betty Crocker's. Her mother had first made them to try to help manage Zeus during Hannah's confrontation with him, and while it was debatable whether they had helped, Zeus had gotten hooked.

So now her mother, effectively a drug dealer to the God of Lightning and Thunder, was called upon to produce for this Fourth of July. Elise, uncertain how to navigate the Greek gods at a holiday party, had insisted that Hannah join them. They had, after all, just finished paying for her education in these people, and didn't they deserve her help? So she had joined her parents, careful to wear the Gorgon necklace that Professor Tetley and Mr. Blean had given her so that she wouldn't be affected by the immortals' illusions. It turned out her mother's social dominance in Cambridge circles had prepared her well for this gathering, and she had not needed Hannah's help in the end. Abandoned by her parents, Hannah had hung out by the water's edge, chatting with Doris and Eunice, friendly nereids she'd met in her earlier trip to the island. They were discussing the relative merits of organic sunscreen when they were joined by the Oak Bluffs art dealer Declan O'Quinn.

She'd first met Declan during her adventure as the Speaker of Truth. She had been looking for information on Zeus, and Declan owned the gallery showing Zeus' photographs. He invited her back to his gallery and attempted to keep her there indefinitely. A descendant of the famous nymph Circe's, he'd entranced Hannah to the point where she had forgotten why she was looking for Zeus in the first place, content just to be locking eyes with Declan. If she hadn't been saved by Doris laying on the bus horn, she might still be mooning over Declan in his art gallery. But she was pleased to see that the Gorgon necklace she was wearing worked to block his powers and she felt no undue attraction to him. She could now dispassionately appreciate his fineness; he was a beautiful man. Her new reaction to him must have been intriguing, because he'd made it his mission for the rest of the party to entertain her. The party had, as he had predicted, devolved into a drunken, brawling mess due in no small part to the brownies laced with pot that her mother had brought. Immortals tended toward the paranoid spectrum when stoned. When the police sirens could be heard approaching he had offered her a place to stay for the night. One thing led to another, and she had been seeing him regularly since.

Gretchen was not a fan of her relationship with Declan. She didn't know about his minor deity status— in fact, Gretchen didn't know about any of the Greek gods and their existence in modern day life. Hannah felt like she had to keep that knowledge away from this new friendship, not sure how she would explain to Gretchen about spending graduation week cursed by the gods. What would happen to their friendship if Gretchen didn't believe her? What if she did? It was not something Hannah wanted to find out. So she omitted any references to the Greek gods when talking about Declan with Gretchen. At first she told herself that it was because of these omissions that Gretchen thought Declan was boring, but eventually she had to admit that Gretchen was right. He *was* boring. In the beginning his tendency to gossip about the gods was fun to hear, but eventually, it all started to sound like tabloid fodder, "You won't believe what Poseidon said about Artemis! Did you know that Hermes is still seeing that human woman? I heard that Hera is trying to get Zeus to do yoga! Can you believe it? Zeus in yoga pants? That is a sight no one should have to see!" She would try to start conversations about art or history; he had been alive for centuries. But he would just laugh and tap her nose and say something like, "Oh, humans are so cute, look at you trying to have a conversation. It makes me want to just hug you." And what would start as a hug would always lead to sex.

The sex. It had been a little daunting to have sex with another man. She had dated Carl Rogerson for three years while in college and had accidentally been engaged to him in June. Carl had been her first. She and Carl had experienced nice sex— mutually satisfying horizontal activity. And she had loved Carl— not enough to be *really* engaged, but still.

She was aware that there was a much wider menu available in the world. Declan was not even a man, but a nymph, a deity known for sexual prowess— even more intimidating. But Declan turned out to be an excellent teacher. He had felt no qualms explaining, correcting and adjusting her efforts. And for several weeks it was great fun. It was just that it was all so *athletic*. He insisted that they stretch before and after and she found herself chanting out counts in her head, like she was in an aerobics class, "and one and two and lift and push and hold, hold, hold..." Despite the good feelings she had after such a workout, she started to dread it all. Which made sense, when she factored in how she felt about exercise in general. When she finally gave voice to this dread in a phone call with Gretchen, she had been met with an exasperated, "Finally! So dump him. Before our trip."

"Dump Declan" was the third thing on her "Greece or Bust" list. An alarm on her phone brought her back to the present. Ten minutes until the library closed and she could finish up her to-do list. First on the list was to call Gretchen. Hannah could see that she had missed several calls while she sat here in the library— a complete dead zone for phone coverage— and she hoped that there wasn't anything wrong with their plans.

Gretchen was the architect of this internet-special-bargain-basement tour of the Grecian islands. Neither of them had a lot of money but they'd been saving up all summer. So what if the airline she was flying on was literally called the Fly-By-Night Airline, and had given her an address near the airport to check-in at midnight and the cruise line was officially in chapter 11 and had advised them that they might want to consider bringing their own drinking water? She was going to Greece. As soon as she finished covering for the head librarian and closed up for the night she would work her way down her to-do list and electronically check-in for her flight, all with a small hand-held piece of genius.

Hannah had always resisted carrying a phone, it had made it too easy for her mother to find her and offer up advice. Like how important it was to have a phone with a pre-set 911 in case she was stranded by the side of the road or jumped in a back alley. She had grudgingly agreed to carry a flip-phone, but it had ended up under the wheels of an SUV. In finding a replacement a salesman had convinced her to try a data phone, and it was a revelation. It was no simple phone, but a *mobile list maker*. She didn't limit her list-making to tasks and errands. She had lists for everyday enjoyment: movies she wanted to see, books she wanted to read, and restaurants she wanted to go to. And then there were the avoidance lists: men with bad breath, spices that make her face break out, or topics never to bring up with her mother. Some lists were maps of her curiosity— one question leading to another question branching out into multiple lists. And with data streaming, she could link her lists to websites and information. It was a beautiful thing. Her love affair with her phone was interrupted by a man's deep baritone.

"Where is Patty? I have tickets to a hot night out— The Roaches in Hartford. They're a Beatles tribute band, you know Beatle covers, but with edge....get it? How about you, hon? Are you busy? I bet you're more fun than you look," and he nodded encouragingly.

Slipping her phone into her pocket she unconsciously touched her hair tucked into a bun. *More fun than you look.* A bun was a very practical hair style when you spent your days among dusty books. She *was* fun. Who was this guy, anyway? She struggled to remember the name of the university security guard leaning across the front desk— was it Bob? She thought she remembered Patty, the head librarian, refer to him as "the silver fox" but that didn't help her at the moment. "Thanks, but I am leaving the country tonight, so I'll have to pass."

Was it Tony? Dave? Why didn't he wear a name tag? She should know his name; she'd seen him every day coming in to work. *Ladies Home and Hearth*, her mother's favorite magazine, had very definite opinions about etiquette among co-workers, and knowing someone's name was non-negotiable. Terry? Gordon? Were men still named Gordon?

"Aw, come on doll, no need to leave the country, I'm sure I'm not more than you can handle. Besides, I hate to go to the show

alone and you look like you could use an excuse to loosen up."
And he waggled his eyebrows at her.

Loosen up? Hannah frowned, looking down at her buttoned
oxford tucked into a cotton skirt with pockets, and hooked her
Keds under the stool. Pockets were useful— it had nothing to do
with her level of looseness. Why was she letting this man, whatever his name was, make her question her appeal? As she raised
her eyes from her own fashion choices, she found that Ted or
Sam or Andy or whoever was now leaning so far forward that she
could see the lettuce wedged between his molars and she leaned
back in the stool to avoid him, mentally noting that she was now
only balanced on the two back legs, "I don't know where Patty is,
she just asked me to close up for her. I'll be sure to let her know
you stopped by."

"Easy Sis, you're gonna fall there. Old Jimmy here isn't
gonna bite, I'm just looking for a little attention, we all need a
little *attention* some times. You've got real pretty eyes."

Jimmy! His name was Jimmy. Wait! Sis, Hon, Doll— *he* didn't
know *her* name. That would make it easier for her to go with the
abrupt ending to the conversation she had just decided on, but
he was still talking. "Just check out those two kids over there.
He'll be getting all the attention he wants, oh yeah."

She'd been studiously avoiding looking at the two teenagers
here for summer school who had been playing footsie under the
study table for the past hour. Following Jimmy's gaze she saw
that the girl, who had stolen the boy's book from him and was
holding it behind her back, was now leaning back in the cage of
his arms as he reached around her. Good lord. The sexual tension was so high, Hannah felt flushed. She couldn't remember

the last time she had experienced the *anticipation* that emanated from the two. It made her entire relationship with Declan feel like an appointment with the dentist; something you'd arranged to do and got through. Looking away from them, she was once again looking into the mustachioed face of Jimmy the security guard and his knowing smile made her feel dirty.

It was time to take the situation in hand and get this library closed. Trying to lower the stool smoothly and demonstrate her lack of concern for the shared peeping that they had engaged in, she stated coolly, "I have all the attention I need, so thank you, but no. I think it's time we lock up," and she flung her bag over her shoulder and leaned forward to get out of the stool. Unfortunately she had miscalculated the weight of her bag and instead of the controlled exit, she felt the inexorable pull of gravity and the cartoonish biological imperative of her arms beginning to pinwheel as she flailed backwards. Luckily Jimmy the security guard had taken her rejection in stride and was back to leering at the hormonal teens, so he didn't witness her absurd fall, but the last thing she saw before flying backwards was the shocked face of her once-nemesis, now-friend/acquaintance and housemate, John MacCallister, as he walked through the main door. *Great.*

The crash of the tall stool hitting the floor echoed in the marble foyer and she heard several things at once. Jimmy let loose a string of expletives starting with the phrase, "What the…" while he apparently hit the ground, yelling at the teens to "Take cover! I've been trained for this!" Then she heard the voice of John MacCallister also let loose a string of expletives starting with the phrase, "What the…" and the distinctive *oomph* of two bodies colliding. She could hear the sounds of an ongoing scuffle and considered making an effort to intervene, but after cautiously reaching around herself and determining that her butt had not been broken by the fall, she let her head drop back and allowed the situation to run its course. Sure enough, she now heard sounds of explanation and apology from both men, and as she looked up she saw four faces staring over the library counter down at her on the floor. The two teens looked shocked, Jimmy appeared to be looking up her skirt, and John was rolling his eyes.

"Okay, okay, show's over, it's not like I'm the first person to ever fall over in a stool before." Hannah tried for a nonchalant tone while simultaneously clapping her knees together and trying to sit up, but she couldn't hold back a low moan of pain as she struggled. She heard a short discharge of breath that she recognized as exasperation coming from John before he took control of the situation. *Great, again.*

What she didn't need right now as she contemplated a ten-hour transatlantic flight on a bruised butt was John being irritated with her. Her history with him was complex. If you had asked her four months ago what her history with him was like, she could have honestly stated that it was minimal. They had been in the same freshman lecture class and it had not gone well. She had avoided him for four years. He was one of those incredibly attractive people who are also incredibly likable and he really irritated her. But then she had bumped into him— literally— in line at the University copy center on the very day that her life had unraveled due to Olympian interference, and aside from being her then-boyfriend, Carl's best friend, he had turned out to be not such a bad guy after all. In fact, he'd been kind of incredible. Carl, John, and she had been a team— working to outsmart the Olympians. And John had almost died trying to rescue her from an Egyptian demon. She had thought that they were friends. How could you go through what they had gone through and not be friends? But he had spent the entire summer impersonating an ass, and when he wasn't avoiding her, he was perpetually exasperated with her. So maybe they were just acquaintances after all.

"Did you break it?" He was kneeling next to her, reaching for her elbow.

She felt momentarily dazed— it must have been from the fall— and she let him help her stand. And some part of her mind logged in his hand on her arm as the first time they'd touched since graduation and she marveled at the fact. Had it really been so long? But his next words brought her back to the present.

"You are lucky the legs are so thick..."

Thick legs! She shook him off, pushing her skirt down and trying to regain her dignity, "The legs may be thicker than most of the waists of the women you date, but I have it on good authority that there are men who like strong women. I have an athletic build. And I did not break my butt, it's just bruised."

"The stool, Summers. I was talking about the stool."

The deadpan tone of his voice only magnified her embarrassment. She lowered her head, her hair effectively curtaining her face while she tried to imagine she could redact the last thirty seconds from her life. "Right. The stool— an inanimate object— is fine. I am also fine, if that concerned you." Opening her eyes she frowned, "What does concern you? Why are you here?"

Looking at him fully for the first time, she saw the stress around his eyes and the tightness of his jaw. He was never this serious. She remembered the missed calls on her phone, and felt her anxiety ratchet up. The thoughts flew through her head; was someone hurt? Her parents? Gretchen? Carl? Carl was still in Japan— had something happened in Japan while she had been in this data-free dead zone? Wasn't that entire country on some massive fault line? Before she could give voice to any of these terrifying possibilities, John spoke up.

"No, Carl's fine. So is everyone else. It's just..." He shoved his hands in his pockets and took a few steps away, and began pacing in a small circle. *This was not a good sign.* John was the poster boy for easy going, always telling other people to "relax." For him to be so tightly wound meant something major was up. The box that she kept locked down in her mind, the box where she kept all things Olympian, started to knock around. And she felt the beginnings of anticipation at the tips of her fingers.

She covered her face with her tingling hands, trying to gain some privacy, uncomfortable with how easily he seemed to read her thoughts. Peeking through her fingers, she saw him watching her, waiting, obviously trying to figure out how to say what he came to say, and she nodded, ready to hear what it was. And then he said the one thing she'd known he was going to say, once he'd ruled out the death and destruction of her family and friends. There was only one thing that would make him act this way.

He leaned in, and in an urgent whisper, said it. "It's *Hera.* She's sent her errand boys— Hermes and Lee— they're at the house. The house we both live in. *Now.* I tried to make them leave. But they insist on talking to you. *On taking you with them.* They said you know all about it, but that's impossible, we all agreed to keep it in the past, to have nothing to do with them.

You said it was *over*."

In her excitement at his words, her hands had formed into fists, leaving her face open for view. And her face must have again betrayed her, because before she could say anything, John burst out, all thoughts of discretion gone, "You *expected* this, didn't you? I should have known. God damn it, Hannah, what does she want? What have you done? Why would you have anything to do with them after what they did to you? To us?"

And he closed the distance between them and that piece of her mind that kept track of John MacCallister noted it was the first time he'd sustained eye contact with her since June. They were very blue eyes. Turning away from him, she made a show of searching for the library keys. She needed time to think how she was going to explain. Yes, she knew that Hera would be contacting her, had actually given her no choice about working for her, sending her a letter on graduation day. The job was a "gift" for her "cleverness." Given the work that Professor Tetley and Mr. Blean had given her to do, they— Tetley, Blean, and she— had decided that she should play along with Hera.

Because, though she was employed by the university to care for its rare book collection, she had also accepted a job offer from Tetley and Blean to monitor the activities of immortals. There was a small stipend that had been established when the Council of Immortals had created the position to enforce the Immortals International Non-Interference Accord of 1783. According to Mr. Blean, the Greek gods, who had recently emigrated to the colonies, had played no small part in the American Revolution. This was not appreciated by other groups of immortals, particularly the Celts and Druids, who had learned the hard way that interfering in human wars often only lead to more instability, war and killing. So they had lobbied the Council of Immortals. Hence the Accord of 1783. The monitor job brought very little power— all she could do was submit reports to the Council. And it brought absolutely no recognition; her anonymity was a condition of her employment. But it was interesting. And she was honest enough to admit to herself that as scary as that week of being the Speaker of Truth had been, it had also been fascinating. This job promised to feed that part of her that liked seeing the characters she had studied alive in her world.

Professor Tetley and Mr. Blean had been doing the job for the last two hundred and thirty years. Two hundred and thirty is a very large number, especially for the human, Professor Tetley. He had started the job as a young man of eighteen. Blean was a centaur, with a life expectancy of over five hundred years. She had dropped those factoids into the internal suppression box where she had hidden all the other things she knew about immortals that made her head hurt. She preferred to think of Tetley and Blean as the kindly, ancient, bespectacled professor and tie-dye wearing aging hippy she had always thought of them as, as opposed to the *actually* ancient professor and the aging centaur they really were.

They had revealed all of this the day before her graduation, informing her at the same time that they felt she was the one destined to take over the monitor job. Her position in the library was a cover, her job as curator technically an internship under Mr. Blean, since she didn't have the qualifications to be hired as a librarian. She only intended to do the work while she was applying to graduate school for classics, but now... Well, now Hera had called.

She switched off lights and used the PA system to announce that the library was closing. Jimmy, the security guard, and the hormonal teens joined the few other exiting stragglers and she set the security system. John was still behind her. Waiting.

John. She and John had visited Carl in the hospital that night back in June when the adventure with the Olympians was over and had all agreed to put it all in the past. To take everything that had happened that week in June and make it an anomaly: a thing that happened once, but was never to be repeated. Never spoken of. John had insisted and she and Carl had agreed.

But then Professor Tetley and Mr. Blean told her who they were, who they thought she was. And they showed her the secret room where she would work. *A secret room hidden behind a bookcase in the university library.* It was like all the books she'd read growing up were coming to life. And she wanted it. And that was the problem, the source of the guilt that had kept her from telling John and Carl. She took the job. And then she got that letter from Hera.

Mr. Blean was concerned about Hannah taking the job with Hera, a notoriously vindictive god, but Professor Tetley had pointed out that it would give Hannah excellent access to the inner workings of the Olympic Immortals, a group that had often violated the accord. He had argued that it would be like being a reporter embedded with the troops. She had agreed, had been looking forward to the time when Hera would make good on her gift. She just hadn't expected Hera to be so obvious. Sending Hermes and Lee was not discreet, which was interesting. She needed to figure that out. She started making lists in her head of things to sort out when John's voice cut into her thoughts.

"Hannah. Are you going to explain?" No longer pacing, he perched on the now-upright stool, arms crossed, waiting.

She had always told people what she thought they wanted to hear. In the short run it had seemed to make life better, but in the long run it had not worked out so well. The lies and avoidances had cost her. So even if John had been obnoxious and distant for the last two months, he was still the person who had stayed by her side when she had really needed him. Grabbing her bag and showing him the key ring, she decided to let him make up his own mind, "I have to lock up." And she started to walk him to the door. Holding the door open for him, she laid it out, "You delivered your message. You are done. You should go home— or go out, if you want to avoid Hermes and Lee. I will deal with them in a little bit. I have something I have to do here first. If you really want to know more, I will tell you. But think about it, John. Because once I tell you, you can't un-know it. And it seems pretty clear to me that in the last few months you have done your best to un-know me. "

He started to protest, but she cut him off, "It's okay. If anyone understands, it's me. We all agreed to be done with them, and I changed my mind. It was my choice. And now you have a choice." He was looking at her like she had two heads, and then it was her turn to read his thoughts, so clear on his face. She smiled at him, "I know, it's called personal growth. I no longer feel the need to try to manage everyone around me and I am occasionally capable of being direct. But I do have a lot to do before I meet up with Hermes and Lee, so...In or out?"

26

He stood there for a moment. He had an excellent poker face. She wondered what he was thinking, what feelings he was weighing. If she had to guess, she would bet that it was his curiosity he was struggling with. He worked as a reporter at the *Hartford Courant* and he spent his days digging past the pleasant face of things to where the dark secrets lurked. Much as she had been pulled back into the world of the Greek gods by her own perverse fascination, she watched him succumb to his love of knowing the *story*. Stepping back he pushed the door closed, taking the keys from her hand. Turning the lock, he handed them back. "I'm probably going to regret this, but I'm in."

* * * * * * * * * *

Apollo
Mid-August on the streets of Milan

Had he remembered to exfoliate? He paused in front of the plate glass window of a shoe store and tried to see if he had any flaky skin. No, of course not. He was Apollo, after all. He was the embodiment of male beauty. Perfection. This window had wonderful reflective properties, so he practiced his model face. Bruno had explained the models needed to look like they found humanity, in all its ordinariness, barely tolerable. But that was a challenge for him; he loved humanity, especially the female portion. The more ordinary they were, the more they loved his perfection. Except Naomi. For some reason, his perfection was not enough for her. Glancing up at his reflection, he was shocked by how just thinking about Naomi had marred his beauty. He shook himself and schooled his features into the expression Bruno had taught him, "Lift your chin, look down and to the side, and imagine you are smelling something unpleasant and waiting for the help to clean it up."

Nailed it! Pivoting in a circle, he tried his other model face; the pout. Pouting was awesome. That was the face he used to get what he wanted from Hera and Zeus. Eyelids slightly lowered, lower lip just a little further out than the upper lip. And then think about something sad. Like those orthotic shoes in the store display. Imagine having to wear such ugly things on your feet. *Yes*. That was it. *Pouty*. Tossing his silk scarf across his neck, he pivoted away from his reflection and crossed the street using his best runway walk. Pouty always worked for him.

He tried to ignore the thought that pouty had not worked that well with his beloved. Naomi Scullerson. Just her name gave him frissons of pleasure. She was the most perfect of human women and she was all his— well, she *would* be all his. Again. Soon. Turning down a cobbled street he couldn't help but admire his own reflection aglow in the early morning light bouncing off the unopened shop windows. His long stride made his ass look great, especially when he turned. It was this ass that had booked a week of runway shows in Florence.

Bruno had made the travel arrangements, but he had switched his tickets to the early train. It was cheaper and the re-fund the travel agent had issued him went right into the bank. *Money saved was money in the bank.* He'd heard Naomi say that more than once. He'd always thought money was for spending. He had enjoyed *that*. Five star hotels, gourmet meals, flying on a private jet. Money in the bank meant living in a one-star hotel, eating tuna fish, and traveling by discount train. He patted his bag, reassured by the clink of his bank hitting up against his hair products. Less fun now, but it would all be worth it once he presented it to Naomi.

He'd met her when he was recovering from an enemy's curse, and she had nursed him back to health with the help of her Amazonian warriors. Warriors who apparently rowed a boat up and down a river, all under the orders of his precious Naomi's commands. Naomi was small and perfect and had the loudest, clearest voice he'd ever heard. He'd recovered and wooed her and had spent the month of June ensconced in a tent with his beloved in the hills of the South Dakota Badlands. It was amazing. But then he'd woken up to her rolling her sleeping bag, and he saw that she had packed all of her things. She'd smiled at him. So he'd smiled back. He used his best smile, the one that had always worked with his loves. But she hadn't fallen into his arms. She handed him a cell phone and a fifty dollar bill. And then she spoke the words that still confused him, even to this day.

"I already called a cab. You can have this phone, it's a burner I keep for emergencies. I think you need it. And I hope the cash is enough to get you somewhere. You are sweet, but I have to get back to the real world now. I have a job waiting for me in Montana, and I have to put some money in the bank. School is not free." Bending down she'd kissed him, "Thank you again for a wonderful vacation."

She ducked out of the tent and was at the trail before he'd understood what was happening. He raced after her and asked her to take him with her to Montana. He loved her, needed her. He used his best pouty face, the one that always worked on Hera.

She'd just shaken her head and patted his arm. "Love? Oh, Apollo. I don't think we need to go there. We had fun, *you* are fun, but I don't have time for a man without a job. No hard feelings?" and she'd nodded at him, so he'd nodded back and watched her jog down the path to the trailhead, visible from where he stood, bereft. She'd looked back and waved before she climbed into the cab of a pickup truck that'd been idling at the opening on the road. And then she was gone.

For a full minute he was distraught, abandoned by his love. He, Apollo, God of the Sun, dumped. He sank to the ground, kneeling in the dirt, cradling his head in his hands. And then the phone she'd placed in his hand vibrated, bouncing off his forehead. He looked down and saw she'd texted him a smiley face. A small yellow circle with sparkly eyes and the upturned mouth and seeing it, his despair was transformed. *It was a smiley face.* He understood. Realized that she hadn't been dumping him, but giving him a quest. A challenge to overcome to win her heart. He replayed her speech in his head. *Man with a job. Money in the bank.* Okay, he could do this.

He'd gone straight to Hera. She had jobs *and* money in the bank. She'd give them to him and he'd get Naomi back. But Hera helped him understand that his beloved probably expected him to get these things for himself. She'd asked him what kind of work he liked to do, and he remembered that his friend and publicist, Archer Adams, had told him he had a face the camera loved, and he shared this with Hera. She had frowned at the mention of Archer, but then she'd hired Bruno to be his manager and had flown him here to Milan to work. As a model. A man with a job. Done.

He'd found the bank at the airport gift shop. It was pink and shaped like a pig, and every time he got paid he folded his paycheck carefully and inserted it into the slot in the top. This week of shows in Florence should fill the bank. And then he could fly back and reclaim his beloved. He leaned back against the train station wall and waited for the conductor to open the doors. The station was mostly deserted at this time of the morning— a businessman in a suit, a cluster of tourists staring at maps. Then out of the corner of his eye he spotted a man in a trench coat, sunglasses, and hat. He was pointing at Apollo, and crooked his finger in a beckoning gesture. Apollo looked behind him, not wanting to look foolish, and mimed to the man, "Do you want me?" The man nodded and then disappeared down an alley next to the station.

He checked the train station clock. He still had ten minutes until his train was scheduled to leave. Maybe this man had important information for him. Regular people did not dress in trench coats and hide their faces. Maybe it was a message from Naomi. A secret message to encourage him to fulfill her quest soon and return home to her. It couldn't hurt to check it out. As he walked toward the alley, he noticed that the doorway was covered in cobwebs, and he carefully avoided getting them on his linen pants. He had to look good. It was his job. He turned down the alley to see the trench coat man disappear from view and before he could call out to him, everything went black.

A mother and daughter arriving to catch the early morning train both remarked on the beautiful silk scarf that was caught in the spider webs just outside the station. They considered for a moment keeping it— it felt like water in their hands— but being Italian, they had a deeply ingrained respect for fashion. Whoever owned this scarf would definitely be looking for it. They did the right thing and turned it into the station master. And though the station master was also Italian, and under normal circumstances would have been more impressed with the fine quality of the silk, he was a busy man, the train was late and his boss had been fussing about timetables recently, and so he tossed it unceremoniously into the lost and found box, where it slid to the bottom, under a pile of umbrellas and used tour guide books.

CHAPTER TWO

Distractions and Escape

* * * * * * * * * *

Gretchen

The Old Bear Bookstore, Farmer, VT

Shifting the wad of gum to her back molars, Gretchen focused on not giving in to the impulse to step across the street to pick up a hard-pack of Marlboros. If she closed her eyes, she could see Shirley, the cashier at Cardone's Grocery, using her key to open the case filled with pretty little boxes of nicotine sticks, her hand hovering over the choices, then settling on the red and white box. She could almost feel the lovely cellophane sliding under her fingers as she took it from Shirley's outstretched hand. Hear the crinkle as she pulled it open…

"Um, excuse me."

Irritated that her cigarette day dream was interrupted before she could imagine a fantasy cigarette in her mouth, she glared at the twelve-year-old girl whose voice had dipped on the last syllable, erasing any possible politeness from the words.

The pre-teen was undaunted by Gretchen's glare, and hands

on hips, demanded, "Bathroom?"

Tilting her head to the left to indicate the general direction, Gretchen narrowed her eyes at the girl, mentally measuring the aura of entitlement that seemed to encircle her. The girl rolled her eyes and took off. Her departure was followed almost immediately by the arrival of a harried-looking woman. Before the woman could say a word, Gretchen turned back to her father's grungy computer, pointing in the direction of the bathrooms, face impassive. She heard the woman mutter, "Rude!" as she scurried after her daughter, calling out "Mercedes! Mercedes! Don't touch the door knob! Wait! I have wipes!"

Gretchen shook her head at the irony of being called rude by a person willing to publicly decry the cleanliness of the establishment she was availing herself of. *The customer is always right.* A sentiment she wholeheartedly despised. Withholding the chirpy salesgirl conversation, which she knew was expected of her in the world of retail, *had* been rude of her. But it had also improved her mood and diminished her nicotine craving. She pulled out the keyboard tray and started sorting through the odds and ends her father collected there, looking for something to wrap her gum in.

The customers. The cigarettes. Her father's store. Locating an old lotto ticket,she spit the gum out and smiled. In thirty minutes she would be leaving them all behind for the Grecian isles. Cerulean seas, sun-kissed days, and men. Beautiful, uncomplicated men. Vacation men were her favorite and since Hannah had finally seen the light and was kicking her boring boyfriend to the curb, she had the expectation of fun with a partner-in-crime. She needed some fun.

She'd spent the last three months living in her childhood bedroom while she filled out financial aid forms, studied for the GRE, and sweated over her application essay. She knew, according to gradschoolandyou.com that she should be applying to several schools of varying degrees of selectivity to improve her chances of success, but there was only one person she wanted to work with. One professor. Angela Gerinvale, the pre-eminent scholar of Bronze Age writings. She was it. Gretchen knew she would have followed Professor Gernivale to East Boondock U for grad school, if that was where she taught. But Professor Gernivale was tenured at Yale. So to Yale she would go. At least that was the hope. She had placed every egg in this one Ivy League basket. It was stage two of her plan to get out of Vermont.

Stage one had been Whitfield University. When she'd left for Whitfield four years ago, she'd reinvented herself; she shelved the supporting role of "sarcastic high school loner on the fringes" in the after-school special for the lead in a multi-arc HBO series on smart, strong women getting what they want from life. So in her first week at Whitfield, she quit smoking. It wasn't so much that smart women don't smoke, it was more that when she smoked, she found herself becoming loner-Gretchen. To distract herself from cravings, she pushed herself to actually participate in Freshman Orientation. It turned out she had a knack for socializing. Finally experiencing the power that extroverts have was addictive, and she said yes to everything. It had been a fun four years.

Stage two required some rent-free time to research grad schools and prepare for the GREs. So back to Farmer and her dad's place. To help out, she'd been setting up her dad with a website for his used book store, cataloguing his inventory, and occasionally waiting on customers. Poorly. And falling back into old habits, some of which were very bad. She hadn't smoked since high school. But twenty-four hours after graduating from college, she was sitting on the edge of her twin bed, contemplating a summer back in Farmer, and she spied the familiar box under a pile of books. She told herself she just needed one. She could smoke just one.

Summer days in Vermont, days spent in your small hometown waiting on tourists, were *really* long, and that one cigarette had turned into a pack a day. But once she and Hannah had started to plan this escape to Greece, she knew she'd have to quit. No one from her life at Whitfield knew that she smoked, and she had internalized enough shame about the habit that she refused to alter that image. So she had quit cold turkey three weeks ago, and now found that she only thought about having a cigarette every twenty minutes or so. When she was awake. In her dreams she smoked like a chimney. It was lovely.

"Excuse me? Were you talking to me?"

Realizing she had been muttering to herself, she pasted a thin smile on her face, and looked up, shaking her head in the negative. The tourist poking through the Russian Lit. section smiled back. Damn. She should have stuck with a glare. This woman looked like a chatterer. Sure enough, the woman took whatever invitation had existed in that anemic smile and ran with it.

"I just love this place. We stop here every year on the way up north. We have a summer place in the Northeast Kingdom. Have you been there? The moose! I just love the moose! Did you know that the plural of 'moose' is just 'moose'? There is a word for words like that...intra-variables...no...invariants!" She smiled triumphantly.

Almost on reflex, Gretchen found herself joining in, "The word 'invariant' may describe the quality of the constant structure of the word in the plural form, but it isn't a grammatical term. Most grammarians simply call them *non-changing plurals*. Less sexy, but accurate. Moose, sheep, fish..." She trailed off at the expression on the woman's face. She was not pleased with Gretchen's contribution.

"No, invariants. I'm sure I'm right. I read it online." The woman's smile tightened and Gretchen reminded herself that she didn't actually want to talk to her. She nodded blandly at the woman's assertion, hoping silence would follow. But the woman resumed talking, "You can learn something new everyday so long as you keep an open mind. Think of that as my gift to you. I believe in the Transference of Generosity. Gift giving becomes gift receiving. Have you heard of that? You should Google it. As I was saying, we love the moose. And every summer we stop here on our way north, to stock up on books for the summer. The owner, John, he's a friend. Are you his daughter? You look like him, except that you are so tall."

There was so much to respond to: the condescension, the inanity, the random assertion of her height. And then there was her amazement at how her father, *Jeff*, elicited this type of reaction from tourists. She had learned her sub-par customer relations from him. He made absolutely no effort to be friendly. She had, on more than one occasion, heard him tell a customer who was asking after a particular book, that the shelves were labeled and he should use his brain. And yet they came back. Year after year. Took pictures of him with their phones. Waited for him to come back from lunch so that could talk to him as they paid for their books. The full measure of his response was often only a raised eyebrow. And they were thrilled. Because of his dark hair and full beard, they assumed he was *the* Book Bear of the store name, not knowing the previous owner had named it after her own self-published children's book. This woman, with all of her crazy talk, was clearly a Book Bear fanatic. It seemed safest to respond to the most neutral of her comments.

"Yep. Tall and his daughter." Her lack of inflection did nothing to stem the tide of chat.

"I knew it! Oh, my husband and I just love your dad's store. It's so great, what with bookstores everywhere closing."

The woman rambled on about the plight of bookstores while Gretchen played her favorite game of guess the books. The woman looked to be in her late forties, her clothes intended to say, "I am of Vermont" but her hair and jewelry screamed, "I live in Connecticut but tell people I'm from New York." She was currently lingering in the Dostoyevsky section, but she held a few battered paperbacks tucked under her purse. A classics tuna melt! When a customer picks two substantial, readerly books to sandwich around books they perceive of as guilty, cheesy pleasures— maybe a real life murder story and a romance novel, surrounded by *Crime and Punishment* and *Anna Karenina*.

"Don't you need to hit the road, Gretch?"

She heard Mrs. Connecticut gasp excitedly at her father's entrance. Oblivious to his groupie, her dad gently hip checked her away from his beloved computer, used primarily for playing solitaire, and wiggled his eyebrows toward the door.

Her dad, the Book Bear. As a kid she had started reading at a really early age. She couldn't remember *not* knowing how to read. It had made life with her father work. It had always been the two of them, parked in a booth at The Common Man diner, her dad with his face in the morning paper, her with a paperback folded back in one hand, coffee in the other. They would order the regular: two eggs, toast and hash browns, and read until they finished, and then they would take turns with the crossword. Sometimes working together, but more often than not competing, racing to see how long it took. They had a running scorecard.

She had vague memories of annoying women trying to mother them both, shocked at a child drinking coffee, eating out for every meal. Cooing about how sad it was that her mother had abandoned them. They would fuss about, trying to impose their norms of orange juice and cheerios around the kitchen table, convinced her father was a fixer-upper. Luckily for her, her father was a rock, unchangeable, and the women never stuck around for more than a few weeks. And that had only been in the beginning. Once she hit school, any attempts to reconstitute the family around a female role model ceased. And if he was seeing anyone, he kept it out of the house, and for that she was grateful. She liked her mornings at the diner. And the crosswords. And the easy space books had always given them.

"You are going to miss me, old man." She gave him a smacking kiss on the cheek. "Your website is up and running. I bookmarked it for you." She rolled her eyes at his glower. He'd been resistant to her summer project. "And I finished cataloguing the last of the books on the first floor." When it became clear that she wouldn't be able to finish cataloging the entire store, she'd hired a former classmate, now the town school librarian, to do it.

"Lisa Maxwell will come and finish the second floor in the next few weeks. Don't forget to pay her, Dad."

"Time to go." Though his words were abrupt, she knew better, and hugged him fiercely.

She caught site of the cash he slipped into her backpack as he handed it to her, using it to break her hold and leverage her out the door. "Dad, I don't need..." but he was turned back toward Mrs. Connecticut who was currently asking his opinion on which copy of Crime and Punishment had the best translation. She could easily picture his inscrutable expression as he said, "Depends." Mrs. Connecticut would probably rave to her friends over dinner that night about the great conversation she had with the Vermont Book Bear.

Dropping her discarded gum in the garbage can just outside the door, she flung the backpack over her shoulder and headed south on Main Street, past the gourmet deli packed with tourists, before slipping down an alley toward the Peter Pan bus terminal. It consisted of a single row of orange plastic seats on the far side of a Subway sandwich shop. It was noon and the line at the counter were all locals. Giving a nod to the half dozen or so people who had known her her entire life, she shifted the pack to the floor and pulled out her phone. Her bus ticket was on her phone, a fact that her father found highly suspicious.

"How will the bus driver know that you paid for that? What if someone steals it off your phone?"

She didn't bother answering her father's questions, he was just expressing his general distrust of phones with data plans. The one thing he'd really enjoyed on the internet was conspiracy theory sites. He refused to even have a cell phone, "You might as well tag my ass and invite the government to explore it with one of those devices."

"So you're leaving us, Holder?" The speaker dropped down into the seat next to her. Flinging his arm across the back of her seat, he drawled, "It breaks my heart. No, truly. How can you leave me?"

Danny Garrigan. Another good reason to get on the bus. He was just as bad a habit as the cigarettes, a semi-regular hook-up since high school. But when she had returned to find him engaged to Christine Baker, she had not indulged, despite months of thinly veiled invitations.

"I'm sure you'll survive, Danny."

"I'm not sure of anything, Holder, except that you don't seem to remember how good we were."

He leaned further back in the seat next to her, stretching his legs, and for just a second she did remember how good it was and how long it had been. Dragging her eyes away from the forbidden fruit, she leant over her backpack, digging through the front pocket. Where the hell had she put that gum? Spying the pack of Doublemint, she missed the danger in front of her until she felt the sandwich bag graze her face and she looked up into the eyes of Danny's pissed off fiancé, Christine.

"Here's your lunch." Christine's face was such a clear mirror of the string of profanities she had left unspoken, that Gretchen almost laughed. Instead she took pity on the squirming man next to her.

"Hey, Chrissy. Danny was just telling me all about your wedding plans. Weren't you, Danny?"

Christine narrowed her eyes at Gretchen, clearly weighing

her dislike against her desire to talk about her wedding. The wedding won out, "Did Danny tell you that we hired a DJ? He's amazing, Johnny Walker, you know, from WKRB? And our theme is Fairy Tale Wedding, but not Fairy Tales the story, but faeries and their tails, you know like with wings and faerie dust and my sister is actually making wings and tails for every guest to wear. And guests will throw glitter at us instead of rice, you know, like faeries. Danny is going to wear a lavender tux, to match the theme. It will be perfect. The reception will be at the Fox and Hound."

Gretchen resolutely avoided eye contact with Danny, schooling her face to express sincere interest, while trying not to imagine him in a purple tux. "The Fox and Hound sounds real nice. Didn't Amy and Matt get married there in April? I heard it was epic." Amy Demers. Another classmate from Farmer Central School. She'd actually heard that Amy's wedding was something of a disaster, an open bar leading to the groomsmen changing the Electric Slide into the Full Monty while Amy, desperate to calm her shocked aunties, tried to cover up the naked men with the train of her wedding dress. The entire performance was caught on one of the guest's phones and posted to YouTube within minutes.

"Oh yeah, did you enjoy looking down your nose at that? Some things never change."

"No, I didn't mean..."

"This has been fun, but we have to go." Reaching down to pull Danny out of his chair, she lifted her chin at Gretchen, "Too bad you'll be gone, or we would have invited you." And with that Gretchen was left alone.

Fingers closing around the pack of gum, she tipped her head back, stared at the ceiling and tried to picture Greece. Far from Farmer, Vermont, where she felt cursed to be perpetually misunderstood. Where local women wished her gone even though she had not acted on the invitations from their men. Though she never broke girl code, never messed around with a boy who she knew another girl liked, she did mess around, and that on its own seemed to place her even further outside of girl world. She was viewed as dangerous. People whispered about her mother, long gone. *The apple doesn't fall far from the tree.* Christine's open antipathy reminded her that the moment she had left for college her tenuous connections broke, and the social circles that had allowed her to orbit, albeit on the edges, had closed up and she was now even further out on the periphery.

Tourists liked to romanticize small town Vermont. With its quaint bridges, charming village greens, and white-steepled churches, they imagined a place where life was simple and neighbors took care of each other. But the reality was that small towns were tough if you didn't quite fit in. From the outside, peaceful was just another word for isolation. The isolation was rarely aggressive. Folks just gave you a wide berth. And for some, like her dad, that was heaven. But she craved contact, wanted to be someplace *teeming*. Teeming with people, sounds, smells, ideas. Because where things were teeming, everyone was caught up in it. At least that was her theory.

College had been sort-of the answer. Whitfield was at least teeming with ideas. If she still felt outside, it was easy to forget when she was in class. Finally she had people who would argue with her, or play off her ideas, or ask her to tell them more. She went to parties and dinners and had tons of social friends, and yet it wasn't until this past June, when she and Hannah had started to hang out, that she had felt *known*. She was self-aware enough to be slightly disgusted at her own sentimentality, but what was that expression from *Anne of Green Gables*? A kindred spirit. Yes. She couldn't quite escape her inner ten-year-old looking for a best friend.

And who knows, maybe they would do grad school together? They were both applying to the same program at Yale. A dream program, possibly the answer to where she would finally fit. Be at the center of things. But first she had to get in.

"Hon, that's your bus out back. Better shake a leg."

Gretchen smiled back at Denise, maker of sandwiches and bus terminal employee, grabbed her bag, and slipped out the back door to the bus that was humming in the alley. Flashing her ticket at the driver, she settled back in her seat, closed the Peter Pan app on her phone, and started surfing for must-do lists for the Grecian Isles. Clicking on a scuba diving site, she read the description of the reef, "Come marvel at the waters *teeming* with fish..." She was resolutely pragmatic, but her newfound *Anne of Green Gables* optimism took that as an omen. Forwarding it to Hannah, she smiled at the swishing sound of her phone as her message winged its way to her friend. An omen for sure.

. . . .

Hera

Alone in her private oasis

Closing the door behind her, Hera leaned back against it and soaked in the blessed silence of being the only person in the room. She hated the office on the last Monday of the month. Full staff meetings to review the issue in minute detail prior to publication. It was a necessary evil. She had to spend all day sifting through the endless words humans used to communicate to be sure that the end result was an issue worthy of her name. There wasn't a second of the day when there wasn't someone requiring her attention, her approval. But now she was alone. In her exquisite loft apartment. The cool air from the AC washed over her as the floor to ceiling windows overlooking the harbor flooded the space with late afternoon sunlight. The warm maple floors contributed to the illusion that the room was glowing. Her home away from home.

She congratulated herself on her brilliant idea to buy this penthouse condominium and to keep it a secret from everyone else in her life. Zeus had no idea, nor did her employees. They all believed that she stayed at the Omni Parker House when she was in Boston for work. Because she had. For years. But recently she had felt the need for something more private, an oasis from all of the nattering humans. So she had paid a very discreet desk clerk at the Omni a ridiculous sum of money to perpetuate the idea that she had a room there and to forward all calls to her phone here. A top floor condo on Rowes' Wharf. She'd also purchased the condos on either side of her to ensure her privacy. Her sanctuary.

Hanging her briefcase and keys by the door, she hit the button on the answering machine and let the messages run while she walked the few steps to her professional grade kitchen, all gleaming stainless steel and pristine marble counters, and poured herself a glass of 2008 Riesling from the Mosel Valley, a decent vintage. The light flavors filled her mouth and she decided to wait on the cold salad she had left ready to eat in her refrigerator; she would have time for that later. For now she wanted to drink a bottle of this excellent wine and unwind from the day. Frowning, she finally allowed herself to consider all of the loose threads that were twisting and warping the fabric of her life. It made her feel unsettled and irritable.

This feeling was magnified as she listened to the endless messages from her staff at *Ladies Home and Hearth*, followed by a petulant complaint from her husband that the AC in her Martha's Vineyard home was not keeping up with the August heat and when was she coming home because there was nothing worth eating in the house and he had needs, woman, and where was she? Narrowing her eyes at the answering machine in the foyer, she picked up the corkscrew from the counter in front of her and flung it at the machine. The force and precision of her throw was impressive, even to her, and the sharp tip of the corkscrew impaled the electronic machine, which made a strangled wheezing noise and then fell silent.

Ah, silence. Wineglass in one hand, bottle in the other, she headed out onto her terrace over-looking the Boston Harbor. The sea breeze lifted the hair off her neck and she leaned out over the railing, the bottle swinging casually from her hand. Looking down, she idly considered what would happen if she let it fall into the swirling crowds of tourists exiting the ferry from Provincetown twelve stories below. While the mayhem would be momentarily satisfying, she instead filled her glass again and put the bottle down on the patio. She had long ago decided not to interfere capriciously with humans. And it was not because of the ridiculous Non-Interference Accord that controlling bitch Athena had shoved down their throats. No, she didn't interfere because it had long since stopped being entertaining. It was just too easy. She liked her pathos with some complexity, some edge.

Reclining back in the deck lounger, she twirled the wineglass in her hand and watched the last rays of sunlight illuminate the pale liquid from within. Simple things were boring. Like her marriage for the last three months. Boring. Zeus had discovered that he liked being married to her again, and after centuries of barely masked indifference and avoidance, he was ready to have a wife. He wanted her at home. In the kitchen and in his bed. She had once thought that would be perfect. A man and a woman bound in matrimony, never to be put asunder. She was the Goddess of Hearth and Home, after all. But she had no idea how tedious it would get. How quickly.

She usually never left the island during the summer. No place was more beautiful than Martha's Vineyard in August. The island was in lush bloom, the scents enticing, the breezes off the water making the warmth of the sun comfortable, and the evening sky a canvas of constellations both familiar and soothing. It was as close to perfection as she had found in this modern world, despite the tourists. And while her office was in Boston, she had relied on telecommuting for years, unwilling to give up a moment of August. But after six weeks of seeing to her husband's copious needs, of having to actually play the role of wife she had written about for so many years, she had manufactured a crisis at work and escaped.

Emptying the glass in one swallow, she filled it again. It would not do for the Goddess of Hearth and Home to resent being a wife, and she wouldn't resent it if she'd had a decent husband. But she had Zeus. It was one thing when he was distant and dismissive— she had enjoyed the challenge of bringing him to heel. But Zeus all needy and demanding, Zeus actually pleading with her, it made her skin crawl. Giving herself a mental shake, she sat upright and looked back into her spare and elegant living room. She smiled. It was completely Zeus-free— not a single reclining chair in the apartment. Sipping, she reflected that it was here, in her private retreat, that she had found the mental space to construct a plan to dissuade her husband from his current matrimonial fidelity, and bring balance and order back into her marriage.

Zeus had to be the one to end this particular phase of their connubial contract; she had a reputation to uphold. And she had devised the perfect solution to make him do it without anyone knowing she had made him do it. But then the lynch pin in her plan had disappeared. No one had heard from him. No one had seen him. So now she had to find him before she could save her marriage by ruining her marriage. But where was Apollo? The question hung out there, the twisting, unraveling thread in the perfect loom of her world.

She had decided to take action. To solve the mystery using the one person who would most like to see Apollo stay gone: Hermes. Hermes was pathetically jealous of Apollo, desperately insecure about his father's affection. Which was funny, because as a son, he was a chip off the old block; a serial cheater, liar and manipulator. Yet Hermes had a basic weakness for human courage. He couldn't seem to stop himself from admiring humans with character. He had made a fool of himself over that gift girl in June. That had been surprising— and it made him the perfect entertainment. Yes, Hermes was the most useful of Zeus' bastards.

As a general rule, she had started out hating all of her husband's bastard children. Athena, Apollo, Artemis... She stopped herself from listing more, knowing too well the aggravation that came when she allowed herself to really think about her husband's extra-curricular activities. *The philandering ass. The vain fornicator. The indiscriminate screwer of all things female. He was the reason the bottle in her hand was empty.* Looking down into the bottom of the bottle, Hera felt the slowing of her thoughts that the alcohol always created. She should get another. Bottle. Now.

Rising slowly from the lounger, she glided rather gracefully, in her opinion, to the kitchen and another bottle of white. Damn, where was the corkscrew? She scanned the contents of her kitchen implements drawer and methodically identified and rejected them: peeler, no, grater, no, melon baller, no, lemon zester, no... wait. She felt something tugging at her mind, and she replayed her previous bottle opening. She had inserted the point of the screw in the exact center of the cork, twisted to the right, pulled the cork slowly out the neck, unscrewed the cork, and then what? Oh, yes. The voices. His voice. She had wanted to stop Zeus' demanding, nasally, irritating voice. Smiling brightly, she remembered.

Removing the corkscrew from the electronic carcass of what used to be an answering machine, she opened the second bottle and poured a new glass. Where had she been? Zeus' bastards! Yes. She had been thinking about how she had hated most of them on principle, but slowly, over time, she had come to appreciate some of them. She respected Artemis as an independent woman who had found her niche in the modern world. Artemis worked for the National Parks, clearing trails and keeping to herself. Artemis was fine. She *should* like Athena, another strong, independent woman. Athena worked out of DC, some political think tank or consulting firm, she could never keep track. She and Athena had a lot in common, they were ball-busters who had triumphed in male-dominated spheres. But Athena liked to think she was morally superior to everyone else, and Hera's bullshit meter went off the charts on that goddess. No one was that cleanly drawn.

Except maybe Apollo. He had no underside to him. He was beautiful, stupid, self-centered and sincere. And despite herself, she had a soft spot for him. When he had come to her looking for money and a job to impress some silly girl he was convinced he was in love with, it had been her idea to help him get a job in Italy. She had some friends in the fashion world and with just a few phone calls, she had him set up with an agent and a line-up of pre-arranged modeling jobs. It was all going smoothly, until two weeks ago when she got a desperate call from Bruno, his agent. Terrified of her reaction to his losing her stepson, it had taken her several minutes to calm him down enough to understand his panicked English. He'd checked all of Apollo's haunts: the hotel he'd been staying in, the studios of his most recent jobs— No Apollo. *Scomparso!* Vanished.

With the sun's last rays moving out over the water, she pulled the light cashmere throw over her legs and settled back into her patio lounge chair, cradling the new bottle of wine. She smiled. She'd called in Hermes. Zeus' bastard she most liked to play with. Then she'd pulled out her little human toy, that gift girl from Apollo's last disastrous venture, and had made her Hermes' boss and set them both to the task of finding Apollo. Two birds with one stone. One of them would find Apollo, so that her plan to lure her husband out of her bed could start, and in the meantime she'd be entertained, watching the tortuous twists of Hermes struggling with his own perverse nature. Maybe she'd been unnecessarily bitchy, giving them such drastically different resources for the job. She pictured Hermes jammed next to his greasy little demon in coach, seething but obedient, while the girl sat in first class. Hera giggled. Being bitchy made her feel girlish. She liked that. She raised her glass in a toast to Hermes, and set about finishing the second bottle.

CHAPTER THREE

Questions and Answers

. . . .

Hannah

In the yearbook archives

"So Professor Tetley is—" John's questions had been cease-less since Hannah'd told him about her *other* job. She was trying to get to her office to check her computer for any immortal alerts that might have been triggered—she'd set up internet activity nets to catch their movements. She wanted as much information as possible before meeting up with Hermes and Lee. But John was at her heels, one question after another.

"Yes. He's two hundred and forty-eight years old. Watch your step." She pointed out the threshold as they passed from the renovated basement back into the original building. The original library had been built into the hill it sat on, with a sub-basement carved deep under the campus.

"But, that's not possible."

For someone who had already met the Greek gods in real life, he was being remarkably obtuse about the parameters of her work as the Monitor. She stopped and turned, needing to end this. She didn't have time to convince him of what *was*. But before she could say a word, he plowed into her, not having noticed her abrupt stop in the dimly lit passageway. They both fell to the floor in a tangled mass of arms and legs. Fortunately they narrowly missed the metal bookcase to the left. Unfortunately, she landed directly on the part of her that had already taken damage not thirty minutes ago.

As she yelped from the pain, John managed to get his footing and dragged her up off the ground, apologizing, "Oh, Han, I'm sorry, are you okay?" And before she could answer, he seemed to be checking her for injuries. His hands sliding over her arms, cupping her head, tracing down her back.

Quickly stepping out of his range, she instinctively covered her backside with her hands and exhaled, "It's fine. I'm fine. Listen, John, maybe it wasn't such a good idea to tell you about my work. About Professor Tetley and Mr. Blean. Maybe you should go home. I have too much to do right now to play twenty questions. In fact, I'm not supposed to tell anyone about this anyway. If anyone found out what I was doing the IC would…"

"The IC?"

Another question. "The Immortal Council, the IC, the governing body of the immortals. I report to them and, well, let's just say that if I was no longer anonymous the repercussions would be complicated." What had she been thinking? She should never have told him. She knew the consequences if her cover was blown, and it occurred to her now that if the IC figured out that she had told John, they might make sure there were no *loose ends*. Pressing a fist into her stomach, she actually felt it turn at the thought.

Mr. Blean had made it clear that once you were the Monitor, you were subject to the decisions of the Immortal Council. They were not known for being generous or remotely balanced and they tended toward teaching a lesson by cursing your loved ones. She'd read the transcripts. They could be brutal. It was part of the reason Professor Tetley had kept the job for so long. He'd started when he was a young man, and had lived a full life during his time as the Monitor. Fallen in love, married, had children and grandchildren. Uncertain how his departure would be taken, he'd simply stayed employed. And alive, long past his relations. He was ready now. The Council had agreed to his retirement. So Tetley and Blean had asked her to step in.

Professor Tetley had arranged for her to be an interim Monitor. She'd work for a year while Mr. Blean searched for the new Monitor. She knew that it was impacting her applications to graduate school, her personal statement unwritten and mocking her, but how could she pass up *this?* And she felt confident that she would not incur the wrath of the Council. She had signed a dense contract outlining her year of employment. But as she stood outside the secret door, about to show this to John, she felt nervous. If the IC found out about her breaking the rules, there was a reasonable chance they would punish him too. And she hadn't warned him. When he said he was in, she hadn't realized how much she had wanted to tell someone. Someone who would understand. How could she have forgotten about the danger?

She was shaken out of her reverie by John's skeptical tone, "Come on, Hannah. I know how to keep a secret. Besides, it's not like they'll kill you." At the look on her face, he let out a low whistle, "You chose to put yourself in danger? After everything we went through to make you safe? You are priceless, Summers."

Everything *they* went through to make *her* safe? Okay, now she was starting to remember why she had avoided him for four years. It wasn't too late to send him home, "Listen, I can handle this. If you leave now—"

He cut her off. "You already gave me an out. And I'm in. I get it. You wanted to do this. I think you're crazy, but I get it. Let's get what we need. Show me."

She absorbed his answer, felt something inside of her relax, and smiled for the first time since falling off the library stool. She put out her hand— he needed to stand back— and she walked to the bookcase lining the back wall, filled with old yearbooks. "Open sesame," and she pulled on the *Olla Podrida* of 1992 and the entire bookcase of heavy red yearbooks swung out silently to reveal a small rounded oak door in the concrete wall.

"Was that always there? Wouldn't I have seen it through the shelves? I don't think it was there before you pulled—" Hannah pointed to the rotated bookcase, and while she waited for him to take in the false back that hid the wall, she discreetly entered the security code and pushed the door inward. John's continued silence made her look back and she saw him staring at the blinking red light of the security camera.

"Don't worry about that, it's on a continuous loop. Come on, we don't know how long Hermes will sit and wait and I have more important things to explain then how to get in and out of my office. Watch your head, it's low for awhile," and she headed down the passageway. She could hear the door and bookcase latch behind them, and she pulled her phone out of her pocket to light the way as they moved deeper into the dark tunnel. She filled him in on the job offer from Hera and her decision to accept it because of her work as the Monitor. Of the internet alerts she'd created to catch unsanctioned immortal activities. He'd been so quiet since she had started explaining that she looked back over her shoulder to be sure he was still there. There were a lot of forks in the passageway.

He was right behind her, and he nodded toward a low sloping tunnel that veered to the left, "Where do they go?" His question sounded more worried than curious. She reminded herself that she'd had months to get used to the idea that these tunnels existed, let alone that one of them led to the secret office of the Monitor of Immortals. Her office.

"I'm not sure where all of them end up. They were built when the school was originally founded. Apparently the students used to travel to class underground in the winter. But they fell into disuse sometime in the seventies. Now they are empty. Mostly. I've started to work on a map. One of them connects up to an exit in the Center for the Arts, and one takes you to the basement of the dining hall." She stopped at the entrance to her office, and dug into her pockets for the key.

"*This* is where you work?" She followed his gaze and understood his tone. The metal door was covered in graffiti and some unknown brown substance that looked sticky, with a faded "Mechanical Room" sign bolted to the center, the padlocks ancient and rusted closed. She had to admit that it did not look promising.

"Books and their covers, MacMan. This," she pulled the door open and gestured for him to proceed her into the room, "is my office." She followed him, carefully locking the door. She turned to see him standing in the center of the room, slowly spinning, eyes wide, mouth open. She took in his stunned silence, his speechless awe. She was oddly satisfied to reduce John MacCallister to wordlessness. She did not regret sharing this with him. It was so *cool*. His eyes met hers and they both smiled.

"Wow." That single word whispered, he walked toward one of the walls and reached his hand out, tentatively making contact. The room was orb-shaped— like being on the inside of a globe. The walls were translucent, slowly shifting scenes moving across the surface. At the moment the image was light and beautiful: sunlight sparkling across the surface of a tree lined lake. Her father's family cottage in Massachusetts. The feeling of light and space were enhanced by the warm golden glow emanating from the edges of the room and it smelled vaguely of freshly washed sheets dried in the sun.

John had stepped back from the wall, and getting a clear view of his face, she saw him trying to form questions. As much as she understood, remembering her first time when Mr. Blean and Professor Tetley had brought her here, they were out of time. With a quelling look she moved past him toward the large wooden desk in the center of the room. "It'll just take a second." She sat down and flipped open the laptop that had been glowing on the desktop, and started checking her nets.

John's voice cut through her concentration, "That's my fishing hole. Right there." Glancing up, she followed his finger to see that the walls had changed; she was looking at a wide, swiftly flowing river, rocks near the shore creating eddies and pools. She could smell pine and hear the noise of cicadas in the distance. She frowned.

"Um, John. Can you stop thinking about that, please. If anyone sees that…" She scrambled to remember what Mr. Blean had told her about the properties of the room. Could anyone else see the walls? Crap. She knew no one could see inside the room, her identity a secret from the IC as well as all other immortals, but Blean hadn't said whether the IC could monitor the room. If they did, they might figure out that it wasn't her thoughts on the walls. "Quick, think about something we did together. Something I would have seen too."

She watched the river morph into the sunset near the ferry on Martha's Vineyard. It was from the first night they'd arrived on the island. She'd finally cracked under the pressure of the SOT, and he had let her. Had sat with her while she'd cried. The red fingers of the setting sun tipping the clouds, the sound of the waves and a light flowery scent. What was that? John's back was to her, hands in his pockets, shoulders tense. Now it was her turn to have a million questions. Why had he thought of this when he seemed to have forgotten it all? Why had he been so great then and such an ass since? Why couldn't she place that smell? It was familiar, but she couldn't put her finger on it. Giving herself a mental shake, she kept her questions to herself and dragged her focus back to the present. She hit a few keys, got what she needed, and snapped the laptop shut.

"We'd better go. Patience is not one of Hermes' virtues." She slipped the laptop into her bag, walking past him to the door, "I promise to answer all your questions about this,"she opened her arms to encompass the room, "sometime. Soon. For now, we should take the passageway to the Center for the Arts exit, it will take less time than fiddling with the library security systems. But stay close, we wouldn't want to run into the troll who lives in the tunnels, he really likes to eat long haired hippies." At his comically wide eyes, she laughed, "Just kidding, John. A joke." She tugged him through the doorway, enjoying having the upper hand, even if it was a little mean, "Everyone knows trolls are vegetarian. Now Snarks, that's what you have to look out for; big nasty teeth..."

* * * * * * * * *

Hermes

Killing time at H's in Centreville

Hermes pushed both hands through his hair, pulling at the ends and growled. Patience was not his strong suit. Neither patience nor humility. Two of the more inane human qualities not particularly common among his kind. He was, though not of the top tier, a Greek *god*. He was not an errand boy. And he most definitely did not play second fiddle to a human girl barely out of the playground. Hannah Summers. The unfortunate human to be gifted by Apollo. The Speaker of Truth. She'd had the decency and wit to give the powerful gift back, making her an unusual human. In their time together, he'd taken to calling her H. H was late.

"Come on, Boss, why can't we go down to Candy's place? I'm hungry."

The whine in Lee's voice made Hermes teeth hurt. He narrowed his eyes at his lumpy assistant. *Man, his human male form was ugly.* Lee, formerly the demon Mott, had been working for him for the last three months, and he had proven to be very useful, especially in his human female form, which was a blonde bombshell, but the estrogen necessary to keep that shape made him irritable. So he tended to stay in his short, fat and lumpy male form unless the job called for something more pleasant. And this job did not qualify.

"Please, Hermes, please, please, please? I'm starving!"

Hadn't he already determined that patience was not his strong suit? "No, Lee, no, no, no! We are going *nowhere*. Not until the girl gets here. Now shut up!" Flinging himself down on H's bed he stared at the ceiling and ignored the mumbling coming from Lee's corner of the room.

H's apartment was in the attic of a house owned by Candy. It was so small Hermes could see the entire place in his peripheral vision as he stared at the sloped ceiling. Bathroom in the right hand corner, the ancient claw-foot tub visible through the accordion door. Windows banked along one side of the place behind his head, books stacked haphazardly to the left, and across the room a tiny kitchen. In that tiny kitchen was a miniature refrigerator and the only thing inside the fridge was a jar of orange viscous *something*. Lee had determined that it was not a member of the cheese family and had not stopped complaining since. They'd been waiting for over an hour and no H.

It was bad enough that Hera had insisted he work with H on this job— what could she bring to the table? But before he could get any clarification on that, it got worse. Hera made it clear that H was to get preferential treatment; first class flight to Milan, a corporate credit card, and an advance to cover her expenses. An *advance*. Hera handed him two tickets in coach on the same flight and a Dunkin Donuts gift card with the assurance that there was enough left on there for him and Lee. She'd handed him the tickets, plastic cards, and an envelope of cash and informed him that he would be working for H, that H was the lead on this job and he was her assistant. He was to go to her apartment in Connecticut and get her to the airport. He'd smiled numbly while he made all the necessary noises to indicate his obedience. As he walked out of Hera's office into the Boston sunshine he took deep breaths. In for four, out for seven. Hera probably expected him to throw a fit. In for four. He would not. Out for seven. But he'd be damned if he was going to work for H.

"I bet Candy has cheese. And booze. You could get a drink and I could finally eat. I have a very fast metabolism and I am wasting away." Lee was patting his significantly rounded hips and pouting.

Dammit, he did need a drink. But all H had was a suitcase full of bottled water. He wasn't sure if that was some new diet fad or if H was a closet Doomsday Prepper. Why H did what she did had never really made sense to him. Now Candy, she was different. She made sense on every level. And she had a fully stocked bar, complete with his favorite Scotch. But as thirsty as he was, there was no way in hell he'd let her see him now. Reaching down, he grabbed the first book his hand touched and expertly whipped *Let's Go Greece!* across the room at Lee's head, "Shut *up!*"

Lee was more agile than he looked and easily sidestepped the projectile. It landed in the sink accompanied by the sound of breaking dishes. Hermes sat up and seeing his miss, cursed, but Lee's reaction was the opposite. Walking toward Hermes, he held his arms out, "Someone needs a hug. What's wrong, Boss? I thought things with Candy were going well."

"What have I told you about hugs?" At this Lee let his arms

drop and his lower lip startled to tremble. Hermes felt a stab of guilt at the dejection on Lee's face. Demons were delicate, emotional. "Don't cry, Lee, okay? Everything with Candy is fine. But we are not going down there, so keep your mouth shut and let me think."

He sprang off the bed and started to pace the perimeter of the apartment. He couldn't see Candy now and explain why he was back working for Hera. They had spent six weeks together on his houseboat in the Puget Sound. It had been a long time since he'd found a woman who was his match both physically and intellectually. *God, it'd been nice.* He'd ended up talking about his work, a lot. And Candy had made him promise to kick Hera to the curb. He could still see her, half dressed, feet up on the railing, leaning back against his shoulder, her tone gentle, "Oh honey, can't you see how she uses you? That bitch knows how badly you want to be loved, and she just dangles their approval just out of your reach. You have to end it. It's that or hand her your balls and be done with it." No. Candy could not know he was here. And the longer they had to wait for H, the more likely it was she might.

"It's Line Boy, we never should have let him go get her, he probably thinks we're here to attack her, *idiot*. It wouldn't surprise me if he is trying to rescue her as we speak. His type always sees women as either needing saving or screwing or both and in that order." Back in June he'd given the "gift" to H when she was waiting in line at the university copy center. She'd fainted and Hermes had watched the long haired boy next to her catch her and carry her off. She called him John, but Hermes always thought of him as Line Boy. Line Boy had been her shadow since then, always trying to rescue her. Hermes smirked, "Remember when you froze Line Boy, Lee? Those were good times." Lee was shaking his head, and Hermes looked incredulous, "It was just three months ago, Lee. You *do* remember, right?"

Lee nodded furiously, "Yes, of course I remember that." He went back to shaking his head, "No, I was just thinking about what you said, that John, ah, I mean, Line Boy, was saving and screwing Hannah. I don't think that's right. I mean I know that he saved her, but I thought I heard some rumor, about Hannah, you know, just gossip and such, but I heard that she was seeing...um..."

"Me. Hannah is my *paramour*." The door swung open to reveal Declan O'Quinn, skeevy art dealer and Martha's Vineyard's very own nymph. Hermes' smirk got wider, came close to a full on smile. Declan walked in, hands on his hips, and in a commanding voice demanded to know why they were in his girlfriend's apartment. Oh, that was funny. Forget the lack of food and drink. The entertainment would make up for it all. H was sleeping with O'Quinn. He would never let her live it down. It almost made up for the money and such that Hera had given H and he had just now decided he was stealing from H.

"I'm waiting for an answer— Hermes? Hermes' *thing*? Why are you here and where is my little Hannah-banana?"

"Lee, my name is Lee..."

Hermes laugh drowned out Lee's tepid reply, "Hannah-banana? Oh, that's great. Please tell me more. Seriously O'Quinn, I want to know. How long have you two lovebirds been together? Is it serious? Tell me it's *serious*, a great guy like you, fantastic gal like her, you're made for each other."

O'Quinn, frowned, confused, picking up on the sarcasm, but

not bright enough to understand it. *Oh this was going to be fun.* Hermes reached down into the suitcase, pulling up three bottles of water, and tried to sound sincere, "No, really, O'Quinn. We want to know. We're just waiting to talk to Hannah. Your *lover.* Have a drink and fill us in while we wait."

CHAPTER FOUR

Denials and Condiments

. . . .

Hannah

Climbing three flights of stairs to her apartment

The heat in the stairwell made the climb slow, and while she could hear John's tread on the steps behind her, he had not said a word since she had lead him through the underground tunnels and out the utility door of Art Building A in the Center for the Arts. The CFA was on the south part of campus, built in the early 70s— grey concrete buildings rising up out of the ground in some modern aesthetic of industrial harmony with nature. She had thought it was bizarrely ugly when she had been on tour of the campus as a prospective student, but it had grown on her over the years, and it was now one of her favorites. It was serene, the lack of ornamentation on the buildings complimenting the space between them. She had tried to chat with John about it, ask his reaction to it, but he had only stared at her as if her attempt at conversation were obscene.

In his defense, it had been necessary to take some evasive measures in the tunnels to avoid some of the nastier rodents that had gotten their scent. It had become old hat for her, but it was his first time. Bound to be a bit shocking. Once they had reached the house, she had expected him to peel off at the second floor landing, where his apartment was, but when she had paused to say goodbye, he had only looked at her stonily and tilted his head up, indicating that she should proceed him up the remaining flight. This had created two distinct sensations in her gut: relief at not having to face Hermes and Lee alone, and dread, as if he were the teacher marching her to the principal's office. Which was ridiculous. She was a fully functioning adult about to immerse herself in the world of the Olympians. If he weren't being so annoyingly silent and condemning, she would be excited. She shook herself mentally. Get excited, Summers. *I am excited.*

She fumbled in her pocket for the key, John now on the landing with her, his body heat adding to the close feeling of what was essentially the attic of this old house, and she was struck by the utter silence on the other side of the door.

Frowning, she tried one more time to talk to him, and whispered over her shoulder, "Didn't you say that Hermes and Lee were waiting in my apartment?" He nodded. "Isn't it weird it's so quiet? If they are in there, shouldn't we hear *something*?" But nodding was apparently all he was willing to offer, because he only met her further questions with an expectant look at the key in her hand. Sighing, she put it into the lock and turned the knob, "Fine. But if we walk into..."

But her words were cut off by a chorus of "Surprise!" and Lee threw what appeared to be a ripped paper napkin at her head while Hermes, lounging on her bed, smirked. Before she could sort out why he seemed so pleased with himself she was startled by John's yell of "COVER YOUR EYES!" and then he tackled her to the floor.

Gasping for breath under the weight of John's body, she pushed her arms up to make room and peered out from under her hair. While John was busy yelling "Get *out!*" the other man in the room was also yelling, "No *you* get *out!*" She sagged back down as she not only recognized the voice but also the size twelve wing-tipped shoes she could see from her vantage point. Dammit. Declan. She had forgotten to break up with Declan.

Hermes cut through the yelling, "Boys, boys, settle down. No need for anyone to leave. But there is also no need for you to protect H, Line Boy. I know you've all met before, but let me make the introductions; Line Boy, meet Hannah's Boyfriend. Nymph boy, meet H's puppy dog. Right, H? You want to climb out from under boy number two to greet your *lover?*" His voice lowered on the final word, all creepy implications clear. She kept her eyes closed, but could only imagine the shit-eating grin on his gap-toothed face. Before she could utter a word, John was all over Hermes.

"You are disgusting, *Messenger Boy*, Hannah would never willingly sleep with that *thing. He is not her lover.*" John's words hung in the air.

As the silence in the room grew, she felt the change in John as he climbed off her. She sat upright, rubbing her left elbow, sore from the initial tackle. She looked up from her position on the floor to see her tiny attic apartment full of men. And all four of them were staring at her: Hermes with his smirk intact, Declan smiling encouragingly, John, the horror etched across his face, and Lee, watching avidly while eating spoonfuls of something orange from a jar.

Lee leaned forward lifting up the half-empty jar, confiding, "I don't know what you call this, Hannah, but it's delicious. Really, very good." And he swallowed another spoonful.

Hannah frowned, "Metchup. It's a mixture of mustard and ketchup. It's meant to go *on* food," *not be food*. She kept that last thought to herself, not wanting to be rude. Man, that demon would eat anything. She wondered if that was typical demon behavior, or particular to Lee, when John's voice again rang out in the apartment.

"Hannah! Are you going to explain? Him?" And his arm swung out, pointing at Declan as if he, John, were in the witness stand identifying Declan as the murderer in a capital trial. As opposed to the completely nice, if somewhat underwhelming, man-nymph she'd been dating. She racked her brain to find the words to explain who Declan was without making too much of it, when Hermes stirred the pot.

"Yes, H, explain. We would all *love* an explanation." Hermes was sprawled across her comforter, head on his elbow, knowing look on his face; the picture of smugness.

She glared at him. Looking back and forth from John's face to Declan's, she considered how to start, what to say. Trying to find the right words in her head before she said them out loud, she tried to buy some time by covering her own face with her hands. Declan jumped into the void.

"Explanations are for mortals. Hannah, my love, you are so much more than most mortals," and he knelt in front of her on one knee. "Meeting you at Hera's party was the best day of my life and having sexual intercourse with you has been great fun, especially once you mastered the more advanced positions, but now I am ready for something more permanent."

Awareness came in a flash: the confetti at the door, the yell of "surprise", even Hermes' smirk. Seeing Declan bend down on one knee brought it into focus. Hannah scrambled to her feet, desperate to stop this, "No, no. Declan..."

Hermes interjected, "Let the man finish, H. You're being *inconsiderate* to your *lover*. Continue, Nymph Boy."

She wanted to punch that interfering winged-shoed god in his gapped-teeth. Clearly this was his design. His production. She knew that Declan was fond of her, but *proposing*—

Declan took her hand and implored, "Look at me, darling."

Looking down at him, she tried to forget the other people present and find the words to stop him before it got worse, "Declan. I *know* that you have been so kind to me, and we have both had fun. But you don't have to let me down easily. I know that you need to have more, to have someone more deserving of your gifts as a nymph. No matter what you say, I am a mere mortal. I totally understand that you have to move on. I mean, I could never expect more from this." She tried to will him to understand what she was saying, but the confusion on his face indicated that he was not there yet.

"But Hannah darling, that's what I am trying to tell you, that you are—"

She grabbed his hands and tugged him off his knee, pulling him toward the door, "Yes I know. I am *dumped*. By you. You have to be fair to all of the other women in the world. I'm sorry, this is too much, Declan. I am going to have to ask you to leave. I need to mourn my loss. Privately." And she pushed him out the door, closing it on his baffled face. Turning to glare at Hermes, she opened her mouth to tear him apart, when she felt the door bump into her back. Dammit. Declan still had her key.

With his face wedged through the doorframe, he seemed intent on explaining, "But Hannah, I don't think you understand, I— "

Putting out her hand, she cut him off, "*Forgot*. You are so right. I *forgot* that you still have my key."

Frowning, Declan placed the key in her outstretched hand and opened his mouth, but never got a chance to speak, "Thank you for returning it, Declan. It was so thoughtful. And now you have to leave, forever. It is the only way I will be able to get over you." She shoved him back out the door and cringed a little when she heard his muffled cry as she turned the deadbolt.

Clapping slowly across the room, Hermes enthused, "Bravo, H, bravo! Maybe you *will* make a useful assistant after all. Wasn't she good, Lee?" Lee nodded at Hermes, the condiment jar in his hands now empty. "Come now, H. Grab your bag, it's time that we get to the airport. You wouldn't want to miss the flight and start out on Hera's bad side. Trust me, it's a dangerous place to be." Hermes pushed her backpack loaded for Greece into her hands. "Lee, go fetch the car, we'll meet you out front."

Lee, waddled over to the door and struggled for a moment with the lock, the metchup on his fingers leaving greasy orange stains on the door plate. As he headed out onto the landing, she heard no sign of Declan. She closed her eyes for a second. At least that seemed to be over. Hermes' snarky voice snapped them open again.

"Sayonara, Line Boy, good luck with your heroics! Next time, maybe the woman in question will want them. Regardless, you are very entertaining for a human. I'll miss you." Hermes grabbed her elbow and started to drag her out the door.

Hannah finally looked at John. She wasn't sure what to expect. Or what she wanted to explain. She didn't regret that she had told him about her work with Blean and Tetley and the IC, or the job with Hera. She was glad that she had shown him her office. Of all the people in her life who knew about her earlier adventure with the gods, there were only two that she felt like she could trust to keep her Monitor secret: Carl and John. With Carl in Japan, well, that left John. She would have told him sooner, except that he had not really spoken to her since she moved into the house, and when he did, he'd been a jerk. But then he had shown up at the library, and she had told him. And even though he had seemed annoyed, it had felt like her was her friend again. That they were on the same team. But now. Now he knew about Declan. The last thing he'd known was that Declan was a dangerous trap they had avoided on Martha's Vineyard, and now he knew, well, he knew enough. She could only hope that he wasn't so angry or disgusted or *whatever*, that he would blow her cover as the Monitor. He was looking at her, shaking his head, frowning. Hannah felt something inside of her drop. Oh. Well. One friend down. She couldn't really blame him. Which is why his next words caught her completely off-guard.

Stepping between Hannah and Hermes, causing Hermes to release his hold on her arm, John poked the messenger god in the chest, "It's your lucky day, Messenger *Boy*, because you don't *have* to miss me. I'm coming. Hannah and I are a team. Hire one, get both. She isn't going alone. So if you don't want me, you can leave without her. Which is fine, right? That won't piss off Hera, will it? It wasn't as if she ordered you to bring Hannah with you, did she? You probably just waited all afternoon for Hannah for your own amusement? Right?"

Hermes stared at the finger on his chest, and Hannah grabbed the back of John's t-shirt, her tight grip enough of a signal that John let his arm drop. Hermes' glare moved from the spot on his chest where John's finger had been to John's face and John stared back, equally silent. Hannah buried her face in John's back and willed Hermes to think. She could only hope that he had worked out that if he hurt John there was no way she would cooperate with whatever plan Hera had. She prayed that his comprehension of this outcome would prevent him from attacking John. Because it was all the protection they had at the moment. Hermes may seem like he was only an annoying messenger, a winged prankster, irritating but harmless. But she knew better. Knew just how casually violent he could be.

The moment seemed to last forever. But then the smirk was back, "*Captain America* is coming with us! Nothing I would enjoy more. Hope you have your passport. See you both at the car— we're leaving in ten." He continued to talk as he walked out the door, "*Captain America*, that is good if I say so myself, I'll have to tell Lee." His smug laugh echoed in the stairwell as he descended the stairs ahead of them.

John left the room without a word. Hannah stared at his back as she followed him to the second floor. He had not said anything remotely encouraging to her personally. Hadn't said anything to her at all since Declan's almost-proposal. Yet he had confronted Hermes, claimed that they, he and she, were a team. Why he had done what he had done was something she would have to ask him, sometime. But for now it was enough that he was coming, wherever they were going. They were a team again. Relief flooded her, pushing all other thoughts out of her mind.

❋ ❋ ❋ ❋ ❋ ❋ ❋ ❋ ❋ ❋

Athena

On the streets of Washington DC

Shifting her briefcase to her left hand, she checked her watch. 6:37 pm. That took seventeen minutes longer than she'd planned. She'd have to have Jessica, her personal assistant, re-schedule her 7:00 pm meeting for 7:30 if she was going to get a chance to return the calls that had been filling up her voicemail while she'd babysat an incumbent senior senator with the moral fiber of a breakfast cereal to keep him from casting an abstention at the roll call for tonight's vote. She had promised her client a defeat on the legislation, and she always came through. Always. Tonight was no exception.

Sidestepping the meandering, ever-present tourists, she cut through the Mall, casting a scathing eye on the other DC professionals rabidly talking on their phones as they also made short work of the flocks of tourists. She disapproved of walking and talking. Not only was it rude and somewhat dangerous, it was primarily inefficient. You could not give your full attention to the person on the call if some part of your brain was busy navigating obstacles. This lack of focus in a conversation could lead to missed cues, mis-statements and ultimately misunderstandings. Which invariable meant more conversations to fix it all. *Ineffi-cient.* She despised inefficiency. She'd sent a crying high school intern home to Connecticut because she had caught her texting during a meeting. The girl had had the same orientation as everyone else in her firm; rules were there for a reason, and the consequences had been clear. Jessica had borne the brunt of the sobbing and apologies from the young woman, but knew better than to ask Athena to reconsider her decision. She would have only had to fire them both if she had.

She allowed a small smile to cross her face. She ran the most powerful political consulting firm in the nation. She was incredibly influential and profoundly discreet. Companies expected the best from her firm and paid obscene sums of money for the privilege of being accepted onto her client list. And she expected the best from her employees. Expectations of excellence only produce results when you have just and fair repercussions for infractions of the rules. This was the ethic that had honed her firm into the instrument of power it was. That Joyce Allston of Wilton, Connecticut, felt her daughter deserved another chance was immaterial. After she had patiently explained to Mrs. Alston that she understood this meant that her daughter would not be graduating from Choate with the rest of her class, and that it could negatively impact her college acceptance to Brown University, her hands were tied. If Ashley was smart enough to get into Brown, she was smart enough to understand the rule that phones were only to be used in private. Not in a meeting. Case closed.

Having arrived at her building, she paused on the sidewalk and took a moment to really look at what she had built. It was a nondescript three-story office building that blended seamlessly into the surrounding neighborhood. A substantial building, devoid of ornamentation. True power in DC was always subtle. The location was ideal. A fifteen-minute walk to the Capitol. She insisted that all of her employees walk to their appointments unless they were more than five miles away. The benefits were two-fold: her staff stayed fit— she insisted they walk at a brisk pace— and they arrived at meetings alert, heart pumping, blood flowing.

Scanning her security card, the doors swung noiselessly open and she felt the instant cooling of the air conditioning that was a necessity in the swampy heat of August. The lobby was clean and modern and empty. There was no need to hire a security guard, with the entire building fitted out with state-of-the-art technology, including a security system to rival Fort Knox. Glancing again at her watch, she could picture exactly what was happening upstairs. Her staff never left until she returned for the night. Tom and Olivia would be monitoring the news feeds, Frank, Ellen and Colin would be working their case files, and Jessica would be at her desk, sifting through the post and answering emails.

Jessica had been working for her for the last three years, and she had been surprisingly efficient. Almost more efficient than she was herself. And yet Jessica was savvy enough to always be deferential. To need her boss's guidance just enough to never make Athena feel threatened. It was perfect. Jessica had most likely noted the delayed vote but had waited to move the 7 pm meeting until she heard it from Athena.

Climbing the central stairs, Athena reflected that *everything was perfect* and she had done it all without once relying on her powers. Yes, she was the Goddess of Wisdom and War, she could have bent politicians to her will, could have easily altered the course of wars, but she was the primary drafter of the Immortals' International Non-Interference Accord of 1783. And she was scrupulous in following both the letter and intent of the Accord. All of her influence, all of her power came from her work. Period. She never broke the law— not even when she was sorely tempted. She had made powerful enemies in her work, enemies who had tried and failed to destroy her and her work. She could have turned them to stone, added them to the Sculpture Garden at the Hirshhorn Museum, but she had relied on legal maneuvers and legitimate force to shut them down. Every time.

Leaning in to submit to the retina scan, she dismissed the nagging thought that she had not been able to uncover who had sent her ransom notes for her half-brother, that she still did not know what level of threat they represented. The light flashed green and she stepped forward through the office door, expecting to be greeted by Jessica. But the order to delay her 7 pm meeting died on her lips. Instead of her staff working diligently on their respective tasks, they were, all six of them, suspended upside down from the ceiling, wrapped in cocoons, hanging from what appeared to be spider webs. Placing her briefcase carefully on Jessica's desk, she stepped forward, and calmly detached the note hanging in front of them.

We will not be ignored. Meet our demands or next time it's fatal.

She raised one eyebrow. She detested threats. Sighing, she started to assess next steps. Of course she needed to release all of her employees who, though terrified, appeared to be alive, eyes wide and blinking, their mouths webbed shut. Walking behind Jessica's desk, she dragged out the Emergency Kit. Pushing aside the semi-automatic and the industrial mace, she pulled out a nine-inch hunting knife and headed toward her dangling staff. She experienced a small moment of entertainment as she saw their eyes get even wider at the blade in her hand, "I'm going to cut you all down."

At the clear relief in their eyes, she suppressed her smile. Humans. Always so dramatic. Sawing through the surprisingly dense webbing, she made the executive decision to remove their gags last to cut down on any caterwauling they might feel compelled to express. And as she released each one from the ceiling, she easily lay them down side by side on the floor as if they weighed nothing more than fish at the market. The orderly act focused her. She started to plan her response to the note. She would have to delay her other work to determine who and what was behind this and how to neutralize them. They were disrupting her world. She would not have it. She would not meet their demands. She never negotiated with terrorists. Never. So she needed to know everything about them so that she could put a stop to this. Her way.

CHAPTER FIVE

Up, Up and Away

* * * * * * * * * *

Hannah

Looking for an empty overhead bin

Her nerves were still sizzling. She'd had what she privately referred to as an "anxiety-demon-sighting" at the airport security checkpoint. As she had bent down to take off her shoes, she could have sworn she saw Sek in the line behind them. Sek. She hadn't told *anyone* about that conversation with Sek. How do you tell people that a sadistic Egyptian demon believed that you were his Mry, his one beloved. It felt weirdly arrogant to think it; she never really had the courage to say it. Besides, Sek had disappeared that night at the Bunker Hill Memorial after trying to kill John. She had checked the immortal chat rooms for word of Sek's movements. Complete silence. He must have gone to ground somewhere. He was probably busy torturing puppies in some far-off corner of the planet. But that didn't stop her from seeing him out of the corner of her eye every once in a while. It was always something else. A shadow, a trick of the light. One time it was just an unfortunately scary looking doorman. After apologizing for screaming at him, she had shoved a twenty in his hand and run away. The man in the airport security line was not Sek. But she still felt skittish.

It didn't help that she had no one to reassure her, but she was glad she'd kept it secret, certain that Professor Tetley and Mr. Blean would have had second thoughts about her being the Monitor if she had a demon stalker. It's hard to maintain anonymity when there is someone following your every move. But that was moot, because he wasn't. And she didn't. It was just her imagination. When she spun around, all she saw was the butt of the man behind her, bending over to take off his shoes. Unfortunately, the guy seemed to think she was staring at his backside as some kind of first move, and started to ask her where she was flying to. She was spared more awkwardness by Lee grabbing her arm to run for the flight.

They'd made it to the gate for the final boarding call, and while Hermes breezed down the walkway to his first class accommodations, she and Lee had stalled for time with the gating agent while John made an emergency pit stop at the duty free shop. He'd claimed he had to buy a last-minute necessity for the trans-Atlantic crossing, and just as the agent was about to lock the door, he'd shown up, the pockets of his sweatshirt bulging. The not-so-mysterious contents were confirmed as he popped open a mini vodka and tipped it down his throat, tossing the empty into the trash can just outside of the plane entrance.

Closing the cabin door, the flight attendant picked up her microphone and made an announcement, "Ladies and Gentleman, the pilot has asked me to warn you that it is very possible that we might have to sit on the runway for an hour because we lost our place in line. Be sure to thank the three people currently walking down the aisle, as it's *all their fault.*" Those last three words spoken with the emphasis of a five year old complaining about her sister.

Hannah, surprised at the hostility of the statement, looked back over her shoulder at the woman making the announcement. Their eyes met and Hannah felt the hairs on the back of her neck go up at the naked aggression in the woman's gaze. The woman's beady eyes bore into her. Turning quickly from her stare, Hannah shuddered involuntarily. She moved down the narrow aisle to her seat and every face on the plane following their progress— every face but Hermes'. He was already reclining fully in his first class seat, silk sleep mask over his eyes. Hannah wished every- one had sleep masks on. The antipathy in the stares of the other passengers was making her feel naked. Naked and slow. Lee was stopping at each row and reading the number out loud.

"Eight. Nope. Nine. No. Ten. Not it."

Checking their seat assignments, she leaned over to Lee, "We are in row thirty-three, Lee. It's all the way back."

"Are you sure? I think we need to read each row, Hannah. We wouldn't want to miss our seats."

Lee seemed to be talking in an inordinately loud voice which clearly carried to the passengers in rows twelve, thirteen and fourteen. The hostility around them now seemed to be tinged with derision. She tried to stare back at the hoard of pissed off flyers, but they were scary. Who was on this flight? Prison pa- roles? Divorce attorneys? PTO mothers?

Ducking her head to whisper in his ear, Hannah tried to gen- tly move him along, "Yes, Lee, they are in numerical order.

Please, just trust me."

But this effort at discretion was undermined by John's decision to join in, "Be careful Lee. Trusting Summers is a gamble." Leaning in to the traveler in row eleven, John passed them a mini bottle of rum, "She lied to me for weeks. Months even." Raising his voice even louder than Lee's had been, "You take all the time you need, Lee. Read each row. Don't let Summers push you around."

The impatient crowd, egged on by John, seemed to be arriving at the irrational consensus that she was the problem, and were now helping Lee read each number, and shaking their heads at her as she passed. A nun sitting in the aisle row crossed herself as Hannah slunk by, shielding herself with her backpack. John was somewhere behind her, drinking and making friends. This was not an auspicious start to the flight.

Luck seemed to finally be on her side as the only overhead bin still open was at their row. Unfortunately, it already had a massive flowered suitcase wedged inside which, if it could be rotated just slightly, would allow enough room for Hannah to squeeze her bag in. It was clearly the property of the little old lady in the center seat of row thirty-two, who was clutching a matching purse to her bosom. Her face was all lovely grandmother, but her eyes were screaming, "Touch my bag and I will cut you!"

Despite the low level hissing which was now emanating from the older lady, Hannah decided to attempt to shift the offending luggage. She dropped her backpack into the aisle seat of her row and reached up with both hands to move the bag, when she was shoved unceremoniously back into her row by a zealous flight attendant carrying extra blankets to the first class customers. Narrowly avoiding sitting on her backpack, she landed in the center seat next to Lee, who smiled and offered her a piece of gum.

"It's ginger gum, good for motion sickness."

She suppressed the instinct to recoil as she watched him unwrap the gum with his teeth and hand it to her after wiping the spit off it onto his pants, "Oh, thanks, but, um, I'll pass."

"Miss!" The same zealous flight attendant was back. How was that possible? Maybe it was a different one. They all looked so similar. Blonde, nominally beautiful women, in grey suits with red vests. They all sported silver wings on their lapels and this one's name tag simply said "Name." Her impossibly thin body seemed to have extra elbows for bending her arms in disapproving ways. Hannah met Name's eyes and realized that this particular flight attendant was angry. "Miss! You need to move your bag off the seat and stow it under the seat in front of you. You are holding up the flight and keeping this poor man from taking his seat. Can you move it, now?!" As she spoke her arms fluttered like wings and, waiting for Hannah to act, she hovered, arms akimbo, perched to strike.

Hannah felt a sinking feeling at the thought of a ten-hour flight with no leg room and leaned forward towards the angry attendant, "Do you think maybe, you could, you know, move that bag so my bag could—"

"No, miss. I could not. The overhead compartments are on a first-come first-serve basis, and you arrived at the gate late, so please stop wasting our time and move your bag to the space in front of you. If I have to ask again, I will need to involve the Air

Marshall." This was all said with an eerily empty smile on her face and Hannah heard distinct cheering from the little old lady with the flowered bag.

Defeated, Hannah shoved her bag under the seat in front of her, "Okay, I'm sorry, I don't want any trouble," but the flight attendant was no longer listening, her full attention on John, who was swaying slightly in the aisle.

"I'm sorry that we don't have any extra seats in first class, sir. But let's get you comfortable here, and we can make sure you have a pleasant flight. Let me take that bag for you, I have a storage compartment back in the galley, you wouldn't want to be cramped for such an extended trip." And she clutched his bag to her chest and flitted away to the back of the plane.

"She's stronger than she looks." John fell into the seat next to Hannah, the smell of whiskey strong on his breath. After fumbling for a bit at his seatbelt, the ubiquitous flight attendant materialized and swooped in to secure it for him.

Hannah realized that this was a different attendant, her name tag said "Tag." She figured she might as well try again, "Um, excuse me, but your co-worker, oh, um co-attendant, took my friend's bag to some storage compartment in the back, and I just wondered if you wouldn't mind taking mine." The steely expression on the woman's face caused Hannah's mouth to go dry and for the second time she felt the hair on the back of her neck go up.

"Miss. If you would stop delaying us, we could prepare for take-off. You and you alone are holding up an entire plane full of people. Now, are you going to follow my instructions and place that bag under the seat in front of you, or will I have to remove you from the flight?" The words seemed to fall out of the flight attendant's mouth with a clipping noise. Hannah shook her head, shoving the backpack under her seat as best she could while the flight attendant stared. Unsure how best to indicate her compliance, Hannah lifted both hands in the air, as if she were being held at gunpoint. This was apparently sufficient, for though the attendant narrowed her eyes, she stalked away to start her pre-flight description of how to attach a seat belt and where the exits are located.

"Man, you are in deeeep, Summers." She felt like she was getting a contact high from the alcohol fumes in John's whisper. With the lack of depth perception that most inebriated people suffered from, he leaned into her face, "She hates you!" God, he reeked. Pushing him back into his own seat, Hannah ignored him, pointedly paying full attention to the terrifying flight attendant demonstrate how to use an oxygen mask.

Lee bent across her lap to offer John a new piece of ginger gum, "You should chew this, John. The combination of muscle relaxants I gave you in the car with the booze you've had since being on the plane might, just might, make your stomach a little *off*. The ginger should help."

Hannah frowned as John unwrapped the gum like it was a puzzle he was having trouble mastering. Hissing at Lee, she ducked down in the seat to avoid the flight attendant's gaze, "What do you mean the *muscle relaxants* you gave him in the car? You gave him *drugs*?"

"He was very nervous about the flight."

Catching sight of the reflection of the flight attendant from hell in the window behind Lee's head, Hannah's face froze in terror, and Lee stopped talking, seeming to disappear back into his seat. Hannah felt a claw like tap on her shoulder. Crap. Turning with a careful smile, she launched into apology and compliment overdrive, "Sorry, please, we're all good here, thanks. Completely ready to take off. That was a great presentation you gave, really great. I feel entirely safe, thank you." But despite her stream of compliant words intended to appease whatever offense she might have given, the flight attendant seemed to be growing more enraged with each word.

She had the surreal feeling that the flight attendant's nose was starting to grow larger and her eyes were getting smaller with each moment. Blinking rapidly, Hannah watched the bright red lipstick thin and stretch as the woman's mouth widened, but the moment was broken by John pulling open her in-flight apron and vomiting neatly inside it. Hannah flinched, certain that this would cause an explosion, but instead, the odd distortion stopped, and the flight attendant rubbed John's back, "There, there, baby, I bet you feel better now. Why don't I get you some seltzer water to rinse your mouth?" John smiled at her and nodded and like that, she was gone.

Pillowing his head on Hannah's shoulder, John gave a thumbs up to Lee, "The gum hit the spot, man. I'm just going to take a little nap and when we land in Milan, we can play our scavenger hunt for Apollo. It'll be fun." Lifting his head abruptly off her shoulder he leaned across her to look Lee in the eye, "It *will* be fun, won't it Lee? This isn't a trick that bastard Hermes made up to lure us into some ancient catacomb and then leave us there forever? You wouldn't do that to us, would you, man?" Without waiting for Lee to answer, John settled back onto Hannah's shoulder, tossing his arm across her lap, "No, Lee is solid.

He gave me these beautiful pills that make me feel like I am made out of silly putty." Wiggling his fingers in Hannah's face he pointed one at her, "While you were busy chatting up the Messenger Boy on the ride over, my man Lee told me that Hera has some *big plan* she needs Apollo for. Bet you didn't know that, did you? I am a *reporter*, Summers. It's my job." Burping loudly, he shook his head disapprovingly at her, "Excuse *you*. Now if you could just stop talking I might be able to get some rest." And with that, he turned his body into hers and seemed to drop into sleep almost instantaneously.

What? Swiveling her head, she looked pointedly at Lee, but he had buried his head in his armrest, snoring conspicuously. The pressure from take-off pulled her back into her own seat and she mulled over this new information. *Hera has some plan she needs Apollo for?* This was exactly the kind of insider info she was looking for to bust Hera for violating the Accord. Why didn't Hermes mention Hera's plan when he was outlining the case? She needed a chance to wheedle the info out of Lee, and this flight was a perfect opportunity to do that.

She leaned over to shake Lee as the plane leveled off, but before she could lean across the seat in front of her suddenly lurched back and hit her knees. The face of the evil granny appeared over the back of the seat, "Move your knees, blondie. They are pushing into my back." At Hannah's mutinous look, the little old lady lowered her voice to a more threatening register, "What? Are you going to complain? I'll do it..." and she held her finger over the flight attendant call button.

Panicking at the thought of another interaction with the terrifying flight attendants, Hannah twisted to let the granny's seat fully recline, but couldn't resist muttering, "You are Satan," at the woman's swirly grey hair. The granny simply lifted her hand and gave Hannah the finger.

In her new position, she was facing directly into Lee's snore with John behind her, his arm curling around her waist. The seat belt was cutting into her hip, and she desperately wanted to release the buckle, but she was worried that somehow the flight attendants would know. She wondered how she was going to survive ten hours in this position, let alone interrogate a demon, when John pulled back, extracting a silently vibrating phone from her pocket.

"Your phone, Han. I think you were supposed to turn it off." He handed it to her and settled back into her neck. "You smell nice." And like that he was asleep again.

Trying to ignore his Jack Daniel's-soaked breath in her ear, she looked down at her phone and felt her blood turn to ice. All thoughts of shifting in her seat and interrogating demons were gone. She felt like she was disassociating from her body, the magnitude of her screw-up incomprehensible. Because somehow in the last three hours of being back in league with the Greek gods she had completely forgotten. And it wasn't like she hadn't had an opportunity to do the right thing. She could have called as soon as she and John had climbed out of the tunnels. She could have called after breaking up with Declan. She could have called anytime in the car ride to the airport. But she hadn't. And now there was no way to fix it. No way to change where she was, who she was with, and where she was heading. She had willingly agreed to all of it. And not once did she think to call the one person whose name was even now flashing on her phone.

Gretchen.

Hovering over the answer button, she tried to imagine how she could possibly answer. "Hi, I know we were meeting at the airport in a few hours, but—" No, she couldn't say that. Maybe, "Gretchen, you won't believe it, but—" No. Terrible. How about, "I know we've planned this trip for months, but—"

And then the decision was out of her hands, as the blondest of the flight attendants snatched the phone from Hannah's numb hand, popping out the battery with one smooth smack. "I'll be keeping this for the rest of the flight."

Holding her breath, Hannah waited for the attendant of terror to leave before she exhaled. Sliding her hands into the unconscious John's pockets, she pulled out a handful of miniature liquor bottles. She emptied one after another she tried out conversation after conversation in her head to explain what she was doing to her best friend. Whether it was the cumulative effect of the alcohol or simply the psychological strain of trying to rationalize inexcusable behavior, she convinced herself that she had found the answer. She would just call Gretchen when the plane landed and tell her the truth. Yep. That would work. She would fix it all when they landed. Lightly dropping the empty mini bottle of bourbon into the bouffant hairdo of the granny, she popped open another. Hey, this one was a bottle of gin. Sipping cautiously, she gasped as the alcohol tore down her throat. Gin is disgusting. She drank it quickly and added it to the growing pile in the granny's hair. From her position, Hannah thought they looked like Christmas ornaments hanging from a hairy grey tree. Pretty.

Satisfied, she fished another bottle out of John's pocket. She just needed to keep her head low and they would give her back her phone when she deplaned. Deplaned. That was such a stupid word. De plane! De plane! Mr. Roarke! Mr. Roarke! We need to deplane! That was funny. She was funny when she drank. Snapping open her eyes, she scanned wildly, hoping she hadn't said any of that out loud. The flight attendants always seemed to be hovering, ready to attack. But the coast was clear. Phew! There was something weird about those scary flight attendants, she felt like she knew what it was but couldn't quite think it clearly enough to know it. Whatever they were, they had her phone, and she needed to get it back, so she had to lay low. Nothing was lower than sleep. Hey, that was a plan. Sleep. Wake up. Get phone. Call Gretchen. Wishing she had her phone so that she could write it down in her little notebook app, she just repeated it in her head until she slipped off to sleep.

* * * * * * * * * *

Athena

Another productive staff meeting

Closing the door carefully behind her, she checked her watch. They would probably be out of it for another half an hour. Long enough for her to clean up all signs of the recent trouble. Settling down at her computer she pulled up all of the surveillance footage and transferred the actual files to her private account while she deleted them from the company system, replacing them with some stock footage from earlier in the summer. She would analyze the images later, looking for more clues as to who she was dealing with. For now, she simply needed to contain the situation.

"Your highness, we're all done out here. Is there anything else you need? Anything we can do for you? We are at your disposal. "

Athena frowned for a moment, could that be sarcasm? No. It was just the natural subservience of lesser creatures. The cleaning company she always used was staffed by Nereids, sea nymphs. She had spent her childhood growing up with them, and she was happy to provide them with work. There was quite a colony of them living in DC; the swampy climate was perfect for their delicate skin. She knew that they had struggled with finding employment in the modern world. Though they looked generally human, some of them still smelled rather like the ocean, despite the use of soaps and deodorants. The current American culture was somewhat intolerant of malodorous humans, which had prevented them from rising in the political economy that permeated all aspects of DC life. It had been her astute advice that they start a cleaning company. The smells of the industrial cleaning products they used tended to mask any other odors. With her connections, she had made certain that their business was thriving. They were deeply in her debt.

"Were you able to remove all traces of the webbing? And did you treat for insects? I don't want anyone experiencing any PTSD if they happen to see a spider scuttle by, or brush up against a web."

"Yes and yes. We did both. There are absolutely no signs left of what happened here."

Rising up from her desk, Athena examined the lobby where her employees had been hung in cocoons. Sliding her finger along the top of the doorframe, it came away clean. The Nereid was right. There was no sign. Excellent. She had wiped each of her employees' minds of their memories of the last two days, just to be on the safe side. This was not the first time she'd had to do it, and she despised the inefficiency of losing their memories as it related to their work, but they had been significantly traumatized by their experiences. Even Jessica was a sobbing, hysterical mess, once the webbing was removed from her mouth. It was a kindness she did for them. That it happened to protect her privacy and business interests— well, that was serendipitous. She did not consider wiping their minds a violation of the Non-Interference Accord. Wiping their memories did not alter the course of human events, except for in very minor and insignificant ways. They would all wake up in a few minutes a little groggy, but she'd left the lights in the meeting room low and the white noise machine on, and they would all just assume they had slipped off to sleep during their weekly mandated meditation time. She had established meditation time for just this purpose. There was no situation for which she did not have a contingency plan.

"Fine. You all did very fine work. You can leave now," and the Nereids started filing out the door. She stopped the tallest one, the one who had spoken to her, as she must be the one in charge, "Here. I know you appreciate the honor of being able to service me, a god, and need nothing more, but I would still like to thank you." Opening Jessica's desk drawer she spied coupons that had been left in the company mailbox. "Take these coupons for your trouble. They are for 50% off at the Shake Shack. But don't gorge. Remember, a minute on the lips, a lifetime on the hips." And she looked pointedly down at the Nereid's ample hips. Holding on to the coupons, she reconsidered. It was not a kindness to give them something they clearly couldn't handle. Withdrawing the slips of paper, she patted the Nereid on the shoulder, "On second thought, please take my gratitude and share it with the others. You are free to go." And she waved regally toward the door.

With one eye on the still-sleeping staff in the meeting room and the other on the security monitor, she watched the last Nereid exit the building and engaged the lockdown protocols. Not only did that make the building impenetrable, it switched the air ducts and plumbing to internal reservoirs, all completely contained. That should keep them safe, even from spiders.

Because it was spiders, hundreds, maybe thousands of them, that had attacked the offices earlier this evening. The security tapes showed every second of it. One moment Jessica was at her desk, typing away at her computer, and the next, she was covered in a swarm of small black spiders, intently weaving a cocoon, trapping her arms at her sides. Her screams to her co-workers were useless. The other cameras had caught the synchronized attack, everyone immobilized at the same moment. The spiders quickly silenced them with webbing across their mouths, and then, in what was truly a marvel to watch, moved each body into the front lobby and then strung them up as if they weighed nothing.

Heading back into her office, she closed her door and opened her safe, the one behind the oil painting of herself. It might be a little obvious, both the location of the safe and the composition of the painting. A tad on the tacky side. But it amused her. She liked playing at being human. Besides, it wasn't like the existence of the safe was a secret. Everyone in the office knew about it. She kept it locked with the traditional combination lock, but she had added a little extra something to the security of it. If anyone touched her safe without her express permission, their skin would start to burn. It would be a burn that would eventually consume their entire body, leaving a pile of ash where a thief used to be. It might seem harsh, but was only just.

Extracting the box labeled "Apollo," she removed each item one at a time, lining them up on her desktop. The first ransom note, which had arrived two weeks ago, demanding her presence in Florence, Italy, or they would mutilate her brother. *Half-brother,* she corrected in her head. It was written on creamy white paper, thick and expensive. The ink had an unusual sheen to it and the handwriting was smooth and accomplished. Whoever they were, they were wealthy. This was further confirmed in their demand. They were not looking for money. They were looking for her. So the agenda was personal.

Then there was the ear. It had arrived the following week with a short note saying simply, "We mean business." She'd had a contact of hers in the medical examiner's office run some tests on the ear and they confirmed that it was a human ear. While the gods *looked* human, they had no DNA in their cell structures. Their cells contained swirling golden fluid, which definitely would have raised a red flag for the ME. So it was an ear, just not Apollo's. The ME had sent it back to her in a mason jar of embalming fluid and it moved gently around inside the jar as she placed it on the desktop. This told her that they must not know details of the gods' anatomy or they would never have tried to pass off this human ear. This had removed from the suspect list the gods of the Greek Pantheon.

And then there was tonight. The spiders. Her connection to spiders was really very obvious and ancient. She had created one vain-glorious spider, not *all* spiders, as their Latin nomenclature, arachnid, would suggest. Some storytellers, Ovid, Hesiod, exaggerated her influence. But it would appear that her sole spider was looking for attention. She nodded to herself, repacking the box, adding a zip drive of the security footage and tonight's note as well. Placing the ear in last, she walked slowly to her safe.

The way forward was clear; she would be ignoring them. Aside from her policy of never negotiating with terrorists, she never looked back on a decision she had made in the past. Being the Goddess of Justice had never protected her from the bitterness of those on the receiving end of her judgement. If only her rightness was evident to all. Until that day, she'd just have to keep her staff safe and wait these idiots out. A knock at the door brought her back to the present.

"Excuse me, but you have a visitor. She says she is your aunt. Oh, and I seem to have missed rescheduling your 7 pm with the Secretary. I don't know how I did that, but I spoke with her assistant and got you in for breakfast tomorrow at Café du Parc. I hope that meets with your approval."

Jessica looked terrible. Her eyes were glazed, her hair was sticking up on one side where the spider webbing had tangled it, and despite Athena's genuine compassion towards her, if she showed any weakness at this point it would only confuse the poor girl more. Using her sternest voice, she set her features in a masque of disappointment, "The breakfast meeting is fine, Jessica, but I expect more from you. You are expressly responsible for maintaining my calendar. I will have to seriously consider your continued employment."

Athena's dressing down of her favorite assistant was interrupted as her least favorite aunt/stepmother pushed her way into the room.

"Fire your staff later, Athena. My sources tell me you have a spider problem. We need to talk."

Hera. Athena ground her teeth and took a slow breath in through her nose. Who had told her? What had she overlooked? Watching Jessica's growing look of comprehension as she touched her hair, Athena cursed under her breath. She'd have to be re-wiped. *Great.* Closing her eyes to compose herself, all she could think is that nothing, nothing, was more inconvenient than family.

CHAPTER SIX

Reduce, Reuse, Recycle

* * * * * * * * * *

Hannah

Desperately seeking fresh air

The taxi driver was bobbing and weaving through the early morning rush hour, the vast network of roads leading out of the airport and into Milan conveying an odd sense of generic urban sprawl. It was not the old world Europe she had expected. It didn't help that she was crammed in the back seat with Lee and John. A particularly nasty lane change made her stomach churn and she felt the cold chills that were the precursor to vomiting. If she could just open the window she could hang on to whatever was in her stomach. As she scrambled for the elusive window crank, she had the hazy thought that the flight attendants from hell had claimed she'd slept through the meal service, so all that was in her stomach to lose was mostly vodka and whatever other bile and fluids were generally in the stomach, all swirling together. It made for a queasy Technicolor image in her mind. An image that triggered a gagging reflex, and coming up empty in the search for a means to open the window, she clamped her lips together and looked desperately at the demon on her right, one hand pressed against her resolutely closed mouth, the other hand pointing to indicate the imminent danger.

"Oh, I have just the thing, hold on," and Lee bent over to rummage in his bag. Hannah looked across Lee's back to see John ignoring her distress, staring out the window at the swiftly shifting traffic. His color was normal and he actually looked good, not as if he had passed out on a trans-Atlantic flight. He seemed to be impervious to the ramifications of his alcohol and prescription drug free-for-all, and if she could only open her mouth without vomiting, she would have demanded to know how that was possible.

"Here." Lee passed her a rumpled air sickness bag, "I rinsed it out after I used it. It's only slightly damp. It should still work just fine."

Shutting her eyes against this knowledge, she tried to focus on outcomes. A recycled airsick bag was better than none. Accepting the bag and holding it gingerly by her fingertips, she was spared the experience of reusing Lee's airsickness bag by the sudden rush of air as the window to her left opened. Leaning out as far as she could, she retched into the traffic, grateful for the movement of the car distancing her from her throw up. Closing her eyes she collapsed back into the seat, mutely returning the used-but-not-by-her airsickness bag to Lee. As he took it back, she opened her eyes to look directly into the smirking gaze of Hermes, leaning back from the front passenger seat.

"Well done, H. Nothing says *buongiorno* like vomit splatter on the windshield." At that moment a car pulled up alongside of them packed with angry Italians, pointing and cursing. Hermes raised the window while Hannah slunk down in the seat and the car drove on, still blasting its horn. "I asked the driver to drop you and Line Boy off at the plaza ahead. Go to Sun Boy's last known address. Lee and I will be at the Four Seasons, researching his electronic trail. Lee, give H your cell number. Don't call unless you find something."

Hannah handed her phone to Lee, " Wait, won't we be staying with—"

But she was cut off by Hermes' laugh, "If you can afford a thousand dollars a night, you are more than welcome to join us. But as I know that's not the case, you'd be better off trying to find something more in your price range. I'm sure Milan has the Italian equivalent of Motel 6."

Before she could argue the point, the car jumped the curb and slammed on the brakes, the back doors popping open. Struggling to grab her backpack without falling out of the car, she felt panic grab her throat. She didn't speak the language, had no idea where she was, and was suddenly wishing her mother was here to make these men be nicer to her. She was tired of John's silent treatment and Hermes' mocking. Lee, with his pre-moistened gum and slightly used air sickness bag, was the only male in the vicinity who had shown her any kindness. But as Lee handed back her phone any kind words he might have said were lost as Hermes, leaning across the seat back and shoving Hannah out the door, ordered the driver to step on it.

She was spared hitting the sidewalk by John's quick reflexes, and he held her under the armpits until she seemed steadier on her feet. In the time it took her to stand on her own, she cycled through a record number of emotions, starting at tears and self-pity, moving through panic and then back to self-pity. She'd been sick, she was exhausted, and she'd just been pushed out of a moving cab. Pulling in the shaky breath that preceded tears, she looked up from her feet to see where she was and she held her breath.

This was Milan. Cobbled streets and ancient architecture that had been present for centuries, now housing cell phone stores and travel agencies. And shoes. Everywhere she looked there seemed to be a shoe store. She was in Milan and it didn't matter if no one had held back her hair when she puked, she was working a case for Hera and she was going to find Apollo. And for whatever reason, John, though he was pissed at her, was here to help. She exhaled tear-free.

Shaking free of John's assistance, she pulled out her phone, looking up her notes on the hotel that Apollo had been shacking up in. "We need to find the *Pigro Americano Ostello*. Hermes said it was in the *Quarto Oggiaro*. But given his general demeanor since our reunion in Connecticut, and the fact that a quick Google search identifies it as the criminal center of Milan, I think we might want to take a minute to get our bearings and check it out before we go. That looks like a coffee shop over there— shall we see if they have wifi?"

She couldn't tell, but she thought she saw admiration in his look as he nodded. At a minimum, he must have been relieved that she had not dissolved into hysterics. She knew her face was expressive enough that he must have picked up on her momentary panic.

"Good idea. I could use some breakfast, too. Maybe they have some eggs."

Eggs? Just the word made her throat close up. Pausing at the street crossing, she stared at him, "Are you the same man who passed out on my shoulder on the flight here? How is it that you are not even remotely hung over? I was there, John. You drank your head size in hard liquor and you took unknown pharmaceuticals from a greasy demon, and yet you don't even smell bad! How is that possible?"

But she was denied a detailed explanation of his recuperative powers as the light changed and the crowd of people they were standing in surged across the street. He smiled back over his shoulder at her, "I have a fast metabolism."

She trudged after his backpack, muttering to herself about men and their glibness. She reached the curb just as the light changed back and she felt the whoosh of the manic cars passing directly behind her. The traffic in Milan was not for the faint of heart or the slow of foot. Trying not to take the deadly pace of the motorbikes personally, Hannah stepped more securely onto the sidewalk and noticed that John was at the café door, chatting with an impossibly beautiful dark haired woman.

Taking in the people moving through the streets of Milan, it seemed to Hannah that all the women were beautiful. How was that possible? Come to think of it, she had a vague memory of her mother quoting a *Ladies Home and Hearth* article to her about European women and their commitment to fashion over function. She wondered if the European Union ever considered holding American women in quarantine at the airports, forcing them to lose their practical travel clothes before entering the country. When they were packing for Greece Gretchen had turned a blind eye to her cargo shorts, but had insisted that Hannah lose the fanny pack, despite its hands-free convenience.

Gretchen. Lee had lent Hannah his phone after the terrifying flight attendants had snatched hers so that she could call. She had planned on telling Gretchen the truth. About everything. Well, maybe not everything, but mostly everything, but when Gretchen answered, Hannah lost her courage and blurted out the first thing she could think of. Death in the family. Beloved great aunt. Funeral on Wednesday. Gretchen was understanding, sympathetic, everything a real friend should be. She even offered to postpone or cancel, but no, Hannah had told her to go and she would catch the red-eye on Wednesday and meet up with her in Volos and finish out the cruise from there. When she ended the call, she found herself looking into the judgmental gaze of John MacCallister. He hadn't said a word to her since then except to brag about his metabolism. And now, here he was, picking up Italians.

Approaching John and the mystery model, Hannah shifted the backpack on her shoulders and tried to smile without opening her mouth, afraid her breath would be rank, even from a distance.

"Hannah, this is Adelina. She was coming out as I was heading in. She speaks English, isn't that great? She's offered to help us, like our very own Italian ambassador."

The woman laughed and put her hand on John's chest. "He's so funny. Is he always so handsome? Mmm, and strong," and her hand slid up and down his chest.

Even saying something so insipid, Adelina was charming. Hannah nodded mutely, caring less about how annoying it was that the members of her sex found John universally appealing and more baffled by how the t-shirt and shorts on Adelina looked like a fashion editorial on the casual elegance of summer while the exact same outfit on her own body looked like the back page of a pamphlet from the government on tourist traps and how to avoid them. It had to be the bone structure. That and the gazelle legs.

"Oh, you look tired. Let me take your bag for you and we'll get you an espresso. Yes?" Beautiful and kind. Well, John had picked up worse. Nodding again, Hannah followed the two of them to a table in the back of the café, sinking gratefully into a chair while Adelina went up to the bar to order drinks.

"She seems nice."

"Listen, Han, we won't have much time alone." He grabbed her hand under the table in a vice grip and yet continued to talk in a relaxed tone, smiling, "We need to get away from *that woman* without her knowing that we are leaving, so we can lose her. Maybe she's just a grifter, but whatever she is, *we* are her *targets*. If she knows that we know, then we're screwed. I doubt she's working alone. If she thinks her cover's blown, she will definitely call in backup. And they are bound to be much less friendly. We only have one shot." John's mouth barely moved and Hannah felt disoriented by the contrast between the alarming words she was hearing and the smiling relaxed face they were coming out of, "When she comes back, act upset. Jealous. Storm off— be sure to grab your bag. I'll go after you. I'll tell her you're insecure, and that I just need to calm you down. She's vain enough to believe that I'll come back to her. It just might buy us enough time."

Their new friend/enemy was heading toward their table elegantly balancing three espressos on a tray. Hannah turned back to look at John, "Really?" She wasn't sure what she was incredulous about, his intense paranoia or the ease with which he suggested she would be insecure.

He was leaning back in his chair, smiling encouragingly at the woman approaching them, all easy–going American hipster, but his eyes momentarily skewered hers, "Pull it together, Summers. This is real." And before Hannah could reply he was up from the table helping Adelina with the drinks, chatting in broken Italian. Hell, he knew some Italian. Of course he did. Her mind tried to skitter off into a list about all the things John MacCallister kept from her when the memory of his urgent gaze penetrated her exhaustion. He had been serious. She needed to get out. Scanning the café for the bathroom sign, she made up her mind.

She bit down hard on her lip, tasting the metallic flavor of her own blood. Grabbing the paper napkin from the center of the table and blotting, she smeared some on her mouth as well. Crying out, she turned the bloody side of the napkin to face out while she kept it over her lower face, grabbing their backpacks with her other hand.

"My tooth!I think it broke! I'm bleeding! I'm bleeding!" Shoving the bloody napkin into Adelina's shocked face, she and yelled back towards the table, "One bite of airplane biscotti and I am a bloody freak!" Then thrusting his bag into his arms, "Enjoy getting to know Italy!" Hannah whined, "I want to go home!" Waving the bloody napkin again at Adelina for good measure, she pivoted toward the bathrooms and stalked in that direction.

She could hear John apologizing to Adelina, saying that they'd had a long flight and promising to be back, but it might take awhile. She turned the corner towards the bathrooms, and without breaking her stride, used the napkin to wipe at her face, and walked instead through the kitchen passway. Pulling her backpack onto her shoulders, she put her hands up at the accusing stares of the kitchen help, "*Tourista. Americano. Exito?*"

Rolling their collective eyes, they pointed her toward a door in the rear, and as she pushed out into the narrow cobbled alley, John was right behind her, but not for long. Taking the lead he looked back toward the door they had just passed through, "Move. Quick. We have three minutes, five max, to put some distance between us and them."

Them? As she jogged behind him through the narrow and winding alleyways of Milan, sweat now pouring down her back in the growing August heat, she wondered, for the first time in her acquaintance with John, if he was mentally sound. Her lip was throbbing, her mouth was dry, and her nausea had finally passed, leaving a massive void in her stomach. She wanted a meal, a shower and a bed. But instead she was running through the back alleys of Milan dodging stray cats and enduring the curious stares of the morning work force unloading produce into the many restaurants they must be running behind. All because John MacCallister believed some random woman, working with some mysterious shadow cabal, was out to get two American tourists. Maybe he'd watched one too many Discovery Channel specials on the dangers of travel. But she couldn't ask him because he was easily half a block ahead.

After ten minutes of darting and sharp turns, she looked back over her shoulder, but the only "them" she could see was an old woman hanging out her third story window, pulling on her laundry line. Her feet flagging, she looked up at the neighborhood they were in and to her surprise, nestled between two ancient buildings, was a narrow passage over which hung the sign, *"Pigro Americano Ostello."* Bingo!

"John! John! Come here!" John spun around, and for a moment that warmed her heart, he looked ready to come to her defense. He was already half way back when he saw that she was not in imminent danger.

"What? Why did you stop? We need to keep moving."

She was also reassured to see that he looked as hot and sweaty as she felt. Her work with the gods had made her aware of the immortals in the world around them and suspicious about any atypical humans. And his sprightly health after a night of debauchery had made her uncertain if there was something off about John. But this sweaty mess was normal. Paranoid, but human. Pointing to the sign, she whispered, "That's the place. Where Hermes said Apollo stayed." Looking over at the street sign she frowned, "But this isn't the address he gave me. I think we should check it out."

Pulling up the bottom of his t-shirt to wipe his face, he nodded, "Okay. But don't tell them what we are looking for. Let's case the joint first."

Hannah smiled, his suggestion lining up perfectly with her ulterior motive. "My thoughts exactly. Follow my lead." She was determined to get to a bed if it killed her. Grabbing his hand she towed him under the stone arch, through a bricked-in courtyard with a broken fountain, home to a flock of murmuring pigeons that didn't even bother to lift when they walked by, to an ancient wooden door with a hand lettered sign that said, *"Americans,*

Come Here Inside." She paused at the threshold, "At least they are clear about their marketing strategy." And she pulled him into the cool, dark interior.

The narrow room had incredibly high ceilings and though the paint was dingy and the windows covered, the floors and counter were made of a beautiful veined marble. A marble so old that the footfalls of centuries had worn paths in it. The only sound in the room was the ticking of a grandfather clock lurking in the stairwell. Intimidated by the silence, Hannah crept up to the counter, peered over and saw an extremely small, elderly man sitting in a hard wooden chair much lower than the counter, his head barely coming to the top. Wordlessly he pointed to a sign that read, "Ring bell for service." She wondered if all of these directions on signs was par for the course in Italy, but when she turned to ask John, he was peering out a peep hole in the door, clearly keeping an eye out for "them." Shrugging, she rang the bell, curious as to what would happen next.

As the bell echoed in the stone room, the elderly man disappeared from his perch. Her hand hovered over the bell, had she done it wrong? Should she ring again? But then she caught sight of him returning with a step ladder balanced over his head. Placing it down, he climbed to the top so that he was just taller than her. She opened her mouth, but before she could speak, he held up his hand, stopping her. Reaching down below the counter he pulled out a large black Victorian ear trumpet, pointing the wide end toward her and placing the small end delicately near his ear. He waved his hand at her.

"Um, hello. *Buongiorno.* We," and she pointed over at John who was still staring back the way they had come, "need a room.

Rooms." She scrambled to try to remember a little Italian, *"Duo room, por favore?"* At his continued myopic stare, she tried to clarify, "To sleep in. Now. We have been flying all night. Also, if you have any food?"

But she was cut off by his singular response, "No!"

"No? But you must have a room free? Yes? If you don't have food, that's okay."

"No! No two rooms for you."

Facing such complete negation and being so close to a bed where she could sleep and have a chance to clear the confusion that had blanketed her since the flight, activated her desperation. In something close to a yell she begged, "John! Can you translate please? I need to sleep." Not waiting for him, she leaned down into the mouth of the ear trumpet, "Please sir, I need to sleep. *Duermo?*"

"Duermo is Spanish, Hannah." John nudged her to the side and engaged in an animated conversation with the frail desk clerk, his Italian peppered with English. It wasn't sounding good from where she was standing. She caught a word that sounded like "no more" and the little old man was shaking his head so vigorously the ear trumpet had become dislodged. John turned back to her and spoke in a whisper.

"Here's the deal. He only has one room available. But he won't rent it to us because he thinks we are... sinners." Suddenly another word she thought she had heard made more sense, "fornicator." This was absurd.

"Just tell him we don't do that." She leaned past John and yelled loudly, "Just friends! No fornicating!"

John, grabbed her arm, "Shh, I already tried that. He doesn't buy it. If you want the room, take it. I'll sit out here in the lobby."

It was the fastest way to sleep, and she was about to agree, when she noticed how anxious and stressed out their escape from the café had left him. Maybe paranoid delusions were his hangover? He looked scared. And the only chair in the lobby looked older than the ancient clerk. And just as unwieldy. As discreetly as she could, she worked the ring off her keys clipped inside her travel shorts and slid it onto her left hand. Charging the counter, she waved her hand in front of the desk clerk's frowning face and did her best to act like a crazy American bride.

"Look! Look! See, we are married! This is our honeymoon!" She elbowed John, "How *do* you say honeymoon?"

"I don't know, my Italian doesn't cover committed relationships." Though he sounded cranky, he must have seen some hope in the clerk's eyes, for he put his arm around her, speaking into the trumpet, *"Luna de matrimonio! La mia bellissima sposa."*

Scowling and shaking his head, the clerk dropped the trumpet, and Hannah felt the defeat in her bones. Suddenly the fake tears she had used at the café were threatening to return in their natural state, and no amount of slow breathing or internal pep talks were going to stop them this time. But she was spared the indignity of sobbing in public by the tiny old man. Coming up from under the counter, he pulled out a heavy brass key with the number four tied to it and handed it to John, while he pushed the leather journal towards Hannah. Pointing at it, he commanded, "Name! Write!"

She resisted the urge to scrawl her name and grab the key before the old man could change his mind, and took her time writing, trying to scan while still keeping her pen in motion, her every move being scrutinized by the little old man.

John leaned over her shoulder and whispered in her ear, "Are you trying to decide if you should keep your maiden name, Summers? We could always combine our names— MacSummers or Sumallister?" She shut him up with an elbow to the ribs and pointed at it. There it was. Proof. In flowery, scrolling script better suited to a pre-teen girl and taking up at least three lines in the register: *Apollo Montgomery*. Whatever his agenda for lying about the address, Hermes had not lied about this. She felt her own relief reflected in John's slow exhale.

"First we sleep. Then we eat. Then we investigate. In that order." At John's nod, she smiled again, and with a flourish in the direction of the staircase, stated in a loud voice for the benefit of the desk clerk, "After you, Mr. Summers."

* * * * * * * * * *

Hermes

Sipping Prosecco at the Four Seasons

Egyptian cotton bed sheets, caviar delivered on a silver tray by a nubile young beauty, and fine Italian wine before noon. Oh, he could get used to Hera's expense account. Twirling the corporate credit card in one hand while he sipped his wine in the other, he tried to imagine what H would do when she realized that the address he had given her was not to Apollo's hostel but to the most notorious criminal quarter of the city. He didn't think she would cower, but she had looked fairly pathetic when he had kicked her out of the cab with Line Boy. His decadent reveries were soured a little by the annoying voice in his head that wondered if she would be okay. Of course she'd be okay. She had the necklace.

"Boss, I am not finding much of a trail." Lee had turned out to be an invaluable employee in the last three months, his computer skills making most cases a point and click success. He was willing to take a pitiably low amount of money for a wage, but Hermes had found that his little demon assistant needed a high level of hand holding.

"Aww, thank you for thinking how valuable I am. You are the best boss I have ever had."

Oh right. And he had the annoying habit of eavesdropping on people's thoughts. *Which would bring him a world of trouble if he ever did it without my permission again.*

"Um, sorry, boss. Um, that doesn't count, right? Because you meant me to hear you think that one, right?" Lee smiled at him, encouragingly.

Rolling his eyes, he suppressed his instinct to throttle him,"Yes. I wanted you to hear that so that you would stop snooping in my mind. Nothing more." Lee was an unusual demon, in his experience. He was this odd mixture of puppy-like optimism combined with powerful skills, all of this focused on serving him. Hermes had found this very helpful in his detective work. Weird, but helpful. "Eavesdropping is rude— unless it's against our enemies. Then go right ahead." Crossing to the other side of the room, Hermes reclined on the couch, "And we wait here, in style, until one of your clever computer nets catches the Golden Idiot, then we swoop in, rescue him and win the game."

"The game, boss?" Lee frowned, obviously confused.

"Yes, Lee. *The game*. The game where Hera tries to belittle me by making me subservient to H." In a high falsetto, "*You* will work for *the girl*. You will help her find Apollo and return him to me." Leaping up off the couch he started to pace. "Screw her!" Candy had warned him Hera liked to play with him, make him her bitch. Well that ended here. "The game where I show that condescending Martha Stewart knock-off how it is done. I'm the professional here. I don't need a child to lead me. But to be on the safe side, I sent H off chasing loose ends while we solve the case."

Hermes didn't need to read minds to understand the look Lee was giving him now, "She'll be fine, Lee. She has Line Boy to help her."

"But, boss, you sent Hannah to the wrong place? What if she gets hurt? Or lost? Oh, I don't like this."

"When did you become the den mother? We are all adults. Why don't you eat, you always feel better with some cheese in you." And he flicked the credit card across the room. Lee caught it easily in one hand. That demon may have questionable gland issues, but he had top-notch reflexes.

"Thanks, boss." At Hermes' sharp look, Lee scuttled to the door, "For the cheese, not for the compliment that I most definitely didn't hear by listening to your thoughts." Lee ducked quickly out the door as the bedside lamp came crashing against the wall, and yelled from the safety of the hall, "I think you are worried about her, too. Hannah. I'll just pop down to the kitchen, just like you suggested, boss. Because you know best."

Hermes scowled at the dent in the wall and the scattered fragments of porcelain from the lamp. He was not worried about

H. Despite being a human, she had game. Hadn't she proved that last June? Hell, she was probably in on the joke with Hera. It was the only way he could think of that H could have come into possession of that necklace. Hera probably gave it to her to use against him. He was done being Hera's entertainment and if that meant screwing over H, well, all's fair in love and war.

Besides, with the Gorgon necklace, H was untouchable. He'd first noticed she had the Gorgon necklace when Skeevy Art Dealer Nymph was proposing to her. While H tended to show less skin than a Benedictine nun, she was too flustered by Art Nymph's proposal and Line Boy's subsequent jealousy to notice that her blouse was made sheer by the bright afternoon light streaming through the windows of her meager little apartment. It was then he caught sight of the small black necklace nestled between her breasts.

Hermes had been there when Medusa met her end by Perseus' sword, and while Perseus was busy snatching up her snake be-ringed head to use as a weapon, Hermes had retrieved the necklace. All three Gorgon sisters had them, and they were reported to contain powerful magic. He was certain that Medusa's sisters, Stheno and Euryale, would be willing to pay a hefty price to have it back. Trouble was, he ran into his cousin, Bacchus, upon his return to Olympus, and one thing led to another, and by "thing" he meant barrels of wine, and he was fairly certain he gave the necklace to a particularly leggy wood nymph who had admired it. She'd been straddling him at the time and it had seemed only polite to let her try it on. When he sobered up, he could never quite remember which nymph he'd given it to. They all looked remarkably similar and they all denied having it. He hadn't thought of it since. But when he was ogling H, he recognized it at once. He never forgot an item he had stolen.

And the flight attendants. Just the latent energy off that necklace had whipped the flight attendants into a frenzy. What would you expect from *harpies*? Half bird, half woman, they were mostly used by the gods to punish humans and snatch food away from them. After the fall, harpies hid out in mountain ranges, trying to blend in with the bird population. But in more modern times, they had found a segue back into civilization with the advent of both the flight and diet industries. If they weren't working for Weight Watchers they were flight attendants. He imagined the harpies on last night's flight would have ripped H to shreds if the necklace hadn't also been strong protection. Which was why he was not worried about sending her off into a notorious part of town in a foreign city without any back up.

The only person he could imagine being powerful enough to have the necklace, and in a position to give it to H, was Hera. Which only confirmed for him that this little expedition to rescue Apollo was fixed from the get go. He expected to be toyed with by his sadistic step-mother, but H? He had thought they had an understanding. Had worked as a team back in Cambridge. He had not imagined that she would be party to humiliating him. But then, he'd been wrong about humans before. Leaping off the bed, he began to pace the room.

He was brought up short by the vibrations of his cell phone. *Hera.*

"Yes?"

"I want to know your progress. I can't reach the girl. I assume you haven't found him yet."

So it's like that. Well, he could play his part, "Well, Hera, I'm not privy to that. H is in charge, I'm simply following her orders."

Hera's voice took on a saccharine tone, he could picture the mocking sneer on her face as she slowed her words, as if she was speaking to an idiot child, "Yes, Hermes, we all know how good you are at following orders. So here is one more, if you can handle it; tell your boss that she needs to call me as soon as possible to fill me in on finding Apollo. Did you get all that? Or shall I repeat it, but more slowly?"

He resisted the urge to smash his phone into the wall. If only he could have resisted the urge to respond at all. Ending the call mid-sentence was probably not the best choice. If it pissed her off that could lead to unpleasantness, but the more likely scenario was that it entertained her, irritating him. What the hell was that breathing thing he was supposed to do to calm down? Where the hell was his happy place?

"Hey, boss. I hope you like olives, because there was this amazing selection of—"

Lee was pushing a silver domed tray into the room, his hands busy and his servile face the perfect target. Hermes let his phone fly, picturing it hitting the demon squarely on the nose. But even this petty satisfaction was denied, as Lee lifted the lid off the food, catching the phone in mid-air, the curve of the lid sending it right back to his hand. Smiling, Lee enthused, "Nice throw, boss! Want me to make you a plate?"

Somehow his little demon's bizarrely cheerful response defused his anger. *Screw them.* "Yes! Bring it on, and then find the Golden Boy, ASAP."

He'd let Hannah wander the hot, humid streets of Milan and

Hera wait for a call that wasn't coming. He would recline in air conditioned splendor eating olives while Lee found Apollo on his laptop. Then he would call them both and tell them where to pick up their sodding Apollo. *Simple enough for you, Hera?* She wasn't the only one who could be entertained. Throwing himself back onto the hotel bed, he grabbed the TV remote and ordered up the finest skin flick the Four Seasons had to offer; to the winner goes the spoils. And he was definitely the winner.

CHAPTER SEVEN

Making the Best of It

* * * * * * * * * *

Apollo

Tied up in a padded cell

One of the benefits of being the God of the Sun was that you never lost track of the days, despite being tied to this chair in a windowless room. He had a flawless internal clock. Fourteen days. Fourteen days inexplicably held hostage. His ankles and wrists were bound by some sticky string that looked like spider webbing, but was so strong it had to be something else. But what? He was a god. He should be able to break free. They must have done something to him when they jumped him.

The last thing he remembered was following the trench-coated man out of the train station in Milan. He had turned the corner, careful not to muss his clothes, when it all went dark. He awoke with his arms bound behind him, his ankles secured to the legs of a metal folding chair. His first thought was of his beloved, Naomi, and with confidence he pulled his limbs in, intent on breaking his bonds and going to his love. But all that had happened was that the chair he was tied to folded in on him, leaving him trapped, flopping about on the floor. He had managed to right himself back into a sitting position, and had spent the unmarked time trying to think his way out of this trap.

Normal bonds could never hold him. Staring down at them he wondered what they were made of. What could be stronger than his muscles? Could it be kryptonite? He'd learned all about kryptonite from a documentary he'd watched. He was not as stupid as Hermes thought. He'd watched it on his phone on the flight to Italy. It was all about a man who was sent here from another planet and though he had amazing powers, there was one thing that could render him weak: kryptonite. Unfortunately he had grown bored by the documentary and hadn't finished it— he had never pretended to be an intellectual— and had spent the rest of the flight texting Naomi emoji that expressed his unending devotion. Kitty cat with heart eyes. Barbershop pole. And of course, the sun. But now he wished he had finished the movie, as it might have given him some ideas of how to break these bonds.

He had no idea why he was here. Were his kidnappers part of some strange cult in love with him, kidnapping him to make him their sex-slave? It wouldn't be the first time. Or maybe they were all part of the hero's quest Naomi had sent him on? Some challenge Naomi had arranged to test his love? They never spoke to him and he'd only seen one person since being here, a lovely dark haired girl who brought him food once a day and fed him by hand. He tried to talk to her, to win her over so that she would free him but she wore headphones and refused to make eye contact, making his most powerful advantage, his awesome charm, useless. If he couldn't sway her with his beautiful face and seductive words, he would do the next best thing. Every time she opened his cell door he started flexing his muscles. His thighs were particularly impressive. He was certain that only yesterday he had caught her staring as he flexed and released. It had to work.

He had been so close to finishing his quest and returning to claim Naomi with his bank full of money, an employed man, worthy of her love. For the first few days he had yelled her name and slammed his feet on the floor, creating as much noise as he could, but nothing. Now he mostly sat silently, waiting for his food, deciding which muscle group to flex to seduce his captor. It was because he was so quiet that he heard the conversation outside of the room.

"You lost them?! Amateur! I knew I should have sent Victor to do it."

"Victor *was* there. We *both* lost them."

"I didn't lose them! I was behind the counter. I was back up, only to be called in by you after you got them talking. I did my part. I drugged the espressos. You were the one who got played."

"What are we going to do with you? First you get all soft on you-know-who because he has pretty eyes and then you can't even manage to dispose of the spies *she* sent to steal him back. I think we need to send you home to Grande Zio."

Apollo frowned. *Grande Zio.* It was the first time they'd said that name. Great Uncle? Who the hell was Great Uncle? And who was the *she* who had sent people to rescue him? If Naomi sent him on this challenge, why would she help him? Unless this wasn't part of her plan and she missed him and sent someone to find him? His head hurt. The pleading tone of the girl only added to his pain.

"No! I can do better. I promise. Please let me stay. I will find them. They can't have gone far."

"Fine. You stay here in Milano and find them. And to be on the safe side, we will take you-know-who to the warehouse in Firenze. But child, do not screw up again. I will not be able to protect you. Grande Zio has waited centuries for the signs to align, for the advantage to be in our favor. We cannot let him down. *Everything depends on this.* "

"I know. I won't let him down. I promise."

"Go with her, Victor. We need Athena's minions stopped."

Athena? Athena was behind his rescue? For the first time since being grabbed he relaxed. If there was one goddess in the world to have on your side, it was Athena. She was even more powerful than Hera, a total badass. She would get him out of here in no time. He heard the key turning in his cell door. It must be dinner time. With Athena on the case, this would probably be his last meal with the girl. Probably. But it never hurt to have a back-up plan.So just to be safe, he clenched his jaw as the girl entered and tried to flex all his muscles at once.

*   *   *   *   *   *   *   *   *

Gretchen

Sipping an Ouzotini in the moonlight

Using the railing of the ship to stretch out her calf muscles after a terrifying ten hour flight on the discount airline, she re-sisted the urge to bum a cigarette off the gaggle of Eastern European twenty-somethings singing ABBA on the aft deck. The moonlight mirrored on the gently moving harbor was ridiculously beautiful, and she should be marveling in the fact that she was in Greece. Instead she yawned. With her travel time and the time difference, it was as if she had skipped an entire day, leaving in the night of one coast to skip right into the night of another.

"Jet lag, love? Here, have another."

At Gretchen's nod, Jillie, the cruise director, handed her a second drink. The cruise line she and Hannah had booked on was called the *Lurve Boat*, everyone on staff sort-of named after characters from the late 1970s TV show of the very similar name. She'd already had her room shown to her by Gapher and Captain Stubbing had been at the gangplank welcoming passengers aboard. The company had gone to only minor lengths to change names from the show, thus leading to a massive lawsuit by the Spelling estate. Court fees alone had pushed the *Lurve Boat* into chapter eleven, and she and Hannah had booked a week, all inclusive cruise of the Greek Islands for $500 each. Which was amazing, except for a few drawbacks.

"We will be setting sail in twenty minutes, so if you need to use the toilet, now is a good time to go."

Like the bathrooms. The *Lurve Boat* had lost its permit to run sanitation lines while in dock, so they had arranged to use other ships' facilities when in port. The other ships would drop a rope ladder down from their main deck, and passengers on the *Lurve Boat* had to climb to get to a toilet. Like a pirate sneaking on board. Which might have been fun, if she had a friend to laugh about it with. The difference between something being awful and something being funny was often the company you keep. Where the hell was Hannah really? Taking a long pull on the strong drink Jillie had given her, Gretchen continued her internal catalogue of awfulness.

The flight. When Hannah had turned out to be a no-show at the landing strip near Bradley Airport, she made the executive decision to climb on board anyway. Hannah's cell had gone straight to voicemail. Whatever had happened, she wasn't filling her in on it. She thought back to their most recent conversation. Had their been any indecision in Hannah's tone? Not that she could tell. So without any other intel, she had to make a choice. Go back to Vermont? Head down to Whitfield? They both seemed like defeats. So she climbed the metal staircase up to the cockpit of the plane. The pilot had handed her a seatbelt, oxygen mask, and bag of peanuts and then given her a small shove through the cargo door, the only words of advice to choose a seat near the center of the plane, as it would be the least cold.

The cargo hold was lit by small blue lights along the ceiling, so she had used the flashlight on her phone to find a seat. The first one she located was attached to the floor with rope. Deciding that she could do better, she searched until she found a seat that was bolted to the floor, the ceiling-high containers on either side suggesting that it would at least be a secure place to ride this out. She thought she heard other people getting on the plane, but her position between the two containers blocked her line of sight. Buckling herself in, she popped on her noise-canceling headphones and lost herself in season one of *Gilmore Girls*.

But Lorelei and Rory, despite their excessive dialogue, were no match for the questions that assailed her. Why hadn't Hannah shown up? Had she gotten a flat tire on the way out of town? Was her phone dead because she lost her charger and so she couldn't call for help? Had the police stopped to help and ran her plates to find that she had unpaid parking tickets? Was she sitting in the Centreville jail waiting to post bail, but unable to afford it because they had spent all of their money on this vacation? What if, by leaving, she had left Hannah stranded?

That thought had coincided with what must have been their final ascent, as the air around her got decidedly colder. Pulling her legs up onto the seat, thoughts of Hannah receded as she focused her energy into generating enough warmth to sleep in the fetal position.

That had worked for at least several hours. When she awoke, the air in the plane was warmer, and she was struck by the possibility that Hannah had just been late to the airstrip, and that at this very minute was somewhere on this plane, hopefully in a seat that was bolted down. That thought had given her the mental peace to dig her phone back out of her bag, just in time to see that she was getting an incoming call from Hannah.

Voice trembling, Hannah had begged her forgiveness. Death in the family. So sorry. Be there by Wednesday.

It was a lie. The dying family member part, not the being sorry or joining her on Wednesday, those sounded like the truth. But why did she lie? What was really wrong? She'd spent hours talking with Hannah this summer and had learned the patterns of Hannah's speech. The way she blocked conversations with politeness and submission. But the more they talked, the less that had happened, and Gretchen had started to feel like Hannah trusted her. But now this. *Death in the family.*

Whatever was wrong, Hannah was keeping her out of it. Which, if she admitted it, hurt. So she had played along with

Hannah's dead aunt story and said all the right things. Sorry for your loss, don't worry, I understand, etc. But as soon as she landed she sent a massive funeral wreath to Hannah's parents' house. Let Hannah explain that to her mother. Finishing off the drink in hand, she wobbled a little on her way back to the bar and felt the first twinges of guilt at what she had unleashed on her friend. Gretchen had only spent a weekend in Cambridge this summer, but that was long enough to know that Hannah's mother, Elise, would be appalled at Hannah's "death in the family" lie. Imagining her friend squirming under her mother's lecture, almost made her regret her actions. But the she remembered that she was alone on the trip they had planned together. Alone and not trusted. It seemed a just punishment.

The bartender, whose name tag said Eyesack, was a beautiful man whose real name, Leo, she had flirted out of him. Smiling at Leo, she decided that she couldn't force Hannah to trust her, but that she could stop moping about it. Hannah would tell her the truth later, or not. Right now she was young and single and in the Grecian Isles. It was time to have some fun. But first, she would pirate her way to the bathroom. Humming to herself, she rearranged the lyrics to *The Love Boat* theme song in her head as she started to climb, "Lurve/ exciting and new/ climb up the rope/ to-oo use the loo..."

CHAPTER EIGHT

Aphorisms and Abbreviations

* * * * * * * * * *

Hannah

Tuesday evening in a hostel in Milan

She woke in the dark; disoriented and thirsty. Luckily, her backpack was crammed full of bottled waters. Leaning over the edge of the bed, she reached down and tried to retrieve the water without waking John. She failed.

"How are you feeling?"

Tipping the bottle back and swallowing, she thought about her answer. "Hungry. And wide awake." Pulling her phone off her travel charger, she checked the time. Crap. They had lost most of the day, and she needed to find Apollo by tomorrow if she was going to make it to Volos in time to meet Gretchen. "It's ten pm. I forgot to set an alarm. I can't believe it." Flopping back down on the narrow bed she pulled the pillow over her eyes and tried to block out the feeling of panic that was building in her head.

Room number four at the *Pigro Americano* was small in actual square footage, but felt more spacious due to the truly epic ceiling height. A single tall window looked out into the deserted courtyard, which might have felt claustrophobic if it weren't for the multitude of stars that were visible through the open sky. What it lacked in the modern amenities— the bathroom was down the hall and there was no air conditioning— it made up for in other ways. The floor was more of the worn marble from the lobby. Its surface stayed cool to the touch even in the heat of August, and seemed to lower the temperature of the room. The double bed— apparently sanctioned only for married fornication— was actually two twin beds pushed together with one large bedspread over them. Making it a simple thing for them to pull apart and each have their own. But the real pleasure of the room were the sheets on the beds. She had never felt sheets so beautifully clean and cool, and after showering down the hall with a hand-held nozzle in an ancient tub, she had slipped on her two-piece bathing suit— it was modest enough for sharing a room with John— and had fallen deeply asleep while John was still down the hall wrestling with the shower head.

"You might want to call her back. Tell her the truth. Or at least extend your lie out to some reasonable time frame."

Flinging the pillow off her face, she turned to him, accusation the primary tone, "I didn't mean to lie to her. I wanted to tell her. I just couldn't. How could I explain? Oh, Gretchen, remember last June? Well actually, you probably don't because most people have very hazy memories of that week, for a good reason. See, I was given the gift of having everyone listen to everything I said in some misguided marketing scheme by Apollo, the God of the Sun, to reclaim his former glory. Now I work secretly to keep the immortals of the world compliant to a non-interference accord. Yeah. She won't think I'm crazy." Flipping onto her stomach, she gave into self-pity and whined into the sheets, "She is my first real friend."

"Oh. So what am I?" He was still lying calmly on the bed, hands behind his head, the sheet draping his hips.

She turned in his general direction and frowned into the dark. Was this a trick question? Though she had decided against honesty with Gretchen, she found herself tempted by John's question. It was their first real conversation since the Declan debacle and she found herself wanting to talk. Besides, there was something easier about talking in the dark, and so she answered.

"*You* are curious."

"Curious like strange or curious like inquisitive?"

"Both." She had spent the better part of the flight here, when she wasn't passed out, trying to figure out why a man who had actively ignored her for the last two months, who was clearly disapproving of her in every way, would risk his safety and max out his credit cards to come with her to Italy to search for a missing god, and all she came up with was *curiosity*. "I think that you came here with me against your own will because you couldn't bear not knowing how this would turn out. "

"You forgot my love of frequent flyer miles, but I appreciate the armchair analysis. Let me return the favor. You deflected my question so that you could talk about me but not to me. Why didn't you answer my question?"

"I did answer your question. If you have other questions, you will just have to wait, because we don't have time. We have to get going." She rolled off the bed and started rifling through her bag for a change of clothes. She did not have many options. She and Gretchen had decided to share clothes for the trip, to cut down on packing. She could put back on the clothes she'd worn earlier, but even the most cursory sniff ruled them out. Leaving her only one choice, unless she wanted to search for Apollo in her bathing suit. "You can use the room to get dressed. I'll use the bathroom." Flicking on the light she ignored his groans as he pulled the sheet up over his head.

She had almost been safely out of the room when she caught sight of John's naked back reflected in the dark window and tripped over the threshold. Catching herself against the wall, she let out an involuntary oomph. She pressed her flushed forehead against the wall, praying that he had not noticed her fall.

"Are you okay over there?" His amused tone confirmed he had not only noticed her fall but had guessed what had precipitated it. Great. More fodder for his ego.

"Fine!" She bolted for the bathroom, the door swinging shut on all that casual nakedness. She headed down the hall, her change of clothes clutched to her chest in a caricature of the shocked maid. Purposefully relaxing her arms, she castigated herself. Why had she spazzed? It wasn't like she'd never seen a naked man before. She was a grown woman, not some prudish spinster aunt from a novel. Her last lover had introduced her to position 87 in the *Kama Sutra*, not that it had been very successful— it had required more core strength than she'd had at the time— but still, she was no blushing maiden. She was a grown woman who needed to get a grip over an ass-sighting. And she would, as soon as she was safely dressed as far from the naked ass as possible. But as she turned the corner she saw there was a line in the hall for the bathroom. Four women, with different shades of short hair, all in Keen sandals and dressed in identical pink t-shirts with "FB's European Tour" printed across the chest. If she had to guess, she would put them somewhere in their late fifties. They were all talking at the same time and she hesitated to interrupt them. She had not anticipated a line, and she wondered what the etiquette was at the *Pigro Americano*. She didn't have long to wonder.

The blonde woman held her hand up in the universal sign for stop, and ordered in a flat Mid-Western American accent, "Take a number." She pointed to a row of what looked like plastic dress size tags. Above the numbers was another hand lettered sign with a long list of rules for the bathroom. She hadn't noticed either the rules or the numbers when she had used the bathroom earlier. Staring at the list while she picked up the number six, she felt a hole starting in the pit of her stomach, only getting deeper as the four other guests waiting in the hall complained, their voices overlapping.

"Can you believe some asshole used up all the hot water?"

"It clearly states on the rules that no hot water can be used between noon and five. What moron can't read?"

"Angela said she saw a man coming out of the shower when she went back to her room during lunch to get her camera. She said he opened the bathroom door and a tower of steam rolled out. A tower. Can you believe it?"

"I can believe it. We should complain to Signor Rossini, he'll set them straight."

"You don't think he'll get them to be whacked, do you?"

"Karen, how many times do I have to tell you? *La familia* don't have people to be whacked. They whack them. Where were you when we were reading *The Godfather's Friend*?"

"For chrissakes, Ellen, it doesn't matter if her grammar is whacked, Signor Rossini is not connected. Any idiot can see that. We should just take matters into our own hands."

"Susan's right. Vigilante justice! Let's fix him ourselves! But, you know, Angela did say he was fine. Like *David on the Half Shell*. So maybe we should talk to him first, you know, just to hear his side of the story."

"Yeah. Let's get the stupid water-hogging frat boy!"

And as if they had slowly reached some inner synchronicity from their overlapping chatter, they all turned to stare at Hannah. The blonde one who had ordered her to take a number, the one whose name was Susan, spoke, "He's probably your moronic frat boy, isn't he?"

Hannah felt a momentary panic, unsure of what the women would do if she owned up, yet realizing there was absolutely no chance to avoid this now. She nodded mutely.

"You and your boy-toy have made us all late for our 9:30 seating at Ricardo's. What do you have to say for yourself?" They had formed a ring around her now, her back up against the wall. All she could see out of her downcast eyes was the logo on their t-shirts. Was she about to be jumped by a gang of angry social-networking middle-aged women? This was not one of the dangers she had read about Milan on the State Department website.

Channeling her mother, she tried a diversionary tactic, "I like your shirts. The FB European Tour. Sounds like fun! Are you all Facebook friends?" She looked up hopeful that they would be more interested in talking about themselves than in beating her up. It had sort of worked, for though they were still angry, it was no longer directed at her. They started to yell at each other.

"I told you FB was a stupid abbreviation. Everyone thinks it's Facebook and no one ever asks!"

"What do you mean, no one asks? She just did!"

"Well FFB is even stupider. People would still think we meant Facebook, but they would just think it was a typo and we were incompetent."

"Girls, we voted on this, so let's stop arguing."

Hannah saw an opportunity to further their distraction, and in her most interested tone asked, "What does it stand for? The FB?" She could change in her room; John's naked butt was nothing compared to this. She just needed to get them to break the circle around her and she could edge out.

The red-headed one named Ellen answered, "Fan Fiction Bitches. It's our book club name. We only read fan fiction and we are all women with healthy attitudes. FB."

"Yeah! We pick a book and then read all the fan fiction about it that we can find."

Despite herself, Hannah couldn't resist asking, "Your book club travels together?"

This time it was Susan who answered, "Well, that is what is weird, right? We were at our June meeting, the first Monday of the month. And we were discussing *Eat, Eat, Eat* by Caroline Carter— a fan fiction of *Eat, Pray, Love*— when we turned to YouTube to watch the latest vlog from the author—"

"But before we could watch it, Ellen, who is obsessed with what's trending, made us watch 'the most watched video.'"

"She thinks it makes her hip."

"No, she does it to stay close to her daughter."

Ellen cut back in, "When we all decided that we wanted to

follow our dreams. Together. Immediately." And they all nodded. They started to talk over each other again.

"It's a little hazy, now, but at the time it seemed clear."

"So clear. We quit our jobs, cashed out our 401Ks and came here."

"We didn't come *here*, we started in Venice."

"We ate *a lot* there but—"

"The antipasto, oh, and the olives and the wine—"

"We ate a *lot* there but—"

"The wine was glorious."

"But—"

"But the canals became tedious."

"And you fell in."

"I did not fall, I was pushed."

"So we came here. To Milano. We stumbled across the *Pigro Americano Ostello*. This is the best deal for long term visits. A steal. We've been here for a month, eating. Milan is delicious."

"Except Angela keeps complaining about the water. And the long lines for the bathroom."

"Made longer by idiots who can't follow the rules."

While they had momentarily been distracted, Hannah watched in dismay as all four women boomeranged back to their bathroom complaint. The circle around her got tighter. A dark haired woman who had been silent throughout now spoke up in a deep, menacing tone.

"What room are you and the moron staying in? We might as well have this out with both of you at once."

Wide-eyed, Hannah held her breath and held up four fingers. She hoped John knew martial arts but worried that his knowledge was limited to yoga. She did not think yoga was going to help them with the Fan Fiction Bitches.

"That was Apollo's room! He must have finished his quest!"

"Do you think he is with his beloved Naomi now? Oh, I hope so!"

"Of course he's with her. That was the plan, Karen."

"Oh, it's so romantic! What I wouldn't give to be a fly on that wall!"

While three of them started to argue about whether it was creepy or not to want to see the reunion, Ellen seemed to finally notice Hannah's panic and interrupted their debate, "You scared her, Maeve. Look how scared she is!" Leaning into Hannah, Ellen slowly placed her hand on Hannah's shoulder, "We aren't going to hurt you honey, just explain the house rules. Oh, poor thing." The remaining women all turned and joined in with general sounds of reassurance.

"Look, she's wearing a bathing suit, oh, she must be afraid to be naked with her boy."

"No, I just—"

"Oh, here comes Angela. Angela, look what we found. She's staying in Apollo's room with her boyfriend but she's too shy to get dressed in front of him, isn't that cute?"

"I'm not too shy, I just—"

And amidst their general chatter they ushered her into the bathroom. They all started to fuss over her and before she knew it they had pulled her dress over her head. They turned their backs while she removed her bathing suit, talking the entire time.

"I saw her man when he came out of the shower. I would be

shy too. Even with a towel on, he made my pulse jump."

"Hush, Angela. How long have you two been together? How did your story start? Did you meet at the airport? Oh, what if they met at the airport and it was love at first flight?"

"We are all done with your puns, Ellen."

"Well, *Karen*, your rhymes are as fresh as yesterday's soup."

"Actually, some soups are intended to be more than one day old, you know, like, pease porridge hot."

But it was Maeve who cut through the noise, "Don't bicker, let her answer. Tell us your story."

And like that, the women fell silent, waiting on her answer. Hannah felt dizzy. Somehow these women had gone from threatening bodily injury on her to fussing over her like a flock of well-meaning hens. It was like she had fallen into a padded cell full of doting mothers. After all of the stress and confusion of the last twenty-four hours, it felt weirdly comforting. On top of that, she had not missed their comments about Apollo. As she laid out her story, omitting all references to immortals and Greek Gods, they listened, an attentive audience.

And they returned the favor, filling her in on Apollo and his hero's quest to win back Naomi.

"It's so wonderful. Apollo and Naomi are star-crossed lovers."

"Star-crossed is not a good thing, Ellen. The crossed part means they don't end up together—"

"That's not true. Look at Romeo and Juliet. They ended up together."

"Oh for god's sake. They only ended up together if you consider being dead a joint activity—"

"You two are way off topic. Apollo is not acting out a Shake-spearian tragedy. He's been cast in an epic hero tale. A beautiful model who is working his way through the fashion houses of Italy and back into Naomi's arms. I see it as a musical. Like *A Chorus Line*, but with male runway models. *A Cat Walk*—"

"Yes! The music could be composed by Lady Gaga."

"Yes!"

As they talked, she became passive under their ministrations. While one fixed her hair, another applied make-up, and a third placed a light shawl over her shoulders, "For when you go into the churches." It was only when Ellen started to lift the Gorgon necklace off her neck that Hannah snapped out of her inertia.

"I only wanted to polish it honey, don't worry."

Hannah's grip on the necklace was fierce, but her tone was easy, "No, thanks, though. I'm sentimental. I mean superstitious. I never take it off." She rose off the stool they had seated her on, and turned to see her reflection in the mirror. It was like they had waved their fairy godmother wands on her. Her hair was lifted off her face and twisted in the back, exposing her neck and giving her the appearance of gracefulness. The make-up they had used seemed to have disappeared into her skin leaving behind longer lashes, brighter eyes and fuller lips. The shawl floated on her shoulders, making her feel winged.

"That is a killer dress, hon."

The dress had been Gretchen's. A simple sun dress fitted close, strings wrapping around the empire waist, tying in the back. But the strings were all that were covering her back, the dress cut to reveal, well, everything, the fabric only starting again right above the lowest part of her back. It was all Gretchen.

Hannah pulled the shawl lower.

"No! Don't cover it up. You got it, you should flaunt it."

Hannah cringed. Flaunting it was not her strong suit. Gathering up her bathing suit from the floor, she thanked the FB women, who all stood in the hall, waving to her as she headed back to the room to get John. Her trip to the bathroom had ended up being the best move she could have made. Not only did she have a detailed account of Apollo's time here at the *Pigro Americano*, but the *Eat, Eat, Eat* women knew everything there was to know about food in Milan.

"Now, remember, Ceres' Table is two blocks south. Great food, cheap prices."

"And candle light."

"No, I don't need candle light."

"Oh, candle light is so romantic."

"No, no romance, we are just friends. Honestly. We just had to pretend to get the room."

"Yeah, yeah, we know. Just friends. Listen, we drink our morning espresso at Carlo's Café in the piazza near the train station. Feel free to stop by and fill us in."

"On all the details! We live for the details!"

Waving a last thank you and good night, Hannah practically skipped down the corridor, the ethereal shawl swirling around her, and smiled as she heard the bantering sounds of the Fan Fiction Bitches resume their natural state of disagreement.

* * * * * * * * * *

Athena

Step-mothers are hard to shake

There was clearly an acceleration factor for stepmothers in Benjamin Franklin's old adage about house guests and fish, because it had only been two days since Hera had dropped in for an impromptu visit and she was smelling to high heaven. Metaphorically, of course. Hera would never *actually* smell. She probably had some ten-part article in her silly magazine about female deodorants and their proper application. Right next to an editorial on the use of beef bouillon; is it a legitimate time saver or the first horseman of the apocalypse?

Athena smirked, grateful, not for the first time, that she was never leg-shackled by such pedestrian female concerns as cooking or house-keeping. Hera can have full reign over hearth and home, she would stick to wisdom, justice and knowledge. And war, she couldn't forget war. While she did not relish personal combat, she was concerned with the strategies of power that war represented. Who has it? Who should have it? What were legitimate ways to get it and keep it? She never had to bother with something so mundane as laundry. That was what other women were for.

Not that she judged them. Other women, that is. For every great thinker there was a small army of lesser people who saw to their personal needs. The everyday woman. They were essential for all the great advances of civilization; she just didn't happen to be interested in them. And she found herself struggling to make conversation with her father's wife, a woman who, though she had amassed no small amount of power in her time since the fall of Olympus, had no real imagination on how to wield that power and instead seemed content to exhaust the topics of hemlines and casseroles, needling other women into submission over minutiae. To spend one's days consumed with such topics would be her own personal circle of hell.

Which might help explain the intensity of tedium she was experiencing with this particular guest. Hera had appeared in her office Monday, implying that she knew details about the spider attack, ostensibly offering help but clearly angling for more information. Though it concerned her that one of the Nereids must have gossiped for Hera to have the intel she had, she would deal with them later. There was no way she would let the Busybody Goddess into her affairs. Since Hera already knew about the spiders, it was simple to acknowledge the attack but deny any knowledge of the reason. She had hoped as she ushered Hera out of her office that that would be the end of that. But she had not anticipated Hera's insistence on staying with her to protect her while such unexplained attacks were ongoing. She could not reject such an offer without raising more questions, so she had feigned gratitude and resigned herself to Hera's presence. But that had become intolerable. She needed to find a way to rid herself of the Queen of Domesticity.

She knew that telling Hera about Apollo's abduction would be the most efficient way to end this torture. It was tempting, as it would solve two of her problems with one elegant choice on her part; telling the truth. Hera would immediately leave to find and destroy the creatures who dared to detain her beloved golden boy. Her annoying house guest would be gone and her enemies would be dust. Tempting. But she did not succumb to temptation. To use Hera in this way would be responding to the terrorist, if only to punish them.

Terrorist were like whiny children. There was no good and bad attention— it was all attention. A response on her part might be perceived as legitimizing their complaint. So despite the convenience telling Hera the tale would create, she could not risk the implications her actions might precipitate. She had nothing to account for in her dealings with that woman Arachne, and she would never cave to those who would try to manipulate her into a manufactured apology simply to rescue her half-brother.

She had done her due diligence. She had reviewed the facts of Arachne's transgression. It had been a long time ago, back in the early time of their reign on Olympus. The facts of the case were clear. Arachne fell victim to her own vanity and arrogance. The punishment she had meted out to her was completely justified. You could make the argument that it had been kind. Really rather poetic. Arachne was allowed to spend the rest of her life weaving, and for a good purpose. Spiders were really rather useful. So, if anything, Athena had improved Arachne's life.

"Do you want me to pull into the parking lot, or is here by the curb good?"

The cabbie's question broke Athena's concentration, and she looked out the window to see that he was not *by* the curb but *on* the curb. The Wednesday afternoon traffic continued to stream by, bending around his car.

"It is illegal to drive on a surface that is not designated as a roadway by the state or federal government."

"Yeah, yeah, yeah. Fine. I'll drop you off here."

Stepping out of the car, she leaned in before closing the door, "You might want to pay more attention to following the rules of the road next—" but her final words were lost as the cab peeled out, the door slamming with the force of the car's acceleration, tires leaving a skid mark on the sidewalk.

Well. Setting her shoulders, she stood still for a moment to let her body adjust to the oppressive August humidity after the air conditioned climate of the cab. The driver had also mistakenly set the temperature of his cab several degrees too cold, but she had erred on the side of politeness and had refrained from pointing that out to him. And after his emotional departure, she was glad she had, as she could tell that any attempt to help that unfortunate man would have been wasted. Some humans were better at taking correction than others.

Straightening her summer linen suit, she walked toward the entrance of the National Zoo, carefully avoiding the stroller moms in their lycra shorts grasping water bottles in one hand while pushing their yelling little monsters with the other. Athena carefully suppressed her disdain. At least on this topic, her stepmother was justified in haranguing women to have the self-respect to dress appropriately. One should never leave the house in clothes you wouldn't feel comfortable being buried in. Did that woman have the word "juicy" written on the seat of her pants? Hopeless. She turned down one of the shadier and quieter paths.

The National Zoo was a favorite of both the ubiquitous tourists and the locals. The masses were drawn to the big ticket animals, the elephants and giraffes, and of course, the pandas. The visitors tended to move in herds, down the paths of least resistance. She always wondered what they looked like to the animals in the enclosures, these half-dressed, excitable creatures thundering through the zoo, pausing once in a while to stare and point. Sometimes she let herself get pulled into the flow of the crowd. It was like surfing on a sea of sub-par intelligence and sunscreen. It could be distracting. But today she needed a little time at her favorite spot to sort through this morning's developments. The situation was reaching crisis point and she needed to analyze it to get some clarity on the best strategy to move forward. Her favorite place in the zoo was in the far southern corner, a fair walk from where the cab driver left her. She would use the time it took to get to her spot to enumerate the relevant events and put them in their proper perspective.

Home. Well, she'd already spent the taxi ride sorting through the irritation that was Hera. She couldn't walk into her house and not be assaulted by the smells of home cooking and the re-arrangement of her furniture into supposedly more pleasing configurations. It was all a not-so-clever campaign to wear her down to get her to divulge the details of Apollo's kidnapping. She knew Hera was suspicious and was not letting up. Hera was a master of indirect relentlessness. Though Athena felt like smothering her with one of the tasteful accent pillows that now brought out the colors of her couch, she resisted. Family drama was an indulgence of the small-minded. Hera could not break her. But to be safe, she had opted to avoid the temptation to lose her temper at home, and had put in extra time at work.

Work. Work had been suffering since the Monday spider incident. Her research staff seemed to be taking longer than normal to bounce back from their memory erase, impacting their productivity. They had failed to provide her with their normally comprehensive briefing on an appropriations bill that was up for a vote. She had almost missed blocking an amendment the opposition had added at the last minute that would have adversely affected her client. She had a zero-tolerance policy for incompetence. She had been forced to fire the entire team. That had been yesterday. And then just this morning the normally imperturbable Jessica had been screening job applicants to replace her research team. Athena was abruptly pulled from her desk by Jessica's hysterics. Athena entered the front office to see Jessica perched on the top of her desk screaming "Spider!" while pointing at something on the floor. It had turned out to be lint. After calming her, she had been forced to dismiss her. She could not have an unstable assistant. So now she had an empty office. That was inconvenient and she resented it.

"Excuse me, do you know where the bathrooms are? This is such a big zoo and we are here from Pennsylvania, and it is so hot, I didn't know it would be so hot, and we all have been drinking so much water and you know what that leads to— bathrooms! We just can't find them anywhere!"

Athena considered the woman in front of her. It wasn't her tacky clothes or bad hair that bothered her, no, for despite her preference for appropriate dress, she was not concerned with the physical plane. What struck her about this particular human was the total lack of intellectual rigor reflected in the woman's speech. Who didn't know that Washington, DC was hot in August? Who chose not to read one of the dozens of maps in the zoo to locate a bathroom but instead accosted a total stranger to find one for you? This woman didn't need a bathroom, she needed a lesson. Reviewing the woman's question in her head, she answered simply, "Yes."

"Oh. Yes?"

The woman was clearly waiting for her to say more, but Athena refused to spoon-feed her. She had not asked for directions to where the bathrooms were. She had asked if Athena knew where the bathrooms were. Which she did. So she had answered in the affirmative. "Good day." And she walked off smiling, leaving a spluttering, angry, bladder-stressed woman and her family behind. She had done the woman a kindness. Though Athena gave her less than a fifty percent chance of figuring out her mistake, at least she had a chance.

Arriving at her bench in a better mood, she checked for gum, and, finding it clear, sat. She was in the large primate section of the zoo and in front of her were a series of tall poles with ropes strung between them. They were built for the orangutans to use to get from their enclosure to the Learning Center, simply another enclosed space where they could play games with the zoologists. Orangutans were incredibly strong, intelligent primates, and their enclosures at the zoo were highly guarded. The illusion of open environments for all the animals at the zoo disguised the high level of security in place to keep the occupants locked in. And yet these poles and ropes were in the open. As they traveled over these ropes there was nothing between them and the freedom of the world. Nothing but their intelligence and self-interest.

She had read all about it. A scientist had designed the ropes to be too far away from anything else for the orangutans to jump to and they were too high up for them to survive the fall. And orangutans were smart enough to know that. So the only force that kept the primates on their ropes was their knowledge of who they were and what they were capable of. She loved to come and watch, imagining the bittersweet feeling the orangutans must experience in the open air on their ropes. And despite the confines of their lives which might drive the most placid creature to desperation, not a single orangutan had ever thrown caution to the wind and jumped. There was something profoundly impressive about that.

She needed to exercise similar restraint when dealing with the descendants of Arachne, for it had to be her descendants who were behind the recent spider attack on her employees, and thus the kidnappers of Apollo. They clearly wanted vengeance. Why else would they use violence to compel her attendance? Vengeance. She understood and approved of vengeance, when it was justified. But in this case it was not. They refused to see that their own limitations had been created by their very nature. It was as if the lesson she had tried to teach Arachne about humility remained unexamined. And unlike their orangutan cousins, these primates were flinging themselves off the ropes, damaging others in their reckless fall. Like her staff. And her livelihood. And her half-brother. They needed a lesson.

As with the woman looking for bathrooms, her response should lead them to learn from their mistakes. Could the imperative to improve the human existence through learning outweigh the principle of not responding to terrorist threats? She nodded slowly. Justice was the process of weighing competing claims for ascendancy, given the context and compelling nature of the claims. If the claim to teach the kidnappers a lesson outweighed the claim to not legitimize their delusions by responding to them, well, then it would be just to teach them. Setting Hera on the kidnappers would be the moral high ground. It would teach them to reconsider the original sin of arrogance in the face of the gods. That it would get the Goddess of Hearth and Home out of her house and stop the disruption of her work, well, those were just unintended benefits. It is not being selfish if a just action happens to serve your needs. It is serendipity. The blessing that comes from wisdom.

She smiled and watched as an orangutan started the climb. Not every primate was blessed with self-awareness. Some needed to be taught. Tonight she would reveal the truth about Apollo to Hera. Everyone should have the opportunity to learn.

CHAPTER NINE

Fight or Flight

* * * * * * * * * *

Hannah

Twelve hours later in Florence

Hannah still couldn't lose the feeling of being hunted, a feeling that had started in the dark on a train platform in Milan. The evening had started over a heaping plate of carbonara as she had filled John in on the information she had learned from the FB women about Apollo heading to Florence by train. Though it was late, John had suggested they check out the station after dinner, if nothing else, to pick up a schedule. The last train of the night was loading, and they found the station master helpful, at least he would have been, if he'd remained conscious. Nothing is more clarifying than watching the person you are talking to, in their case the station master, fall to the ground, a dart in his neck. Correction. Watching a second dart hit the wall next to you is more clarifying. And motivational. Adrenaline gave them the speed they needed to make it onto the moving train ahead of their assassin. They collapsed, winded, and as the train pulled away, their pursuer a lone, dark figure, remained behind on the platform. John had caught a glimpse of her face as he pulled Hannah onto the train. It was the woman from the café, Adelina. That John was right about her was the only upside to this development. All they knew was that she was hunting them— for who and why was a mystery.

That was midnight in Milan. Now it was noon in Florence, and she was trying to blend in with the tourists lining up to enter the Uffizi art museum. Twisting the ends of her borrowed shawl, she tried to find some shade in the shadows of the massive building to her back, but with the sun directly overhead, she was out of luck. Still, she tried to be inconspicuous and blend into the Florentine architecture while she watched the plaza for Gretchen. After the events at the train station, it had become clear to Hannah that she either had to call Gretchen and kill off another fictitious relative, or tell her the truth. She opted for the later. After a surprisingly short list of questions, Gretchen told her to stay put, hung up, and texted her with a travel itinerary. So here she was, waiting for Gretchen's train to bring her up from Rome, where she'd flown during the night.

Hannah slipped further into the shade of the Uffizi. She needed to be able to see Gretchen, but not be seen by the dart wielding Adelina. Hiding in Florence wasn't that hard. The ancient city seemed filled with nooks and crannies built for concealment. Add in the secret tunnels built by the Medicis, and Hannah couldn't think of a more fitting place to be living out a cloak and dagger scenario. Folded into all of the ancient structures were the casual displays of beauty: the statues by Michelangelo, the paintings of Botticelli and Raphael, the lush gardens and elaborate palaces. It was a sumptuous location. But her appreciation of it was mitigated by her growing exhaustion. Having fled one city in the dark of the night to arrive in another hoping that, in transit they had lost their enemy, had left her with an adrenalin hangover. The rush was waning and the only thing keeping her focused was meeting up with Gretchen. Noon at the Uffizi. There were supposed to meet outside, right? Gretchen's text had said *at* the Uffizi, not *in* the Uffizi, right? It was noon, so where was she? John would tell her to relax, remind her that the trains in Italy were notoriously behind schedule, maybe even distract her with a running commentary on the tourists filing into the museum. But John wasn't here either.

He had said something about getting food in the market across the bridge. She hoped he meant the bridge spanning the Arno river directly across from the Uffizi. Florence was full of bridges and she wished he was back already. She had the distinct feeling that something was watching her. Watching and waiting. And now that she was alone, she had the impending sense that whatever it was, it might consider this a good time to strike. She caught herself reaching up to check for the Gorgon necklace and resisted. If there was something watching, she did not want to do anything to reveal her one advantage. For a moment the absurdity of such a dramatic thought struck her, and she smiled. Hadn't she once seen a t-shirt proclaiming that it isn't paranoia if they *are* out to get you? She had a visceral understanding of that particular slogan. Because there were definitely people out to get them.

The number of their adversaries seemed to have increased exponentially since arriving in Italy. And that was not an exaggeration. They had entered Italian airspace with a job to locate a god gone AWOL with exactly no known enemies, and now they had two confirmed enemies. Hannah still wasn't sure who Café

Girl really was or why she was chasing them. What she was sure of was that Hermes had given her bad information. The FB women had confirmed that the address he'd given her was to a notoriously dangerous part of Milan. Hermes was not on her team. And that was a problem. Hermes with an agenda was a dangerous competitor.

She shaded her eyes to scan the now-quiet streets. The Italian day paused around noon. Shops closed up and everyone seemed to evaporate for an hour for the midday meal. It was one of the delights of Italian life the FB women had regaled her with in the bathroom at the *Pigro Americano*. Tugging on the hem of her sundress, she thought longingly of her backpack, abandoned along with John's bag, in their midnight escape. All they had were the clothes on their backs and their basics: phone, wallet and passport. They'd only planned to go out for dinner and discuss the information she'd learned in the bathroom. The FB women said Apollo had bid them goodbye the night before as he always took the discount train first thing in the morning. He was headed to Florence for a modeling job. It was a place to start looking for him.

She had felt excited about both the meal and the lead. She was also pleased to finally be neither hungover nor jet-lagged, and with the FB women's help she had felt pretty in the sundress and borrowed shawl and eager to be going out into the night of Milan. That was last night. Now she wished she had worn the stinky shorts and t-shirt from Monday. This sundress was useless. Gretchen clearly had not considered the lack of pockets important when she bought it. Pockets were not only good for carrying things, but also for shoving your hands into when you felt like bolting but needed to wait. Trying not to jump out of her skin, she wrapped her hands in the ends of the shawl and pulled it across her shoulders.

"Hey Hannah—"

John's words caused her to twist, her nerves frayed. "Easy, Summers. You look like a bird." Placing his hands on her shoulders, he lead her to a shaded part of the wall, "Aren't there bird women in your classics' books?" He leaned back against the stone wall with her, holding open a bag of fresh cherries. "Here. Eat. No sign of Gretchen?"

"Thanks." She closed her mouth around a deep red cherry, pulling off the stem. The cherries were perfect, juicy and cool. It filled her mouth with sweetness and provided her with a moment of normalcy as she rolled the pit around her tongue. "Harpies. The bird women. They snatched all the food away from Phineus, King of Thrace, as his punishment. They were thought to be sharp gusts of wind." She felt a momentary sense of déjà vu, an idea close but just out of reach, and then shook it off. "The trains are probably late. At least that's what I had you tell me in my mind."

They exchanged smiles and Hannah took another cherry. John's anger or resentment or whatever it was that had driven him to freeze her out at the start of this job had long since passed, and communication between them had become easy. She supposed one of the side-effects of the fight or flight instinct was that it cleared out emotional baggage and simplified relationships. Now that she thought of it, the thaw had started earlier in the night, over dinner. Hannah was pulled out of her reverie by the growl of her stomach. Pressing both hands over her midsection, she caught sight of John's amused expression.

"What? I get hungry when I'm tense. It's biological."

"Of course. Science and all." Handing her the bag of cherries, he rummaged in his pockets, " I also grabbed some bread." He reached in and pulled out a short crusty roll and tore it in half.

"Grabbed? Do we have to worry about the *garda?*" She hoped if he did steal it, that he had more. The bread tasted wonderful. Flaky on the outside, airy and chewy on the inside. Italy had not been a disappointment in the food department. "Thanks. This is perfect. You wouldn't happen to have a water bottle in one of those pockets?"

"Gas or no gas?"

Laughing, she chose the carbonated water bottle and took a break from looking for Gretchen to eat. They both slid down to sit against the wall, splitting the remaining cherries and using the now-empty bag to collect the stems and pits. John produced a hunk of cheese from one of his many pockets and they took turns biting off the cheese and bread. She shouldn't be so hungry. She and John had eaten a huge meal the night before. It had started out somewhat awkwardly, which had been her fault. In between the first two courses, despite the inherent rudeness, she'd answered texts, as her phone had finally adjusted to its new European location, and a flood of delayed texts started rolling in. Professor Tetley checking in on the assignment. A terse request for an update from Hera. A ridiculously long message from her mother demanding to know where she was and why wasn't she in Greece like she said she would be and did Hannah have an explanation for why that lovely friend of hers had sent a funeral wreath and condolence card to their home in Cambridge and just who exactly had Hannah fictitiously killed off and did she know that *Ladies Home and Hearth* reported that women who lie to other women have a sixty percent chance of never meeting the right man. It was scientific. The text ended with an exhortation to consider her actions, ending with the quote, "Oh, what a tangled web we weave when first we practice to deceive." Capped off with a smiley face emoticon. Classic Elise.

At her expression, John had asked if the fish course hadn't agreed with her, and on an impulse she handed him her phone. Scanning the message, he had looked up at her and for the first time since this had all started, she was a direct recipient of the charming MacMan smile. It made her feel a little lightheaded. Raising his wine glass, he proceeded to perform a dramatic reading of her mother's text, complete with a spot-on Elise impersonation. He really had her mother's inflections down. They both dissolved into laughter, cut short by the arrival of the pasta course, and the phone went back into her purse. They spent the rest of the meal talking through everything— from the initial visit of Hermes and Lee all the way up to the Fan Fiction Bitches in the bathroom. She showed him the Gorgon necklace and told him what it was capable of. He confessed that he still woke up freezing cold most mornings, the residual effect of having spent so much time frozen back in June. And sometimes he thought he'd seen Sek in Connecticut— at the grocery store, or in line at the bank. His mom, a psychiatrist, had reassured him that it was probably an echo of the stress he'd experienced. It's not every day you encounter a demon.

After dinner they stopped by the train station. They had shown the station master a photo the FB women had shared with her of Apollo from a modeling campaign he'd done that summer in Florence. While the Station Master didn't recognize

Apollo, he did recognize the scarf Apollo was wearing in the print. Digging down into the lost and found box he had pulled out a long silky scarf, an exact match to the one in the picture. As Hannah was examining it, the dart took down the station master. When a second dart skimmed by her face they ran for their lives, still clutching the scarf.

"Isn't that Gretchen?" John's voice brought her back to the present, and he pointed across the plaza at a dark haired woman striding confidently down the street toward them. Gretchen was one of those women whose confidence illuminated her features. She had a long straight nose set over a somewhat wide mouth. If the Queen of Spades jumped off a playing card and cut her hair short, you would have Gretchen. She was tall and angular and she wore clothes that made the most of her height. In her ankle boots and short shorts her legs were epic and elegant even with the massive pack on her back.

Scattering the cherries from her lap, Hannah leapt up to meet her friend, sprinting across the plaza, anxiety about how mad Gretchen might be at her eclipsed by the relief at seeing her. Flinging herself at Gretchen, Hannah hugged her fiercely. Excited, she started peppering Gretchen with questions and exclamations, "You're here! Was the trip hard? What is Rome like? Was the flight expensive? I'll pay you back! Are you hungry? We have cherries and bread and cheese and water and some of the water is fizzy, is that big in Greece too, or just here?"

Gretchen gently disengaged from her grip and laughed, "No, big, no, and yes— I'm starving! But should you be talking so loudly, Han? Aren't we supposed to be, I don't know, discreet or something? On the phone you mentioned several enemies I thought we were concerned about, I mean, providing you haven't gone bat shit crazy on me, which trust me, I considered, before I decided it didn't matter because either way I wanted in."

Hannah must have looked hurt, because Gretchen grabbed her back into the hug, "No, no, I don't think you're crazy. I'm here, okay?" Leaning back to look Hannah up and down, she let out a low whistle, "That dress looks good on you, Han. I have good taste." Gretchen's eyes widened as she looked past Hannah's shoulder. She lowered her voice to a conspiratorial whisper, "John MacCallister. Now that is how to travel, Han. He didn't bring a brother, did he?"

Hannah shook her head, turning to watch his approach, "He did not. He is definitely an only child."

But before she could discourage Gretchen's train of thought, Gretchen tossed an arm around her shoulder, and waved at him, calling out, "Hey there John." Catching herself short, she looked around surreptitiously, lowering her voice, "Um, sorry, are we not using our real names? Because if so, I came up with an awesome alias on the ferry over." Dropping her pack to the ground, she struck a pose, "I'm Calista Dreamstar. My parents were 60's radicals deported for anti-American behavior and I have grown up in coffee houses around the world, always on the move, my education consisting of late night *tête-à-têtes* with the literati on philosophy and politics and wandering through the museums of the world. I am in Florence to meet up with my Midwestern cousins, you two, who are looking to get off their conventional Rick Steves-inspired tour of Europe and really live. What do you think?" Waggling her eyebrows, she stepped back to look at them together, "I think I nailed you two."

John retrieved the shawl that had landed on the ground during Hannah's exuberant greeting, his own greeting to Gretchen as warm as Hannah's, but not involving quite so much physical contact, "Hey. I'm glad you're here. Real names are probably fine, but you do have a point about taking cover. Why don't we catch up in the Palazzo Vecchio, that castle place over there behind the David? It's pretty deserted about now." John slipped the shawl back over Hannah's shoulder and picked up Gretchen's backpack, smiling at them both before heading off across the piazza. Gretchen linked arms with Hannah and they followed at a distance so as not to be overheard.

"So what is up with that?"

"With what? John? Nothing. I mean, we're just friends, he's helping."

"Please tell me you are on top of that."

"What? No! I mean, we're friends...I think. It's complicated. But it is not *that*."

"Why not? Wait, you are unattached, aren't you? You did dump what's-his-name, didn't you?"

"Yes. I did. It was awful, Gretch. I had to stop Declan from *proposing*."

"Proposing what?" At Hannah's nod, Gretchen laughed, "That is perfect. Wait. Didn't you tell me that what's-his-name was a nymph? Wouldn't marrying you break the Non Interference Accord?"

Hannah frowned, "You're right. I hadn't thought of that. Talk about the theater of the absurd." Trust Gretchen to think out all the implications of a situation. If she had married Declan she would have also been obliged as the Monitor to report him. That would have made for an awkward conversation with Tetley and Blean. She was already lying to them, and it made her feel slightly nauseous. They had sworn her to secrecy about the Monitor job, so she had to omit any references to working with John or Gretchen in her text updates. It was complicated, but worth it. Tugging Gretchen into a faster pace, she pulled her up the marble steps, "I'm so glad you're here. I have a lot to fill you in on and as much as I would love to continue talking about my disastrous personal life, we need to focus, *Calista Dreamstar*."

Putting her hands up, Gretchen muttered, "Fine. No more talking about how obvious it is that the MacMan is into you. And for the record, I would be happy if you called me Calista. I wouldn't mind having a double life, too."

Ignoring Gretchen's John-bait, Hannah focused on the idea that she had a double life. She had never considered her work with Tetley and Blean in that light, but now that she thought of it, she was managing a lot of different covers. Only John and Gretchen knew about her work with Blean and Tetley, but Blean and Tetley didn't know about John and Gretchen. Hera didn't know about any of them, except John. Hermes and Lee were equally in the dark; all of the Olympians thinking she was merely the former "gift girl" working for Hera. And none of them knew about the demon Sek declaring that she was his Mry— his one, true love. It made her head hurt.

She paused to look up at the interior of the castle, the Palazzo Vecchio. The original fortress was built in 1229, and it had undergone many renovations since then, most notably under the ownership of Cosimo de Medici. It was straight out of a child's story book— crenellated ramparts and a soaring tower overlooking the piazza. You could almost see the knights in armor riding out, banners flying.

John walked over to join them. "I chatted with the guard; he tells me there is a small room on the mezzanine with a view of the plaza. I thought you could fill her in, Han, and I would keep a lookout. What do you think?"

He was just looking at her for agreement, but Gretchen's questions and innuendo swirled through her mind, and she felt herself blushing under his gaze. "Yes, yes. Good plan." Pushing him forward into the castle, she sent a quelling look over her shoulder at Gretchen, who was smirking, "We'll follow you."

The mezzanine was between the first and second floors, consisting of a series of interconnected rooms constructed in the fourteenth century, which according to the signage, served as the living quarters for Cosimo's mother. John walked to the back of the first room, to a series of steps leading to a small annex. Unlike the room they had just passed through, which had held dozens of religious oil paintings of the Madonna in various stages of distress, this room held no framed artwork. The stucco was painted pale blue with small birds, fish and animals playing among vines twining along the walls. It was simple and childlike, a relief from the heaviness of the religious imagery in the outer room.

John nodded toward the window on the far wall, "I'll keep an eye out front. I can see everything from here." The window in question was small and high and clearly built for the purpose.

Hannah looked back into the room they had passed through and, confident no one was near, pulled out Apollo's scarf, handing it to Gretchen. "This is it. It's our only clue to Apollo's disappearance."

Gretchen slid the scarf between her fingers, her first reaction one of pleasure, "Oh. It is so smooth. Is this silk? It feels lighter and smoother than silk. How is that possible?"

As she spread it out, Hannah pointed to a series of symbols lining the edge. To the casual observer, it might look like simply a decorative border, but she suspected they were runes of some sort. Some kind of ancient language. And if anyone would be able to recognize it, it would be Gretchen. "What do you think of these?"

Gretchen squinted, "At first glance, they could be anything. Someone at the textile plant could have used a computer program to make a border design. But look at that," she ran her finger under one section of the pattern, "That is familiar. I know I've seen it before. I just can't remember..."

Hannah grabbed Gretchen's shoulder, pointing in horror at the ceiling over John's head. Feeling Gretchen's entire body stiffen, Hannah knew that what she was seeing was not her imagination. Lowering slowly over John's head was the largest spider she had ever seen in her life, its body roughly the size of a soccer ball. John, staring out the window, was oblivious. As she stared in shock, the spider swung to the left of John, attaching a thick string of web to the wall. It gathered its red striped legs into its massive black body and seemed to vibrate. Understanding broke Hannah's shock, and she sprang forward, grabbing John's hand and pulling him away from the window. Yelling at Gretchen to run, she watched, horrified, as the spider launched itself across the room towards her. Acting on instinct, she flung her arm out, blocking the spider's path. It sprayed a cold sticky fluid directly in her face, blinding her. She clutched her face and screamed.

John was now the one doing the pulling, his grip fierce on her arm and though she couldn't see, she followed him. She wiped violently at her eyes, but found it impossible to clear the stickiness holding her eyes shut. John was flying through the room, dragging her behind, and she bounced off the door frame. She tried to stop, to tell him she couldn't see. She heard him urging Gretchen to go down and, realizing they had made it to the stairs, she dug her heels in, needing to explain that she couldn't see. Before she could speak, she felt herself pulled out into thin air and felt the sick jolt of not touching ground. An image flashed through her mind of plunging through a void, crashing, breaking. Except she didn't. One of John's arms swung out around her shoulders, the other swept under her knees, and apart from the loud exhaled "oomph" that escaped him as he lifted her, neither of them said a word. She buried her head into his chest and focused on his heartbeat. She tried to not think about the horrifying sound that had emitted from the spider when she had hit it or the scuttling sounds she had heard as they had fled from the room.

She felt the warmth of the sun on her face, so they must have made it out of the castle. She heard Gretchen call, "Over here!" and felt John bend to pass her into what had to be a taxi. Gretchen's breath was coming in shallow pants, and she could hear John giving the taxi driver instructions in Italian. Then he was back beside her, all three of them crammed in the backseat. The lurching movement forward stilled her immediate panic, as she tried to reassure herself that even an obscenely large spider could not outrun a car.

"Gretchen, help me with her. Hannah, sit back, I need to see your face." John's hands gently lifted her shoulders and she realized that she had balled herself up into the fetal position.

"What the hell was that? What's wrong with Hannah? Did it bite her? Hannah, did it bite you? Try to tell us what... Oh my god." Gretchen's voice trailed off.

At Gretchen's obvious dismay, Hannah felt panic grab her throat and her entire body started trembling. John's voice cut through her terror, "Easy, Summers. It's okay. I think it's some kind of webbing. Hold still." She could feel his fingers probing the edges of her face. "She can breathe. I see her breathing. Hannah, can you talk?"

That was silly. Of course she could talk. Hadn't she been talking the entire time? Wasn't she talking now? But then she heard Gretchen gasp, "I think her jaw is trapped in the web. Oh shit, oh crap, oh..."

She strained to reply, but couldn't utter a sound. At the realization that she could not open her eyes or her mouth, Hannah felt the shaking start in her limbs again. The fact that her breathing was limited to her nose, which was underneath the webbing, caused her breathing to ratchet up into short fast inhales. She pulled at the stickiness on her face, desperate to be free, as spots started to explode behind her eyelids.

John caught her hands, "Easy. It's okay, Hannah. Easy. Try to breathe slowly, you are fine. I need you to stay as calm as you can. We are going to get this off of you, okay? Right away." He was slowly rubbing her wrists and he sounded so certain. She felt herself ease back from the edge.

"Good, that's good. I am going to ask you a question now, so

I need you to nod or shake your head, okay? Good. You're doing great. Think back, Han— when you hit the spider, did it bite you?"

She could feel him sliding his fingers over her arms, and now Gretchen was checking her legs. She forced herself to relive it. When she had hit it, the spider had seemed surprised. Was that right? It fell back, spewing as it went. Then they ran. There would have been no chance for a bite. She shook her head.

"No? No bites? That's great. Really. So all we have to do now is get this off you." John was holding her hand now, talking softly, and she could hear Gretchen arguing with the cab driver in English with some Latin thrown in.

"She is *not* evil. Just drive, *veho, veho*. Do not stop this car, *facta non verba!* Mac, can you help me here? He got an eyeful of Hannah in the rearview mirror and he is trying to kick us out." She went back to arguing with him in her English/Latin pidgin.

"I told him to take us to the Pensione Ferretti. It's near the train station. Just keep him driving, Gretchen, we're almost there." He turned back to her, his tone shifting from gentle to practical, "Here's the situation, Summers. I think a little olive oil will do the trick to get this off your face, but we need privacy if we want to do this without alerting the police or scaring the locals. So we're going to get a room, okay?"

Before she could nod the cab pulled to an abrupt stop, and all three of them were tossed forward. While Gretchen cursed at the driver, John helped her regain her seat, and then eased her out of the car, "This way, Hannah. It's just another block or so. I'm going to wrap the shawl around your head, okay? Good. Okay, take my arm and follow my lead."

Stepping out of the cab she had felt a little shaky, but Gretchen came and took her other arm. Leaning across Hannah, she addressed John, "That cabbie was on the phone to his parish priest as we were leaving. I don't know any Italian, but I am pretty sure *opera del diavolo* does not translate well. Oh shit, he's coming back. What is that he's swinging?"

"That is a rosary. Let's just go, come on."

"No, wait." Hannah could hear the thunk of Gretchen's backpack hitting the ground and the distinctive sound of zippers, and then Gretchen was turning her, "I am just slipping some sunglasses on your face, Han. There, perfect." In an urgent whisper, Gretchen talked past her, "We can't outrun an angry mob. I have an idea, but I need you to translate. Tell the avenging cabbie that she's an American actress recovering from a face lift. It's a revolutionary new procedure, guaranteed to reduce swelling. Go on. Talk."

"I don't know if my Italian—"

Hannah could now hear the man yelling, "*Diavolo! Diavolo! Opera del Diavolo!*" John stepped in front of her, Gretchen guarding her side. Both murmuring words of reassurance at her, but she found she didn't need them. Being unable to neither see nor speak had created a bizarre feeling of detachment once she had mastered her fear of suffocation. She felt like she had become some prop in a play being acted by others. It was with the curiosity of a bystander she listened to her friends.

"Try, MacCallister. He is literally foaming at the mouth and he's drawing a crowd."

As John started talking, Gretchen leaned in, and whispered into her ear, "John is great, I think they are listening to him.

They seem more interested than angry now. Damn, I am so glad I came. This is no midnight buffet overlooking the Acropolis, but it sure isn't boring. What the hell was that spider? Fascinating! I don't remember super-sized spiders in my text books."

While she was also glad to have Gretchen there, she would have liked to point out that being attacked by a super sized spider was more terrifying than interesting but since her jaw was webbed shut, she'd just have to think it. At a resurgent yell of *"Opera del Diavolo!"* she only hoped that she would have a chance to discuss the relative merits of midnight buffets and not experience first-hand the ancient practice of exorcism.

*   *   *   *   *   *   *   *   *

Lee

Crafting the spin on an express train

Hermes had fallen asleep legs outstretched, arms crossed, and Lee, seated on the bench across from him, beamed. Even asleep with his head thrown back, snoring, Hermes looked cool. Lifting his butt to release another stream of gas, Lee reflected that the bruschetta he'd eaten earlier in the day was probably a bad call on his part. Olive oil always made him gassy. On the plus side, Hermes' aggressive snores and his own unique body odor had cleared the compartment on an otherwise packed train. He turned on the bench, putting his legs up and kicked off his shoes, adding yet another layer to the signature stench in the space. A tourist, tapping determinedly at her phone, had wandered in, taken one sniff, and turned tail, all without looking up from her screen.

Popping open his laptop, he considered how best to complete the work Hermes had assigned him. His exact orders were to "get that goddess off my ass" and then he had fallen asleep. Frowning down as Hera's email loaded on his screen, he saw that all of the messages were marked "urgent." Not that he would ever consider criticizing the goddess, but when every email is urgent the category loses some of its, well, urgency. Opening them chronologically was like being yelled at over escalating degrees. Though they seemed like questions, they were, by all accounts, accusations of failure. *Where are you? What are you doing? Where is Apollo? Why haven't you found him yet? Tell me EVERYTHING! NOW!!!* At least she was brief.

Considering his answers before typing, Lee decided it was in his best interest to answer only the specific questions Hera had asked. *On a train bound for Florence.* Send. *Answering your emails.* Send. *We have no idea.* Send. *Ditto.* Send.

Responding to the last email demand to "tell her everything" was more complicated. Lee squashed the whining inner voice that accused him of selling out Hermes and began typing. He knew that if he didn't give her something, she might show up and take over. So he would tell the truth, just not all of the truth. Tapping efficiently at his keyboard, he started with Hermes stealing Hannah's plane ticket and sending her on a fake lead, and ended up with his description of how Hermes had trashed the hotel room when Lee had reported that not only did he have no idea where Apollo was but that they had also lost Hannah. She and her friend, John, had disappeared in the night, leaving all of their bags behind. It was only after Lee found them on the train station security cameras running from a tall woman and escaping on a train headed for Florence that Hermes had ceased smashing lamps and vases and such. He concluded the update to Hera with the optimistic assessment that they were certain to find Apollo in Florence. Send. That should keep her away.

Closing his laptop, he stored it back in his bag and winced at the pain the movement caused. He slid his fingers lightly across the burn marks on his right shoulder under his t-shirt and stared out the window at the passing scenery. Sek had always been good at hurting him in concealed places, so that no one could tell. Even if he healed faster than humans, the pain he felt was just as real. And Sek knew how to cause pain.

Lee and Sek had been assigned by Apep, Egyptian god of chaos, to humiliate the Greek god Apollo, for some perceived insult Lee had never quite worked out. It didn't matter. Gods insulted required sacrifice. Part of the plan had involved manipulating Apollo into giving a human the power to have everyone listen to everything that human said. Then he and Sek were going to have her say awful things about Apollo. A straightforward plan. But the human picked for the gift was Hannah, and Hannah had the bad fortune to be Sek's Mry.

Every demon has a Mry. A Mry is the mortal manifestation of an immortal demon's one true love. Because the Mry is mortal— it takes a new form each life cycle— it can be hard to find among all the mortal creatures, but when a demon sees it, he knows it. Lee hadn't found his own Mry for decades. When he had heard Sek confessing his undying love of Hannah back in June, his stomach sank. Sek was a profoundly evil demon. It was very bad news for Hannah. But then John arrived to rescue Hannah. Hannah turned away from Sek, and ran towards John, to protect him from Sek. Lee witnessed Sek's pain at her choice— a clear rejection of the love he had just offered her. Rejected, Sek had sent a killing curse at John and disappeared. It was only by freezing John that Lee had been able to save his life. Lee let himself believe that Sek was too proud to ever show his face around Hannah again.

But that was then. It had been so quiet since then that Lee had hoped that maybe he had imagined the entire thing. But now he knew differently. The first morning in Milan he had gone down to the hotel kitchen to see about getting a small plate of cheese, meats, and olives for breakfast. But before he could get the attention of the kitchen staff, he found himself cornered in the linen closet, Sek searing his skin, grinning at the pain he was inflicting. Sek looked terrible. Thin. Disheveled. Crazed, even for a demon. He demanded to know where Hannah was. After several excruciating minutes Lee reluctantly gave up the name of the hotel Hermes had sent her to. Sek had laughed maniacally and disappeared, leaving Lee to console himself with the thought that, seeing how unbalanced Sek was, maybe he would kill Hannah and John quickly.

And honestly, when he found that Hannah and John had disappeared from the hotel in the middle of the night, he had assumed that Sek was responsible. He'd been shocked by the video footage of them at the train station. He had no idea who the woman chasing them was, but it was clearly not Sek. Which meant that they were both still alive somehow. But that only raised more questions. Sek was a level thirty-six demon of the Egyptian Order. He was formidable. Even for someone with Hermes' powers. How had two young humans escaped Sek? And who was the woman at the train station? And why were Hannah and John going to Florence? Was Apollo there? Questions made him hungry.

Opening his pockets, he pulled out a dry smoked salami and started chewing. He was glad Hannah and John were alive. He liked them. And he was more than a little curious about their relationship. He fancied himself a romantic and hoped that Italy would work its magic on them. But they had better move quickly, because if he could find where they went, then so could Sek. And if Sek used him once to try to get them, then he should expect he would be asked to betray them again. Taking a larger bite of the cylindrical meat, Lee tried to focus on chewing and ignore the throbbing of his shoulder and his conscience. If only he didn't know himself well enough to know that he would definitely crumble under the threat of pain. He struggled to swallow the spicy meat. It was not working. Even eating couldn't distract him. Groaning, he shoved the salami back in his pocket.

CHAPTER TEN

The Calm Before

* * * * * * * * *

Hannah

The cheapest room at the pensione

She was still imprisoned under the spider web and could neither see nor speak, so she shook her head and took both of John's wrists in her hands, moving them away from her face. He had been working the olive oil into the webbing for the last half hour, gently lifting the edges, only to stop and rub more oil in. She had spent the time concentrating on breathing through her nose and being patient. But she was done with that. John was protesting, clearly anticipating her next move, but she ignored him. She had a plan. Just like a Bandaid. Or an eyebrow wax. Gather your courage and then pull without mercy. Sliding her fingertips under the outer edge of the web, she mentally reviewed the plan. Grip on the inhale, pull on the exhale. Good. That will work. She could do this. Okay, on three. One, two, three.... Okay, on the *next* three...

John's hands on her own were gentle, "I know it's taking a long time, Han, but it's working, I promise, just give me a bit

167

longer." And disengaging her hands from the web, he went back to working the edges, "Gretchen went to the library— oh right, you know that. I forget that you can hear." She heard the sound of him unscrewing the oil bottle, "You know, I could make all kinds of outrageous statements and not hear a word back from you. I should take advantage of it, but it takes all the fun out of irritating you if you can't complain about it." He started working on the webbing under her jaw. "I miss your voice, Summers. I guess because I have never spent so much time with you when you haven't spoken. It's odd."

It was odd. Not that she wasn't speaking, but that John would view her silence as an anomaly. She had spent most of the last decade not speaking much, keeping her thoughts to herself. She had definitely found her stride as the nice but quiet girl. But clearly John saw her differently. Unless she was different with him? Carl had been the talker in their relationship. *Carl.* She hadn't thought about him since this started. What would he think of the situation they were in?

"I got an email from Carl. He heard through the grapevine, which could only mean *our mothers,* that you and I were here to-gether. Did you know they've been talking since graduation— all of our moms? They, our mothers and Carl, they all suspect the Olympians are messing with you again. He had a lot of ques-tions."

She hadn't talked to her mother once since landing in Italy. She shook her head again, wondering how Elise had convinced Carl to snoop.

"I got the distinct impression that Carl was fishing for an-swers for them. I wonder what your mom has on him?"

That was weird. Could John hear her thoughts? Ow! John had just experimented with pulling at the webbing under her chin and Hannah was grateful she had not had the courage to execute her rip-it-off plan.

"Sorry, Han. I got a little ahead of myself there." He went back to slowly rubbing her skin, "I lied to them all. I really don't like lying to Carl, but I didn't know what to tell him. There are so many secrets and most of them are yours. So I told him we were looking for an ancient Italian manuscript the University wanted to acquire, I was here to translate for you. You know, for your *official job* as the curator of the University's classics collection. Carl will report back to the mothers. I don't know if they'll buy it. Carl and the mothers are a fairly skeptical audience."

Carl and the mothers. There was a complication she didn't need. How was she going to keep her anonymity as the Monitor if they were suspicious?

"You know, until I heard you trying to order a gelato I had no idea how hopeless you are with foreign languages. How did you get the curator job? I would assume that you would need— Oh wait, I think this is it, Han. Hold still." She could feel him lifting the webbing further, felt a loosening under her chin. "I spoke too soon, sorry."

He switched sides and rubbed in more oil, "Gretchen's already picked up more Italian in the last three hours than you have in three days. Speaking of Gretchen, that was clever of her, to think up the cover story about you being an American actress who'd had a facelift. That cabbie was trouble. I thought they were going to burn us all at the stake for consorting with the devil. Gretchen's quick. And that work she's doing with the patterns on the edge of Apollo's scarf. Amazing that she recognized them as runes. That is hard core. You never mentioned that she was a genius."

Hannah felt a little deflated and oddly irritated hearing John talk about Gretchen. Brilliant and quick? Well, she agreed, Gretchen was brilliant but wasn't she, Hannah, sitting here trapped in spider webbing because she was the one who'd been quick?

"Easy, Summers. I think you are smart too. And quick. If it hadn't been for you, I'd be the one trapped in webbing, or worse."

This was getting unsettling. How was he reading her thoughts?

"I have never met anyone in my life with a more animated forehead. It's like your thoughts are being broadcast by each frown or lift. Even your hair follicles are expressive." Placing both hands on either side of her face, his tone lowered, and Hannah felt his breath on her exposed forehead, "Okay, Summers, I have good news and bad news. The good news is that—" and then without another word he ripped the webbing off her face.

The rush of air and light was disorienting, but it was not enough to compensate for the breathtaking pain of every hair under the webbing parting ways with her face. She wanted to yell, but it was like she had forgotten the mechanics of opening her mouth. John's hands were back on her face, now tracing her jaw, sliding back under her hair and as she looked into his eyes, she felt everything go quiet.

"Hannah Marie Summers, thank you for saving my life." And

then he was kissing her.

She stayed in the kiss for a long moment, caught by the heat of it, and as the kiss deepened she felt the twist in her gut, the yearning. He tasted familiar and unknown at the same time. And she was shocked at the depth of her response. While he seemed content to continue kissing, she found herself needing to get a handle on this. Lowering her head, barely breaking the contact of their mouths, their foreheads still touching, she took a shaky breath. They were alone in a hotel room in Florence, Italy, sitting on a bed, and the idea of leaning back and continuing filled her with confusion. What did it mean? Was this how he said thank you? She struggled to find the track back to normalcy. She couldn't seem to force her body to move away from him, but she could try to gain some control of the situation with words.

"What is the bad news?"

At his bemused expression she continued, "You said you had good news and bad news. I assume that the good news was that you could get the web off my face, so what is the bad news?"

Hannah jumped as Gretchen answered, leaning against the doorframe, "The bad news is that we are likely to see more nasty spiders if we keep looking for Apollo." She slammed the door behind her and paced to the windows, pulling the curtains closed.

How long had she been in the room?

"I got through the first side of the scarf, and you are not going to like this. It is a retelling of the Arachne myth. Though given what we've seen today, we can safely assume that it is less myth and more like history. And it is one dark history." Pulling the scarf out of her bag, she unfurled it on the bed, "If Apollo is mixed up with these people, we are not simply locating a missing party boy. Look at this line," and she ran her finger under a series of symbols. "If my reading is accurate, these say 'Justice through blood.' They don't say whose blood, but I think it is safe to say that our eight-legged hairy friend at the castle may not be the last time we will meet up with monstrous spiders while working this job. So if you two are done canoodling, we might want to come up with a plan to avoid death."

"Did someone say they needed to avoid death? I am an expert at that and I charge very reasonable rates." Hermes sauntered into the room, Lee following him, loaded down with bags. Were there no locks on the doors in this hotel? Kicking the door closed, Hermes smirked at her, "Oh, H, really? Line Boy? I thought you were more discriminating." Crossing the room to take Gretchen's hand, he bent down and kissed her wrist, "And who are you? You are a definite upgrade from Former Boyfriend in H's Three Musketeers." Without pausing for a reply, he plucked the scarf from the bed, "Did I hear you say you had deciphered an ancient language printed on a fashion scarf last worn by our golden idiot? Beauty and brains. Definitely an upgrade."

Lee shed the bags at the door and shimmied between Hannah and John on the bed, patting their knees and grinning like a child on Christmas.

"Hi, Hannah. Hi, John. I am so glad to see you two alive, being a twosome. I always thought you'd be good together." Pulling what appeared to be a long sausage out of his pocket, he pointed it at her, "You don't happen to have any of that delicious metchup with you, do you Hannah? I have a dry salami that could really use something to bring out its meatiness."

But before she could respond to either the worrisome notion that Lee had been prepared to find them dead, or the misperception that everyone seemed to be under after one simple kiss, or even to say no, she did not have metchup on her, everyone started talking at once. John, leapt off the bed, confronting Hermes, and engaged in the age old "You need to leave/who's going to make me" male dominance dance. Gretchen dropped down on the bed next to Hannah and was going on about how wild it was to actually meet Hermes, isn't it weird that he looked exactly like he did in all the old paintings, except that he was way hotter than she had expected, and who was this other guy? Which prompted Lee to introduce himself and offer Gretchen a bite of salami. As the volume between Gretchen and Lee got louder and the tension between Hermes and John got tighter, Hannah felt stuck, frozen and mute, in the middle of it all.

That was until she saw a completely normal sized spider slowly lowering itself from the ceiling on a single translucent thread, and acting on instinct, she grabbed the nearest thing, which in this case was Lee's salami, swiped the spider on its thread onto the meat, ran to the window, flung it open and tossed the meat and spider out into the late Florence afternoon, just missing a tour group leaving the train station. She heard their gasps and ducked quickly back into the room, pulling the curtains tight. Turning round, she saw every eye on her, expressions ranging from concern (John and Gretchen) to amusement (Hermes).

Lee was the first to speak, his expression one of dismay, "I know I said it wasn't the best salami, but you didn't need to throw it away!"

"There was a spider. Here. You were all so busy chatting and fighting you didn't see it. A spider. Here."

Hermes smirked, "Yes, and I am sure there are bed bugs too, H. Do you want us to help you toss the mattress? Since when did you lose your mind?"

Hannah caught Gretchen and John exchanging a look, and she bit down on her instinct to plead her sanity. She pointed to the scarf in Gretchen's hands, "Justice through blood. Isn't that what you said those runes mean, Gretch? Didn't you say it was a retelling of the Arachne myth? Add that to the freak of a spider that attacked us at the Vecchio, and I think it is safe to say we should be suspicious of all spiders, regardless of their size."

Hermes eyes narrowed, "What attacked you?"

Gretchen was frowning, "A spider, about this big." She circled her arms. Lee's eyes widened, and Hermes looked like he was going to argue, but Gretchen ignored him. "Why didn't you kill it, Hannah? It was so small. If you think it is somehow connected, why throw it out the window? Won't it just lead bigger, badder spiders here?" She tucked her feet up under her on the bed, her eyes scanning the corners of the room.

John was the one who answered, "Because we don't know why the spiders are after us. And if we arbitrarily kill one, they might take that as an act of aggression."

"Yes. That's it exactly." Hannah smiled at John, and as their eyes met, the memory of the kiss came back to her in full force and she no longer felt confused by it. At the darkening of his eyes, she blushed.

"Can you two do that later? The killer spiders? What is our plan?" Gretchen was now standing on the bed, holding out a pillow like a sword.

Before Hannah could respond there was a sharp rap at the door. They all looked at each other, alarmed for their own reasons. Lee jumped up on the bed and hid behind Gretchen, John stepped closer to Hannah, putting his arm out to prevent her from going to answer. A second rap made the them flinch, and Hermes finally moved.

Muttering under his breath about useless humans and demons and that god damned Apollo, he opened the door, "Yes?"

Standing in the hall was a short man with pince-nez glasses perched haphazardly on the end of his sweaty nose holding a battered salami aloft like a standard. As he spoke, once he caught his breath, Hannah recognized his voice as belonging to the desk clerk, whom she hadn't previously seen as she had been under the web when John had checked them in. He looked angry. Pushing the door wide, he pointed at all of them with the now dirty, broken salami, "Get out! Now! This room is no longer for you. *Perdersi!* Leave!" He punctuated each word with a shake of the salami.

Hermes nodded at the clerk, "Yes, yes. I completely agree, good man. We were just leaving." Turning to look at Hannah, he addressed only her, "What's your call, H? You can all come with me and Lee, we have a suite at the Savoy." His disparaging look took in the room, the somewhat shabby walls, small bed and exposed sink and toilet in the corner. Lowering his voice, he leaned into her, and she wondered vaguely if he was trying to use any of his mind tricks on her, "We could work together to finish this job. Lee and your brilliant friend there could go to the hotel and finish deciphering the scarf and you, me, and Line Boy could check out the fashion house it came from and see if we can't figure out where the hell the golden idiot is. It's a plan. Do you have a better one?"

Fingering the Gorgon necklace, Hannah reminded herself that she was safe from enchantment, she could rely on her own assessment of Hermes' offer. She looked at her friends' faces and could see they were waiting for her, trusting her. Even the desk clerk seemed to be waiting for her to answer. She closed her eyes and tried to sort through the options. It was her fault that they were in the position of having to depend on Hermes again. He had come through in the end back in June when Sek had kidnapped her, but not without a lot of lying and a tremendous amount of self-interest, and she wasn't sure he wouldn't sell her out again.

"It's not just spiders you need to worry about, H. That woman on the train platform in Milan, whoever she is, she is on her way here. That dart in the station master's neck, it was poisoned. Lee read the coroner's report. If we found you, she could find you too. It's just a matter of time."

Hermes' tone was casual, as if he didn't care how she answered, and while the news about the station master's fate was discouraging, Hannah was encouraged by Hermes' efforts to convince her. It meant he needed them, and that was probably the only assurance they were going to get that he wasn't going to screw them over, at least not right now. Besides, he had a good point. There were an increasing number of threats. She looked at John, putting her hand on the Gorgon necklace, tipping her head toward Gretchen. She saw him nod ever so slightly.

"Okay, Hermes, your plan sounds fine for now." Crossing the

room, she held out her hand to Gretchen and helped her down from her perch on the bed. Slipping the necklace off, she held it out for Gretchen, "Here, Gretch, take this and go with Lee. It's a family heirloom, and I'd hate to lose it if we run into trouble at the fashion house. Wear it for me?"

Watching Gretchen place the necklace over her head, Hannah felt better about leaving her alone with Lee. Responding to the desk clerk's repeated *"signorina"* she turned to the desk clerk and with John's help translating, they negotiated how much to pay him for the time they'd spent in the room.

"Wait, um... I, um... Hannah, um..." Lee was pulling on her sleeve like a five year old needing to use the bathroom, "We should talk...you shouldn't...maybe it isn't wise..."

But Hermes' voice drowned Lee out, "Good call, H. You won't regret it." Putting his hand on the small of Hannah's back, Hermes looked over his shoulder at the stuttering Lee, "Be a gentleman, Lee, and carry the bags. We need Genius Girl to carry the scarf. Oh, and yes, *you*. Come on, Line Boy, let's get a move on. Unless you want to stay? I could take care of H."

"Hannah, I have to talk to you, um... about... um... you really shouldn't...um..."

Not bothering to respond to either Lee's stuttering or Hermes' provocation, Hannah knocked Hermes' hand off and walked through the door, John and Gretchen at her back. She could hear Hermes demanding to know why Lee was trying to sabotage a perfectly good plan, and Lee's indistinct response, and then she, John, and Gretchen were down the stairs and out of earshot. Arriving at the lobby before the demon and god joined them, she took advantage of the moment, "Gretch, whatever you do, don't take that necklace off. It's a Gorgon necklace. It will protect you from enchantments. And maybe more."

Gretchen couldn't hide her fascination with the object, but she frowned, "Shouldn't you keep it then? The jumbo spider seems to have a bead on you and John."

Hannah started to answer her, "You need it—"

John finished, "Because we can't trust Tweedle Dee and Tweedle Dum up there and you'll be *alone* with Tweedle Dee, so you should have it. Tweedle Dum is a self-serving ass, but Hannah and I have each other. We'll be fine."

Despite the tension of the situation, Hannah looked at John and smiled. To have someone so completely in synch with you when everything was becoming increasingly perilous made her feel simultaneously safer and more optimistic. John smiled back. Gretchen rolled her eyes, "Fine, I'll keep it on. I know you two have played with the gods before, but be careful. The text I've been able to translate from the scarf is not warm and fuzzy, and you might run into trouble at the—"

"I am a god, Genius Girl. I can keep your friends safe from angry spiders. No matter the size." Hermes had joined them in the lobby with Lee on his heels, "Though I'll only do it because I am a professional. One of the perks of being a god is excellent hearing, Line Boy. Tweedle Dum indeed. Let's move."

The three of them exchanged a look and then turned to join Hermes on the sidewalk. Hannah walked right past Lee, not noticing his frantic attempts to silently get her attention.

* * * * * * * * *

Hera

Waiting in the airport bar

"Another. Like the last. And one for my friend here." Masking her cringe, Hera sipped at the sub-par merlot the bartender topped off in her glass, and tried to focus on cracking the shell around the goddess of war. "Drink, Athena, I insist. The least I can do is buy you a drink when you are going out of your way to help me find Apollo. Besides, it has a very nice bouquet, I think you'll like it."

Sipping at the wine, Athena blanched. "This is awful, Hera, really, I expected you to have a more informed palette."

"Oh? This isn't good wine? I never really understood wines."

"Given your responsibilities with your magazine, that is an unforgivable lapse in your education. We have time before our flight. Let me educate you. Bartender, I need to see your wine list."

It was so easy to bait arrogant people; they readily believe that the people around them are idiots and are completely willing to demonstrate their own superiority by "helping" them. Hera hid her smile in another sip of the dreadful wine and watched Athena demand to taste all of the wines prior to using them for Hera's education. Excellent. Human alcohol took some time for immortals to adjust to, and if one were an infrequent imbiber, well then the metabolic process was even more unstable. Based on Athena's past performances at the Fourth of July parties on the Vineyard, Athena was a lightweight and should be sloshed in less than twenty minutes, at which time Hera intended to get some real answers from her.

Athena had come to her late last night and claimed that she had intel that Apollo was mixed up with a terrorist cell in Italy. And in her most condescending "I hate to be the bearer of bad news" voice, she had explained to Hera that many young men get caught up in political activism, and it was nothing she, Hera, should feel ashamed of, knowing how involved Hera was in Apollo's life. Athena was sure that given Apollo's innate gullibility and general lack of good judgement, combined with overly-protective parents, this was an unintentional alliance. She, Athena, had struggled with her conscience about whether to intervene, because it went against not only her personal morals to respond to terror, but it also could be considered an infringement of the Non-Interference Accord. But she had been moved by Hera's concern and was willing to help her find Apollo. *Help her find Apollo, my ass.* This tightly-laced sanctimonious goddess of self-righteousness was hiding something. Maybe a lot of things. And she was going to get the answers.

Athena was now ordering the bartender to open a bottle of '82 Chateau Ste. Michelle, arranging glasses on the bar from chardonnay to cabernet sauvignon. Hera took advantage of Athena's preoccupation to take a more thorough look at her step-daughter. She was less put together than normal, her carry on bag bulging, a loose thread on her suit lapel. When Hera had casually pointed out that Athena's assistant, who Hera had met several times, was off her game, Athena had blandly replied, "I had to dismiss Jessica. And I have not had time to hire a new assistant. I had planned to this week, but here I am with you."

It was true that Hera had strong-armed Athena into coming on this trip. Athena had wanted to simply give her the information she had gathered on the terrorists Apollo was supposedly with and send Hera off to take care of the situation. Athena wasn't nearly as skilled at manipulation as she thought she was, and Hera was no one's attack dog to be sent off on an errand. So she had met Athena's pretense with one of her own, bursting into tears at the news, begging Athena to help her. Athena was the one to cave, revealing much more than she realized. Clearly this situation wasn't one she could walk away from.

So what was the truth? Athena had shown her the terrorist's letters demanding an ouster of the Italian government, or Apollo would be hurt. And then the ear, belonging to some unfortunate human, which Athena said the terrorist claimed was Apollo's. While the ear was real, nothing else was. The letters Athena maintained her team had analyzed were clear forgeries. She'd done an article in *Ladies Home and Hearth* about online services that could scan documents to determine if they were plagiarized. A quick scan had confirmed that eighty percent of the letters Athena claimed were from Italian terrorists were taken directly from *The Communist Manifesto*. Nothing was more tedious than the lies of the arrogant, so it was only fitting that she use that arrogance to take her down, hence the wine tasting.

"Okay, now Hera, we are going to start with the Chardonnay. It is important that you not just drink it down, but first you should swirl it, and then..."

Hera steeled herself and feigned ignorance of a subject she could write a book about. "This is a lot of information for me to take in. Can you show me how? I'm a visual learner."

Athena patted Hera gently on the shoulder, "Admitting your weaknesses is the first step in becoming strong. I'm proud of you. Watch carefully, and if you need me to, I can repeat it until you understand." She burped lightly, the alcohol already affecting her, "It's so refreshing to see someone willing to humble themselves in front of their superior. You know, you aren't nearly the bitch everyone says you are."

Hera smiled, and this time there was nothing forced or artificial in her expression. "Oh, Athena, you say the nicest things. I can't wait to learn more from you. And I just got an alert that our flight has been delayed, so we have plenty of time for you to relieve me of my ignorance."

Athena would be putty in her hands.

CHAPTER ELEVEN

Lost in Translation

* * * * * * * * *

Gretchen

The most expensive suite at the Savoy

Tugging on the necklace around her neck, she tried to zone out the little demon-guy Lee, who had been acting weird since they got here. First he had gone into the bathroom, come out and stood on his tiptoes affecting a Marilyn Monroe pose and asked in a high falsetto if he looked good. At her confused, "Sure," he had cursed and started pacing around muttering about how was he supposed to do anything and how was he going to protect her, and every once in awhile she heard him say the name "Sek" but she couldn't waste time trying to figure out a clearly disturbed demon when Hannah and John needed her to decipher the scarf. Watching his spastic pacing made her grateful for the Gorgon necklace and she slid it under her shirt. She offered up a silent thank you to Hannah and turned back to the scarf.

After Hannah had called to confess to her lame dead aunt story and then proceeded to tell the unbelievable story of the Immortal Council, her job as the Monitor and their two hundred and forty-eight year old professor, and outlined her current adventure as an undercover agent supposedly working for Hera, Goddess of Hearth and Home, looking for Apollo, God of the Sun, in Italy, while being hunted by some Italian model/hit woman, she had found herself wondering if she wouldn't have been better off not hearing the truth. It would have been much simpler to assume this was another lie and keep cruising the Grecian Isles with Jillie and the crew of the *Lurve Boat*. But after a summer of talking non-stop with Hannah, she could read her, and knew that despite sounding certifiable, Hannah was telling the truth.

She'd had time to consider what this all meant on her trip from Thessaloniki to Florence. She'd had to wonder about Hannah's experience as the Speaker of Truth. What if she'd been given the power to have everyone listen to everything she said? Would she have worked so hard to give it back? Why had Hannah given it back?

She couldn't handle it.

Who had said that? The demon guy was back in the bathroom. Get a grip, Gretchen. Tracing the rune that was stumping her, she tried to refocus on the scarf, but found her thoughts slipping. She had always viewed herself as the badass in their duo, now she had to revisit that idea. In the small amount of time she'd been on this caper with Hannah, she'd seen more than enough danger. She had almost peed her pants when that monster of a spider had lowered over John, but Hannah had sprung into action, smacking it with her bare arm. And that web on her face; if that had happened to her she would like to think she could have been as calm as Hannah, but she didn't give herself very good odds. She had felt so freaked out just seeing it on Hannah. No, Hannah had more edge than her cotton skirts would imply.

So if Gretchen wasn't the badass in this adventure, she could at least be the brain. She was the one who had recognized the pattern on the edge of the scarf as being a language, and not just some graphic design. She had decoded that language, at least most of it, and that had felt good. Like she wasn't the most useless person on the team. She had definitely made it to Velma status in the Mystery Gang. And now she had to finish it. The little demon guy seemed to have taken up permanent residence in the bathroom.

He's just a distraction. You can think more clearly without him, without any of them.

When had she started talking to herself in the third person? It must just be her subconscious mind trying to protect her from stress. And it was true that she liked to work alone. Spreading the silk out on the table in front of her, she reviewed her notes and reoriented her mind around the patterns. Tracing her finger over the symbols, she frowned. These runes had a different base shape than the ones she had translated into the story of Arachne.

Deciphering language had always been fun for her. Riding in the back of her dad's van on the way to some book auction in Maine or New Hampshire, she would stare at the dots on the ceiling panel. If you concentrated on them and then relaxed your eyes, the dots would lift off the ceiling like a 3D illusion. Language was like that for her. She could look at a sentence and see how the shapes and frequencies of the letters lifted off the page, just like the dots. It was easier to see them when they were written, but with a little practice, she had learned to hear them as well. She had found a ticket out of her small Vermont town by excelling in foreign languages, several colleges offering her a full-ride based on her SAT subject tests in French and Spanish.

Her advisor at Whitfield had encouraged her to become a world languages major, extolling the many exciting opportunities for translators in the foreign service or in teaching, of all the traveling she could do simply based on her gift with languages. But she had resisted. She knew herself, and she was too opinionated to work for politicians in foreign service, incapable of translating their words without adding her own snark. And she was way too impatient with the slow progress of others to consider teaching. But then in the fall of her sophomore year she had stumbled across an example of an Ancient Greek translation from an urn in her history textbook. Staring at the twisting symbols, they lifted off the page and she was hooked. She changed advisors and became a classics major. She didn't have to worry about being patient with the other students, because, generally speaking, the annoying people majored in English. Or Economics.

Other people are a waste of time.

Well, not everyone. Not Professor Gerinvale. The thought of studying with her, deciphering the beginnings of language, made her feel giddy. She had labored over her application to Yale, forcing Hannah to listen to her essay time and again, worrying that somewhere in the far reaches of her mind lurked the perfect anecdote, the illuminating description, that would bring her application to the top of the pile.

Hannah was also applying to Yale for the Classics program,

but she was much more circumspect about her essay. Gretchen had always presumed that was due to her more private nature, but now she wondered. Was it because she was using her first-hand knowledge of the Olympians to shape her insights? That seemed a little unfair. Not every student has the chance to chat with the immortal players in ancient Greek myths. That might give Hannah an advantage that she had not really earned.

We wouldn't put it past her. What do you really know about her?

The pragmatic part of her, the part that had to wrap her own Christmas presents, or make her own birthday cupcakes to bring to school, the part of her that figured out early on to pretend to other people that her father was doing these things, that part of her wondered if it wouldn't be right, in the long run, to claim her own work, even if it exposed Hannah's secret. And what if Hannah was using her position to get an advantage at Yale? If she was honest, she had thought Hannah's thesis was boring. While it had been carefully executed, there was no intellectual originality to it. She had written it prior to the Speaker of Truth gift. What if now, Hannah had some special benefit from her work that artificially enhanced her application? What if, because of that, Hannah got accepted to Yale and she didn't? Exposing Hannah's secret by capitalizing on her own translation work all of sudden seemed less wrong.

You should get the credit you deserve. You earned it. Like everything else in your life.

The necklace felt uncomfortably heavy against her chest. Sliding it out of her shirt, she shifted it so that no part of it was directly against her skin. She needed to get a grip. It was unlike her to go down such a dark hole. Hannah wouldn't manipulate the admissions board. And so what if her thesis had been dry. Hannah had legitimate skills and knowledge and it was none of her business what Hannah put on her application. She could not put this translation on hers. She had promised to keep Hannah's secret, and the scarf was part of that secret.

The scarf. Staring at the final line of runes, she idly ran her fingers around the faces of the Gorgon sisters on the necklace and tried to relax and let the meaning lift off the silk. But her attempt was disrupted by a loud shout from the demon dude.

"It's mine!"

Lee lunged from behind her and she felt his hands scrambling for purchase on her neck, but before she could respond she felt the necklace heat up and she heard a cracking sound and the little demon's hands were no longer on her. Spinning in her chair, she looked to see him crumpled up on the floor by the door. Damn it. He looked broken. She hoped it hadn't killed him. *It?* When had the necklace become an *it?* The demon on the floor moaned. She should help him, he was part of the team, even though he had tried to jump her, but she really didn't know much about the Egyptian gods, let alone demons. Could they die?

"I am not doing mouth to mouth. Just for the record." She stopped herself from talking and gave herself a mental shake as she crossed the room to assess the damage. She had the strangest thought that she had been talking to the necklace, but that was ridiculous.

"Or is it?"

Slapping her hand over her mouth, she stood frozen where she was and looked around the room. Had she said that? Lifting the necklace up, she looked at their images. Gorgons were often represented as evil faces with oversized mouths and pinwheeled eyes, used by Ancient Greeks to ward off evil. But the Gorgons on this necklace were beautiful. Three women, their faces serene, looking inward, their hair twining and locking. The three Gorgon sisters, Euryale, Stheno, and Medusa. Many people thought that Medusa had always had snakes for hair. But according to Ovid it had been Athena who had turned Medusa's hair to snakes for the sin of getting it on with Poseidon, who was into Medusa's long blonde hair. Unfortunately they had had the bad taste to get it on in one of Athena's temples. The virgin goddess was rightly annoyed. But instead of punishing Medusa by having her spend a century mucking out the stalls of the sun horses or some other disgusting task, Athena had given Medusa a permanent bad hair day, cursing her to turn any man who looked at her to stone. Gretchen smiled, wondering if Athena was aware of the double entendre in that outcome. Probably not.

We hate Athena.

Gretchen wasn't a fan of Athena either. Either? Who else was she imagining disliked Athena? The Gorgon sisters? She sank down, staring at the necklace, and only realized that she had forgotten about the demon when she heard him groan again. She dropped the necklace, but stayed sitting.

"The little demon. I should check on the little demon."

Why? He was trying to separate us. Leave him.

"Us?"

Yes. Us. You and us. He is nothing. We are everything.

Gretchen blinked. Us? We? Though the faces on the necklace were carved in stone, she knew it was them. *The sisters.* She tried to quickly review what she knew from myths about cursed objects that talked to you without letting on that she was thinking about cursed objects. Um... She should keep it talking.

"Yeah. Right. We rock. Um, so what should we do now? I'm feeling sort of tired. Maybe we should take a nap?"

She stretched her arms up over her head being careful not to think what she was planning, on the chance that if she did the necklace would hear her and it would stop her. She feigned a yawn while the voice demanded, *No! Don't sleep until you have finished him off. Take the table lamp and smash his skull. End him forever!*

"Oh yeah, good idea. I hadn't thought of that. But first—" She paused in her stretch to rip the necklace off and over her head, flinging it across the room. She held her breath and waited, but the only thing she heard now was the whimpering of the little guy. He was cowering, his hands over his head. Except he was no longer a he, but a she. A blonde bombshell. She rubbed her eyes and looked again. Still a woman. Oh. Hadn't Hannah said wearing the necklace would protect her from immortal enchantments? This would explain his earlier 'Marilyn Monroe' behavior. He looked like Marilyn's prettier sister.

"Hey, buddy, um, miss, um..."

"Lee. My name is Lee. And I don't want to hurt you, you don't need to smash my skull, please."

"Lee. Right. Don't worry, Lee. I don't want to hurt you either, it was the necklace. It wanted me to use the lamp, but the necklace is off. Look, it's over there on the floor. See? Are you okay?" She decided that caution was the better part of valor in this circumstance, and stayed on her side of the room. The little guy had attacked her, and she no longer had the protection of the necklace. She slowly started to put herself within reaching distance of the necklace, in case she really should bash his head in. Hadn't Hannah insisted she keep it on? Did Hannah know that the necklace was possessed? She tried to remember if she had seen Hannah having conversations with herself when she was wearing it, but she didn't think so.

"I'll be okay. Just a little sore." In front of her eyes he morphed back into the Lee guy, and she found that oddly reassuring. "We need to get the necklace back to Hannah. She *has* to wear it. It's a matter of life or death." He was staring at the necklace, dread etched in every line of his face, "Can you hand it to me?"

Gretchen shook her head, "I don't think I should touch it again." He nodded and but still didn't move. She leaned closer to him, dreading the answer to her next question, "Why does Hannah need it? What, in particular, is life or death for her?"

Lee was shaking his head, but also standing up, a new look of determination on his face. "I can't say. *You* have to trust *me*. She has to wear it. It was the only thing keeping her safe. I can probably touch it now that it isn't on you."

Gretchen had also stood up, in front of the necklace, blocking his path to it, and she felt an irrational urge to punch him in the face. To gouge his little red eyes out. Where was her pen? Could she reach the lamp? She could still smash his head in. He stopped in his tracks.

"I can read your mind. I thought you said it was the necklace that wanted to hurt me? You aren't wearing the necklace. Those are your thoughts."

"It was. It did. But now, when you said that you were going to take it, it was like all those thoughts were mine. Oh, that can't be good." She turned her back on him, and grabbed her head. Something in her had reacted badly to the necklace. This could not be what Hannah experienced when she wore it, or she would have warned her, would never have given it to her. Whatever old magic was in this necklace, it must be volatile, interactive. And on her neck, it unleashed her inner Gollum. But with Hannah it had been protecting her from something this demon knew about.

"Does Hannah know about this danger, the danger she needs the necklace to protect her from?"

"She did. But she thinks it's gone."

"And you know it's not."

"I do."

"But then why didn't you tell her? Why won't you tell me? Is she in danger from Hermes?"

"No. Hermes likes Hannah. We have to hurry. The *danger*, he could be here, in Florence already. I have to get it back to her. She should never have taken it off. She has to put it back on. I don't have time to explain anymore. It would only take a moment and she would be lost to us forever."

Forever. Gretchen tried not to imagine Hannah being gone forever. But the voices in her head took over.

She lied to you about her aunt dying. She ditched you and your plans for Greece so that she could go to Italy with a man. She wasn't a real friend. She ignored you for years at Whitfield. If your positions were reversed, she wouldn't give up her beloved necklace for you.

Wait. That was completely wrong. Hannah *had* given it up. She had given the necklace to her, wanted Gretchen to have it, to protect her when she would be alone with Lee. Hannah was her friend.

We are your real friends. We would always protect you. Always put you first. And we would never lie to you or take away your most precious desire.

Hannah had apologized for lying about Greece and Italy, she told me everything. And haven't I always known that she liked John? I definitely knew that he liked her. So if I harbored some latent fantasy where John was into me, well, that's my fault.

Not the boy. Your heart's desire. You both can't have it. She will take it from you. We've seen it. You have to take it from her or lose everything. You need us!

Oh, shut the hell up! Gretchen clenched her jaw and concentrated on making a wall in her mind, blocking out the crazy voices. Hannah was her best friend. If she believed Lee, then Hannah's life was on the line. And if her own disassociated thoughts were any indication, part of her, the necklace part, had become an obstacle to protecting Hannah. Well, that was bull-shit.

The little demon guy said he could read her thoughts, so she concentrated and *thought* as loudly as she could, "The Gorgon necklace is seriously demented. It has a voice that reaches me, even when I'm not wearing it. It wants to make me keep it at all costs. So I am going to go into the bathroom and lock the door. Run the shower. Anything to block out the idea that I am letting it go. You'll have to move quickly. Get it to her. I'll stay here and work on deciphering the last runes on the scarf. If I don't chase you down the street."

She forced her feet to carry her to the bathroom door. She threw the lock and grabbed the edges of the sink, her arms shaking with the effort to hold herself in place as she heard the running feet of the demon as he grabbed the necklace and fled, slamming the door. As the Gorgon sisters moved further away, she felt them flailing at her to give chase, but she slid down the back of the door, legs outstretched on the marble floor, and buried her face in the plush white bathrobe hanging there.

• • • • • • • • • •

Hermes

The lobby of San Marciano's Silk House

"Tell me again how the spiders play into the golden idiot's disappearing act?"

H and Line Boy exchanged a look. Screw them. So what if he was having trouble getting his mind around this case. *Humans.* There were at least a dozen painful curses he could inflict on them; he could make Line Boy's ears fall off, he could freeze H's tongue to the roof of her mouth, he could make them both lose all their hair with the snap of his fingers. *All* their hair. See how much they like looking at each other then.

"We went over that on the way here. We can talk about it again, but this isn't exactly the place for that conversation. Let's just wait for the receptionist to come back." H's entire speech had been whispered through clenched teeth, her lips stretched into a frozen smile. And she looked pointedly at the security camera mounted in the corner of the room. Line Boy simply stared at him. God damn humans.

Rolling his eyes in reply, Hermes resisted the urge to stamp his foot and demand an answer. Not wanting to be in striking distance of either of them, but of Line Boy in particular, he strode across the vast white marble lobby to the display of textiles on the far wall. As he feigned a deep interest in the silk-making process, he tried to get a grip on how this whole job had gone wrong. It was beyond galling that he couldn't seem to put the pieces together. From the very start he had been two steps behind and now he couldn't even grasp the apparently obvious connection between a woman cursed to be a spider several thousand years ago and the God of the Sun vanishing off the streets of Milan. As far as he knew Arachne had nothing to do with Apollo.

H had surmised that it had something to do with Athena. And sure, Athena was the goddess who had done the deed to the weaving chick, but what could that have to do with Apollo? Usually, when he was on a case, the story unfolded for him with the ease of opening a newspaper. Motivations and outcomes lining up in predictable patterns. He had built a very nice life on his ability to read humans and gods alike. So why the hell was he floundering?

He heard, clear as day, Candy's voice in his mind telling him that this was all Hera's fault.

"Hera set you up, baby. She planted the idea that you were incompetent back in Boston, and now you can't get that out of your head. She is toying with you."

"Yeah, but I toyed back. I stole the plane tickets, the credit card…"

"What?" H's voice cracked across the room, and he realized he had spoken out loud. *Get a grip.*

"I said that we are being toyed with." Crossing back to the two of them perched on the ridiculous white marble divan, he continued, "That receptionist went to get the manager ten minutes ago. They are playing us." Sure, when he had started speaking, he had only been covering for his insane conversation with the Candy in his head, but as he had continued he became more convinced that he was right, "If you two want to sit here and wait, go right ahead, but I am done being polite." And he walked around the white wall divider behind the receptionist counter, coming face to face with a massive steel door, locked.

"Can you open it?" H was to his left, Line Boy behind her. They appeared to be looking at him now for answers. That was better.

"Of course." He quickly assessed the locking mechanism. Reaching into his pocket he withdrew the appropriate pick, and disabled the lock. The doors swung open silently to reveal an enormous warehouse space: long white tables covered with bolts of silk, a bank of sewing machines in the corner and several industrial sized looms dominating the far end. Everything was still, the looms frozen in mid-weft, the sewing machines abandoned with silk under the needles. The only things moving were scraps of silk spinning out into the corners of the room.

"You were right! They must have bolted while we sat there in the lobby like idiots."

He allowed himself a small smile at H's words. Yes. He had been right. And they were idiots. That felt better. Narrowing his eyes, he noticed a stairwell at the far end of the room. "Well, you only gave them a head start. Being idiots." Lifting his eyebrows towards the stairs, he put his hand out, preventing them from coming into the room. "There can only be one boss. And that's me. If you want to come, fine. But you do what I say when I say it." They exchanged another long look and he felt his irritation surge, "Or you can stay here. That lobby was bland, it could use some new statuary. Though I'd have to knock your noses and sundry off to have you fit in with the other Florence statues."

Line Boy started spluttering and puffing up, but H kept her cool.

"Fine. You are in charge. For now." She shot Line Boy a "keep your mouth shut" look— at least that was his interpretation of it.

This was much better. Hermes strode across the room, almost to the stairs, when Line Boy called out, tackling H and pulling Hermes' ankles out from under him, causing Hermes to hit the floor on his knees. Almost simultaneously he felt a rush of air raise the hairs on his neck, and twisting his head saw the dozen or so darts impale themselves on the wall next to them. H was buried under Line Boy who was checking her for injury.

"If you ever touch me again, it will be the last thing you do, human." Standing up, he dusted the threads from the warehouse floor off his knees.

H's voice incredulous, she sprang to her feet, poking him in the chest, "Are you kidding? You're threatening him? You should be thanking him! He saved our lives, well, my life, seeing as how you're immortal and all. But John spared you some pain, at least. No doubt those darts were poisoned, like the one that killed the station master in Milan. I am still new at this, but I am pretty sure Mr. Blean told me that immortals suffer when inflicted with human mortal danger."

Line Boy's face blanched at H's words and Hermes rewound the tape. New at what? Mr. Blean? Isn't Mr.Blean her hippy boss at the college library? Why was he teaching her things about the immortals? In a series of flashes several truths revealed themselves to him. *New at this.* H was not just the girl-formerly-with-a-gift, she was the *Monitor.* The top-secret, anonymous Monitor who had the ability to report on immortals breaking the Non-Interference Accord. And Blean, that tie-dyed hippie, was not just some annoying liberal with Birkenstocks, but he was the Council's centaur. He had to be. Why the hell else would he be teaching her about immortals. As he watched H's face drain of all color, he knew he was right. He smirked, this was the mother lode of leverage against H. This job just got much better. "Oh, H, you're the Monitor? Really?"

Her eyes flashed, and he could have sworn he saw panic on her face, but her words were angry, her stance aggressive,"*Monitor?* Is that what you call being in charge of this investigation? Because it's pretty clear from your little outburst in the lobby that I was supposed to be in charge of this case. Had to steal it from me, Hermes? I wonder what Hera would think of that?" She leaned in close and lowered her voice, "Don't worry, I'm no snitch. But I am also not the same girl you gifted back in June."

Hermes frowned. He was an expert at lying. Could he have been wrong? Had H only been talking about being new at this, where the "this" was detective work? That still didn't explain her comment about Blean. If he concentrated, he could read her mind. If she was the Monitor, he could blackmail her to keep her secret or use her to bust his enemies or simply expose her for the fun of it. But if he tried to do any of those things and she wasn't the Monitor, and the real Monitor caught him at it, well that would mean a century in Tartarus. Staring into her eyes, he pushed past her defenses, her thoughts just seconds from his reach, when Line Boy again interrupted.

"Listen, can you hear that? Hannah, we have to go. Now!"

Looking past Line Boy at the lobby, Hermes could see the rug moving towards them. Trust Line Boy to be afraid of furnishings. Staring a moment longer, he realized that what had appeared to be a moving rug was a mass of spiders, now half way across the warehouse. He hated spiders. And while H had been right that he was immortal, he was not looking forward to experiencing the pain that thousands of spider bites would inflict. Turning, he fled down the stairs, on their heels immediately. The landing opened up to two tunnels, each heading off in different directions, both heading down into the ground at a rapid descent. The clicking and slithering of thousands of spider legs was growing louder. Monitor or not, H was no snitch, and regardless of how she got there, she was on his team. Damn it.

"You two go left. Now. I'll stay here until the spiders are almost on me and lead them down the tunnel to the right."

"But what about you? If they web you, you'll be all alone, trapped."

"That's sweet, H. It is nice to know you care. But don't worry. Remember, I am the god with the winged sandals. I think I can stay in front of a herd of spiders. Is that what you would call them? A herd? Maybe it is a flock of spiders? Oomph—"

H had hugged him, hard. "Thanks." And like that they bolted down the tunnel to the left. Hermes tried to shake off the warm fuzzy he'd felt at her hug, to keep the edge of his cynicism sharp, but it became moot, as the swarm of spiders descended the stairs above.

"Come on you disgusting arachnids. Let's play tag. You're it."

He sped down the tunnel, being careful to keep close enough to the spiders to keep the chase, but far enough away to avoid the lunging front line. While he couldn't be sure that they were all following him through the dark, dank tunnel, it looked like it was all of them. A swarm. Definitely a swarm.

CHAPTER TWELVE

Under Florence

* * * * * * * * * *

Hannah

Grabbing a stitch in her side

Running at full speed, they never once paused when the tunnel split. Whichever one of them in the front at the time made the choice, the other pulled along by hand. At first it had been Hannah in the lead, the adrenaline giving her feet wings almost as real as Hermes'. Her speed was motivated by both the mass of spiders she had spotted over her shoulder when John had grabbed her arm and the all-too-recent memory of her entire face being trapped under spider webbing. But as the adrenaline wore down, John took the lead, and while they were still moving without pause, she had to grab the stitch in her side to keep moving, unable to stop and stretch it out.

The tunnel from under the warehouse had eventually opened onto a larger passageway, cobblestones under foot, brick ceiling overhead. John had managed to open the flashlight app on his phone, and every once in a while she spotted what looked like an ancient wall sconce. It had felt like they had been slowly climbing in the last few minutes when John abruptly stopped. Trying to halt her momentum she flung her arms out, but the stitch in her side flared, and she doubled over, her heading making contact with his side, knocking him onto the floor.

"Sor... ry... are... you... o... kay?" Trying to apologize and catch her breath at the same time, Hannah used both hands to press her sides and bent her knees. John shook off her question, having leapt back up to a squatting position. Putting his finger to his lips to silence her, and using the other hand to light up the tunnel behind them, he was focused on figuring out if they were being followed by a horror swarm of spiders, and she tried to swallow her gasps for air. They held this pose for what felt like twenty minutes, but it must have been only twenty seconds.

With no imminent threat behind them, John shone his phone on the door before them. It was skinny, wedged into a bend in the tunnel. The wood was covered in peeling red paint, the handle a heavy iron ring. Hannah reached out a hand to pull the ring, when they heard angry voices on the other side. She stepped back, John's arms coming around her as he placed himself between her and the door. Without a word they agreed to stay mute, and they leaned in together, trying to listen.

The voices rose in volume and clarity, but unfortunately for her, she also realized they were speaking Italian. As she waited for John to listen in, her mind wandered. She briefly thought of her grad school application to Yale and her sheepish blank in the "foreign languages studied" line. It was not the only aspect of her application she had felt uncomfortable with. She had tried to tell herself that everyone felt that way about grad school applications. But she had hours of listening to Gretchen work over her application as a counterpoint to her theory.

Gretchen had never struck her as uncomfortable with the process. Anxious, yes. But in the many phone calls when Gretchen had read her essay, she had seemed so convinced that Yale was the right place for her. The only place for her. Hannah had wanted it too— who in the classics world didn't? But she had felt oddly removed when she had tried to write her essay. She had told herself that it was because she was uncomfortable with selling herself, but standing here in the tunnel unable to decipher a single word being said on the other side of the door, she realized that maybe it was hard to sell herself to Yale because she wasn't actually good enough.

John's arm tightened around her, and her thoughts of her intellectual inadequacies were swamped by the fireworks going off in her body. They had had absolutely no time to be alone since that kiss, no time to talk about it, and yet she felt like she knew exactly what it meant. It was like the steam finally clearing on the bathroom mirror, and what had only been a murky indistinct image before was now clear.

She looked up, his face a study in concentration. She could see his mouth moving with the words, his eyes staring at the door. It gave her an unguarded moment to really look at him. His eyes, lips, nose, skin. He had the most beautiful face. Seeing it so close, she realized that he actively tried to downplay his beauty, that he must have spent his youth mastering the art of appearing more normal. Crinkling his eyes to mask their intensity, pulling faces and using sarcasm to distort the perfect symmetry of his features. Focused on translating the voices on the other side of the door, he was unaware of her stare and she felt a deep sympathy for the Mac Man. It must be hard to be so pretty. She smiled at the thought of him wanting people to listen to him and having to realize that all people wanted to do was look at him. That must have driven him crazy.

He looked down at her, the smile still on her lips, and in the silence he smiled back. The voices on the other side stopped, and he leaned down, kissing her. It must have been the run, the breathless feeling that filled her as the kiss made her legs tremble, and she slid her hands around his neck. Without thinking she pulled his head down more firmly and lost herself to the rush. She felt the whip-like reaction in him, but as his hands lifted her hips against him, his phone fell from his grip, the flashlight beam careening wildly against the walls of the tunnel on its trip to the ground. They both froze as the phone clattered on impact, the sound echoing in the tunnel.

"Hannah." He looked down, avoiding eye contact, his breath ragged.

"I know." But she didn't move away. Yet. She leaned her head against his chest, gratified to hear his heart racing. Although that could also be from the dash from death they had just made. Scrambling for perspective, she forced her mind to the present, "What did they say?"

"There were two people, I think. A third person came in at the end. One of them was yelling at the other, about how they would both be fired." While he talked he ran his hand lightly up and down her back. "And the other one said that no, he wasn't getting fired because the caterer was an idiot. Then there was some cursing about northerners, and I think some sort of slur, I'm not quite sure, but I think that they were talking about a missing truck and a missing caterer. Then they were interrupted by a third person saying it was time, and they all left."

"Do you think it could have something to do with Apollo and the people in the silk house?" She whispered her questions. "Could they have left through this exit? Used the truck to move him?"

His hands were now sifting through her hair. He was slow to respond. The phone was still on the floor of the tunnel, the light warming the red brick walls, casting a circle around them. "That seems like a stretch. We must have passed a dozen forks in the tunnel." He had started to kiss the edges of her ear.

"Yes, but isn't this the first door?" She lifted her head off his chest and kissed him. Doors, tunnels, spiders, all fading. As he worked his way down her neck she slid her hands into his back pockets. The Mac Man in her mind always had a condom in his back pocket.

"Whoa, Han. Not that I'm complaining— the State Department warnings of pickpockets in Florence never even hinted at it being quite so erotic— but what are you looking for?" John held her shoulders in his hands, his face bemused.

"Uh, protection? I assumed you carried some in your back pocket, or maybe in your wallet?" The blurry edge of embarrassment started forming on the sides of her mind and she took a small step away from him, crossing her arms behind her back.

"Here? Oh, Hannah, we are not going to have our first time together in some bizarre Medici tunnel under the streets of Florence."

There were only two options at this point; minimize the embarrassment by agreeing, or saying something to somehow deny that she had intended to do what they both now knew she had wanted to do, this option buoyed up by the notion that clearly he had *not* intended to do what she had intended for them to do. She could back away from the moment and somehow try to save face. It was what she should do. But then two things happened simultaneously that lead her to take a third option. His bemused look blossomed into a full-on amused look, which was irritating, and she remembered that she had a condom in her purse. Gretchen had insisted. She smiled, sliding it out of the travel bag hanging around her neck. He was going to regret being amused. And she was going to enjoy it. She waved the condom at him playfully.

"John MacCallister. I promise that for our second time together we can have white sheets and rose petals." She reached down, lifting her sundress up and over her head, "We can even have candle-light and wine." Dropping her dress on the ground, she smiled, "But right now we are going to have to make do with brick and dust and—"

Her words were lost in his mouth as he finished the sentence for her.

* * * * * * * * *

Lee

Searching for Hannah's cell signal

Lee paced in circles at the entrance to the Boboli Gardens. Hannah should be here. Right here. The sun was starting to set and there was clearly a wedding taking place in the Pitti Palace behind him, men in black pants and white shirts impatiently stepping around him, arms laden with trays of wine glasses, muttering about tourists. The Pitti Palace and the adjoining Boboli gardens were open to visitors during the day, for a price. Lee had to buy a full day's ticket even though the woman selling tickets to the museum had told him that all visitors must leave by sunset.

He stared at the tracking information on his phone, as if it would somehow tell him more. Hannah's cell phone should be here where he was standing. But there was nothing but a marble statue of Artemis, bow lifted. He cocked his head to the side. It was a decent likeness. He had met Artemis at Hera's Fourth of July party. Apollo had made the introductions.

"Lee, my main man. This is my beautiful sister Artemis. Arty, this is Lee. Watch out, he is quite the ladies... um, thing, um, demon. You're a demon, right Lee? Lee here has a thing for cheese. Isn't that fascinating? I'll leave you two to it." Apollo had sauntered off to the bar without a backward glance.

Lee had tried his best. He remembered asking her if she found the human hunting seasons annoying, but she had simply stared at him, unblinking. He slowly reached his hand out to her wrist to check for a pulse when Hermes had swooped in.

"Hey there, party-goers. Artemis, looking lovely as usual. You don't mind if I steal my friend here away for a minute? Fantastic!" Hermes had dragged him to the sea wall by the scruff of his shirt collar. "You are one bold little demon my friend. No male, human or otherwise, touches Artemis. Period." Hermes had proceeded to educate him with tales of males who had fallen afoul of Artemis. She was one terrifying goddess.

"The gardens are closed. You must leave. Now." The woman

who had sold him the entrance ticket not fifteen minutes ago was now brandishing a broom at him, as if she could sweep him away, backing him toward the statue. He dodged to the side, still terrified of touching even a stone version of Artemis. "We have an event. It is invitation only." She swung the broom back and forth.

Lee raised his hands, "Okay, okay, I'll go. In just a second. I just have to wait for my friend to come back. She went into the palace to use the bathroom." Something about the lie he had just told tugged at the corner of his mind.

"She cannot be in the bathroom. I have just checked and they are empty." She was shaking her head now in rhythm to the broom sweeps, getting closer and closer to whacking him.

"Could she have used a different bathroom? Is there a basement level to the Palace?"

"Of course there is a basement level. And below that, another basement and from there there are tunnels that travel underground throughout the city. If you had paid for the guided tour you would know all this. I am sorry to say that I think your friend has left you." Her look was one of both derision and pity, "I doubt it is the first time this has happened to you, yes?"

Lee felt a sharp hatred for the ticket woman. Humans, as a species, were so casually mean, so shallow. He knew that she said these things to him because he was considered by humans to be ugly, and therefore worthless. Some immortals were rude or cruel to him, but it had almost nothing to do with how he looked. They could separate out his ability to contribute from his physical appearance. Hermes was put off by his smell, but he valued his cleverness. Humans, on the other hand, almost always equated their revulsion with his appearance to his value as a being.

Except Hannah. She had always been nice to him. In June she had carried him in her arms when he was hurt by his fall down the stairs in the monument; she had pleaded with Hera to heal him. And even though he knew that it had all been part of her lie to fix things, she had raised him up as the hero in front of everyone. She was his *favorite* human. He needed to find her, make her wear the necklace. Protect her from Sek.

"Looking for me?"

Lee turned at the voice and smiled. *Hermes.* He seemed a little dusty, but none the worse for wear.

"*This* is your friend? I thought it was a she? How many friends do you have?"

"Lee! You're here!"

Turning back, he saw Hannah and John calling and waving as they exited the palace. They were also disheveled, but somewhat more chipper than Hermes. Hannah ran up to Hermes and hugged him, and then bent down for a quick hug for Lee. Lee took advantage of the hug to whisper, "Hannah, you need to be careful..."

But she had only laughed and walked back to John, kissing him. Hermes groaned and muttered something cynical about true love, but Lee was filled with terror. If Sek saw that, if he was here, he would kill them both. Maybe attack them all. He would definitely kill John. But it was like he was in the wrong movie. Everyone around him seemed to be in a great mood, the great mood that comes when danger is past. Except he was the only one still stuck in a horror movie, when the music is building and

you know the guy with the pickaxe and hockey mask is somewhere in the house. He needed to talk to Hannah without John
or Hermes hearing him— John, because he would only be noble
and brave and get himself killed trying to protect Hannah and
Hermes because Hermes would learn that he had been talking to
Sek and not telling Hermes about it. He would never trust Lee
again. Lee would just have to get Hannah alone to warn her.

The ticket woman swept at his feet, "Well, you are all found
now and you must all leave now. Good bye. *Buona Notte. Adio.*"

They started walking down the road leading to the bridge
that crossed to the Uffizi, the piazza on their right starting to fill
with evening vendors. Lee tried to position himself next to
Hannah, but she was busy skipping and swirling and dipping her
head into John's shoulder. He pulled on the hem of her sundress
when it swirled into view, and that got her attention. She smiled
down at him.

"How did you know where to find us, Lee? It was the best
feeling to come up out of the tunnels into that beautiful palace
and see you standing there, waiting."

"The *best feeling*, hmmm, H? I think you had better work on
your technique Line Boy. I am fairly certain that—"

Hannah hit Hermes in the gut— playfully? Lee frowned. She
had linked arms with both John and Hermes, effectively keeping
them from snarling at each other. The three of them were walking so fast and they all seemed to be talking about something he
didn't quite get and how the hell was he going to get her alone?

"Hey! Can you all slow down a little? Some of us have short
legs."

Looking back over her shoulder, Hannah stopped abruptly

and apologized, "Sorry, Lee, that was so rude of us. I guess we just got a little carried away. It is so nice to walk in the open air, un-chased by hundreds of spiders."

"Make that thousands of spiders, Han." John was shaking his head.

"Our H does not have a head for numbers." Hermes smirked.

"Or languages. Have you heard her trying to ask where the bathroom is? She told the poor doorman his mother was a library." Now John was the recipient of the playful gut punch.

Hannah pulled them all to a stop. "Why don't you three grab this table," they were at one of the many restaurants ringing the Piazza del Duomo, "and have a drink while you dissect my flaws. I am going to run up to the room and get Gretchen. She texted me that she had finished decoding the scarf. She *is* a genius. We can all download together and then come up with our next step. Who knows? Maybe we can enjoy an evening in Florence." She waltzed away, not waiting for a response.

John and Hermes exchanged a slow look and then both shrugged and sat down, Hermes calling for the waiter. This was Lee's chance to catch her alone.

"Um, I have to run back to the room, too, I need to get my... I need a new... um..." but it turned out Hermes and John weren't even listening. They had started to argue over the wine list. Trying to weave through the growing crowds in the plaza, he dodged high heels and swinging purses with a stream of *scusi*.

Breaking through the crowds, Lee could see Hannah entering the lobby. He called her name, or would have, except he was suddenly incapable of breathing, and therefore silent. Gasping like a fish and grabbing at the vise grip around his neck, he heard the voice he'd been dreading since early this morning.

"Why aren't you in more pain?" Sek's question sounded petulant.

Why *wasn't* he in more pain? And come to think of it, he could breathe. Why? He'd been on the receiving end of Sek's scorching grip before. Why was this so different? Like a voice in his head he heard the answer.

We are here. We will protect you.

The necklace. If Sek knew about it, he would steal it. Screaming at the top of his lungs, Lee writhed and twisted, drawing on a long history of being tortured by Sek to feign his reaction.

Releasing his stranglehold, Sek grabbed Lee's arm, dragging him back away from the crowd. "That's more like it. And there will be more like that later, I promise. But for now, I need to be a little more discreet. You are going to be the tasty bit of cheese that brings me my beloved mouse."

The Gorgon sisters in his mind were asking him what to do.

Shall we hurt him for you? Burn him? No, I know, we can break all his bones. Would you like that?

Would he *like* that? He would love that! Except then Sek would know that he was using magic to hurt him. And Sek would stop at nothing to find the source and take it from him.

Not necessarily. Tell him you moved up in your demon ranking. That you are now more powerful than he.

He would never believe that. I mean look at him. He is the most measly of demons I've ever seen.

You always were so judgmental. It's why you never could land a man.

Yeah, well, at least I'm not a slut.

Shut up!

Lee blinked rapidly. While the voices from the necklace argued in his head, Sek was busy grabbing a local boy and giving him a letter with instructions to deliver it to Hannah. He had to get the Gorgon sisters under control before Sek turned his attention back.

Get us under control. Look who's getting a big head.

It would be the only thing big about you.

There you go with that judgy thing again. It would make any man shrivel.

You want to know what makes a man shrivel? How about your voice? It sounds like a thousand cats crying.

A thousand? Really? Do you have any idea what a thousand really is?

Lee thought as hard as he could, *Ladies. Please stop. I need to get you back to my friend, so to do that, I need you to let him hurt me, just a little.*

Oh! Your friend? The one from the hotel? Oh, we would love to go back to her! She was the best!

She really understood us.

We could do great things together.

Sek was sending the boy off and Lee realized that he didn't have any more time to try to explain to the Gorgon sisters who he meant. It was better just to agree. He thought, *Yes. Her.*

Fantastic! We'll do whatever you want.

Yes. We promise to help.

Anyone but the other one.

Yeah. She ignored us. All the time.

It wasn't just that she ignored us. She controlled us. Without even a hello or a please or thank you. Work, work, work, all the time. And she was always in danger. It was exhausting. But the other girl, now she was someone we could have fun with.

Sek grabbed his elbow, twisting it behind his back, pushing him through the plaza, "You are being weirdly quiet. Not that I'm complaining. It's just that I expected you to plead for her life or at least whimper and cry. This is an improvement."

"How are you going to get at her? She has protection." Hermes had taught him that egomaniacs like Sek enjoy talking about their plans. A good detective can get anyone talking.

Sek stopped short, spinning Lee around to stare at his face, "Do you know what her protection is?" At his mute head shake, he flung him forward and continued across the cobblestones, "It doesn't matter. My little note told her to give up her protection and come with me willingly or everyone she cares about dies. Starting with you."

Oh, he is so pompous. "Everyone dies."

What a drama queen.

Yeah, come on, little demon, let us hurt him. It would be fun!

Fun! Fun! Fun!

Lee tried to think of the options. Hermes had taught him to play out the consequences, to consider each outcome of his possible moves, but it was hard to concentrate with three Gorgon sisters yelling in his head. He would need a diversion to get Hannah away from Sek. Maybe the sisters could do it for him. He would also need a diversion to get them back onto Hannah's neck.

"Yeah, sure. But wait for my signal."

"What are you babbling about?" Sek was forcing him up the steps of the massive cathedral that dominated the plaza.

"Just whimpering, with fear. Um, why are we going in here?"

Sek had dragged him to the rear of the church, past a velvet rope with a sign stating in several languages, "Closed for construction."

"I thought that would be obvious, idiot. We are going to get closer to God." Pushing him up the winding staircase, Sek's eerie laughter echoed in the domed ceiling, setting pigeons roosting in the rafters to flight. They probably only numbered a dozen or so, but covering his head with his hands to avoid their flapping wings and screeching beaks, it felt like a thousand.

CHAPTER THIRTEEN

Never Have I Ever

· · · · · · · · · ·

Hannah

Riding down in the elevator

"When dealing with immortals, try to empty your mind of the human norms you carry. What is persuasive or significant to a mortal is immaterial to the gods. Their norms are centered on identity, ability and, above all, power."

Mr. Blean had spent several weeks at the start of her job pushing her to reframe her analysis of hypothetical scenarios involving the immortals, patiently explaining what she misunderstood or in what ways she had failed to properly assess not only what they were doing but how she might interact. She traced the edges of the note in her pocket, a note that a scruffy Italian boy had shoved into her hands as she had waited for the elevator to carry her to the penthouse suite. She'd read it on the ride up, overwhelmed by terror. Just thinking of it made her breath catch. That was *before*. Now she was riding back down, Gretchen at her side, trying to remember everything Mr. Blean had taught her about immortals. She forced her mind to stay calm. She had a plan. She needed to stay present.

"Are you sure?" Gretchen's expression was casual, but her tone was strained, worry radiating out of each syllable, and Hannah, giving in to a surge of affection for her, hugged her. It was a testament to the level of her distress that Gretchen allowed the hug to last until the doors opened on the lobby.

Letting go, Hannah straightened her shoulders. "We talked about it. I've got this." Smiling, she linked arms with Gretchen and crossed the foyer, pushing out into the Florence evening. As they strolled across the cobblestones of the plaza, Hannah noticed that the crowds had changed. No longer dominated by packs of tourists in their travel sandals, it seemed to be a much more native Florentine crowd, well dressed men and women flowing across the plaza, not a Velcro-ed shoe in sight. Some were dancing to street musicians, most drinking and laughing and smoking. She wanted to hit pause and simply stand in this moment, savor the novelty of being someplace so completely *European*.

"For crying out loud, Han, stop staring or they will think you want them to talk to us." Gretchen looked pointedly at a pack of Italian men who appeared to be actively deciding which one of them had dibs.

"Talk to you, you mean. That dress is ridiculously hot, Gretch." They had both taken the time to change clothes from the pack Gretchen had brought from Greece. Gretchen was wearing a silver body-hugging bandage dress. Hannah had opted for a pair of slim black capris, with pockets, and had conceded to Gretchen's choice of an electric blue silk tank. In the warm evening air it slid over her body in a way that almost made her blush, "I'm sure they're not looking at me."

"Really, Han? I can't tell if you're being falsely modest or just absurdly insecure."

The memory of her time with John in the tunnel flooded her and she laughed, "Fair enough. I can hear Elise quoting *Ladies Home and Hearth* at me— Women who run themselves down deserve to sweep the floor alone— does that even make sense?"

Pulling up to stand in front of her, Gretchen held her by the shoulders, her gaze probing, "Nothing in that magazine makes sense. Even the recipes are judgmental— add sugar at your own risk— it's fucked up. Are you sure about this plan? You don't have to go alone. We could tell the boys—"

"No. I'm fine." Spying the flock of Italian men approaching, she took advantage of the impending invasion to force herself to get to it. "Sorry to leave you to fend them off. John and Hermes are in the far right corner of the plaza. I'll meet you there. I promise."

Nodding, Gretchen hugged her again, a stark sign of the level of danger she was in, "Kick his demon ass."

Pivoting, Hannah walked resolutely to the central entrance of the Duomo, a set of massive bronze doors. Staring up at the statues of the twelve apostles and the Virgin Mary holding a baby Jesus arrayed across the front facade of the cathedral, Hannah tried to empty her mind of fear and doubt, silently offering up an apology to the array of Christian saints for what she was about to do in their house of worship. Pulling on the heavy door, she opened it only enough to slip in, letting it close behind her. The nave and the sanctuary were lit by overhead fixtures, but the dominant impression of light was formed from the hundreds of votive candles filling the side alcoves and lining the sacristy. The candles emitted a flickering warmth which only made the expansive central dome seem even more awe-inspiring. Hannah paused for a moment at the center of the dome and tilted her head back, turning in place to take in the elaborate frescoes painted on the ceiling. She tried to imagine the very human artists, artisans, and laborers who had made this structure possible. The love required to build something so beyond necessity, so clearly a statement of passion for God. Such a human accomplishment.

Exhaling slowly she centered her mind on releasing all such concerns and reminded herself of the strategy she and Gretchen had come up with in the hotel room, after she had showed Gretchen the note and told her the entire Sek story. It had felt good to finally talk about it with someone she trusted.

They agreed that she needed to work against Sek's expectations, unseat his presumptions. The note had said to meet him at the top of the dome or he would rip Lee's limbs off. On the eastern wall she spied a velvet rope stretched across a set of iron steps spiraling up into the darkness. There were a few people in the cathedral at this time: a handful of men and women kneeling in pews, praying, an older man in clerical robes in whispered conversation with a security guard near the altar. They seemed to be discussing locking up, the clergyman pointing to several doorways, the guard nodding slowly. Slipping under their shifting gaze, Hannah moved toward the bank of red votive candles nearest the spiral staircase, digging a dollar bill out of her purse to put into the money box. But instead of taking one of the long matches to light a candle, she kept walking calmly toward the roped-off area.

Without pausing, she ducked under the rope and began her ascent up the stairs. In seconds she was beyond the sight of anyone in the church, the way above her dark. The staircase felt unstable under her feet, the entire structure swaying slightly with her climb. Reaching the top, she found a door with a heavy brass padlock hanging open. Pushing, Hannah watched the door swing open to reveal a landing. Following the faint light from several small square windows set high in the wall, she came upon another ancient door. Opening it, she found herself outside on a narrow ledge with a high metal railing. The evening air was fresh, and she inhaled deeply while getting her bearings. She was on the top of the building's facade. Far below her was the Piazza del Duomo, filled with small sparkling lights and the sounds of people enjoying the night. Somewhere out there were John, Hermes, and Gretchen. Above her was the arching structure of the dome, curving into the blackness, illuminated only by patches of light from the moon and stars breaking through the heavy cloud cover. There, at the top, in all that darkness, were Lee and Sek.

She wished her mother was here. Elise would have some pithy expression picked up from decades of reading *Ladies Home and Hearth*: "When facing an unpleasant task and your resolve is hazy, delay only makes you both dirty *and* lazy," or, "A moment spent dallying yes or no is only another moment for dust to grow." Hmm... Those seemed to all be about cleaning. There had to be better inspirational gems from her mother stored in her memory. A stitch in time saves nine? No. A spoonful of sugar? Completely unhelpful. Then she heard it, her mother's voice, clear as day, "Life is for the living, Hannah, get in there and get it done." Wiping her sweaty palms on her pants, she reached up and grabbed a rung just above her head, the way up a series of metal bars bolted to the side of the building, a long curving ladder to the apex of the dome.

As she reached the top of the dome the rungs were replaced with steps, a skinny iron railing offering meager help. Standing on the top now, she could see two figures black against the rising white cupola, lit up by spotlights. One was tall and blade shaped, the other short and crumpled. Oh, poor Lee. She found it easier not to be afraid of Sek when she could be angry at the pain he undoubtedly had caused her friend.

As she approached, his voice cut across the distance between them, "*Darling*. You came. That is perfect. I would have hated to have hunted you down. Although there is something to the pleasure of the chase." And he licked his lips, his tongue long and thin.

She had to steel herself not to cringe in revulsion. She had to play this smart. Sek's face was partially visible from the refracted light of the spotlights on the cupola. He was hanging onto his human form, no horns in sight, but she could see his pointed teeth through his smug smile, his red eyes glowing slightly. Lee was not so composed, his horns protruding through his thin hair, his cloven feet uncovered, and his expression was far from smug; he was stricken and anxious. He opened his mouth to say something to her, but Sek lashed out and hit him hard in the face, "Not a word, Lee. This is between me and my beloved."

"Did I give you permission to call me your beloved?"

Her words had an almost comical effect on both demons. Sek opened and closed his mouth several times, as if words were beyond him. Lee looked truly appalled, then she could actually see the lightbulb go on over his head and caught the briefest of smiles before he went back to his first expression of shock. She saw him slide his right hand down to tap his pocket. Excellent. She just needed to get close enough.

Striding toward Sek, she raised her chin and imagined her mother on their family vacations, complaining to one of the many hotel managers that the room was filthy and the pillows were insufficient. "I did not expect to see you until you had redeemed yourself in the eyes of your overlord, Apep. You have not proven yourself worthy of me."

"I—? What—? You?" Sek was actually backing away from her as she stalked him. She needed to get to Lee, and the only way was toward Sek.

She mimicked him, "I? What? You? If I wanted to bind myself to an idiot, I would have chosen Apollo. At least he looks pretty when he's babbling incoherently. You disappoint me, Sek." It was just a few more steps now.

"No! This is wrong! You are wrong!" He had stopped moving back, narrowing his gaze on her, he cocked his head to the side, "This is an act. Some kind of game you are playing to—"

She cut him off, "Well, that makes sense. You see this as a game, Sek? Is that why you've been playing hide and seek with me for the last three months, hmm?" Just a little closer, she would have to get a little closer. "Did you think I couldn't see you? In the movie theater? On the ferry? At the airport? Please. Always lurking, never having the guts to approach me like a proper demon."

He snarled, but his voice sounded more resentful than angry, "I couldn't approach you. I tried, but I kept getting pushed back.

You have some sort of trinket from Hera that protects you. I know you do. You have to take it off, or I will kill everyone you know, one by one." As he talked he got more confident and now it was she who wanted to step back. But she held her ground.

She had to hope that Lee would take advantage of the distraction she was about to create. For the second time that day she reached down and pulled her top off, waving the silk tank in the air like a banner of war, "Does it look like I am wearing a trinket?" She reached out and grabbed Sek's shirt front, praying that Lee would act, terrified that Sek would, "Do you really think there is some bauble that keeps you from approaching me? You can't approach me because you are pathetic, broken. Even here, inches from each other, you can't touch me. I dare you to try."

In the split second before he reached for her she witnessed a slew of emotions distort his features. Distrust. Fear. Hatred. Awe. He landed on pleasure. "I almost believed you." Leering at her chest, he stepped closer, "And I appreciate the level of your commitment to the con. It only makes me love you more, my beloved," and he slid a single finger along her collarbone.

The reaction was instantaneous. He was flung backward in the air, hitting the stone walls of the cupola with enough force to make sand fall from the mortar. Suspended off the ground, his limbs twisted and flailed as he cried out in pain. The sound of his screams were so inhuman it made all of the birds roosting in the nooks of the cathedral take flight, their panicked calls adding to the din. Hannah covered her ears.

"Silence!" His screaming ceased. She thought that winning would feel better, but she had started trembling all over and she worried she would lose her grip before she could finish the plan.

She knew what a completely evil creature Sek was, and yet she had not been prepared to see him in pain. Pain she had caused. She felt her stomach clench and small explosions of light in the back of her eyes warned her that her hold on consciousness was fragile. It had been so close. He had touched her, and then she had felt the weight of the necklace in her pocket, and he was gone, just like that. But what now? He was still convulsing, pinned six feet high against the wall, and she was about to vomit.

"Here, Hannah."

Looking down, she saw Lee holding her tank top out for her. Staining the silk with the sweat from his overactive glands. He waited while she slipped it back over her head, and then he took her hand. Whispering to her, he guided her, "Just think it. They have to obey you."

She closed her eyes and commanded the Gorgon sisters to stop hurting him, just hold him. His flailing stopped.

"I hope this clears things up for you, Sek. I may be your Mry, but you are not mine. At least not yet." She and Gretchen had argued about this part of the plan. She had wanted to send Sek to do one hundred years of kind acts to be worthy, but Gretchen had insisted that that would only make him suspicious. Gretchen thought she needed to send him to do demon worthy things, but Hannah hadn't wanted to be responsible for more evil in the world. When she framed it that way, neither had Gretchen. But then she hit on it, the suggestion that would be demonic enough but not hurt others, "You must be punished for your failings. You must go away from me and earn your name. Go to the Under-world and call on Hades. Offer your services to him. Ask him for the lowest job, the most demeaning work. You must do every task he sets you to, no matter how degrading. When you think you are ready, you may return, but if you find you cannot approach me, you must go back and work until you are worthy."

Sek was staring at her, the longing in his eyes unnerving. It was almost more terrifying than when he had been threatening her. His silence worried her until she remembered that it was her command that had left him without words. Get a grip, Summers. It would completely ruin the plan if she acted freaked out now. Straightening her shoulders, she tossed her hair back, "I am leaving now. We are leaving." She looked down to see that Lee had reclaimed his human form and he smiled up at her. "Do not think to try this again. Do not lay another hand on anyone close to me or I will never accept you. Never. Am I clear?'

Watching him slowly nod, his gaze never wavering from her face, she wondered if they had made the right call and momentarily feared for the unintended consequences of this charade. But then Lee tugged her hand and she turned her back on Sek, ordering the necklace to keep him there until they were away from the cathedral. She followed Lee back down the way she had climbed, until they were once again in the main church, now empty. All of the electric lights were off and the nave was awash in shadows, the lights from the votives glowing red. What had once felt peaceful and expansive now felt closed-in and oppressive.

Acting purely on instinct Hannah bolted for the doors and finding them unlocked, she burst out onto the plaza, weaving through the crowds to the table where she'd left John and Hermes, hoping to find Gretchen there with them. But they weren't there. An older couple was half-way through a wine bottle, arguing in sharp words. Panting from her sprint, she scanned the crowds. She couldn't see them anywhere. Spinning in circles to find them, she felt the tingling in the back of her head intensify. She bent over, bracing her hands on her knees, and tried to fight off the faint. And then she heard it. The sweetest, snarkiest sound.

"Still looking for religion, H?"

"Hermes!" She seized him, holding him close, and then, almost as quickly, shoved him back, panic giving her voice an edge, "Where are John and Gretchen?"

"It's nice to see you, too."

Though his tone was sarcastic, she felt him assessing her. She had to get herself under control, or he would start asking questions. "Sorry. It's just, I get lost so easily, and we are here in this foreign city, and you were all supposed to be here..." and she pointed at the bickering Italian couple.

"You can blame Line Boy for that. Your gal pal said you had ducked into the church to pray. I speculated that you were full of regret for your underground hook-up and had decided to take the veil. He didn't take kindly to my playful banter and went after you. Then she went after him. I went after her, at least I started to, but then she had him wrangled back. Long story short, we lost the table."

"Hannah!"

And then she was tackled by Gretchen, her hug bone-crunching, and she could hear Hermes ribbing Lee about always getting to the party late, and over Gretchen's shoulder she saw John. The thought that somewhere out in the night Sek might still be watching caused her to stay where she was and simply nod at him. His smile was careful, and it made her want to rush over and explain. But not now. She would fill him in later. Much later. For now they had work to do.

"I think we should head back to the suite. It's too noisy out here to talk anyway. Besides, the wifi is much better in the hotel, and I have a hunch, based on Gretchen's brilliant translation, on where we can find our golden friend." Gretchen and Lee were quick to agree, and the three of them lead the way back to the hotel, Hermes and John silently following in their wake.

* * * * * * * * *

Athena

Wishing she'd packed sunglasses

"What do you mean, I'm already checked in? That is impossible, as clearly I am standing here before you, waiting to do precisely that."

Hera's voice berating the desk clerk was like a wrecking ball in her skull. Athena suppressed the instinct to grab her aching head. She refused to reveal her discomfort, especially to Hera. She was appalled to consider how much she had already let slip on the flight over. If she didn't know better, she would think Hera had pretended to be ignorant of wine just to get her drunk so she could take advantage of her and fish for information. But that seemed unlikely for one very good reason: that plan required a perspicacious level of intelligence the publisher of housekeeping dreck clearly did not have. Now, if Hera had needed a devious plan to braise a chicken leg…

"No, I will not wait while you call the manager. You will tell me right now which room I am apparently already checked into."

The pitch of Hera's voice was rising, and it made Athena want to cry. Stepping away from the altercation, she feigned an interest in the lobby's marble columns, but the morning sunlight that was flooding the foyer cut through her like a sword cleaving her head. Needing to hide, she clenched her jaw and stepped into the shade of the potted palm to the left of the front desk, pretending to examine its leaf health. Swiping her finger along its length she held it up and announced, to no one in particular, "Dust. Typical."

Hera looked over her shoulder at her only to roll her eyes and turn back to berating the front desk clerk at a decibel that threatened to split Athena's skull. The wave of nausea came out of nowhere, and she bent over and neatly vomited in the dusty palm's pot. Ah, that felt better. Delicately wiping the side of her mouth with an airline napkin she'd found wadded in her pocket, she deposited that into the beleaguered palm's pot as well. Feeling better, she joined Hera at the desk.

It was time to take the situation in hand. "Young man, pursuant to international law as constituted by the EU, of which Italy is a member, you must provide full information to the named card member, as confirmed by legitimate legal identification, of all the details of a given charge, including rooms. If you indeed charged this woman's credit card, then she has every right to know which room the charges originate from. If you have any questions, I suggest you confer with your corporate counsel. But if you make us wait for that, you might as well also inform him that I will be filing a lawsuit against your establishment for reckless and illegal corporate financial practices. Desist from your stuttering and provide the information."

With shaking hands, the clerk passed Hera a printout, avoiding eye contact with them both. She attempted to read the paper over Hera's shoulder, but Hera had already crumpled it in her fist. Stalking to the elevator, Hera threw over her shoulder, "I was handling it."

"Not very effectively." *Someone* was defensive. What did she expect, the Goddess of Marriage was probably in a perpetual state of PMS. It was Hera's hysterical tears that had prompted her to come on this ridiculous errand. Following her to the lifts, she decided that she could be magnanimous and let her rudeness pass unremarked. Vomiting had significantly improved her stomach, and if she could simply get to a dark place to sleep for an hour, she would be fine. Then she could point Hera in the direction of the blackmailers and let her do the dirty work. Hera, in her present emotional state, would probably curse them all to dust before they could utter a word. Threat contained and problem solved.

The elevator doors opened, and she followed Hera in, watching her jab the penthouse button. "Any idea who we might find when we get to the room?" Ignored. Fine, she would have to try to talk to her on a womanly level, "I can see that you are upset, Hera. I'm sure you can handle this, but if you tell me what to expect, I might be able to help you." There, that would probably get through to her estrogen-addled brain.

Hera turned to look at her, her eyes narrowed. Was she about to cry? God, she hated it when women cried. If only more women could access their intellect instead of their—

"You have vomit on your chin."

"Oh." Searching her pocket for another airline napkin, she almost missed exiting before the doors closed. Wiping at her chin, she lengthened her stride to draw even with Hera without appearing to rush. *Why didn't she wait for me?* She had the uncomfortable feeling that she was the one who was acting emotional. It was just the hangover. It made her weak. She caught up just as Hera started banging on the door. All pretense at being composed was lost as she grabbed her head to contain the pain, dropping the napkin on the floor. She moaned and my have even begged her to stop *for all that is holy*— she couldn't tell if she said it aloud or was only thinking it. It was immaterial, as Hera continued pounding until the door swung inward and a short, lumpy man stood on the other side.

"Hera. It's nice to— ," but Hera shoved the oddly greasy man aside

"Where is that thieving, good for nothing, lazy—"

"Well, hey there, boss. I wasn't expecting you. Have you come to Firenze on business or pleasure? Business probably—" His words were cut off in mid-sentence as Hera turned him to stone.

Athena stared at her half-brother, Hermes, leaning negligently back on the pillows, arms behind his head, frozen in stone. *What a sloppy curse on Hera's part. He would not make a good garden ornament in that pose.* A quick assessment of the room showed that Hermes was not alone. Along with the lumpy little man, who was clearly not a human, there appeared to be quite a human contingent present: a man and two women. One of the women, dark haired and taller than the other, pointed at

Hermes' stone figure and started screaming. Well, if Hera could toss around curses, so could she. Staring at the screaming banshee Athena sealed her mouth and it was instantly quieter. Hera had the audacity to look annoyed at her.

"What? I have a headache. Besides, you were the first to curse. I'm just following your lead. At least I didn't make a completely useless statue. Where would you put him while he is in that prone state?"

"I cursed a *god*. He'll be fine. She is a *human*. You aren't too hungover to understand the difference?"

"Fine. I'll undo it." She pointed at the other two humans, "You two. Stand next to your friend. Don't worry, when you wake up, you won't remember any of—"

But Hera grabbed her arm in a vise-like grip, "Did the wine kill of all of your brain cells? You can't wipe their memories. They are working for me. Or at least that one is," and she pointed to the blonde. "Just undo your curse."

"And leave them to report me to the some ridiculous tabloid? All I need is for the Monitor to hear about this and I am screwed. I have a reputation to protect. I have to erase their memories. It's that, or kill them. Or hey, you could turn them into shrubs. Florence is filled with gardens that could use some new topiaries."

Before Hera could answer, the blonde one spoke, "My friend promises not to make any more noise. She was startled, but she is fine now. Please don't erase our memories. We have worked so hard to find Apollo, and we are so close. When the job is done, if you feel it is necessary, well then, I am sure you would do what you must, but for now…"

Athena stared at her. Who was this human who, in the face

of all that had just transpired, could so calmly make her case? Now that she was really looking at her, her face seemed vaguely familiar. Where had she seen her before?

"How do I know you?"

"She's working for me. Just do what she says and let's get on with this." Hera crossed the room to a side chair and waved in the vicinity of the laptop glowing on the desk, "Report."

The boy was looking back and forth between Hera and the blonde, but the blonde was only looking at her. She was even more impressed. The girl's gaze was direct without being impudent. She was waiting for her decision. A glance at the dark haired girl proved that she was no longer hysterical, so her ears would be safe from the din of screams. Fine. She restored her mouth. The girl gasped slightly, but then settled down, sinking into the couch behind her. The blonde and the boy exchanged a look, and then he joined the girl on the couch. The blonde nodded politely in her direction and then turned to address Hera.

"What would you like to know first?"

Hera's gaze took in the opulent room, and she flung her hand out, "Why don't you start by explaining this. And them," pointing at the two humans on the couch.

"The Savoy has the best security in Florence. And the most thorough housekeeping, which, given the reach of our kidnappers, is essential. We have already been attacked twice while in Florence, and that was after fleeing from an assassin in Milan. We needed a secure location to plan the extraction of Apollo. And they," here she pointed at the two humans on the couch, "have been invaluable contributors to this investigation. You did put me in charge. I assumed that included bringing in the necessary staff."

Damn it. This crew of misfits seemed to have figured out significantly more than she had anticipated. She would have to determine the extent of their knowledge if she was going to keep her own role out of this. On the plus side, the blonde had a nice speaking voice, low and fluid. She could listen to her speak without wanting to kill her. Now all she needed was less light. Crossing the room to close the drapes, she probed, "Assassins and kidnappers? Hera and I were under the impression that Apollo had joined a fascist cell." She sank onto the couch next to the dark haired girl, who visibly flinched. "Oh calm, down." The silence in the room penetrated her exhaustion. Hera was staring at her, stony faced. "What?"

"Apollo joined a fascist cell?" Hera's voice dripped with sarcasm.

"Inadvertently. I mean, we all know he isn't bright enough to understand—"

Hera laughed, leaning back in her chair, crossing her legs, "Another lie and I will report you to the Monitor myself. Imagine that, the Goddess of Justice, the principle author of the Non-Interference Accord punished for chronic abuse of humans. Oh, the irony. You will be the butt of every joke by every immortal. They will relish in your fall. And don't waste any breath trying to deny; aside from the ample evidence I found when I searched your offices, the Nereids you exploit for your office cleaning are ready to testify against you at my word."

Was the room spinning? When had she lost control? Bolting up from the couch, she grabbed the vase of flowers and flung it at Hera's feet, the crystal shattering into hundreds of sparkling shards with a satisfying explosion, "How dare you threaten me!"

Hera slowly rose from her chair, lifting both arms, and a wild wind whipped through the room, flinging the drapes back and flooding the room with a sunlight that grew in intensity as she spoke, "Who do you think I am?" Athena cringed back from the blinding light, "Sit your ass down and tell the girl everything you know so that we can find Apollo. Now!"

Covering her eyes, Athena nodded slightly and turned to the blonde, who was still standing by the desk. Every other occupant of the room was cowering behind the couch. Who was this girl? Her composure bordered on the unnatural. "Yes. Apollo was kidnapped. They sent ransom notes to me two, maybe three, weeks ago. Along with a severed ear. Oh, and when I ignored them they cocooned my staff and hung them from the ceiling." At a gasp from behind the couch she clarified, "They were *fine*. Listen," she turned to address Hera, "any military expert will tell you, you can't negotiate with terrorists. It only opens the door to more attacks. On the other hand, they were attacking my people, and keeping Apollo captive, so what could I do? When you showed up worried about Apollo, I thought I could give you the proper motivation to obliterate them. Apollo would go free and the terrorists would be punished and I could stay above the fray. It's called plausible deniability. Try not to take it so personally."

Hera looked ready to retort, but the blonde stepped between them, "So, we had already figured out the general coordinates of where the Arachnids are." Pulling a scarf out of her pocket she handed it to Hera, "Apollo was wearing this when he was taken. It was made in a fashion house here in Florence. Gretchen noticed that the pattern on the scarf's edge was a story in an ancient language. She deciphered the runes; they tell the story of Arachne's," and here she paused, looking down, "the story of Arachne's *encounter* with Athena. Think of it as the company history. The other runes provide the latitude and longitude of what we assume is their silk farm. We think they have taken Apollo there. Unfortunately they also seem to have a massive army of spiders that not only attack, but appear to warn them of our movements. They have been one step ahead of us and every time we get close, they move him."

Why had the girl called her schooling of Arachne an *encounter*? It had clearly been a lesson about the dangers of arrogance and pride. Maybe her voice wasn't so mellifluous after all, because Athena wasn't too hungover to pick up on the implication of that carefully chosen word. *Encounter.* Just as she started to visualize the blonde as a pile of ash, Hera's voice cut through her thoughts.

"I assume you have a plan. Tell me."

That blonde girl was now informing Hera that she needed her full team for the plan to work, and had the gall to insist that Hera return Hermes to his animate state, which to Athena's surprise, Hera did. As the blonde girl talked them through the plan, Athena started to compile a mental list of the girl's presumptions. Apparently Arachne wasn't the only human who needed a lesson in humility. She would let Hera get her precious Apollo back, and then the blonde was going to have her very own *encounter* with the Goddess of Justice.

* * * * * * * * *

Apollo

In the back of a van

It was surprisingly comfortable, being suspended by webbing from the ceiling of the van. The slightly stretchy nature of the strings served as a kind of shock absorber, and while he could hear that the van was traveling over uneven surfaces at a high speed, he was only rocking gently in his cocoon. Of course he couldn't see or speak, so his sense of time could be off, but it seemed to him that they had been driving for at least four hours. Sniffing, he picked up the light scent of lavender. The girl had come with him. That was good. If only he could be free of this webbing, it would enhance his ability to seduce her. As it was, he couldn't even flex his muscles in this situation. He would have to wait for his next chance to woo her.

She hadn't been in the room when they had webbed him. Athena must have gotten close to finding him, because the guards who came in were clearly in a panic. One minute he was sitting on the wooden chair, hands and feet bound, working on his marriage proposal to Naomi, visualizing his dramatic bend of the knee and her swooning acceptance. She would be so overcome by his bravery and beauty that she would beg him to take her right there on the campus green. He would sweep her up in his muscular arms and carry her off to the bushes so that they might have some privacy as he— and the next minute he was grabbed by two dudes and held upright while hundreds of spiders swarmed over his body. Instant Apollo burrito. Arms and legs strapped flat, webbing over his eyes and mouth as well. While he couldn't see, he assumed it was the same two dudes who had grabbed him who now flipped him like a surfboard and carted him out of the room.

For the first few minute of his trip, he half-hoped to hear Athena yell out, "Release him!" and come to his rescue, but as time slid by, he realized that rescue was not so near. When they loaded him into a van, he accepted that this game was going to be played out for a while longer. No one had said a word since they had started driving, but in the last few minutes he had heard someone moving into the cargo section where he was hung, and that someone was his best bet for an inside assist. He had heard one of the dudes call her Adelina.

"I hope you are okay in there."

Her voice was barely audible over the noises of the road.

"I convinced them not to hang you by your feet. I would hate to think of you being uncomfortable. You are so brave and beautiful." She must have slid her hand down his chest, the pressure so slight, her touch shy. "If only he knew how wonderful you are, I am sure he wouldn't do this, not to you, no matter what she did to us."

Apollo frowned within his spider sack. It sounded like he was in some sort of actual danger, and that was ridiculous. He was Apollo. God of the Sun. On a sacred quest to win the heart of his beloved, Naomi. He was not destined to have *things* done to him. He was the doer. The hero. If only he could talk, he could explain this. Get her to understand. He could convince her to set him free.

A loud, masculine voice let loose with a string of Italian curses ending in a demand for her to return to the front or a series of equally unpleasant expletives would rain down on her.

"I have to go. I just wanted you to know how sorry I am. If only she had answered. Grande Zio has waited so long for justice. It shouldn't be at your expense." And she pressed a kiss in the general vicinity of his hand. "*Addio.*"

Apollo breathed a sigh of relief. He had been worried there, with all of her apologies and regret, that something bad was going to happen to him at the end of this ride. But then it all made sense. This would be at his expense. Adelina, just like Naomi, probably assumed he didn't have money and thought he wouldn't be able to pay whatever her Grande Zio wanted, but he had a piggy bank full of money. Problem solved. Of course, depending on how much expense it would cost him to get out of this situation, he might have to work a little longer to fill the bank again to reclaim Naomi, but he had learned from his many times of being in love that the journey to true love was never direct, and often suffered setbacks.

CHAPTER FOURTEEN

A Train with a View

* * * * * * * * * *

Hannah

In which Hannah lies to Gretchen, again

"Are we going to talk about this?"

Hannah trained her eyes on the swiftly passing landscape outside the train window and avoided Gretchen's gaze. So she would have to start lying now. Fine. She might as well attempt to misunderstand, "The plan? Is there some part of—"

"Not the plan. *John*. Are we going to talk about John?"

Hannah slowly turned her head to meet Gretchen's gaze. They were sitting in a private compartment on a high speed train bound for Como, compliments of Hera. There were no other people in their car; nevertheless, she lowered her voice, "Why would we talk about John?"

"Come on, Hannah. One minute you two are engaged in an end-of-the-movie-they-finally-did-it kiss and exchanging significant soulful looks and the next moment you are doing that weird friendly/cold thing you do. Then you pair him up with the terrifying twosome, Athena and Hera..." She raised her eyebrows and looked expectantly at Hannah.

"Come on, Gretchen. Since when does one kiss constitute anything? He's John MacCallister. He probably kisses more women than he doesn't, on a purely mathematical level. And any significance you read into our looks probably had something to do with the situation we are in. You are just doing that 'seeing sexual tension in every situation' thing that *you* do. Besides, what do you mean by 'that weird friendly/cold' thing?"

"Um, the thing you are doing right now to me?"

"Now?"

"Yes, now. You get all calm and analytical and answer questions with more questions. Try to distract me all you like, but I can read body language and I know when two people have had sex. You and John found the time and space somehow in the last sixteen hours to have sex." She leaned across the aisle and put her hand on Hannah's knee, "Was it bad? Is that the problem? That doesn't mean it can't get better, Han."

"It wasn't bad." Lies are more believable with some truth. To keep John safe from Sek, she couldn't let anyone think there was anything between them. Even Gretchen. So she needed to sell this lie. She wasn't proud of it, but it needed to be done. Emotions like guilt and shame were luxuries at this stage, so she cleared her mind and focused on selling her story of failed love to her best friend.

"I knew it! Spill, Han, I want all the details. Some people say that and they don't really mean it, but I do. It has been a stressful forty-eight hours and I could use some steamy entertainment." She leaned back in her seat and nodded encouragingly, "It was good, wasn't it."

"It was fine." The key was to spool it out slowly.

Gretchen narrowed her eyes, "We have two and a half hours left on this train ride and I can be unrelenting, so why not spare us the tedious back-and-forth and just divulge."

Hannah heard her mother's unwelcome voice in her head, chiding, "Tangled webs, Hannah…"

"It was dirty, and not in a hot way. We had sex in the tunnels under the streets of Florence and I think I still have grit under my… *fingernails*. And before you get any ideas, it wasn't an important relationship event. Think of it as stress release. We had just been chased by a swarm of spiders and survived. Any college psych major can tell you that surviving a life-threatening event can trigger unexpected sexual drives. When it was done we were both a little embarrassed and we agreed to forget that it ever happened." Hannah stared back out the window, unable to look into Gretchen's face, feeling a little dirty herself. It had the unintended benefit of triggering Gretchen's compassion.

Gretchen crossed the aisle and squeezed into the seat next to her, wrapping her arm around Hannah's shoulders, "That is a terrible lie, Hannah. Tell me what *really* happened."

Hannah stared into her friend's eyes and all she saw was sincerity. *Crap.* She did not deserve this level of concern. Maybe she didn't need to lie about it. Maybe… Looking back out the window, she answered and found it wasn't as hard as she thought to tell the truth to Gretchen, "It was lovely. He is lovely. It was so sweet, Gretch, I think he was nervous. He wanted to wait until we could do it someplace nice. Or have a date or something. But it was like I wasn't myself, and I just insisted. I know that you have been needling me about him for months, but I honestly had never thought of him that way." At Gretchen's snort, she clarified, "I never thought of him that way *with me*. But when he kissed me in the room, it was like all of a sudden everything came into focus. And then all of you came in. And the rest is like I told you, only it was dirty in the hot way, too."

Gretchen squeezed her shoulder, "So why give him the Elise Brush-Off?"

Hannah turned to stare at her, "The what?"

"The Elise Brush-Off. I saw your mother dispatch a pair of Jehovah's Witnesses when I was at your house this summer. Your mother is a virtuoso of the Brush-Off; polite acknowledgement with a distinct undertone of 'remove yourselves from my property *now*.' You have been giving the MacMan the Elise Brush-Off since you got back from...Oh." Gretchen started shaking her head, "I thought you said our plan worked and that psycho demon stalker was sent to the netherworld?"

"It did. Sek's gone. But I think he is even more obsessed with me than before. When I told him he was unworthy of me, he *loved* it. And if he found out about John..." Jumping up, she started to pace in the tiny space of the train car. She forced herself to say what she'd been thinking since seeing Sek on the rooftop of the Duomo, "He's already tried to kill John once. If he succeeded..."

Gretchen didn't tell her not to worry, or assert that she was overreacting. She simply nodded. "So the official story is the isolated hook-up? Stress release? And in reality?"

Sinking into the seat opposite of Gretchen, Hannah smiled bitterly, "In reality, John insists we can make it work. Keep it secret. But I'm not so sure— there is too much at stake. If he got hurt..." She leaned across the seat, hands on Gretchen's knees, "You are the only one who knows."

Gretchen's head lowered until their foreheads were touching, "Your secret is safe with me."

They stayed for a moment like this, not speaking. Passing tourists looking in might have imagined they were praying, so still and intent was their pose.

An announcement that the dinner car was open broke the spell, and Hannah sat back, "So, now that you've exposed my secrets, can we talk about something else? Are you hungry?"

Gretchen put her feet up on the seat across from them and put her head on Hannah's shoulder. "Always. But first tell me again what Professor Tetley said when you showed him the translation of the scarf."

Grateful for Gretchen's topic change, Hannah launched into a full-on impersonation of Professor Tetley, "Hannah dear, that is simply fantastic! That you even recognized the runes on the scarf is beyond astute, but your translation is nothing less than brilliant! Top drawer, Hannah, top drawer." Dropping the elderly professor's slightly affected British accent, Hannah turned in their shared seat to look Gretchen in the face, "I wish I could have told him it was your work, Gretch."

"I know. But if you did, you'd lose your job. I don't want that. I like being on the inside of this crazy immortal thing." Touching her lips, she frowned slightly, "But I could have done without the first hand experience in curses. I like having a fully functional mouth. Damn, Athena is strung tight! They should call her the Goddess of Instability. And did you see the looks she was giving you? She does not like you."

That was an understatement. Not only had she seen the reflection in the mirror of the rage on Athena's face, but Hera had even taken the time to warn her to not be alone with the Goddess of Justice. She had been tempted to file a Monitor report in her conversation with Professor Tetley and Mr. Blean. She'd been holed up in the marble bathroom Skyping them on her phone. But she had held off. If she had filed the report, the Council would have immediately dispatched minions to bring Athena in for judgement. There were no trials at the Council of Immortals, just degrees of punishment. If she had done that, she would have been safe, but the Arachnids would have lost out on the chance to hold Athena responsible. And Hannah could not let that happen. Somewhere between being attacked by the spiders and meeting Athena, she had found her sympathies shifting. The spiders deserved an audience. So she held her tongue. For now.

Reaching down into the backpack she and Gretchen were sharing, she pulled out a Toblerone candy bar she'd lifted from the mini-bar and unwrapped the front, breaking off a triangular chunk and handing it over to Gretchen. Letting the hazelnut flavored chocolate melt in her mouth, she agreed with Gretchen, "Athena doesn't like me, but I'm not too worried. She might want to incinerate me, but she has too many witnesses, and her reputation matters to her— as long as she's thinking straight. It was one of the reasons I paired John up with Athena and Hera. He's charming. Maybe he can calm Athena down. She seems to do better with men than women."

Gretchen passed the chocolate bar back, a substantial amount in her mouth. She mumbled through chocolate-filled cheeks, "But Hera, too?"

"Hera wants Apollo found. Why, I'm not sure. It could be some odd mother instinct. She does have a soft spot for the golden idiot, as Hermes would call him. But I think there might be more. Tetley and Blean are convinced Hera has something brewing, it was why they were so eager for me to work for her. Hera's name has been mentioned by immortals filing anonymous reports more than a dozen times in the last month, but no proof, all rumor."

"Did you have any idea that Athena was off the rails, in the non-interference department? Hera seemed to have some prime blackmail material on her."

"No. Athena's reputation is pristine in the immortal world. She was the primary author of the Accord. She sits on the Council in perpetuity. What she did to you blew my mind. For that alone the Council would strip her of all her powers for a minimum of a century. Ironic, really, since she is the immortal who has pushed for mandatory punishment terms. In my first week on the job Tetley and Blean made me read the Council minutes for the last hundred years. Athena is black and white about it. You break the Accord, you pay the price."

"Bitch."

"No. She never seemed to take pleasure in it, but she also never allowed for the intentions of the accused." Hannah smiled. In this way, Athena reminded her of her own mother. *We have rules for a reason, Hannah. If they were up for debate they'd be called The Ten Suggestions.*

But Gretchen was frowning. "Han, this is bad. *Really bad.* If the Goddess of Mouth Sealing finds out you are the Monitor, that you can and, according to her own inflexible standards, *must re-*

port her, ruining her, there is only one way out for her."

Hannah had thought of this, and hadn't really come up with a solution to it yet. But Gretchen didn't need to know that. Sliding the Gorgon necklace out from under her shirt, she tapped it lightly, "Don't worry about me, I've got the sisters on my side. At least while I have the necklace."

Gretchen's eyes went wide, and she sprung up from the seat, frantic, "Good point, Han. Hey, I overheard the porters talking up the sandwiches in the dinner car. And now that the dinner car is open... The candy just isn't cutting it. Can I get you anything? No? Okay, see you soon!"

And she was gone.

That was slightly weird, but it did spare her answering any awkward questions about the limitations of the necklace. Limitations she had no understanding of. When she had pressed Mr. Blean about it, he'd gotten all vague and quoted Confucius at her, "The superior man is distressed by the limitations of his ability; he is not distressed by the fact that men do not recognize the ability that he has." That hadn't helped at all.

Ping.

Looking down, she saw a message on her phone.

How r u?

She smiled and stared at it for a second.

OK. How r u?

She sent the message, watching the bar fill along the top of her phone, confirming the message's journey, wishing she could follow it, wishing that for a moment everything could be stopped, everyone's eyes closed, ears covered, and she could just curl up for a moment in the protection of that small message.

OK.

She smiled again. Poised to type some other generic exchange just to keep the contact open, she was caught off-guard by the simultaneous vibration and ringtone of an incoming call and almost dropped the phone on the floor. It was Professor Tetley, the picture on her screen one she had snapped back in June at her graduation brunch. He was holding a champagne flute filled with mimosa in the air, the image on her phone a kind-hearted toast every time he called.

"Hi! Is everything okay?" Hannah's mind was in express sort mode, trying to identify the most likely reasons for this transatlantic call. Professor Tetley's enthusiastic response put an end to her macabre imaginings.

"Everything is fantastic! Absolutely fantastic! I have the most exciting news, my dear. I am not going to even give you a chance to guess, or really reply, for that matter, as this call is brutally expensive. I showed your scarf translation to one of my former students, now a brilliant academic in her own right, and she has offered you a fellowship; full ride, stipend to boot, along with a guaranteed spot on her research team. Angela Gerinvale at Yale. She's the best in her field of Bronze Age Writings. And she wants you. It's her only spot. But she needs you to start ASAP. She has a massive grant from the NSF to work with the Russians on deciphering the Trojan Script on vessels excavated in Anatolia. She'd like to get you up to speed before you leave. When she saw the work you did on the scarf, she was over the moon, in her reserved, dry way. She won't even think of taking on another grad student; you are it. I told her you would be thrilled! So hurry up and get back here. This is a once in a lifetime opportunity, and you deserve it, my dear. Blean and I will find another Monitor, no worries. This is your dream, you must follow it. Really stellar work on those runes, dear. You'll have to tell me how you did it over a pot of tea when you return!"

He ended the call and she was left holding the phone, staring now at the front screen, a selfie with Gretchen on the steps of the University Library. The compartment door slid open and Gretchen pushed in, hands full of sandwiches, bottled water, an apple, and a banana.

"I didn't know whether you would want an apple or a banana, so I got both, you choose and I will take the other." Dropping the food in the seat next to Hannah, she tilted her head, "Did you get a phone call? I thought we weren't linking phones until we got there?"

Hannah shoved the phone into her pocket, "It was my mom. Typical Elise wanting to be sure I was wearing sunscreen, you know, her concern primarily that I not develop freckles, because while they are cute on some people...."

Gretchen laughed. "Well, that would explain the look on your face. An Elise worry-nag tends to make you look like you just lost your best friend. But of course you didn't. Your best friend was busy gathering food and fixing your life. Here," and she passed a sandwich. "Eat. Then you can put on the sunscreen. Because Elise is not wrong about you and freckles. Not a good look. And after the sunscreen we can go back to discussing how my academic acumen saved the day." Unwrapping her own sandwich, Gretchen continued in a tone that sounded a little forced, "It's too bad I can't use the translation in my grad school application. It's not like you need it. Not everyone is lucky enough to have an in with the Greek gods by virtue of birth. That is going to have to help you get a spot, don't you think?" Reaching down to snag the apple, she twirled it in front of her, "You don't even have to finish your essay. You could always walk into the interview and use the Gorgon necklace to persuade the committee to admit you."

Hannah stopped chewing, the bread sticking in her throat, "I think my chance at grad school will be based on my abilities and—"

"Oh, yeah, of course," and Gretchen bared her teeth, taking a bite of the apple, "I didn't mean anything by it. Of course you could get in based on your own accomplishments. I'm sure you've written a kick-ass personal statement. Not that I would know, you never having shared a word of it with me." She looked up, and there was a flash of something feral in her eyes, but then it passed, "Ignore me. I think I am going to grab some shut eye. I'm so tired, it's like I'm hearing voices." And like that, she tossed the half-eaten apple in the trash bin in the corner and closed her eyes, arms crossed.

Whatever was happening, all Hannah could see was red. She stared down at the sandwich in her hand and felt an overwhelming urge to smash it into Gretchen's smug face. Where did she get off? Luck? Gretchen thought she was lucky? She hadn't asked for the gift, and she had worked damn hard to give it back. She'd been forced to confront forces Gretchen had only read about. She'd been in grave danger from impossibly powerful immortals, and that was a plus? And what did she mean by that comment about her personal statement? So what if she still hadn't written it? It didn't mean that she wanted to get into grad school any less. Okay, well maybe she did want it less than Gretchen, but she still wanted it. Was it reasonable to compare herself to someone unnaturally obsessed?

It wasn't her fault Professor Tetley had shared the scarf translation with the woman from Yale, or that Professor Gerinvale had only one spot and she wanted Hannah. And then there was Professor Tetley. She had never had a grandfather, both her parents' fathers having passed away when she was little, but that was what he felt like to her. In the last four years at Whitfield, Professor Tetley had always been there for her, with his kind and optimistic counsel. He had always seemed to think she was delightful. And because of that, because of his unfaltering admiration, she had *felt* delightful, even when she knew better. She hadn't asked him to share the translation, and now, because of his belief in her, because it had lead to her getting the one thing she knew Gretchen wanted, she would have to tell him she had lied? To him? Her jaw clenched and she put down the sandwich half she'd been about to bite, feeling ill.

Fingering the Gorgon necklace, she replayed Gretchen's words, "You could always walk into the interview and use the Gorgon necklace to persuade the committee to admit you." She stared at Gretchen's face, across the car. Even in the early stages of sleep, she radiated confidence. She had always admired that about Gretchen, but now she felt oppressed by her arrogance. Was it really Gretchen's academic acumen that had saved the day? She had already figured out the Arachne connection by herself. It was possible she could have used that knowledge to figure out the runes on the scarf, wasn't it? Her stomach rolled in protest. If she told the truth about Gretchen's translation, she would lose everything: her job, her grad school, her future. If she said nothing, it was all there for the taking. But what if it wasn't hers? What if it all belonged to Gretchen? But should Gretchen get everything and she end up with nothing? She needed some air. Rewrapping the sandwich, she dropped it in her seat and headed for the open car at the rear of the train, knowing that no amount of scenic countryside would be able to distance her from the stark choices in front of her.

* * * * * * * * * *

Hermes

In which Hermes' best friend tells him the truth

"Are we going to talk about this?"

Hermes frowned and pointed to the chopper blades overhead, making an ungodly noise.

Lee persisted, "You can hear me just fine through the headset. It's why we are wearing them."

Hermes frowned deepened and he pointed to the helicopter pilot.

Fine. I'll just talk directly into your head. Then we can be sure no one is overhearing us. Are we going to talk about this?

Hermes glared at his assistant.

I'm not just your assistant, but your friend, too.

Then get the hell out of my head, friend.

Hannah took the hit; for everything. The hotel expenses in Milan and Florence. Not to mention the flight, or the misdirection to the Hotel Apollo was staying in, which almost lead to them getting kidnapped themselves. None of it. She didn't give you up, and she could have. She could have told the truth. Thrown you under the boat. But she didn't, boss.

It's bus. You throw people under the bus, moron. And what was this huge accomplishment on H's part? This clear demonstration of her saint-hood? if she had tried to sell me out to Hera, I would have—

You would have what? Hera had turned you into a prone piece of concrete at that point, boss.

Marble. I was finely veined Italian marble. And I have a long memory and a history of holding a grudge. She didn't sell me out because it was in her best interest. You heard her tell Hera. I am essential to the plan.

Not hearing a reply in his head, Hermes turned to look at Lee and witnessed an epic eye roll from the demon. He thought in his loudest, rudest tone, *You are rolling your eyes at me? Really?* But the pilot's voice interrupted what would have been a scathing put-down with directions to check their seat belts as they were preparing to land.

But she clearly isn't working with Hera against you. You were wrong about her.

If that is true, who gave her the ugly piece of Athenian crap she wears around her neck? That is one powerful piece of antiquity. No way she picked that up on Craigslist. I recognized it. Hell, I would still own it, after I stole it of course, if I hadn't given it to some nubile wood nymph who was busy making me forget my name—

You know about the necklace?

I know I've been off my game on this case, but I'm not an idiot. Of course I know about the Gorgon necklace. I noticed it on the plane. It was what set the harpies off. I assumed Hera gave it to her, but you don't think so, do you? You know where she got it, don't you? He'd turned in his seat to stare at his assistant at an unfortunate time, as the force of the landing tossed him forward, torquing his neck.

Rubbing the spasming muscles, he transferred his glare to

the pilot, who appeared unperturbed behind his mirrored aviator glasses. His internalized interrogation of Lee would have to wait while he played nice with Hera's celebrity friends who had flown them up in their private helicopter and would be cruising them around the lake on their private yacht. H's plan was actually decent. They knew, based on both the scarf coordinates and tracking the caterer's truck that left the palace, that the spider folk had taken the golden idiot to Lake Como. The lake was shaped like an upside down Y. H and Genius Girl would travel up the lake from Como in the western leg; Hera, Athena, and Line Boy would travel up the lake from Lecco in the eastern leg, and he and Lee would move down the lake from the top, all the while making sure to draw attention to their movements, counting on the spiders to report back to their human kidnappers. This should trigger the kidnappers to move the Golden Idiot. Lee would track all forms of transport, looking for any anomalous movements, and then they would all three converge on them. They would use the kidnappers' best advantage, their nasty little spiders, to force them out into the open.

Luckily the celebrity was off shooting a film somewhere and Hermes had to make only minimal small talk with the servants to get set up on the yacht and confirm that the captain was to make frequent stops on their way down the lake. The staff were remarkably compliant and completely incurious, one of the unexpected benefits of borrowing the toys of the famous— the well-heeled prioritized discretion in their hiring practices. Hermes, leaning on the railing of the upper deck, looked out at the ice blue lake, ringed by mountain peaks and the palatial estates of the wealthy and felt a little homesick for his modest house boat on Puget Sound.

Thinking of his home made him think of Candy, and her gentle but unvarnished truth telling, "As long as you look to be someone to *him, she* will own you."

It was true that he wanted Zeus to look at him. With what? Pride? That Hera knew this about him, and exploited that knowledge, that was his own fault. He continued to play to Hera's tune.

"Boss?"

Hermes spun around to see Lee in his rumpled greasiness looking completely out of place on the pristine luxury yacht. Something in the earnestness of the little demon's face touched him, and he decided to throw him a bone, "You were right, Lee. H isn't working against me. Yay for the home team."

Looking down, Lee fiddled with the buttons on his Hawaiian shirt, "Not that I'm eavesdropping on your thoughts or anything, but, if you ever wanted to do something else, work for someone else, I'd go with you."

He couldn't deny that Lee's little loyalty speech had made him feel oddly braced up. "Shall we check out the galley before we get underway? I'm betting Mayor Megabucks has a fine selection of scotch which I can evaluate and I'm sure he has to have some kind of cheese, too."

Lee, beaming, nodded enthusiastically and skipped on his way below deck.

CHAPTER FIFTEEN

Instruments of Torture

* * * * * * * * * *

Gretchen

Arguing in a café in Como

Hannah had buried her head in the menu and had already waved off the waiter twice. What was she doing? The plan was to alert the spiders to their presence by talking about Apollo in the spiders' vicinity and wait for word from Hermes that the kidnappers were on the move. Instead Hannah had been blathering on about how the tragedy of Arachne might not have been Athena's fault. "Since when did you become an apologist for the insane goddess who sealed my mouth? Or did you forget that she did that? And threatened to do worse."

She is ignoring you.

Just like she ignored you for years at Whitfield.

Clenching her fists, Gretchen waited for Hannah to answer. The voices of the Gorgon sisters were incessant. Needling. They had been since the moment Hannah had shown her the necklace on the train. She'd feigned sleep on the railway because she found herself saying things to Hannah she never would have said if they hadn't been driving her crazy. Resisting them was making her itch all over. Rubbing her hands along her legs, she tried to focus on her argument with Hannah.

"I thought we were on the same page on this one, Han. Athena, confronted by the superiority of Arachne's weaving, cursed her out of jealous spite. Then rationalized it."

Hannah snapped down the menu, "Well maybe it wasn't like that. Maybe Arachne wasn't any better than her friend. Maybe her friend would have figured it out on her own if Arachne hadn't been such a show off. Maybe what looks clear cut is really more complicated. Maybe Athena was doing Arachne a favor by teaching her to back the hell off and give someone else a chance to, you know, *weave*."

Maybe Hannah was insane? What the hell was she talking about? As she tried to frame her response in the form of a question that didn't make things worse, the waiter approached, having taken the lowered menu as an opening, but Hannah waved him off again, and aggressively reinstated the menu in its up and locked position.

Look at how she treats you! She doesn't deserve your loyalty. You know you want us back. Just take it. Take us. You can take her. Just hit her on the head. We won't stop you.

We won't?

No. Tell her her shoe is untied and when she is looking down, strike. One quick hit. Aim for the spot where the head meets the neck.

With her out, you can just grab the necklace and go.

But aren't we sworn to protect her? How can you encourage this girl to violate—

Ignore her. She's on the bottom of the necklace, upside down. She gets confused.

Yeah. We belong with you. Don't you feel it? Think of what we could do together.

Take us. Take us now! Just do it!

No, that would be—

Yes! Do it now!

What are you waiting for? Now!

"Shut up!"

Hannah lowered the menu and scowled at her, "I wasn't talking. What is your problem?"

The couple having tea at the next table looked over; even the waiter was curious, looking up from his phone. Gretchen scrambled to cover, "Um, I just meant the opposite. You know, like calling something bad when it is really good. 'Shut up' means 'answer me!' It's a Vermont thing. We say 'shut up' when someone just sits there, not responding after their friend asks them a perfectly reasonable question like why are we sitting here arguing about Athena? I thought we had a plan? To talk about you know what." She leaned across the table, her voice an urgent whisper, "What is going on with you?"

Gretchen felt her hands clench as she caught sight of the Gorgon necklace swinging on Hannah's neck as Hannah leaned across the table to snap back, "I asked you first. And you can drop the weird Vermont vernacular excuse, you've been bizarre since we got on the train. You are yelling at me and you are all twitchy and now...." Gretchen found it hard to follow Hannah's words; the image of her knocked out on the ground, the necklace in her own hands floating in front of her like some kind of astral projection.

Yes. A sharp undercut to the jaw should do it.

She grabbed the underside of her chair and tried to refocus on the words Hannah was saying, but Hannah's litany of complaints was cut short as the waiter materialized. Whether to eavesdrop more effectively or hopeful that they would actually place an order, he had clearly decided to assert himself, "What can I bring you ladies?"

Bring her a nice bottle of Pellegrino to hit the blonde on the head!

Bring her the courage to take what is hers!

No! Bring her the strength to ignore my sisters—

Shut up, you ninny!

No, you shut up!

"Please bring us *due caffe con latte, molte grazie.*" At the waiter's grateful nod, Gretchen smiled. His relief at finally getting a billable response from their table was matched by her relief when she realized that talking quieted the crazy Gorgon bitches in her head. She needed to keep this going, "Talk with me, Hannah. You've been the weird one since the train ride. Is this about you know who?"

Hannah was looking past her, her face a study in irritation. Her voice was oddly flat and distant in her response, "Why did you do that? Just order for me? I am perfectly capable of ordering for myself. You always take over, it's so arrogant. For the record, I hate *caffe con latte*. You can drink them both yourself."

What the hell was wrong with her? Could the Gorgon sisters be driving her crazy too? Because if they were saying half the things to Hannah that they had said to her, "Listen, Hannah, when I wore the necklace—"

Gretchen felt her jaw slam shut, and heard the sisters' warning fill her head.

I wouldn't do that if I were you.

You can't trust her.

You are her only hope. Find a way to tell her— umph.

Ignore her and listen to what the blonde girl is saying. She isn't your friend. She hates you.

"When *I* had the necklace... you have to be the expert on everything! Why did you order for me? I never asked you to." No longer was her tone aloof, the words hissing out of her, her nostrils pinched, her mouth pursed, "I know that Hermes calls you Genius Girl, but you really shouldn't let it go to your head. He's being ironic. In case you missed that."

Gretchen felt something inside of her snap, "Yeah, I got that. But then again, I also get how to order a simple coffee in Italian. I ordered for you because that poor waiter has been waiting almost half an hour for you to figure out how to say hello in his native tongue. I was *helping*. What the hell is wrong with you?" She realized that she was grabbing the table with both hands, her own voice an angry hiss. While the Gorgon sisters stayed mute, she felt her anger growing, filling her, and she wondered if they were helping.

"Yeah. That's right. I suck at Italian." Then in a mockery of Gretchen's voice, eerily on mark, Hannah flipped her hair back and thrust her breasts out, "Poor Hannah, she needs to be rescued by me, her brilliant friend, or she might inconvenience a waiter. It's lucky for her that I am so incredibly smart. And beautiful. What would she do without me?"

"I don't do that with my hair!"

"Oh, please. You're doing it right now!" She launched back

into her mimicry, "I'm so sexy, even when I'm being a pretentious know-it-all my tits look great." Hair flip. "Yes, Professor Tetley, that was *my* brilliant insight. I can't help it. It's my burden to share my every thought with the world and cast the light of my astounding intellect across the dark waters of ignorance. Oh, yes, I am poetic too. So many gifts for just one mortal, it doesn't seem fair."

They now had an avid audience, the other diners at the café openly staring. The waiter hovering on the sidelines, their drinks on his tray. Gretchen felt physiologically displaced. Hannah's snipes were cutting deep. Some part of her was insisting that this was not real, that it was something contrived. Hannah was never nasty like this, was she? Could the necklace be pushing Hannah to say these things? But everything Hannah was saying was too much like the voices she sometimes imagined might be mocking her behind her back. Gretchen bit the inside of her cheek and tasted blood, desperate to orient herself to something she recognized.

"Hannah, why are you doing this? I don't get it." She was embarrassed by the pleading in her tone.

Hannah's bitterness of the last few minutes coalesced into a more aggressive condescension, "For someone so brilliant, you really are slow, Gretch. I thought I made it clear that it is you who are the problem for me. You, always taking over. You, always assuming that you know more. About everything. This summer, how many times did you force me to listen to your list of astounding accomplishments in your application to Yale? Was that really because you weren't sure if the wording was elegant enough? Or were you really just making sure I knew exactly how much better you are than me? Why is it that the people who like to see themselves as confident always need to have someone close to them they can confidently *condescend* to? Do you really think I hadn't noticed how much you enjoyed being the voice of experience? Just because I don't drone on about my dreams of grad school doesn't mean I don't have them. And that I don't deserve them." Pulling her phone out of her pocket, she thrust it into Gretchen's face, "Remember that call on the train? That wasn't my mom. It was Professor Tetley. I got into Yale. It's mine. Professor Gerinvale has one spot and she wants me."

Gretchen stood up, her chair clattering on the cobblestones, and in the background of her mind she could hear the Gorgon sisters.

Yes! Now! Slap her!

We warned you! Rip it off her scrawny neck!

Oh, no! Don't—

She opened her mouth, wanting to deny what she'd just heard, but breathless with the realization that it must be true. A million comebacks flooded her mind. Countless ways to cut into the underbelly of the insanely obnoxious woman sitting across from her. She could eviscerate Hannah's personal life; one failed relationship after another. She could highlight her screwed up family; point out how much like her crazy controlling mother she really was. She could even point out what a mediocre academic she was, despite getting into Yale: her boring thesis, her clear lack of original ideas, her overly safe and pedantic writing. The only thing bringing Hannah on par with her in the classics was the random luck of being a passive nobody descended from Cassandra. A nobody the Greek gods choose to gift because they thought she'd be easy to control. Everything she had now she got because she was so pathetic. Hannah was nobody. Nothing.

That's right.

Tell her that. You won't even have to hit her to get the necklace. Say everything you really think about her and when she is crushed, you can just take the necklace. Destroy her with the truth.

Mrphm! Dngth!

The dissenting sister had clearly been silenced somehow. The other sisters were right. Who was Hannah Summers to keep her from what was rightfully hers. Who was she to mock her? She would destroy her with the truth. And then she would take the necklace and she would have all the power.

"Oh yeah! Well, you—" The truth. Cut her down. "You are —" To the quick, Holder. Cut her to the quick. "You are... On your own." Pushing away from the table, she stalked across the plaza. Ignoring the gasps of the onlookers and the cries from the waiter, demanding she pay. Ignoring the now wailing Gorgon sisters, begging her not to leave them and the pointed silence of the woman around whose neck they hung. But mostly ignoring her own hurt at the hands of the one person she had come to think of as a sister. Ignoring that would require a distraction, and this being Italy, it meant that her options were between gelato or wine. She didn't care which.

* * * * * * * * * *

Hera

Nothing going as planned in Lecco

"I have found that humans, as a lot, struggle with taking responsibility for their actions. Take these spider-people. While I am sure that they have convinced themselves that their ancestor, Arachne, was some innocent victim of mine, we know that is simply not the case."

"Uh huh." No amount of rudeness on her part was slowing Athena's self-serving monologue. It was like standing in line at the grocery store behind an overly chatty octogenarian. All you wanted was to pay for your produce, not inadvertently learn the tedious accomplishments of her clearly mediocre granddaughter 's recent middle-school production of Annie. But her voice was impossible to tune out and you found yourself humming "It's a Hard Knock Life" in the car. Athena's bullshit was impossible to ignore. Here she was wasting time in Italy listening to this drivel while everything in her life was going to hell.

Hera had been the CEO of her own company for the past eighty years and knew when an employee was preparing to quit. There is a vindictive lack of fear in their eyes that can't be ignored. She had seen that light in Hermes' gaze when they were leaving Florence, and she knew that it was only a matter of time before he made the break. It was annoying. He had been a reliable distraction for years. Such a satisfying plaything; a challenge to manipulate, and so gratifying to demean. She idly wondered who had given him the backbone to even consider standing up to her. Could it be the gift girl? She certainly seemed to have his back in Florence, even after he'd screwed her over.

Hera's phone buzzed, and hoping it was Hermes giving the word to move, she glanced down only to see that it was Zeus. Again. She had been gone for three days and he had texted her over three dozen times. From wanting to know how long he should microwave a hot dog to how to apply Preparation H to his hemorrhoids, he seemed incapable of functioning without her constant interaction. That she longed for the simple days of his marital indifference was the understatement of the century. But she refused to be the one to break. It was his fault that their marriage was failing. He was going to get the blame. She had a plan. A plan that revolved around Apollo. So she was here, listening to the Goddess of Wisdom drone on. She texted Zeus a series of emoticons she hoped would make clear the application process of Preparation H, and tuned back in to Athena's prattle.

Athena continued lecturing an invisible audience, her gaze aloof, her tone professorial. "Arrogance. Pure and simple. I showed her mercy by making her a spider. I could have simply killed her, ending her line forever. I thought the lesson I taught was clear. And yet here they are, centuries later, some distant relative of her family in cahoots with the spiders, daring to question my role in the events."

Hera snorted into her glass, "Cahoots? Really? All that wisdom and knowledge and you use a word that connotes cartoon alliances? Name me one reference to a serious person using the word 'cahoots' and I will buy the next round." Waving to catch the waiter's eye, she raised her empty glass at him.

Athena's gaze snapped down to meet hers, and she frowned. "No more rounds." She had the gall to put her hand over Hera's glass, and with a flick of the wrist, dismissed the waiter poised to refill, "You are past your limit." Athena's disapproving tone was made all the more unpalatable by her wagging her finger in Hera's face, "You of all people should appreciate what I have done. What I had to do. Or did you forget the obscene images

Arachne wove into her tapestry? My father, your husband, the God of Lightning, in compromising positions with human women. I was defending his honor, and by association, yours as well. But do you have the grace to be appreciative? No. You just wallow in drink and snipe at my word choices." Lifting her hand off the glass, she signaled back to the now anxious waiter, and continued in a loud voice, dripping with condescension,"Please fill my companion's glass with more alcohol. She is good for nothing but whining anyway, and if she is inebriated she might eventually pass out, sparing us all."

Hera tasted metal and felt a rush of rage. So this was happening now, was it? Athena wanted to dance? Hera smiled at the waiter, holding her glass aloft as he filled it cautiously, his hand visibly shaking. Several of the other patrons had slipped out the side door during Athena's last words, and if Hera wasn't mistaken, the bartender had removed what appeared to be a cudgel from under the bar and was tapping it lightly in his hand. The tension was delectable. Anyone could engage in a physical fight. Hera much preferred to attack people psychologically. Who needed Hermes for entertainment? Taking a delicate sip, Hera patted Athena's arm, "Oh, poor Athena. No one ever takes the time to really appreciate how right you are, do they?

Athena's brow furrowed, she clearly hadn't anticipated this response, "No. They don't. But that matters very little."

"Because you don't do these things for your own selfish reasons, right? You do them because they are just and fair. Moral, really."

Athena nodded slowly, clearly wary of Hera's intent. Hera lowered her gaze, she even bit her lip for extra measure. "You were right, you know. I have had too much to drink. I think it has been the stress of this trip. I was feeling so confused by all of the competing interests in this situation. I mean, we have the kidnappers, who are clearly bad, and Apollo, who is clearly the victim, but then Hannah, you know the blonde girl working for me, she called your punishment of Arachne an 'encounter' and I got all confused. Her use of the word seemed designed to question the morality of your actions. Could the Goddess of Wisdom and Justice, you, beautiful and fair, could you have done something to *deserve* this? I couldn't sort it out. I am, after all, only the Goddess of Hearth and Home. The most complex analysis I engage in is how to best seat divorced parents at a wedding. It hurt my head trying to determine who was right. But I should have known that you were right. You know that girl Hannah is a lot like Arachne, isn't she?"

Nodding slowly, Athena sipped from Hera's full wineglass, "I thought I was the only one who picked up on that. You have more astuteness than you give yourself credit for, Hera. You just lack the originality to apply it to truly important subjects. The hearth and home are nice, but, really." Swallowing more wine, Athena's tone grew contemplative, "That girl and Arachne are truly the same." After tipping the glass all the way back, she put down the empty wineglass with force and sneered, *"Encounter. "*

The blonde girl had impressed Hera back in June. She had lied to Hera to save her friends and family and assumed all the fault for the Speaker of Truth debacle, astutely ascertaining that Hera needed someone to blame to save face— all that skilled lying and noble sacrifice had impressed Hermes— making her the perfect instrument to humiliate him on this job. But the blonde had been oddly loyal to the messenger god. That was unfortunate. And boring. Hera just needed to spice things up. "Yes, I think it was clear to everyone that she was looking for the most polite way to say that you screwed over Arachne. That you acted out of jealousy. She's clearly a spider sympathizer. You should *deal* with her."

Making anyone squirm required using something, or someone, who posed a real enough threat to that person's insecurities to cause them to twist. And though Hermes' time as her plaything might be coming to an end, Athena was turning out to be just as entertaining. How lucky that the girl was as effective an instrument of torture for the Goddess of Wisdom as well. Well, lucky for her, not so much for the girl. Athena was much more unstable than Hermes was. All Athena needed was a small push.

"If I were the Goddess of Justice, I might think it was my responsibility to teach the blonde girl a lesson. Shh... Look, he's coming back." The boy was returning and her fun would have to wait. He had ducked out almost immediately upon their arrival at the bar in Lecco, phone plastered to his face. "Quiet. He's her friend. We wouldn't want them to know what you plan to do to her."

"Sorry, the call was important—"

Athena cut him off, her tone imperious, "I was under the impression that Hermes would be texting us, not calling."

"No, of course. You are completely right. That is the plan. I'm so sorry, I didn't explain that well. The call I was on, it was from my mother. She's taken ill. I have to go to her. Now." Then he batted his substantial eyelashes at Athena, "If you would allow it. Please. I wouldn't want to leave you if you needed me."

The boy's pandering charmed Athena, who was even now

sending him on his way. She always was a fool for a pretty face. Hera could tell he was lying, but she didn't care what he was up to. It suited her to have him out of the picture. It would make it easier to egg Athena into an ill-advised attack on the girl, a violation of the Non-Interference Accord significant enough to provide her with compelling leverage with which to make the bitch dance for decades to come. It was the first bright spot in her day. As the boy left the bar, Athena returned to expounding on the ways in which the girl was now even worse than Arachne, and deserved a lesson, the severity of which would be impossible to ignore.

The vibration of her phone alerted her to an incoming text, and to her delight, it was not from her imbecilic husband, but Hermes giving the word that the spiders had taken the bait. He sent them a series of coordinates which, according to her phone's GPS, lead to a small island just north and east of here. All of them would converge on the island from separate directions, preventing the kidnappers' escape and hopefully driving them into a trap on the island itself. The girl Hannah and her friend would be meeting them there, completely unaware that they were about to face an Athena whipped up into a frenzy of crazed self-righteousness. What would happen? It was better than dinner and a show. She paid the bill and gave the message to Athena, graciously letting her take charge of the situation and lead the way to the waterfront, content with her view from the rear.

CHAPTER SIXTEEN

The Dye is Cast

. . . .

Hannah

Riding a tourist ferry as a thunderstorm rolls in

Hannah closed her eyes against the sight of the tall clouds, their lower layers black with rain, and almost wished for the storm to arrive sooner than later, as it so perfectly matched her mood. It had been her first fight with Gretchen, and she couldn't shake the pessimistic thought that it would be their last. She still wasn't sure why she had gotten so angry.

Liar.

Liar? She wasn't the liar. Liars are people who actively distort the truth to further their own ends. She was a *concealer*. It wasn't her fault she got Yale. She had to *conceal* Gretchen's contribution to translating the scarf. If she had told Professor Tetley the truth, he would have had to report her to the Council and she would be stripped of her job. Is it wrong that on her first major assignment, her first international job, which she had been sent on undercover and completely alone, she had asked for help from her friends? Maybe. But one mistake shouldn't mean you have to lose everything you care about. Especially when the lie doesn't hurt anyone.

Except one person.

It's not like she asked Professor Tetley to show the translation to the Yale woman. She didn't actively steal Gretchen's work. Because of actions beyond her control, actions taken by a third party, she had been given a future based on the aforementioned unavoidable concealment. She was not a liar because she would not let herself benefit from the lie. She would turn down the Yale woman without letting Blean and Tetley know about her breaking the anonymity rule by involving John and Gretchen in her monitoring work. She would just work as the Monitor for another year and apply to grad school later. Then no one would get hurt.

Liar.

Sure, in the short run Gretchen would miss out on this "perfect" opportunity. But in the long run, would she really be hurt by this? Gretchen was brilliant. She'd do some other brilliant translation and go to the graduate program of her *new* dream. Maybe this would even be a good thing for her. Like sometimes you are so focused on the thing you think you want, you almost miss the thing you need.

She needs a dose of reality.

Yeah! Maybe Gretchen needed to have a little disappointment to let go of her so-called dreams and face the here and now. It seemed to Hannah that all her life Gretchen seemed to get what she wanted. She had talked her way through every class they'd had together, basking in the golden glow of professorial approval. And she only had to point to the guy she wanted and she had him. And Hermes, her Hermes, had given Gretchen a nickname within minutes of knowing her. *Genius Girl.* Please. She wondered if she shouldn't take the Yale offer, just to show Genius Girl that there were other smart people in the world. It would be such a screw-you-Gretchen act.

Yeah!

No! No. She had decided not to do that. For several reasons, not the least that she wanted her own future to be hers based on her own work, and also, if she was honest with herself, she wasn't really that interested in Yale. No. She'd looked at the situation and determined the path of least destruction, and she was taking it. She'd turn it down as soon as she got back to the states.

Boring.

That was weird. She'd had some pretty heated arguments with herself before, but Hannah could not remember her inner voice being quite this rude. The first drops of rain hitting her cheeks distracted her from this train of thought, and she lifted her face into the wind. She had remained by the prow's railing when most of the tourists on the ferry had retreated to the canopied seats to get away from the incoming squall. She idly wondered if Hermes and Lee were being drenched at this very moment, as their boat would be heading south toward the island. Unless her perception was way off, they would have to be traveling directly under the storm. Even if their boat did not have cover, Lee and Hermes were immortal. It's not like they could die of pneumonia. Besides, Lee could probably use a thorough washing anyway.

Hera and Athena were most likely already at the island by

now. Though the town they had left from was further away, she doubted Hera was traveling via public transport. She probably hired some hover boat flying over the surface of the lake at insane speeds and was even now sipping wine at the island's sole restaurant. From what she had read on her phone, the island the spiders had moved Apollo to was some kind of tourist trap. The only island in the lake, with one restaurant that served one meal, twice a day, to a herd of tourists willing to eat overly-salted fish and wilted salad. Well, at least that was according to MississippiQueenB's TripAdvisor review. Hannah's stomach rolled thinking about it.

"Do you really think it is the food that is making you feel queasy, my dear?"

Hannah hung her head, instantly recognizing his voice and wondering how much Mr. Blean had already plucked from her unguarded thoughts.

"Not much, my dear. That necklace you are wearing protects you significantly, but I could gather enough to know that you are struggling with more than physiological distress." Placing an arm around her shoulder, he squeezed lightly, "Roger, I mean Professor Tetley, called me to come check on you. I was in Sardinia. Small dispute between the mountain satyrs and the river nymphs over fishing rights, nothing that can't wait. From what little I could discern of your thoughts, I see our learned friend's worries were not unfounded."

Hannah scrambled to sort out what the arrival of Mr. Blean might mean to her plans for Athena without thinking loudly enough to be heard. At least she didn't have to worry about John and Gretchen. When she had called John and told him how

Gretchen had abandoned her, he had offered to come to her, but she had insisted he go home, and he had agreed. Which was what she had wanted, right? She needed John to be safe, and if he had been surprisingly easy to persuade, that didn't mean he didn't care about her, did it?

It most definitely does mean that.

No. It means he respects my feelings. He was, after all, the MacMan, fluent in modern relationship power dynamics. She'd asked him to leave, so he did. If she could only dispatch Mr. Blean as easily.

"Am I to take from your continued silence that you are not simply trying to find words to answer me, but the words to answer me and get me gone? Oh, don't look so worried, I already told you that your actual thoughts are protected by the Gorgon sisters. You have a very expressive face, Hannah." He looked out across the water at the rain now covering the island they were quickly approaching. "Why not start with a status update on your assignment. Have you figured out Hera's endgame?"

She tried to wipe the stress from her face and channel her mother's best Chair of the Historical Commission voice. She focused on what she had gleaned of Hera's plan, "I think Hera needs Apollo for a larger plan down the line. She's fond of him, but not *this* fond. Hermes was confused by her actions too. I overheard him talking to Lee in the taxi in Milan." Cocking her head to one side, she did her best Hermes impersonation, "The golden idiot has disappeared for years in the past, and she-who-shall-not-be-named didn't lift a single manicured finger to find him. So why now?"

Mr. Blean's expression remained impassive, with the exception of a single raised brow. Clearing her throat, Hannah plowed on, *sans* impressions. "Um, right. So Hera's interest in Apollo is suspect as is her involvement with Athena. She didn't spend more than five minutes with Athena at her own Fourth of July party, but now she is velcroed to Athena's side just to rescue one of her husband's bastards? Come to think of it, even given the Arachne connection, I don't think for a minute that Hera wouldn't have been able to retrieve Apollo on her own, so she must have plans for Athena as well. Hera is all about Hera. "

Avoiding Mr. Blean's gaze, Hannah leaned out over the railing, "They are a volatile pair, Hera and Athena. We should split them up. They almost totaled the Savoy in Florence in a pissing match." She now had his full attention, and they were both getting wet as the first few drops had reached them. "I know, Monitor protocol dictates I file a report when I witness immortal destruction of private property, but I didn't want to blow my cover by reporting them. I was the only one who saw it, besides Hermes and Lee." Feeling more confident that she could face his direct gaze, she looked him in the eye and used the truth to help her convince him, "I've made some rookie mistakes, but I have it under control now. When this is over, I will make a list of Hera's potential grudges; work, family, personal. You might want to get back to those satyrs and nymphs. I'll file a full report when I get back to Whitfield. I promise, boss."

Her interest in whether she had succeeded in alleviating Mr. Blean's concerns was lost as a violent crack of lightning followed almost immediately by a deafening report of thunder rent the sky. The gaggle of tourists in the covered seats let out a collective gasp, and the sounds of incipient panic escalated. The ferry captain's voice crackled over the intercom, imploring the passengers to stay calm, but the translation of his message into the English, Chinese and French languages was interrupted by a rapid series of strikes that lit up the blackness and seemed to reach down into the depths of the lake, making it feel as if they were in the center of a Tesla coil. Now there were some definitely hysterical passengers. As the majority of tourists pushed inward as far from the exposed edges of the boat as they could, a few were running wildly to the railings, as if they might escape overboard.

Despite the danger in the situation, Hannah felt removed. She found herself comparing the actions of the tourists to the movements of an amoeba under a microscope. The panicking majority forming the nucleus, while the outliers moving like pseudopods pushing out to the edges of the slide. One woman stood out, waving her hands over her head. Dressed in white capris and a leopard print tank top two sizes too small, she was moving with alacrity on the stiletto sandals strapped to her overly tanned feet. She was yelling at her husband, Vito, screaming about how her astrologer had predicted she would die a watery death, how she had wanted to go to Palm Springs but no, you had to visit the Motherland, even though the only motherland you really had was your effing couch. He was yelling back at her, "Teresa, get your goddamn head together, woman!" His words were having no effect and in her hysteria she was heading directly towards a crew member who was leaning over the railing, attempting to toss the tow rope to men valiantly trying to dock them in the now wildly choppy water.

With the same dispassionate perspective in which the woman appeared to be a single celled organism under a microscope, Hannah could anticipate that in less than three seconds, the woman's frantic path would intersect with the leaning worker, certain to send him overboard. Not sure if she said it aloud or simply thought it, her exact words were, "Shut her down." The result was instantaneous. The woman's arms snapped to her sides, her body rigid, her mouth clamped shut, and her eyes went wide. She dropped to the deck like a tourist-torpedo. The rain was now a deluge flooding the deck, and as the boat pulled against the front moorings, the ferry tipped. The effect was of one large water slide, and the unnaturally stiff woman was buoyed up on the water and sliding feet first toward the stern of the boat.

Before Hannah could connect her thoughts with what had happened to the woman who was now doomed to fulfill her astrologer's prediction, Mr. Blean flung himself at the Teresa-projectile, just catching the top of her head before she shot into the lake. His hands full of her very large, dark hair, he turned to yell at Hannah, "Fix it! Now!"

The command from Mr. Blean broke her disconnected trance and she gasped as she was re-engaged with her own mind. In a tone that brooked no objection, she yelled, "Stop it. Make her normal again," Hannah ran to help Mr. Blean pull the reanimated Teresa firmly on deck. Jumping to her feet as the sky was once again filled with lightning, Teresa seemed unfazed by her experience of being cursed, driven as she was to get the hell off that boat. She smacked Mr. Blean's hands off her, and, shoving Hannah aside, ran to join the throng of tourists exiting the now docked ferry, yelling, "Vito! Wait for me! Vito!"

Hannah stared after the woman as she elbowed her way through the crowd, and turned to Mr. Blean, "Did I do that? I did that, didn't I? But how? I've been wearing this necklace for months, I've thought thousands of things, but that never happened. Why now?"

Mr. Blean was staring at her, his brow furrowed. Grabbing both her arms, he leaned toward her, urgent through the downpour, "You haven't *used* the necklace, have you Hannah? Asked it to do something *for* you?"

Of course she had. When Gretchen had told her about the things the necklace had done to Lee in the hotel room, it had seemed like a literal god-send for getting rid of Sek. But she had never told Mr. Blean and Professor Tetley about her demon problem. And she couldn't start now. "No. Not that I know of. Why? Would that matter?"

His expression was so clearly disappointed, she felt the flush of shame at being caught in a lie heat her cheeks. She was spared further lies by the vibration of her phone in her pocket. Pulling it out, she scanned the text. Each team was reporting in their location. Hermes and Lee were scaling the coast on the northern end of the island, and Hera and Athena were, in fact, sipping wine in the restaurant lounge. But then Zeus had joined them. Apparently he'd been all alone at home and couldn't find the nail clippers. He'd come to fetch Hera back to her *rightful place*. Athena's sparse text indicated that he and Hera were having "words." That would explain the storm. Holding the phone for Mr. Blean to see, she sounded forced, even to herself, "Look. All this," and she waved at the black sky frantically, "It *is* Zeus. Mystery solved, right?"

Mr. Blean just stared at her, waiting, she knew, for her full story about the necklace. If Mr. Blean thought that the silent treatment would shame her into confessing, he had under estimated her skills at resisting shame. She was the daughter of Elise Summers. She only buckled for the best, and Mr. Blean had nothing on her mom in the shaming department. Feigning regret, she looked down at her phone as she typed her location, "They are all here. It's time to rescue Apollo. I have to go. I guess we'll have to talk about the necklace back at HQ, right? I'll be careful not to use it again, Mr. Blean, I promise." Before he could reply, she started running toward the dock, yelling over her shoulder, "You'd better disappear. If you-know-who sees you, it might blow my cover as you-know-what. Cross your fingers, um, and get dry!"

She watched him disappear off the deck. *That was weird.* She had never seen him travel so carelessly in the potential view of humans before. So why now? She was distracted from this by the strangled cry of the crewman she'd saved as he grabbed her arm and pointed at the spot where Mr. Blean had just been. Without pausing a moment she thought, "Make him forget seeing Blean," and as his hand went slack on her arm she joined the herd of soaked tourists crowding the island dock. She had it all under control.

* * * * * * * * * *

Hermes

Practicing quitting while rock climbing

"I could stick to the classics."

"Yes! Make it classy. That's a good idea, boss."

"Not classy. Classic."

"I don't get it. What's the difference?"

Hermes paused in his climb. The wild storm made flying too dangerous, so he and Lee were working their way up the rocky cliff on the north side of the island, the boat anchored in the rocks below looking smaller and smaller as they climbed. It was a pretty crappy day for a climb. The pouring rain was not only making it hard to see potential foot and hand holds, but a small stream of sediment was now pouring over the face of the cliff as the ground above had reached saturation. Gesturing with his free hand, he attempted to explain the nuances of the English language to the demon.

"You call something 'classic' if it is generally accepted to be a superior way of doing something."

"Oh! Like serving haggis with neeps and tatties!"

Hermes frowned through the rain. Neeps and tatties? That sounded like the candy in an adult-only Easter basket, but whatever."Right. *Classy* is something that is done in good taste."

"Ohhh...Like the mints they left on our pillows at the hotel. Those were classy, right?"

Hermes nodded and turned back to the climb. "Exactly. Classy things are often classic, but classic things aren't necessarily classy. Take quitting, for example," and he levered himself up to a new foothold, "A classic way to quit is to walk up to the boss and tell her to take her job and shove it. Classic, but not what anyone would call classy." Pulling himself further, he muttered, swinging hand and foot to each word, "Which is exactly what that controlling, manipulative, harping bitch deserves. Umph." And he pulled himself onto the top of the cliff.

Looking down he could see that Lee hadn't moved since his mints comment,"Lee! Climbing! This century please!"

Lee looked up at him bemused and yelled, "But how would something so unclassy become classic? Isn't rudeness always bad?"

"If you don't start climbing you're going to experience some classic rudeness firsthand, demon. Move!" He threw a handful of mud down, hitting Lee square in the face. Damn. He really shouldn't have done that. While it had gotten the results he was looking for— Lee was now climbing at an impressive clip— he felt like the asshole dad that hit the family dog on the nose with the newspaper just because he'd had a crappy day. Nice. He could add self-loathing to his cocktail of dissatisfaction with this entire job. Reaching down and lifting Lee up the final few feet, he wiped the dirt from Lee's face with his fingers. "Sorry, man, I'm a real dick." Setting Lee on his feet, Hermes knelt in front of the demon's face, "Would you like to take a swing at me? I deserve it."

Without another word Lee hauled off and punched him hard in the nose. The pain was instant and blinding and he tasted blood in his mouth. "Damn it, Lee! You broke my nose!"

"Ooh!! I get it now, breaking your nose was *rude*, which means it was not classy of me, but it is the superior way of dispensing retribution. *Classic!*"

"Yeah, Lee. Great job with the vocab lesson." Hermes focused on straightening his nose as best he could and shoving some grass clods into his nostrils to stanch the bleeding. Sitting back on his haunches, he stared hard at his assistant through the rain, "Now that we've sorted that out, do you have any pointers on how to tell Hera I'm quitting? Should that be before or after we play our parts in H's secret little plan?"

"Secret plan? There is no secret plan! We are here solely to get back Apollo. This has nothing to do with the Immortal Council."

"The *Immortal Council*? H is the Monitor! I should have known! I did know, but I believed her lies." Hermes turned his back on Lee and tried to work through the angles on this new intel without letting the slippery little dude into his thoughts.

"No! I mean, nooo, of course Hannah doesn't work for the Immortal Council. If you must know, it's me. I work for the Immortal Council. I doubt she even knows it exists. But you can't tell anyone I'm the Monitor, or I will lose my job."

Hermes stared at Lee. It was possible Lee was the Monitor. He had it on good authority that the Council had been keen to bust Hera for a while now, and when Hera had put the word out that Lee was no longer under Apep's protection but her own, they might have made Lee an offer he couldn't refuse. Turning back to Lee, he probed, "If you are the Monitor, tell me who is on the Council."

"I don't know. Just like they don't know it is me. It is a double blind situation. I file reports that go straight to the council on a dedicated line, and get assignments from my handler, one of the centaurs. His name is Bruce. In his modern life he works in accounting." Lee's face had a clarity that could have been because he was telling the truth. Or it could have simply been that the rain, which was now slowing, had washed away not only the mud but a few greasy layers of grime as well.

"Bruce, in accounting?"

"Yes! Bruce in accounting. He enjoys role playing at Medieval Fairs and collecting baseball cards. Oh, and he has his own butterfly conservatory."

The more Lee talked, the less Hermes believed him. It all sounded like soundbites from online ads. Bruce in accounting, my ass. On the other hand, he seemed to be quite confident about the way the job works, which means Lee must know the Monitor to have learned that. And that brought him back to H. Maybe if he played along, he could learn H's game plan. "Did you report Hera for turning me to stone in Florence?"

"I had questions about that, too, but, technically speaking, immortal-on-immortal cursing is only a misdemeanor in the Non-Interference Accord of 1783. It is within my discretion to report such incidences. And given the bigger issues at hand—"

"Like busting Hera?" Hermes could not keep the hope out of his tone.

"Like holding Athena accountable for her transgressions against Arachne. True, it pre-dated the Accord, but still, she should have to answer for it. Not to mention her rampant use of her powers against humans. When she sealed Gretchen's mouth, well, that alone would get her removed from the Council and sentenced to one hundred years hard labor."

"Who the hell is Gretchen?"

"Genius Girl."

"Oh, right. H's friend got cursed by A?" Damn. You miss a lot when your eyes are made of stone. "Okay, so if you already witnessed Athena's curse on Genius Girl, then why all the drama over Arachne? Why not just let her hang for her present day wrongs and tack on a reprimand for the spider chick?" Hermes felt his irritation level rising with the heat from the August sun. What the hell was wrong with H? This could have all been over this morning and he could be halfway to his houseboat by now.

"Because she thinks that it's important that Athena learn from her mistake." Lee closed his eyes, clearly replaying a conversation he'd had with H, "That Athena's rationalization of her actions against Arachne is emblematic of her distorted sense of her own superior morality and at the core of her dysfunctional relationships with others." Opening his eyes, he nodded vigorously at Hermes, "I think that Athena needs to learn a lesson. That is why we are here."

Hermes sighed. He sincerely liked H. Because despite having an incredible power gifted to her last June, she never used it to screw anyone over. She didn't even try to use it to make the world a better place, she just wanted people to think for themselves. And she told a hot mess of a lie to Hera and Zeus to save and protect everyone else, even the Golden Idiot. It had impressed him. Not enough that he was going to take orders from her on this job, but still; respect. That was then, and now, well now she had clearly let the job of Monitor, because there was no way II was not the Monitor, she had let the job go to her head if she thought that she could stage an intervention for Athena to confront her so-called mistreatment of some weaving chick from Lydia, and expect to walk away from it. He had hoped to quit before the confrontation. Just walk up to Hera right before the party with the spiders started and say "See ya!" and fly on his trusty winged sandals right out of this story, but now, now it was different.

"That is a terrible plan, Lee. Why the hell didn't you talk H out of it?"

"Talk who? Talk what?" At Hermes' knowing look, Lee's

shoulders slumped and he leaned forward, his hands on Hermes knees, "Wait, why is it terrible? Hannah made it sound so reasonable. No, not just reasonable. Just. This will help Athena, in the long run. Won't it?"

"Right. Because powerful people with a god-complex love being humiliated publicly and having their delusions of justice ripped from them in front of the very people they've wronged."

"They do? Well, then, you agree that it's a good plan?" Lee had started to smile, his look hopeful.

Hermes made a mental note to explain sarcasm to Lee on the flight home. "It's a plan, Lee. It's a plan." Looking across the field, Hermes could see a small stone church set amongst some straggly trees. He squinted, frowning, "Well, at least we know where the plan will be unfolding. I'd better text the others. It looks like they're expecting us." The walls of the church had seemed to be undulating in the heat waves, but upon closer inspection Hermes could see that it was not some illusion of movement from disruptions in the thermal fields, but actual movement on the walls. Thousands, maybe millions of spiders were crawling over every surface of the ancient building. Great. A doomed plan with only disastrous possible outcomes compounded by an epic creep factor. Just the kind of job any sane god would quit.

"When did you know I was lying?"Lee had found a dry rock to sit on, his tone curious.

"The Bruce in accounting shtick. It sounded canned. Phony." Hermes joined him on the rock, content to discuss the finer points of lying with his demon assistant while he waited for the others to arrive for H's crusade for Justice with a capital J.

CHAPTER SEVENTEEN

The Things We Value

* * * * * * * * * *

Hannah

Trudging uphill

Walking in the wake of Zeus, Hera, and Athena was less than ideal. She stubbed her toe for the third time since heading out from the restaurant after getting Hermes' text. She had scanned an aerial image of the island on her phone, and with the exception of the restaurant and the ferry dock, the island was one rocky outcropping after another. The paths meandering through high grasses and scrubby trees lead to the only other structure, a crumbling stone chapel on the northernmost tip. Hermes and Lee were waiting for them there, as were the spider folk, presumably with Apollo. She should feel nervous, they were walking into what was bound to be a volatile situation, and yet she wasn't remotely anxious.

Bring it on!

Yes. She was ready. "Ouch!" Except for these stupid rocks. She accepted that the rocks were only being rocks, she just wished they'd do something useful, like form steps.

285

A loud rumble filled the air and Hannah looked skyward to see if Zeus was gearing up to strike again. Her eyes dropped quickly to the ground and her mouth fell open at the sight.

"What the... Was that really necessary?" Zeus glared back at Hera and Athena. The path in front of them was now a series of stone steps, rocks breaking free of the earth and wheeling in from all sides to shape the stairs. Hera and Athena rolled their respective eyes in disgust, clearly convinced that it was the other's doing. Feeling a rush of pleasure, Hannah bit down on the instinct to yell, "It was me! That's right, I did that!" She needed to keep her newfound powers under wraps, but she did allow herself a small smile. The rest of the climb was significantly less painful.

As she reached the top, she joined the others, who were silently staring at the church, its every surface, including the entrance, covered with spiders. Hermes and Lee were sitting on a boulder on the far edge of the clearing. Hermes casually sidled over, chewing on a long piece of grass, and murmured in her ear, "Are you out of your mind, H? Just report A to the Council and let's get the hell out of here."

Now it was her turn to roll her eyes. *Lee.* She should have known better than to confide in him, but she hadn't really had a choice, she had needed his help with Sek.

Calm down. Find out how much he knows.

Right! Pointing at the church, she spoke in a voice designed to carry, "So that's the place, huh? You think Apollo is in there?" Then under her breath she hissed through clenched teeth, "I don't know what you're talking about."

Athena and Hera stared at her for a second. She watched

their estimation of her drop as they considered her asinine statement, then returned to arguing about the best approach to the arachnid lair. Lee was scuttling between their legs, cleaning the gods' feet with the hem of his shirt.

Hermes wrapped his arm around her, his tight grip on her arm at odds with his relaxed expression, "The plan. Athena. Getting justice for Arachne. Your job as you-know-what. I know it all. And this is a terrible idea. Call it off. Let the Council deal with Athena. Zeus and Hera can rescue Apollo and the three of us," and he nodded at Lee, who had slinked over and was standing by his side, "can get the hell out of Dodge."

The goddesses' argument was escalating, and Lee was starting to whimper. Smiling into Hermes' face, she spoke through her clenched teeth, "I could do it your way. But I think," and here she used her thoughts to make him release her arm. He gasped as his fingers sprang open, "That today, we are going to do it my way. Don't you agree?" Not waiting for his response, she focused her thoughts on the spiders swarming the chapel and told them to please move aside to let them enter. Like a curtain pulling back, the spiders parted.

Well done!

Lee let out an amazed, "Ooh! Look!" and the three Olympians who had been arguing about how to remove the spiders stared open-mouthed at the entrance to the chapel, now clear.

Hermes grabbed her shoulders, his breath in her ear, "This is bad juju, H. You're using the necklace, aren't you? Those bitch sisters are in your head. You aren't strong enough to control them. You have to take it off."

Silence him!

No. She didn't want to silence him, she wanted to win him over. It was suddenly important that he understand. She pivoted to look into his dark, angry eyes. She leaned up, grabbing his shoulders, their foreheads almost touching, and urged him to believe in her, "I *can* handle this. I may not be able to order a gelato in Italian, or decipher ancient runes, or even finish a grad school application, but this," she waved her hand to encompass the scene in front of him, the seething gods, the spidery chapel, its insides dark and menacing, "This I can handle. I know what needs to happen to make this right, and I finally have the ability to do something about it. *Trust me.*"

He shook his head, "How? Those Gorgon bitches have you convinced that you are doing all this. Don't think for a minute they're on your side, H." And now he was holding her shoulders, shaking them lightly, "They are an-*cient*. Gaia made them to protect the *Titans*. You know, the ones Zeus and his sibs destroyed. They are all about destruction, now. Their name, it literally means *dreadful*. You think you can control them, but—"

"Because I do." She did. Everything they had done had been on her command. She was sure of it. She no longer cared if he understood.

He's not important.

Hermes opened his mouth to argue, but Hera's imperious tone ended the debate. "If you two are quite finished exchanging sweet nothings, I have decided that you will lead the way. I did, after all, hire you to find Apollo, and I always get my money's worth. Step to it!" With her arm extended out, pointing into the dark entrance, the lowering sun lighting her from behind, she looked exactly like the illuminated images of her in museum paintings. Hannah decided to take that as a good omen.

Because it is a good omen!

Looking both at Lee and Hermes, she nodded, "It will work." And without waiting to see if they followed, she walked confidently into the dank darkness, the only sound that of the dry sliding and clicking of thousands of spiders' legs.

* * * * * * * * * *

Mr. Blean
Arguing with his best friend

"That is precisely what I am asking you, Roger. Where the hell am I? No, there are no landmarks. No, nothing. I can see exactly nothing. Because if I light up the space I am in and I trigger some chain of events, I could be stuck here for eternity. Yes. Well, I wouldn't put it past them. They are Gaia's creatures after all. Try that computer program Hannah wrote for tracing cell phone signals. Yes... Yes, she is very clever."

But even clever, lovely young women can't be expected to hold their own against ancient powers. He had precious little time to get back to Hannah. He still couldn't believe he hadn't foreseen the dangers of the Gorgon necklace. He was a centaur of the Fifth Order, known for the depth and breadth of their knowledge, he should have anticipated the necklace's powers. Instead it had been he who had suggested they give it to her.

They had picked it up fifty years ago in a raid on a commune in the Utah desert. A group of particularly bold nymphs had conned a dozen or so humans into being their slaves, sexual and other. They might have flown under the radar if they hadn't gotten greedy and applied for tax exempt status as a religious group. The IRS agent sent to investigate never came back. When he and Roger heard about the agent's disappearance, they moved on it, and found the agent in a dog collar and diapers. Roger had filed a report with the Immortal Council and the nymphs had been convicted and sentenced to twenty five years labor in Hades for each human they had enslaved.

Before the human authorities were called in, he and some nereids working for the council cleaned up all signs of immortal and immoral activity. Nymphs, by their very nature, are slobs. So while the nereids made sure all the humans were dressed and their memories were cleaned, he'd gone through the piles of garbage the nymphs had left laying about. He found the necklace in a wooden box of whips and chains. He couldn't believe his good fortune. He'd read about it, of course, but no one had seen it for more than three centuries. He'd hidden it from the council, wanting to study it himself. When Hannah had first started working with them as the Monitor, he'd been so worried about her safety from the demon Sek that he had turned to the necklace. In his time studying it he had determined that it had the power to protect against immortal illusions, but never had he imagined it could do the things he had seen it do with his own eyes on the deck of that ferry. And now he stood completely still in the utter darkness, wondering where the Gorgons had sent him when Hannah told him to disappear.

"What? Yes. That little spinning donut means the program is running. Really, Roger, you need to take a weekend to master the rather obvious conventions of the...I know. You'd be surprised, they've really upgraded their wifi. Since we are on that topic, are you sure the timing is right? I just think she might need to process this with *you*... No, she did not confess to either yet... Well, I was hoping to avoid all that... I know. I'm very fond of her too... I know, I know, but if you remember I was the one who said we should tell her everything and you were the one who said we might scare her off... No, no, it is not your fault. No. I will fix it, I promise... Wait, do you have it?"

He had to get back to Hannah quickly, before anyone could figure out that she was using the necklace. It would be a fatal mistake. He held his breath as he waited for Roger to read him the coordinates.

"I'm in the what? Well, that's inconvenient... I didn't know they had cell service either, but I told you Hades had upgraded the wifi... My plan? I plan to stop her. Or more accurately, *them*. I promise to take care of her, Roger. We should be home by tomorrow morning, noon at the latest... Roger, I know that we don't often speak of our feelings... Yes, well, indulge me this once. I am very fond of you, too... Yes... Goodbye, dear friend."

Closing his phone slowly, he debated calling back, telling him more. But that would only embarrass him. The best thing he could do now was save their favorite young woman from a terrible mistake.

Knowing where he was, he felt safe calling forth light. A floating orb of blue lit the space around him. He was standing on the brink of Tartarus, a misplaced step would have sent him plummeting to the depths. Moving with confidence, he stepped quickly over gaping holes until he was clear of the pit. It was a shame he didn't have time to make nice with Cerberus, the three-headed dog that guarded the gates of the Underworld. He had most certainly become aware of Blean's presence, if the whining he was hearing was any indication. The beast was a creature sensitive to slight and slow to forgive, but he would have to make it up to him later, as there was a long way to travel to get out of the Underworld. He only hoped he wouldn't be too late.

* * * * * * * * *

Gretchen

Slowly putting two and two together

"Why are we leaving again? I mean, I'm leaving because, *screw her* and her crazy Olympian problems, but why are you leaving her?" She squinted at John, his back to the now lowering sun.

"Um... I'm doing this... because she told me to." John closed his eyes and shook his head, "We were on the phone, and she was telling me about your argument, and I offered to go to her, and she told me to leave, and I agreed." He frowned at her, "But that would leave her all alone with the gods, wouldn't it?"

"Ah... *yeah*? Which is why I'm surprised at you agreeing to it. I mean, I know the two of you aren't married or anything, but I've seen the long looks you send her way, not to mention your underground hook up," His frown deepened significantly, "*Please.* Women tell each other these things all the time. You wouldn't believe the things she told me about that art nymph dude... what was his name? Declan? Oh, the things he would have her do!"

His frown morphed into a full fledged scowl, "Your point?"

"My point being, I am fairly certain you have more than casual feelings for her, and unless she yelled at you and told you you were an arrogant, insecure, controlling know-it-all whose life-long dreams she'd stolen, I don't get why *you* are so keen to leave her."

"But I'm not keen to leave her. I have to do this. Wait, why do I have to do this?" He was holding his head between both hands, as if he could fix what was wrong with physical pressure. Some of the other passengers waiting for the train were slowly moving away, and Gretchen saw one of them head toward the ticket office. When he spoke again, his voice was angry, causing the circle of people near them to retreat even further. "This is one of those things, isn't it? Some trick of Athena or Hera's? I don't *want* to leave her, she's in danger. She needs me. But I can't seem to do anything about it."

Oh no. This had the Gorgon sisters written all over it. Except she couldn't remember if John knew about them? Wasn't that one of Hannah's secrets she was supposed to keep? Before she could decide whether to tell him or not, John slammed his hands down on the bench, and then suddenly he was clinging to it. "I want to stand up and walk away from the train station and get to Hannah, but if I let go of this bench I am going to get on that train." His voice had risen with each word and his bizarre battle with his own body was definitely going to raise a red flag with onlookers. He looked psychotic. She wished desperately that he had found her prior to her making her way through an entire bowl of chocolate chip gelato. The sugar floating through her bloodstream was making the entire situation feel like a Japanese game show. She tried to force her brain to sort through the possible options, but her thoughts, fueled by a sugar rush and a healthy dose of panic, were racing randomly and time was running out.

The train had pulled up on the tracks, and passengers scrambled to get on while avoiding their bench. As John's agitation grew, Gretchen noticed the police officer heading their way. That couldn't be good. She knew enough from the movies that it might be bad for John if the local authorities got involved—maybe not Turkish-prison bad, but still bad. What could he say in his defense? "Sorry for acting homicidal, but my girlfriend used an ancient necklace on me to make me go away and I really wanted to get back to save her." She needed to help John. Hell, she needed to help Hannah too. Think. Think.

Smiling broadly at the worried passengers, she hugged John, whispering, "I can't explain now, just go. Take the train, get to the airport and go home. You won't be able to fight it anyway. I'll go back and help Hannah. I promise. Keep your phone on. And try to act normal, the cops are coming." She jumped as the billy club tapped her on the shoulder.

"Is there a problem here?" His English was flawless and aggressive and though his face was carefully bland, he was now tapping the club in his hand with deliberate intention. This was bad.

"No, no, officer, no problem. Just hard goodbyes. You know how it is." She leaned toward him as she reached behind her and pushed John off the bench in the direction of the train, "Breaking up is hard to do, am I right?" The officer's eyes didn't move. Not even to blink. Firmly placing herself between Officer Dead Eyes and John, she turned and waved to John as he boarded the train. "Get home as quickly as you can. You should feel much better once you do. Call me, anytime." At the officer's suspicious grunt, she turned on him, "What? Just because I don't want to be his girlfriend shouldn't mean we can't be friends." Upon closer inspection, Officer Grim was six feet two inches of fine Italian male, "You know, if you smiled once in a while, I might invite you to call me anytime."

The officer raised an eyebrow and removed what looked like a handheld citation computer from his belt and started typing. Crap. Could you get a ticket for flirting with an officer of the law? That seemed ironic in a country so flagrantly sexualized as Italy, but what did she know. Oh well, at least John got away. Looking back in the direction of the train, she could see that it was slowly pulling out of the station, John's anxious face pressed against the window. She waved again with as much optimism as she could muster. Officer Too Hot cleared his throat and handed her a ticket.

"Behave." He turned and left, only to be stopped a few feet away by an American woman with a broad Southern accent asking if he knew where the "Puerto de Toilet" was. Gretchen looked down to see that instead of a ticket, there was a short message: *Call me 441-889-6702. Alfredo.* He looked back at her as he led the tourist toward the bathrooms and winked. Damn. If only she didn't have to help her best friend deal with monster spiders and vengeful goddesses. Hannah had better appreciate this.

Looking down at her phone, she scrolled through the text messages the group had been exchanging. *Isla de Comacina.* She needed to get there, and fast. Sprinting over to the ferry terminal, she scanned the schedule, but the next ferry wasn't until six o'clock. Hoping to find another ferry service, she walked down to the waterfront and was inundated with offers from water taxi drivers.

"*Bella! Bella!*"

"Over here, beautiful girl!"

Okay. More Italian males. She could handle this. "*Excusi*, can one of you take me to *la Isla de Comacina, pronto*?"

"*Si, si, va bene*, I can take you. But it will cost forty euros."

Digging in her purse, she felt her stomach drop. *Oh no.* Money. She had none. Her purse held only her passport. John had found her at the train station buying yet another cup of gelato and she had thrown her wallet at him when he had asked her about Hannah. She could remember him picking it up off the ground, but he must have pocketed it. And now all of her money, and all of her ways of getting money, were traveling on an express train to Milan.

"No, no, don't go with him, *bella*, I will take you for thirty euros."

"I will take you for twenty! That is your best offer, it is almost like a gift. Come, come, we go now."

The water taxi drivers were waving and preening and from her position above them on the dock they looked like a flock of roosters angling for attention. Though her instincts balked at getting into an enclosed space with any of these men, she had to get to the island.

"Um... I have no money. My friend, she is on the island. I need to get to her. Please..." Her voice died out as she watched the previously avid men turn back to puttering on their boats at her admission. Sinking to the dock, she let her legs dangle and considered just calling Hannah on the phone. Would she pick up? Would the Gorgons let her? It was worth a try. She started to dial when she felt someone tug on her shoe.

"I will take you to your friend. *Gratuito*. For free."

Even from this angle Gretchen could tell her was at least a foot shorter than her and probably weighed less too. His upper lip was home to a sadly thin mustache and his smile revealed a row of desperately mangled teeth. He couldn't be more than sixteen. His entire appearance screamed harmless. And he was offering her a life line. "Thank you. Yes! Can we go now? Can we go fast?"

He nodded to both and she jumped up and ran down the dock to follow him to his boat. The other water taxi drivers started hollering at him in Italian, and Gretchen was grateful that she had not let on that she spoke the language, as the graphic crudeness of their comments would make a stripper blush. Marco, she deduced from their catcalls that her new friend's name was Marco, was doing his best to ignore them, but his ears had turned bright red. Following him into the boat, she waited for him to start the engine and cast off. As they pulled out of the slip she turned around and in her loudest Italian asked the heckling roosters if they kissed their mothers with their filthy mouths. At least that was what she hoped she said. Their silence and Marco's laughter gave her some confidence.

"Did I say that right?"

Marco looked at her, "Well, it depends what you were trying to say. If you were trying to tell them that you kissed their mothers'... how you say... the bottom hole... the dirty bottom hole with your mouth, then you said it right. Is that what you meant?"

Goddamn pronouns. "Not exactly."

Marco put his right hand around her waist as he drove the boat at a terrifying speed toward the island. He was even now sliding it down to her ass. So much for harmless Marco. Well, she had filled his head with weird images of woman on woman oral/anal action, so she would just have to take care of this the old fashioned way.

What had Hannah said she did? Toss her hair and push out her tits? Fine. Maybe that was her signature move, "Marco? Could I try steering the boat? It looks like fun!" At his enthusiastic response, she slipped in front of him and ignored his second hand on her ass. She took a moment to orient herself, then she opened the throttle and threw the wheel left and right, causing the boat to fishtail wildly.

Marco yelled something unintelligible in Italian and shoving her out of the way grabbed the wheel with both hands, pulling the boat back under control.

Mission accomplished. The island was close, it would only be a few more minutes now. "Wow! I'm terrible at that. I'd better sit down and leave the steering to you." Settling into the seat, her ass now firmly out of reach, she added light molestation to the list of things that Hannah had better appreciate when this was all over. That and what was certain to be a massive sugar hangover. She needed to get to Hannah before she could enumerate all of the debts she had accrued. But first she needed to vomit just a little off the side of the boat.

CHAPTER EIGHTEEN

Celebrity Rehab

* * * * * * * * * *

Hermes

The view from the rear

Hermes stood as still as possible, trying to fight the urge to flick the spiders off his shoulders. At the moment there were only a few spiders climbing over his skin, but he need only look up to see that any action he took that could be perceived of as aggressive toward these few spiders would be followed up by an overwhelming attack by the hundreds of thousands hanging from the rafters.

They were nothing compared to the massive spider swinging from the crossbeam in the front of the church. It was the size of a cow, if cows had eight hairy legs and deadly mandibles sliding back and forth. Under the spider stood what looked to be an ancient man, his face hidden by layers of thin scarves, his arms and legs appearing stiff, as if his clothes were webbed to hold his body upright. Half a dozen thugs in various sizes stood behind the old man, and to his right was a tall, beautiful young woman, her hand on his elbow.

Apollo was hanging from the ceiling, arms and legs splayed across a massive tapestry hung behind the altar. Hundreds of spiders were sliding in and around him, trapping him into the fabric. Every so often the big spider would make an low guttural sound and the spiders on the fabric stopped moving around Apollo and would pierce him, sliding their threads through his body. Apollo's initial scream had indicated the intensity of the pain this action caused, but his mouth had been webbed since then, and the only sign of his pain now were the increasingly limited movements of his limbs within the tapestry. It was horrific. Even for the idiot.

Zeus, father of the year, appeared to be taking a back seat on the Apollo rescue mission, sprawling casually in one of the remaining wooden pews, lacking only a box of popcorn and a soda to complete the picture. Hera was still standing but she also seemed to be removing herself from the action, after shoving Athena toward the altar. Athena had shed her human clothes, and resplendent in her goddess robes stood ramrod straight, arms crossed in judgement, her height exaggerated by the speared helmet she now wore. Hmm... That helmet was a good idea. It would give the spiders pause before crashing down from above.

"There are so many thoughts in this space, Boss, and most of them are centered on eating us. I can't tell what is happening."

Lee tried to jump up to see, but the little chapel was definitely at capacity, and his view was blocked by Athena's voluminous dress. Hermes considered lifting him up, but Lee's nerves had kicked his adrenal glands into overdrive, and he had a distinctly oily sheen to him.

"Where is Hannah? What is happening?"

H was standing between the creepy old dude and the brimstone-breathing Goddess of Justice. She raised her hand and all the sounds died off. He wondered what the Gorgon bitches were telling her to do.

"Athena. You stand accused of the misuse of your powers against Arachne of Lydia. How do you plead?"

"Who exactly is accusing me?" Athena's voice rang out, causing a massive shuffling from the rafter spiders, and Hermes felt a few of them fall onto his head, one of them crawling in his ear. This job was the worst.

The girl next to the old man started to speak, but H ignored her, "*I* am accusing you. I've read all the accounts. It is so obvious what you did to Arachne. And why you did it. So clear why these," H flung her arm out to encompass the room of spiders and friends of spiders, "relatives of hers were driven to hold Apollo captive. To bring you to justice!" H had walked to the center of the room, and with a total lack of reasonable fear, was pointing her finger directly in Athena's face.

The girl again tried to gain the floor, but this time it was Athena who cut her off. "Seeing as you are so clear on this, why don't you walk me through the specifics of my transgression."

Lee pulled on his sleeve, "You have to stop her, boss. Hannah has no idea what danger she is in. I may not be able to sort through all of the spider thoughts, but I can hear Athena's loud and clear. She is considering how much pain to subject Hannah to before she turns her into a spider! You have to do something. You can't let her down."

"Why not?" It wasn't his fault H was a on suicidal power

trip. "Don't look at me like that." Honestly, he wasn't sure if he could help H. He was certain that the necklace was hell bent on playing this scene out, and if he tried to stop it, he had no doubt they could shut him down. H was midway through her retelling of the Arachne myth, clearly favoring Ovid's story.

"Then you challenged her to a contest, assuming you would win. And when it became clear that you were going to lose, you were so embarrassed you claimed that she had been disrespectful to the gods. So you tore up the proof that she was better than you and then condemned her and her descendants," H spread her arms to take in the chapel, "To a life of misery. All to assuage your pride."

"Is that it then?" Athena's voice was calm, her face and body still. The hair on the back of Hermes' neck stood up.

"No! Then you went on to tell yourself that it was okay. That what you did to Arachne was not only necessary, but it was right. It is a pattern with you. You justify your actions and lie to yourself over and over. To the detriment of others less powerful than yourself. *You, the Goddess of Justice,*" H's voice dripped with sarcasm. "And I am going to put a stop to it."

"Boss. *Do something.*"

H was insane. She was inches from Athena now, and perilously close to Athena's spear. He knew he had to extract her, but he had to do it carefully, diplomatically, or this could come back to bite them all in the ass. Lee's whining had progressed to whimpering. He needed to shut the demon up. Looking down to do just that, he caught sight of what had to the most unfortunate tourist on the island. A leggy brunette had just ducked in under the spider curtain and she was now staring in horror at the scene playing out between H and Athena.

"Lee, freeze her quickly. Then get her out of here."

"You'll save Hannah?"

"Yeah, sure. Now get that girl out of here."

Lee sprinted over, but did not freeze her, and instead was whispering frantically to her. Looking closely Hermes could see that the female was H's friend, Genius Girl. She may have thought she knew what she was getting into, but he couldn't be responsible for keeping two women safe in this setting. He'd have to get Genius Girl out of the way first. He was just about to take care of it himself when things for H got even worse.

"*Scusi—*" the Italian beauty standing under the massive spider tried once more to speak.

"Not now!" Both H and Athena yelled in unison at her. A mass of spiders lowered threateningly at their aggressive tone toward the girl, but neither woman seemed to care, so intent were they on their own argument.

Athena was speaking now, her voice filling the church, "Do you actually think that a nothing like you," she lowered her spear to point directly at H's heart, "a blip on the human scale, has any insight into me and my world? All this is," and she swung her arm out to encompass everyone, "is a massive inconvenience. There has been no injustice here, unless you count the wasting of my time and energy responding to it. I'm done."

Athena raised her spear, slashing it across the tapestry and Apollo dropped to the floor at her feet, his mouth still encased in webbing, eyes bulging. Hermes smirked. He had to admit that that visual was going to entertain him for some time. Grabbing his ankles, the now furious goddess flung him across the chapel in Hera's general direction, "Here's your precious boy. And now to take care of all of you." Her robes rose up swirling around her, power surging in her eyes.

Yep. He was not paid remotely enough for this crap. He'd have to grab both girls and screw diplomacy. Before he could move, he watched in horror as a prone Apollo flew back across the room and landed at H's feet.

"I'm not done with you, Athena. You can't bully me. We still have to discuss the charges I brought against you. See, I know a little about immortal justice and you can't just dismiss me because you don't like what I am saying." H rested her foot casually on the now limp and unconscious god in front of her.

Athena's face twisted in rage. Damn it. Hermes knew that if Athena found out that H had the Gorgon necklace and was using it against the gods, she would kill her on the spot. And be within her rights. This was so unlike H— it had to be the Gorgons. Oh shit, now he had to help. Well, better that Athena blame an immortal. What's the worst she can do?

Flying between H and Athena, Hermes snatched Apollo up and tossed him into the rafters, where hundreds of spiders responded by swiftly spinning a net to catch him. He turned to H, hoping his words could reach her, willing her to understand and play along.

"I can't keep helping you anymore, H, *pretending* to give you powers. You are just a human, powerless, and we can't trick Athena. She is one of the smart goddesses. So no more games. Just talk to her, human to goddess. She's a reasonable woman, it's not like she's being controlled by some horrific demon creatures." Hermes felt his throat close. Goddamn Gorgons. He knew they would shut him down, he only hoped he'd said enough to get through H's crazy power trip. He stared at her, felt his own eyes bulging as the Gorgons choked him. He only had a minute before he would pass out, and he tried to use every angle of his eyebrows to drive home his message to H. Crap. The edges of his vision closed in. He had failed. Lee would never let him hear the end of it.

. . . .

Hannah

Like waking from a dream

Was Hermes choking? Who was choking him?

You wanted him to stop talking. He was ruining your plan.

Did you hear him? Taking credit for your powers. Classic Hermes.

Actually, that wasn't classic Hermes. Why was she thinking these thoughts? It didn't make sense. Hermes was staring at her as his lips turned blue. What had he said? "Being controlled by horrific demons." He had been staring at her neck. Did he mean the Gorgons? Could *they* be in her thoughts?

Don't be stupid. They are under your control.

You are finally the one who can make it all work out.

Finish it with Athena. Make her pay for everything she's done to me, I mean to us, or her, or whatever makes you finish her off!

The voices. They weren't her own. Hermes eyes rolled back in his head and she thought with as much force as she could, *Let go of him. Now!*

She leapt forward and caught him as he fell, gasping for air. He opened his mouth, but no words came out as he massaged his throat. Whispering in his ear, "Sorry," she turned her back on Athena to help him stand on his own and the magnitude of the danger she had created listening to the Gorgon sisters swamped her.

You can blame us if you want, but it was your thoughts we acted on.

Yeah. You wanted this. This is your party, bitch. Have fun!

Hope you like Justice served cold. Dead cold!

That was a good one, sis.

Fair enough. It had been her party and she had liked the vigilante rush, but she was done being judge and jury. Now to shut down the Gorgon sisters. *Stop talking and I forbid you to act!*

Ahh... The silence of the sisters filled her with the sudden awareness of how present they had been in her mind. It was a relief that she could muzzle them, but now how was she going to get out of the fire with Athena? What had Hermes said? "She's a reasonable woman." She *was* a reasonable woman— correction, goddess. *Reason.* She just hoped it would work.

Turning to face Athena, she tried not to panic when she saw the murderous rage in her grey eyes. Here it goes, Summers, speak the truth. "I know what you did and why you did it, because I have done the same thing." She looked quizzically back at Hermes, and was encouraged by his look of disgust. Hermes hated I-statements almost more than he hated the truth. She smiled at him and turned back to the terrifying goddess, "When you realized she was better than you, you were embarrassed. Sure. And it wasn't like it was even something, that if you were honest, you really cared about. I mean, you are the goddess of war and strategy and weaving should fall under Hera's wheelhouse, but still...You set yourself up to be compared to Arachne and she was better."

It wasn't working. If anything, Athena seemed more incensed. Panic initiated a flight instinct and she looked to the door where she saw a familiar figure standing in front of an undulating curtain of spiders. *Gretchen*. She was standing next to Lee, her white tank top seeming to glow in the gloom.

"How are you here?"

From across the chapel, Gretchen smiled, "Did you think I'd let one small fight scare me off?Of course I'm here. I'm your wingman."

Hera chose that moment to chime in, "This is all very touching. But let's get back to the part where you try to lie your way out of having accused Athena of being unjust and selfish. You were in the middle of trying to distract her with false compassion. What do kids these days call that? Oh, right, *empathy*. Please continue."

Hannah narrowed her eyes on Hera, who smirked. Of all the immortals she'd met since June, Hera was the worst. But the snarky little speech gave her an idea. Turning her back on Hera, she addressed Athena,"I'm not going to deny that I accused you of being unjust and selfish. I did because you were. Hera is right. I do have empathy for you. I understand why you did what you did. I understand it, because I've acted out of jealousy too. I represented work that my friend did as my own, for reasons I won't go into, but then, when my professor shared the plagiarized work with a colleague, and I got a grad school offer, I didn't correct him. I let the lie stand, and I came up with a lot of plausible excuses for it. I mean, I know that by a lot of measures she is better scholar than I am, but for just a moment, I wanted to be better than she was... or at least as good. I was willing to steal her future. I didn't, I mean, I won't, but the point is, I understand the temptation."

At the complete silence in the room, Hannah stopped talking. She could feel the Gorgon sisters pushing to be unleashed and she felt Hermes' hand on her elbow and his silent urge to escape. But she ignored these forces and stared at Athena, waiting for her verdict. Unfortunately, her answer came as the goddess lowered her spear, the tip resting just above Hannah's breastbone. The time to run was past. With a face of stone, Athena lifted the spear and Hannah felt the cold tip press through her sundress, feel the tension on her skin. She was flooded with regret, things said and left unsaid. Her brain scrambled to pull together a plea for mercy even as it registered that it was too late.

"Athena! Remember me? The human you cursed back in Florence? I just thought you should know that I took a little photo of that trick of yours with my handy phone."

Gretchen, the same Gretchen whose future she had just admitted to stealing, was now flashing her phone in front of Athena's face, her other arm draped casually around Hannah's shoulders. The spear did not move.

"How about we report this bitch to the Immortal Council? Oh, did you hear that Athena? Yes. Hannah here is the Monitor for the Immortal Council, *your* Immortal Council, and she's already written a full, detailed report on your activities. You are familiar with the Non-Interference Accord of 1783? Banning the cursing of humans? Our friend, John, he's waiting for us in the airport in Hartford, and if we don't show up, he's going to place that report in the hands of the Immortal Council directly. Think how much fun the Council will have busting you. I doubt they will show you mercy. On the other hand, we arrive in Connecticut free of spear holes, and that report disappears. Forever."

Hannah felt her stomach clench at the disdain on Athena's face. If they had learned one thing on this trip it was that Athena did not respond to terrorists. Blackmail probably fell into that category. *Oh, Gretch.* She wondered what the karma ramifications were for causing the death of a friend? What could she do to save Gretchen?

We could save Gretchen. Just give us the word, and she is safe.

Hermes' grip on her elbow tightened, "Don't use them. Whatever you do. Your friend with the spear would definitely run you through and be in her rights."

A million questions flooded Hannah's mind, but before she could form one, everyone, even the spiders, jumped at an inhuman noise that filled the chapel: low, wet grunts followed by a high-pitched vibrating noise. It sounded like a drowning walrus using a busted electronic toothbrush. All eyes landed on the snoring god in the pew.

Hitting the recumbent Zeus in the arm, Hera snapped at Athena, "I know the wheels of justice turn slowly, but will you get to the part where you kill them all, please?" She glared at Athena and Hannah felt all hope exit her body at Athena's assenting nod.

Athena turned to Hannah, "Notwithstanding your vulgar friend's attempts at blackmail, your little story has persuaded me to reconsider my actions." Hera could be heard muttering from the back of the church, but Hannah's full attention was on the tip of the spear Athena was removing from her throat. Athena pointed it at the group surrounding the altar, "Sure, maybe I was a little jealous of Arachne's skill, but at least I never stole someone's *ideas*. Compared to that depravity, my fit of pique is not so bad. I suppose I could consider making reparations. But first I'd like to know exactly who I am dealing with."

"That wasn't really the point of my story I mean— Ow!" Hermes kicked her in the shin.

The decrepit shell of a man began to speak in a voice that was dark and thready, as if it were spun out of his barely moving mouth. "They call me Grande Zio. They," and he gestured to the girl and the thugs, "are my descendants." Turning to look with reverence upon the gargantuan spider, he continued, "She is La Grande Madre, and *they* are her descendants." As he spoke the giant spider over the altar started to vibrate, and in response, all of the spiders in the rafters seemed to drop down, spinning, now hanging only feet away from their heads, the darkness in the chapel deepening.

Through the thin layers of webbing that seemed to hold his face together, Hannah thought she saw a skeletal smile on the ancient man's face, "But you might recognize her as Arachne, and I am her son, Closter."

There was an audible gasp from Lee, who had started to fan himself, his eyes glued to the altar, "I did not see *that* coming!"

Hannah felt a hysterical laugh push up at Lee's telenovela reaction, but it died on her lips as Gretchen's grip on her hand tightened. A quick look at her friend revealed she was not holding up well. Spiders had started to spin webs over her head, the gossamer threads shining in her dark hair. Gretchen's arm was trembling as she knocked them away, her teeth audibly chattering. Hannah needed to get her out of here. Gretchen looked like she was seconds from a breakdown.

But then Athena spoke, and Hannah paused, finally about to hear the words she had worked so hard for, "Arachne and Closter, I apologize to you both. This woman," she pointed again at Hannah, "has helped me to see that my actions were wrong, not as heinous as others' might be," and she tilted her head ever so slightly in Hannah's direction, "but still *wrong*. I will now return you to your human form."

"Oh please, don't do that!"

They all stared at the young woman. Hannah felt her victorious moment become hazy with confusion. The old man was whispering violently in the young woman's ear and Arachne had begun to vibrate and buzz. In fact all of the spiders seemed upset, the ones suspending Apollo appeared to be spinning him into a tighter and tighter cocoon. And then the truly bizarre happened. The young woman, the same young woman they had run from in Milan, the shooter of poisoned darts, *that* woman, Café Girl, pulled a laptop out of her shoulder bag and opened it.

"You could turn La Grande Madre back into a human, or..." and here she paused dramatically, and with a flourish hit a button on her keyboard, pulling up a title slide in what was clearly a Power Point presentation, "you could be a ground floor investor in the future of Arachne Global Textiles."

CHAPTER NINETEEN

Modern Business Fundamentals

* * * * * * * * *

Gretchen

Trying not to hyperventilate

The beautiful Italian woman was still talking, "I, um, *we*, are honored by your apology and your offer to return La Grande Madre to her human form, but we, I mean, I, think we would be missing out on a really tremendous opportunity to dominate the world silk market by expanding the applications of our unique thread. We at Arachne Global Textiles have blended spider webbing with silk worm threads to create a super fine silk that is incredibly strong. The commercial applications for it are infinite. With our product and your investment, we could make millions."

Gretchen watched in dismay as Hannah stalked over to the woman, all accusation, "Then why did you kidnap Apollo and ransom him to Athena? And what about the story on your scarf, 'Justice through blood.' How is that *not* looking for vengeance?"

Gretchen turned to Hermes, "Is it the Gorgon sisters? Are they making her crazy?"

Hermes looked at Lee, who shook his head, "Nope. That's

one hundred percent H. I think it might be time for us to go. We just need to grab H and—"

But the Italian woman was talking again, "The scarf does not say 'Justice through blood.' It says 'Family through blood.' *Family*. Like all of us."

Family through blood. Gretchen grimaced. "Oh, that makes more sense. I was stuck on that first rune. so I tried to use context..." Gretchen's voice died out at Hannah's stare.

Athena cut her off, her impatience clear, "So you don't want justice. Then why kidnap Apollo? Why send all those letters demanding my presence? And the ear?"

The girl nodded, "Yes, the ear. Well, my marketing professor said that sometimes you have to think outside of the box. I tried to set up a meeting, but your assistant refused to give me access, so, we, I, launched this initiative to get an audience with you. I may have implied to my great uncle that we would be looking for justice, because I needed the help of La Grande Madre and her children, but when you are building alliances, you sometimes hook people with what they think they want and then you have to help them see how this new plan benefits them." She turned from Athena to the decrepit old man, "We will all be better off this way, Grande Zio."

Then several things happened at once. The old man, the thugs and the girl all started arguing in loud voices, hands flying in the air. Athena stated that she hated working with indecisive clients and they should call her when they were of one mind. She rose up in a swirl, nabbing Apollo's webbed body and exiting through the chapel roof with the aid of her spear, displacing thousands of spiders and splintering the rafters. All of them had to duck to avoid the falling slate from the roof. But the most alarming was that the spiders had started spinning a web around the entire chapel, the diaphanous threads closing closer and closer in.

"Hannah! We have to go!" Gretchen had wanted to yell this, to reach Hannah over the din of the arguing Italians, but her mouth had gone dry, and all that had come out was a whisper. She felt the first threads from the wildly spinning spiders landing lightly on her hair, and this time she did scream. In fact, she couldn't seem to stop screaming.

Hannah ran to her, holding her close, "It's okay. You're okay. Sh, sh... That's right. You need to breathe in, Gretch, or you're going to pass out." Something in Hannah's voice cut through her terror, and she took a shaky breath, "That's it. Good job. Okay. Let's get out of here."

Together they turned toward the back of the chapel. Zeus and Hera were gone, they must have slipped out during the chaos. The pews they had been in were covered in spider webs so thick they were almost invisible. The exit was completely obscured. Only Lee and Hermes were left. Lee, Hermes, and hundreds of thousands of spiders.

Gretchen turned to Hannah, "What do we do?"

Hannah scanned the room, moonlight visible through the hole in the roof. The din of the argument and the humming of the spiders made it hard to hear, so she motioned them all closer, and they huddled, like a football team before the hike. Hannah was their Quarter Back.

"Hermes, can you get through the spider webs?"

"On my own, probably. But if I have to transport the rest of you? No."

"Okay. Let's use the Gorgon sisters. They could get us out of here."

Except you forbid us to act. Your words. Bet you wish you'd chosen better.

"So now you'll never act again?"

You aren't very smart, are you? No wonder you had to steal Gretchen's work. Cursed necklaces have rules. All commands reset within twenty-four hours. Unless of course you want to give us to Gretchen. Then we could get you out of here.

"Why didn't you say so? Here," Hannah reached to pull the necklace off, but couldn't move it, "Why won't it come off?"

"It will, you just have to die first."

Hannah seemed to be contemplating this answer. Gretchen shook her by the shoulders, "Focus, Summers. The Gorgons are not the answer. There has to be something else."

Hermes' voice was sour, his face resigned, "There is no answer. We become cocoons, eventually eaten. At least you two will get to die."

Gretchen covered her face with her hands, unable to process what she was hearing, and realized that her lips had gone numb, a numbness that seemed to be spreading across her face, "They're biting us! Oh my god! Little ones, they're already on us!" She frantically swatted at the webs that were now clinging to her clothes, but for every spider she knocked off, more were lowering from the ceiling. "Hannah, *please*. What else can we do?"

Hannah had knelt down in front of Lee, her fingers sliding over him. "Lee, why aren't the spider webs bugging you? There are no webs on you at all."

"I don't know. I'm so nervous right now I can't even think. Oh, Hermes, we never got to quit our jobs. I really wanted to quit with you. There were so many things I wanted to do with you— geo-cacheing, bar trivia, mani-pedis. But now we'll be stuck in spider webs until someone comes looking for us, and there is no one who will come looking for me but *you*," Lee started to cry fat, greasy tears, his face glistening.

The incongruous sound of Hannah's laughter stopped Gretchen's own tears.

"Look at Lee! Oh my wonderful, beautiful, oily little friend! Don't you see!" At the blank looks from the others, Hannah launched back into QB mode. "Gretchen, wrap your arms really tightly around Hermes from the front. I'll grab him from the back. Lee, I'm going to need you to rub, um, *yourself*, all over our backs. Then Hermes, lift Lee up and hold him in front of you as you fly us out of here. With Lee's um, *slipperiness*, on us, we should be able to pass through the webs covering the hole in the roof. That's the plan, and it's going to work. Now!"

It was a beautiful thing, how it all came together. With Hannah calling the play, they all snapped to. Gretchen and Hannah locked arms around Hermes, Lee wiggled and rubbed and hugged and coated them in whatever was coating him. Then holding Lee aloft like a shield, Hermes flew them up and out, webbing sliding past them, impervious to the trap the spiders had woven.

They hung for a moment in the night air, the spider chapel roiling below, the feeling of freedom a revelation, their escape complete. Gretchen considered saying something, wanting to thank Lee and Hermes, but especially Hannah. Before she could, the massive shape of Arachne climbing up the steeple became visible. She heard Hermes mutter, "Not today," as he flew them at a breakneck speed over the cliff and down to the yacht, still moored by the rocks.

It was a rough landing on the deck, and when they let go of Hermes, both she and Hannah slipped and landed on their backs, the Lee-grease making it difficult to get traction. Hermes offered them both a hand, but his arms were too slippery from having held Lee, and as his arms slipped out of their grips he stepped back and into the oil they had tracked on the boat, also landing on his back. There was a moment when she couldn't tell if Hermes was angry, the only sound after he hit the deck was the gentle lap of water against the side of the boat. And then into the silence, Hannah started laughing.

"Look at me! I'm making a Lee-grease-angel on the deck!"

Gretchen craned her neck to see Hannah on her back, swinging her arms and legs out, leaving a smear shaped angel in her wake. The full force of their escape washed over her, and Gretchen stopped trying to get up and started laughing too, followed by Hermes. Lee, the only one still on his feet, stood over them all, beaming.

* * * * * * * * * *

Lee

Buying a sandwich at the Milan Airport

"Oh yes, extra mortadella please." With the prosciutto on the crusty bread, *heaven*. Watching the young man layering his sandwich, he couldn't help adding, "Oh, and a little more mayonnaise too. You wouldn't happen to have any ketchup, would you? If you mixed it with some mustard... Oh, no ketchup?" At the boy's offended frown, he quickly changed tack, "Never mind the metchup, just add a little more mayo... a little more... a little more...Yes! That looks delicious. *Grazie.*"

It was his third sandwich since arriving at the airport this morning, but he doubted he'd have time for another before they had to board their plane. As he ambled back to the gate, he saw that Hannah and Gretchen were still tethered to the charging station, trying to get their phones back up to full battery before the long flight. Gretchen appeared to be in the middle of a long story, her face animated, Hannah nodding and smiling. He caught a few words, and surmised that Hannah had managed to get her friend the job with the professor she worshipped. Gretchen reached the end of her story with a flourish and Hannah laughed and applauded briefly. After bowing, Gretchen headed towards the bathrooms. As her friend walked away, he saw Hannah's hand slide down to the necklace, her face wan. Something in the angle of her neck made his heart hurt.

Lee looked down at the sandwich in his hand, already half eaten, and crossed the lobby to Hannah, "Here. You should eat a little something." He settled in the seat next to her and placed it gently in her hands.

"Thanks, Lee."

She took a large bite and leaned back, stretching her legs out in front of her. Slowly she let her head lower to his shoulder.

"He's not here, you know. Just in case you were worried." He could always sense Sek's presence, the violence of his aura preceding him like a red vibration.

Hannah lifted her head to look at him, her smile thin by any measure, "Well that's something. Do you know where Hermes went?"

"He had a job. He'll show up again, probably when we get back to Connecticut."

She wrapped the end of the sandwich back into the cellophane and placed it in his hands, "I was thinking, maybe, if you guys were interested, that I might be able to, you know, work with you? Would you talk to Hermes? See what he thinks? I need something to do, now that I no longer have a future and all."

Her sad little speech was interrupted by the short hairy mancentaur, Mr. Blean, running towards them, yelling Hannah's name and waving a boarding pass in the other. He reached them just as Gretchen returned and they all launched into versions of the last twenty-four hours, the centaur's story one of tedious escape from Tartarus in time only to catch the flight home with them. Hannah went last, describing Hera's withering email firing them all, and ending with her thought to talk to Hermes about possible work, assuming that her job at the university would end now that her anonymity as the Monitor was blown.

"Oh my dear, I'm sorry to contradict you, but your obligations to the Immortal Council are not quite at an end yet, so you are not at liberty to seek other employment. Contractual details and all." Mr. Blean's explanation was cut off as the airline attendant started to announce the boarding groups for their flight. "We have a long flight. I'll explain. For now, shall we board?"

Lee watched the three of them proceed down the runway, Gretchen and Mr. Blean keeping up a stream of travel-related pleasantries. Hannah stood between them. Pensive. And even though Hermes had told him it was rude to do, he slipped into Hannah's mind, rooted around her memories, and then finding what he needed, flooded her with the image of sunlight reflecting back on tree-lined lake, a thousand diamonds on a deep blue surface. From his spot at the back of the line, he caught sight of her smile.

"Sir, you can not take that sandwich on the plane. The FAA has passed recent restrictions on foods that surpass eighty olfaction units in smell. You are going to have to relinquish your sandwich before entering." The flight attendant lowered the beeping wand in her hand and showed him the read-out: one hundred and sixty five Olfs.

Humans and their rules were so interesting. Lee'd never heard of an olfaction unit before. Oh, well, he had Hermes' first class ticket. Hermes promised that they fed you well in first class. He dropped the sandwich in the bin the attendant was holding at arm's length. All he wanted to do now was kick back, take off his shoes, and air his feet out for the next seven hours. The FAA had said nothing about *bodily* odors exceeding eighty Olfs.

CHAPTER TWENTY

Airports are Public Spaces

* * * * * * * * * *

Hannah

Rethinking her offer to help Lee find his bag

"Black with wheels?"

"Yes. But not small wheels. Big wheels. Like those. But not that one." Lee pointed at a black wheeled bag as it passed by for the third time on the luggage carousel.

No one else in their party had checked bags for this flight. She didn't even have her backpack any more, traveling only with her passport and the clothes on her back. Now that she thought of it, when had Lee had time to even get a bag, let alone check it in? It must make sense, but she was too tired to piece it together. It was enough that Lee had seemed confused by the directions to the baggage claim. She had felt badly for him and offered to help. After arranging to text Gretchen when they were done, she had brought Lee down here to baggage hell, avoiding the escalators as Lee was unsure if he could exit them without getting sucked in. While some moments are ripe for teaching, this seemed like a time to simply take the stairs.

The upper levels of Bradley airport had undergone the requisite renovations that made it look like every other middle sized airport in the country. Grey carpeting and off-white walls with massive photos of either jet equipment taken at such close an angle as to appear artsy or pictures of the Connecticut Capitol Building in Hartford, a Willy Wonka like structure with a towering gold dome, ornate scroll work, and granite gewgaws. All it needed was a fountain of chocolate and candy trees to complete the effect. The artwork served the dual purpose of alerting you to the location you were in as well as masking the now-ubiquitous security cameras recording every passing face. Lee had pointed out that the spoke in the photo of the airplane wheel had a flickering red dot and had made a point to stop and wave. Gretchen gave it the finger. All very modern.

But down here in baggage claim, it was the airport time had forgotten. Unlike the space age donut-shaped luggage carousels in more modern airports, where you could imagine that incredibly intelligent machines had sorted and carefully guided your suitcase to appear magically through a hole in the donut, Bradley's baggage claim department was gritty. Large s-shaped conveyor belts protruded from holes in the wall, the over-sized doggy doors covered in plastic flaps that lifted to reveal the hairy arms of workers tossing peoples' bags haphazardly into the metal chute.

Mr. Blean and Lee had agreed to split a cab, while she and Gretchen were being met by John. She checked her phone for messages; one, from Gretchen, saying she and John were circling the airport and to text her when they were ready, the airport cops quick to harass any car that lingered for more than a minute. The other from Hermes, saying simply, "We need to talk."

She was too tired to talk to Hermes, too vulnerable since learning that she was indebted to him for her life. She had taken the time, on the flight home, to confess quite a number of things to Mr. Blean, not the least was that she had become enthralled by the Gorgon sisters in the necklace and had used her borrowed powers against Athena. Mr. Blean had left her no illusions about the painful death she would have experienced if Hermes hadn't been able to cover for her.

As if the airline ginger ale was a truth serum, she also found herself owning up to the Sek story. It turned out both Mr. Blean and Professor Tetley already knew. Unfortunately, her use of the Gorgon necklace to send Sek away was another potentially deadly exposure, and had bound her to the necklace, all attempts to remove it from her neck having failed. So, to sum up, she had endangered her friends, exposed her role as the Monitor and thus losing that job and become indebted to the council for breaking her contract. She had admitted to academic plagiarism and lost out on grad school, and had made her already-terrifying demon problem worse with the added fun of binding herself magically to the homicidal Gorgon sisters. Not a great week.

She just wanted to get home, shower and sleep. She would face the ramifications of her trip tomorrow. Mr. Blean had explained that she had to make recompense to the Immortal Council for breach of contract. He was vague on the details. Whatever Hermes had to tell her would have to wait. She texted back to Gretchen that they were still looking for the bag and to let Mr. Blean know. She was starting to despair of finding it. Every other passenger from their flight had gotten their luggage and left by now.

"They haven't added any new bags for a while now. Shall we check with the airline? I think that is an office over there." Hannah headed off toward a door on the far side of the room with the picture of a mangled suitcase next to a stick figure with his hands in the air taped to the door. In her opinion, it was not the best image to project to the public. Someone should talk to their marketing department. She resigned herself to wait as she joined the end of a long line spilling out of the unfortunately marked door.

The woman in front of her seemed intent on voicing her displeasure with the airline, tossing out comments, waiting for someone to take the bait. Hannah often fell victim to this type of gambit, uncomfortable with the silence meeting this woman's rhetorical fishing, but today she was simply too tired to feel guilty. She avoided eye contact and waited. Waiting made her mind slip back to yesterday's confrontation in the chapel.

Business Italian style. This was the second time in her experience with Olympians that her and her friend's lives had been endangered for something remarkably pedestrian. With Apep, the elaborate "gift" scam to embarrass Apollo had been over a misnamed Egyptian God of Death in a B-movie about Sherlock Holmes. Now a kidnapped god was all a ploy to get a sit-down meeting with an investor. Surely there had to be more important issues confronting the Immortal community? She wondered if the pettiness of the gods' problems was in direct relation to the unending length of their existence. She should make a list. She had a sample size of two, but for now, it seemed a solid hypothesis. Which made her wonder what Hera's end game with Apollo might be. It bothered her that she had never figured that out. And since she was no longer the Monitor, she was unlikely to ever learn. Given her theory of inane Olympian problems, Hera probably had an overdue library book or an unpaid parking ticket she needed Apollo to fix for her. She laughed out loud at her own joke, incurring the wrathful stare of Complaining Woman.

"You find this funny?"

Hannah found it funny that she had picked up Hermes' habit of naming people based on first impressions or locations of sighting them. She had named that amoral Italian model with a degree in marketing Café Girl. Now she was looking into the irate face of Complaining Woman. "By *this*, are you referring to the line? If so, then no, this line is not funny. Definitely a serious line. But I did have a funny thought—"

As she revved up to unleash her line frustration on her, the Complaining Woman's mouth was opening and closing like a carp. Oh, that would have been a much better name! *Carp Woman.* Before Carp Woman could achieve her goal, Hannah heard Lee's triumphant yell.

"I found it!"

She turned to see him pull the very same black suitcase with large wheels they had been watching for the last twenty minutes off the carousel. Lee had yanked it onto the floor and before she could reach him, had unzipped it and started to inventory its contents. She had a profound moment of confusion, wondering if the Gorgon sisters were messing with her mind.

"Cheese. Check. Wigs. Check. Mouthwash. Double check, hotel shampoo—" He was speaking in an undertone, clearly working his way down a mental list.

"Lee? Lee? Lee!" He looked sincerely hurt by the sharpness of her last "Lee" and she felt regret fighting with impatience. Regret won out, "Sorry, listen, why don't you wait for the taxi to go through your things." She didn't wait for his reply, just started to push items back in, "Ouch! Did something bite me?" She sucked on her finger, tasting blood.

"Possibly. They don't like having their space invaded." Lee bent over the still-open bag and started cooing at it.

"I know I should ask you like a thousand questions, not the least of them is whether this bite is poisonous, but I am too tired for reason, Lee. Just zip it up! Let's go meet the others on the curb." Impatience now had a healthy lead over regret, her hand throbbing. She wanted to get home and see Professor Tetley. She needed to apologize to him in person for lying about the translation. She knew Mr. Blean had already filled him in, but when Mr. Blean had tried to put her on the phone to talk to him she had waved Blean off.

It wasn't that she didn't want to talk to him, really. It was just that she felt like she could handle his disappointment better if she could see his face. Mr. Blean had assured her that Professor Tetley understood and forgave her. But she needed to see that forgiveness firsthand. And then maybe share a pot of tea.

In her senior year they had met weekly in his office, ostensibly to work on her thesis, but inevitably they settled into an easy chat, the wing chair in his office feeling like it belonged to her, the seat the perfect size for tucking her legs. It might be irrational, but it was the first place she wanted to go once she got back to Whitfield. To do that she had to get out of this godforsaken airport.

Muttering to herself about the bag and the wait and the bite, she pushed through the double glass doors to see her parent's

SUV waiting in the far lane. John and Gretchen were standing next to her mother, who was bent over; Gretchen looking frozen, John grim, his eyes going straight to her face, the concern in them made her feel light-headed. Something was very wrong. Her mind started to fly through the list of people she loved. Just as she registered seeing her father at the wheel of the car, her brain insisted that she process what she had already seen. What she already knew, but didn't want to be true. Her mouth went dry as she refocused her gaze on her mother. Her mother was holding Mr. Blean in her arms. Mr. Blean's sobs were wrenching, shaking his entire body. Her mother looked up from rubbing his shoulders to look her in the eyes, and she mouthed the words, "I'm sorry, honey."

Lee had trundled his bag next to her and stared for a moment, then slipped his hand in hers. Ever so gently he lead her between the airport shuttles to her friends and family, and to the grief and regret waiting for her in the loading zone. And the pot of tea that would never again be shared.

* * * * * * * * *

Apollo

On Hera's private jet

He waved at the flight attendant, and when she came near, he asked her for another hot chocolate. With marshmallows. Though he could see the hesitation in her face, she nodded, patting his hand before leaving. He was sitting as far as he could from Hera and Zeus, whose constant sniping was making him miss the peacefulness of his kidnapped time. Aside from the time they had woven him into a tapestry and then suspended him upside down from the rafters in the church, he had been comfortable being kidnapped. Hera had insisted on flying him home, claiming a week on the Vineyard was just what he needed after his ordeal, but ever since they had taxied on the runway in Milan, Hera and Zeus had exchanged one nasty comment after another. He had quietly moved to the furthest seat, his retreat going unnoticed as Hera and Zeus continued lobbing insults.

Reaching down into his carry-on, he pulled out his piggy bank full of checks. Adelina had saved it for him. That and his phone. She was beautiful and so obviously in love with him. Definitely his type. Except he was on a hero's quest for his beloved Naomi. He hugged the bank to his chest and imagined their reunion. He would take the bank to Naomi and show her his undying love. She would take him back and they would live happily ever after. At least that was the plan he had texted to his friends from his hotel in Milan, the Fan Fiction Bitches. He had found a dozen or so messages from them when he had turned on his phone. They filled him in on everything and were waiting to hear the end of his story. They had all taken turns posting their own versions of his reunion with Naomi. If he had time, he would check them out before seeing Naomi; there might be some helpful advice in their stories.

Advice might be needed. Somehow the experience of being kidnapped had allowed doubt to creep into his certainty that Naomi was waiting for him to fulfill her hero's challenge. He pulled the airplane blanket up around his shoulders and stretched his legs out, reminding himself that he was a successful male model, the scarf king of Firenze, and that Naomi was bound to fall at his exquisite feet. Except what if she didn't? He needed to talk to someone. That girl Hannah seemed to have good advice. She had definitely helped Athena understand the Arachne problem. Maybe he should talk to her. Before he talked to Naomi. He made a mental note to get her digits from the Fan Fiction Bitches. She had stayed at the same hotel he had in Milan. Apparently she had been looking for him. He had worried that she was another woman madly in love with him, but the FBs insisted that she had her own guy, and she seemed to sincerely want to help him. He would contact her and make her dreams come true by letting her help him win Naomi. Yes. That was a good plan. He felt a little better.

Until then, he would try to nap. The flight attendant returned with his second cup of cocoa. Sipping slowly he closed his eyes, content to let the warm chocolate cover up his insecurities about his beloved's response to him fulfilling her quest. The marshmallows were there to fill the hole made by the incessant viciousness of the two gods in the front of the plane. He gulped more, filling his mouth with small marshmallows and rich chocolate. He smiled as the marshmallows melted in his mouth. Everything had to work out. He was Apollo, god of the Sun. He would get the girl. He always did. Eventually.

* * * * * * * * * *

Hermes

On the bank of the Okeanos

"You're certain, Professor? Because this is a one-way ticket and you still have other options."

Professor Tetley patted his hand, "It's quite all right, Hermes. I worked out a deal with Hades a century ago." Pulling a scroll out of his coat pocket, he unfurled it and showed it to him, "See, corner unit, third floor, with a view of the ocean."

"In honor of over two hundred years of service to the gods, we hereby grant Roger Tetley, Professor of the Classics and Monitor for the Immortal Council, an afterlife in the Elysian Fields."

It looked legitimate. But still. "Elysium isn't all it's cracked up to be, you know. What did Hades tell you? He didn't quote Homer did he? All that crap about the rivers of honey and cooling winds, never to toil, blessings for ever, etc, etc."

At the Professor's patient look, Hermes' irritation flared, "Every hero I have ever transported there was so convinced they'd made it to the promised land, literally. But there is a dark underbelly to Elysium. They have *community potlucks*. Every Thursday. Mandatory. And don't get me started on their monthly poetry slams. At least in Hades you can stop pretending to be moved by someone rhyming 'soul' with 'old' while they hit the bongos."

"Oh, my good man. Please. I was an academic. Potlucks and poetry readings are my bread and butter. Besides, I was promised an endless supply of Earl Grey and free wifi. And my bride awaits me there. It's been one hundred and eighty years since I've seen her. I feel like a school boy."

"Oh, I didn't realize your old lady was there. How did you swing that?" It was highly unusual for there to be any modern residents of Hades, let alone the Elysian Fields.

"Maggie and I discussed the various options for the afterlife, and we agreed not to interfere with our children and grandchildren's faith, but that for our own afterlife, we wanted to spend it together. In Elysium." The Prof looked over his shoulder and then lent forward, whispering, "Let's say I had a little leverage with Persephone. I was a guest at President Van Buren's Inaugural Party where a certain goddess punched her Presidential card. She was not eager for her husband to learn of her, shall we call them, *political activities*. It wasn't hard to swing."

"Sounds like you thought of everything Professor." Hermes bent down to lift the professor up and cradled him in his arms, this final passage one only Hermes could move through.

Professor Tetley grabbed his arm, "Wait. Tell me again."

Hermes had told him variations on this story several times since getting the call in Milan to come and deliver the Prof Man to Elysium. It was the story of how Hannah talked Athena into taking responsibility for her Arachne gaffe. How she and Gretchen had told the truth to Blean, whom Hermes now knew was the centaur handler for the Monitor. Had been the Prof's handler for all of his two hundred and thirty years. How all of them would be fine. He was sure of it. He had opted to leave out the problem of H's indentured servitude to the Council, her evil necklace problem and its possibly fatal outcome and her persistent demon suitor. The dude deserved some peace. Besides, he was due to find out about it all, in good time. It wasn't like Elysium was Tartarus. Elysium was wired with all the modern tech. He was bound to read about it on the net.

"Hannah will be fine. I promise. But that reminds me, you need to read through the Elysian Field Guide," Hermes shifted the dude to his left arm and reached back into his pocket, pulling out a thick binder. "There are strict rules limiting communication with the living. And now with wifi, well, the rules are complex. You will be visited by the Welcome Wagon tomorrow and they can go through it with you. If you have questions, that would be the time to ask them. Remember, break the rules and it is down to Hades proper, no do-overs." He looked down into the Professor's face, trying to gauge if he was ready. At this stage it was not unusual for souls to hesitate, torn between the living and the dead. "I'm sure your gal Maggie is a pro at all this."

Mentioning his wife's name seemed to help him, the Professor's face clearing, and he nodded, "Yes. Let's get to it, then."

Hermes flew over the river, the islands of Elysium approaching. He could see a figure waving from the golden fields in front of them, and heard the Professor let out a short exclamation of joy. As he set him down next to a spry chick with long white braids, the Professor turned back, "Be sure to visit my gravesite. Tell them all that I am happy, that I want them to be. Oh, and I left you a little something over my eyes for your trouble." Reaching out to shake his hand, he looked Hermes in the eye, "I have known a lot of gods in my life. You, sir, are an excellent Messenger God. Thank you." And then he was embracing his lady.

Classy.

EPILOGUE

Endings and Beginnings

* * * * * * * * * *

Hannah

Sunday afternoon

She hadn't bothered to change out of her funeral clothes. She found the black wool dress perversely satisfying to wear while she packed. She wiped the dust from her books onto her skirt before she placed them in one of the dozen or so moving boxes littering her tiny apartment, satisfied by the smear of dust across the dark fabric. She could hear her mother's voice in her head scolding her for the unnecessary cost of dry cleaning her dress, especially now that she was working for free. As if from under layers of cotton batting, she could also hear the Gorgon sisters agreeing with her mother. She was in no mood to humor them.

"You had better watch yourselves, or I will shut you down for good. You wouldn't like that very much, would you? And agreeing with my mother about laundry? You might want to rethink that. If you are trying to get back in my good graces, that is not the way to do it."

"Han?"

She jumped, startled, instinctively flinging the book at the source. John caught it before it hit him in the face, looking down at the spine, "*Heart of Darkness?* I shouldn't take any hidden message from your choice of projectile, should I?"

"No." Crossing the room, she locked the door behind him, putting her hand out for the book, "It was just what was on hand when you scared the crap out of me."

Putting the book on the counter behind her, he slid his hands up her arms, "Are you okay? With everything?"

Leaning into him, she closed her eyes. "Yeah, I'm fine. Just angry with the *girls*. And everything."

That morning they had all been at Professor Tetley's grave, following his detailed last wishes to the letter. He had been laid out in the university library the day before, as people gathered to mourn. Then at dawn this morning the women carried his bier in a procession to the cemetery just north of campus, where they placed him in a tomb next to his wife. Her mom and dad were there for it all, her mother standing next to her lifting the bier, Candy and Gretchen on the other side. Halfway there the mourners began singing, the procession lifting from a dirge into a celebration. The crowd were mostly university types, colleagues and friends. But she had a slight advantage, wearing the Gorgon necklace, and saw through quite a number of immortals disguises to see that they were present in large numbers.

Hannah had worried what would happen to Professor Tetley, wondered where his soul would go, but then she saw Hermes slip into the tomb just before it was closed and nab the gold coins off Professor Tetley's eyes, and she had her answer. Well, part of an answer. If Hermes took payment, then he had done the job. Now that she thought of it, her mother had said that according to the Medical Examiner's Office, they believed Professor Tetley had suffered a massive stroke late Thursday night, around the same time Hermes left them at the airport. She made a mental note to interrogate Hermes about the details of Professor Tetley's final resting place at the first opportunity.

She had hoped to get answers when they were at the reception following the burial, Mr. Blean having invited people back to his home. But Hermes had spent the entire time talking with Candy, who looked so happy to see him that she hadn't wanted to intrude. Besides, in all the confusion since learning of Professor Tetley's passing, Hannah still hadn't thanked Hermes for saving her from the Gorgons, a conversation she knew would have to happen before she got any other answers. So she had mingled.

The reception at Mr. Blean's was not your typical post-funeral affair; wine was flowing freely and an impromptu open mike had materialized in the sitting room, folks lining up to share their favorite Professor Tetley stories. After listening to the first few mourners, she had had enough. There were some things she preferred not to think about when it came to her beloved advisor. She certainly hadn't expected a triad of wood nymphs to burst into a decidedly bawdy song they claimed was inspired by their favorite weekend in the Ozarks with the Professor. Leaving the room, she had bumped into Hermes, who had only smirked at her, and then joined in the chorus with the other mourners.

Checking her watch, she had realized that she had to go. She had slipped out of the reception telling her mother to let John and Gretchen know that she would be back soon, not seeing them anywhere. A process server had found her at the wake last night and handed her a summons. It informed her that she was mentioned in the will and invited her to attend the reading on Sunday at noon in the university library reading room. Cutting across campus, she entered the library just as the clock began striking twelve. The Library Reading Room was on the second floor, and she made it before the final bell. Tapping lightly on the heavy oaken door, she was taken aback to see it opened by a very large, hairy satyr who demanded to see her summons and a photo id, all in a thick Ukrainian accent. At least she guessed it was Ukrainian. In her brief time as the Monitor, she'd read about the large satyr population in the Carpathian Mountains, but she had not imagined that they were both large in number *and* size. This satyr was imposing.

"It's all right, Vlas, she's with us. Since we are all here, will you please guard the door, from the other side, and make sure we are not interrupted. *Daiakuji.*" Mr. Blean took her arm as he lead her into the room.

As she scanned the faces at the table, she stated the obvious, "This isn't the reading of the will, is it?"

Mr. Blean walked her to a seat at the head of the table. To her right were Gretchen and John, to her left were Hermes and Lee. Mr. Blean sat at the other end, "To be precise, it isn't *only* the reading of the will."

He pulled out a single sheet of heavy paper and read, "I, Roger Harmonious Sebastian Tetley, of sound body and mind, leave all of my worldly possessions to my dear friend, Charnous, son of Chiron, known among humanity as Mr.Tobias Blean, to dispose of as he sees fit. With the exception of my yellow wing chair, flowered tea pot and Titian painting, which I leave to the young woman who was like a granddaughter to me, Hannah Marie Summers."

Mr. Blean lowered the paper and looked about the room, "Will read. Now let's get down to business. First, Hannah, I suggest you give a direct order to shut down the Gorgon sisters. You can do that, can't you?"

She had. At least she hoped she had. She was not sure how much control she really had when it came to the Gorgon sisters. It seemed to have worked. They had then spent the following hour discussing how they were going to work on what they had agreed to call, "the troubles" with "the girls" and the "puppy dog." It had been Hermes' idea to refer to the Gorgon sisters and Sek that way. Each person would, based on their unique skill set, focus on an aspect of the troubles without exposing her to fatal charges from the Immortal Council, or getting any of them killed by Sek. It required a profound level of secrecy. Which they had all pledged. John had thought of an ingenious way for them to communicate about it.

Mr. Blean had ended the meeting informing her that she needed to pack her things, as the Immortal Council had met that morning and decided her fate. Six months as an unpaid intern in Washington, DC. Working for Athena. Mr. Blean was doing a bad job of masking his worry about this verdict, and Hannah had to admit the prospect seemed fraught to say the least. She had not reported Athena to the Council but both she and Athena knew Hannah knew about Athena's infractions. If that made sense. Gretchen's attempt to rescue her by blackmailing Athena had kept Athena from outright killing her, but Hannah knew that a threatened goddess was a dangerous goddess.

"What are we going to do about Athena?"

John's question in her ear brought her back to the present in her apartment. And to the fact that he was ridiculously adept at reading her thoughts. "Don't worry about Athena. If I follow the rules, I think she will too. I don't want to talk about her." Burying her face into his neck, she blocked out thoughts of both the past and the future and focused on the present. He had the nicest smelling neck. She breathed in slowly.

"Um, Han?" He cupped her shoulders, leaning her back to look into her eyes.

"Yes?"

"Aren't you worried that it will make you a target? Athena knows that you know. What if she decides you are a liability she needs to eliminate? Have you thought about reporting her?"

She knew that look on his face. And as much as she enjoyed arguing with him, she found that her mind had slipped to a completely different topic. She needed to put an end to the issue of Athena. At least for now. "I'm going to rely on her sense of justice. It's what she's known for. Can we change topics?" She started working on his jeans, noting that he had changed out of his funeral clothes.

He paused for a moment, as if he were weighing his options— continue talking or join in the undressing? Not surprisingly, he tried to do both, "Okay. Topic change." He slid his fingers under her hair, "What are you going to do with the Titian?" He made quick work of her dress, lowering the zipper with a quiet whoosh, the dress sliding down her body.

She stepped out of it, picked it up, and rolled it into a ball, "I'm bringing it with me to DC. I'll stick it in a cheap metal frame. No one will think an unpaid intern would own a priceless painting. Hidden in plain sight. " Smiling for the first time since she had stepped off the airplane she tossed the dress into the garbage can beside the door. Two points!

Lifting her up onto the kitchen counter, John started kissing her, his comments coming in short breaths as he removed her remaining clothes, "Hiding in plain sight. Like us?" Slip pulled over her head. "Are you sure they bought it? Us as *friends*?" Bra joining the slip on the floor. "Are you sure you want to do it like this?"

"Up here on the counter? It could work..."

"No. Not that. I mean, yes, I think this will work very well, but—"

His next words were lost as she pulled his shirt off over his head.

As soon as his head was free, she saw that he was serious about his question, and that she was unlikely to be able to move this forward unless she answered him. "I think it is the safest way, given Sek's murderous jealousy. Everyone by this point either knows or suspects that something happened between us in Italy. But they also suspect that it was a fling. A one-off. You should have heard my mother. She is not a fan." She pulled him closer, "I am not ashamed to admit that only enhances your appeal for me." And she set about to illustrate the ways in which her interest was enhanced, not ashamed either by her opportunistic attempt to distract him from the conversation. But he was persistent.

Disentangling her arms, he held her at arm's length, "Then why lie to everyone and tell them we're just friends?"

She rested her head against his and knew she needed to confess, "I told Gretchen. She knows the truth. About you. About us."

John's laugh surprised her. At her frown, he explained, "I'm just glad, I guess, that you told her. I told Carl." At her worried look, he continued, "He was pretty shocked, but he seemed happy for us. And he understands about keeping it secret. His only concern is mine; if I have to pretend we're just friends, how can I be there to protect you from Sek?"

Sighing, she cut to the chase, "You can't protect me from Sek." At his attempt to object, she looped her arms around his neck, "No one can, John. Not Hermes, or Lee, or even Mr. Blean. The only thing keeping me safe is the very thing that puts me at risk." They both looked at the necklace resting just below her collarbone. "If Sek suspects that there is more than friendship between us... I need you to be safe." And just like that, everything that had happened in the last twenty-four hours washed over her, and she felt her shoulders begin to shake.

He pulled her into an embrace, lifting her off the counter and carrying her to the bed, nudging off a stack of books before lowering them both to mattress. The books spilled into a box labeled, "Cookbooks I Should Read."

"Oh! I had sorted those by subject and—"

"Summers, please be quiet." His voice was patient, as was his mouth as it moved over hers. He divested her of her remaining underwear, his hands caressing her in a way that was both deeply comforting and exciting at the same time. The analytic part of her brain registered that it was a common human reaction when confronted by death, to reaffirm that you are alive by engaging in activity that stimulates the pleasure centers. Like an instinctive drive towards life. It probably was also part of the limbic brain's survival of the species. Reproduction. *Oh.* All thoughts of the biological imperative of their activity was eclipsed as John seemed to have found more than one pleasure center at the same time. Shutting down her own brain, she was lost in sensation.

Except there was something off.

Ignore it.

There was a noise her mind was struggling to identify.

Please ignore it. It will go away.

He is very good at this.

Isn't he, though.

A little to the left, a little more…

Pushing on John's shoulders, he lifted his head and registered the sound, whispering, "Someone is knocking on your door. Are you expecting anyone?"

Shaking her head, she scrambled up, grabbing a towel from the back of a chair and wrapping it around her body, "Just a second!"

John was already pulling his clothes on and stepping barefoot out of her window onto the fire escape. Their eyes met, and he smiled, made the international sign for "call me" and disappeared. Hannah felt some weight inside her lift, and she shook her head, smiling.

You are the worst. How bad would it have been to let that beautiful and talented young man finish?

Hannah grimaced, only now aware that the girls had resurfaced during her time with John. "It's time for you to take a nap.

Now!" Silence. Resentful silence, but silence nonetheless. She would have to figure out how they had joined the party. Later. Now she had to deal with the person on the other side of the door, who had progressed from knocking to kicking.

"I am not particularly tired, H. Though I will grow old waiting for you to open the door. And Lee here has to use your bathroom. Open up unless you prefer demon vomit on your welcome mat."

Damn it. Why were they here now? Flinging the door open with one hand while she clutched the towel to her body with the other, she was knocked aside as Lee bolted past her to get to the bathroom.

"He has trouble holding his liquor." Hermes looked her up and down, then slowly lifted her crumpled dress out of the garbage, "What exactly is going on here?" His smirk morphed into mock distress as she pulled the dress out of his hands and slammed it back into the garbage, "I declare, Hannah Summers, that is positively wasteful! It gives me the vapors."

Tucking the edges of her towel more firmly under her arms, she tried to take hold of the conversation, "What are you doing here? And what's with the tragically bad Southern accent?"

Lee's excited response was muffled by the bathroom door, "We're all moving to DC together!"

"Yes, it's true. We are all heading South of the Mason-Dixon line." Hermes executed an elaborate stage bow, "Allow me to introduce myself, H. Say hello to your new boss."

Hermes was interrupted by Lee, still yelling even though he now stood outside the bathroom, "Your new *bosses*. Athena is staying on in Italy indefinitely to help the spider people and has asked me and Hermes to run her consulting firm. And you are our intern. Won't that be fun!"

Hannah's relief at not encountering Athena on a daily basis was profound. Touched as she was by Lee's enthusiasm, she couldn't help voicing her concern, "What do you two know about political consulting?"

Hermes sprawled in her one chair, "Well, that's your job to sort out. You're the intern."

Lee crossed the room to burrow into her fridge, pushing the contents around, "Don't listen to him, Hannah. Athena gave us the lowdown, and her private cell. This is going to be fun! All three of us, working together, just like you wanted." Poking his head out, "You don't happen to have more of that delicious metchup, do you? I think it would settle my stomach."

Hermes leaned forward in his seat and pointed at the stacks of books, "Forget the condiments, Lee. Just pack her up. We need to leave now, that's why we're here. To get you down there. We all punch the clock on Monday. And we thought you might be dragging your heels."

"You are going to have to push that start date back a week, Messenger God." Standing in the doorway, Gretchen looked at her, "You do know your door is open and you are standing there in only a towel? If you were on the way to take a shower, make it a quick one. Our flight leaves in three hours."

Gretchen closed the door behind her as she crossed the room to the dresser, pulling out handfuls of underwear and shoving it into a bright yellow backpack. "You know that travel insurance you insisted we buy?" She turned to Hermes, "I thought it was a complete waste of money, but you know how stubborn she can get? Well, it all turned out for the best." She held out a black one-piece bathing suit with a skirt running along the bottom, "Seriously? We'll buy you a bikini when we get there." She tossed it across the room, where it landed in the garbage can on top of the black dress. Focusing back on Hannah, she nodded to the bathroom, "Tick tock."

At Hannah's continued stillness, Gretchen slowed in the pillaging of her underwear, "I can see we are not going anywhere until I explain." Unzipping a front compartment on the backpack she pulled out a thick manila envelope, "It was sent to my dad's address. He arrived this morning with it. The travel company we booked through cut a deal with the Feds to plead guilty to fraudulent insurance practices. Part of their plea involved reimbursements of affected travel itineraries. Long story short, they offered us a refund because we had purchased their crappy insurance. Not cash, but in travel vouchers. I had to choose between a week at an all-inclusive in Jamaica or a week at Disney World in Fort Lauderdale. I picked Jamaica." She smiled encouragingly, holding out the papers.

Hannah looked at them, "Are you sure you want to travel with me? I mean, our last trip was—"

Gretchen rolled her eyes, the move softened by her smile, "I am good with what happened. But if you want to talk it through, what better place to do it than on the beach in Jamaica with a dark and stormy in hand? Yes?"

Hannah paused for just a moment, weighing her choices. Responsibility would dictate that she finish her packing and show up for her job on Monday. She always did the responsible thing. Screw it!

"Don't forget to pack my sunscreen. It's in the top drawer. I'll be quick." She turned to face Hermes and Lee, "The books are sorted to match the boxes' labels. Thanks, guys!" And she bolted for the bathroom, snagging her phone off the counter and leaving her incredibly competent best friend to handle the two immortals in her living room. As the water rushed out of the shower head, she could hear Gretchen ordering them about and Hermes complaining. She tapped out a quick message to John to let him know where she was going. Balancing her phone on the edge of the sink, she looked at her reflection in the mirror as it slowly filled with steam. She fingered the necklace around her neck. She had problems, but she also had friends. A boyfriend. Secret boyfriend, but still... and a best friend.

She had said horrible things to Gretchen. Horrible things she kind of meant. But not meaning to say them in such an awful way. And despite claiming that she was over their fight, Hannah suspected that Gretchen had some legitimate complaints as well. She started making a mental list of topics she and Gretchen should cover to be sure they were done fighting. She smiled as she stepped under the spray. A week in Jamaica was plenty of time.

ACKNOWLEDGMENTS

My husband and I have an ongoing joke about acknowledgements. When our children were in elementary school, their school hosted an annual Spring concert. One year the hardworking music teacher, in giving her closing speech, thanked the classroom teachers for their "constant support." For some reason, this brought up an image in my mind of the teachers *constantly* holding the music teacher up in the air *supporting* her. Whether it was the saturation point of Spring school events, or the effects of sleep deprivation from raising two young children, the phrase and the image made us laugh.

But the truth is that creative work *can be* like being held up in the air by the people in your life. I have to thank the people who held me up during the creation of this book: Lily, Ethan, Steve, Clare, Barbara, Rebecca, Sue, and Tia. Thank you all for your support— writing can be fraught with turbulence, and though sometimes I dropped, because of you all, I never really hit the ground.

REVEALING HANNAH

The Greek Myth Series

. . . .

Book One

Revealing Hannah The Myth of Cassandra

April 2015

Book Two

Revealing Hannah The Myth of Arachne

May 2016

Book Three

Revealing Hannah The Myth of Echo

coming Spring 2017...

COMING SOON

the 3rd book in the Greek Myth Series...

Revealing Hannah The Myth of Echo

The adventure continues for Hannah— Though if this is an adventure, she wants her money back. Doing grunt work for the Immortal Council, working as an unpaid intern, and having no idea what to do with her life was more like the fate of Sisyphus than she had hoped for at the start of the fall.

Add to that boyfriend troubles, thinly-veiled disappointed texts from her mother, and the ever-present danger of an obsessed, sociopathic demon and something has to change.

But she is not without a plan. She has to get out of DC and find a nymph who's only a voice. Echo was last heard from at the Grand Canyon, but Hannah's sources tell her Echo is on the run. Hannah is determined to find her, and with Echo's help, get rid of her own demon problem. Then she can focus on what to do with her life. So she reserves a very practical Toyota Tercel from the car rental agency— reliable and small, perfect for one person. But when Hermes and Lee offer to pick it up for her, they show up at her door behind the wheel of a Delta '88- a whale of a car. Hermes and Lee are on the run from the Vitamin Mafia and need to get off the grid and out of town, preferably in a car that predates GPS.

Did someone say road trip?

ABOUT THE AUTHOR

Laura Fedolfi grew up in Chichester, NH. She attended Phillips Exeter Academy in Exeter, NH and Wesleyan University in Middletown, CT. There she wrote a senior thesis in her dual degree of Philosophy and English. She went on to receive a Master's Degree in Conflict Analysis and Resolution from George Mason University, Fairfax, VA. She has lived for the last eighteen years in Chelmsford, MA where she and her husband have raised two children. She has held many different jobs, done a wide array of volunteer work, and is involved in the life of her Episcopal church, All Saints'. Though she has always been telling stories, she began writing them down only recently.

She is happy to hear from readers and can be reached through her website: www.revealinghannah.com